IMPLODE

The Completionist Chronicles Book Eight

DAKOTA KROUT

MOUNTAINDALE
━━ PRESS ━━

ACKNOWLEDGMENTS

Many thanks to all of my supporters, especially those that have been here since the beginning.

To my Patreons, thank you for wanting to be the first to have eyes on the work, and for giving me tips to make it all better.

Finally, to William Merrick, Samuel Landrie, and Zeb Foltz… thank you for doing so much, and asking for so little in return.

PROLOGUE

Ooph!

The humans had returned as conquering heroes—at least in their minds—so being forced to their knees was the last thing they expected. When they hit the ground and felt the pain spiking through their limbs, their moods shifted directly from confusion to fury. Four of the six began mouthing off, yelling at the people they had been expecting rewards and gratitude from.

The Elves didn't waste a single breath on explaining themselves, instead slapping the humans the rest of the way to the ground, then driving long blades through their torsos to pin them there. The angry shouts became gasps of pain, and the two that had remained quiet allowed themselves a moment of smugness when they were left merely kneeling. Only a *hint* of amusement, certainly, as neither wanted to draw the sudden and confusing punishment onto themselves.

"Prepare yourselves for the words of... *the Ascetic*," one of the guards announced in a sonorous voice, almost as though he were singing praises. After he bowed thrice, he personally pulled out a series of earplugs and pushed them into the ears of the captives—a move that had the guards muttering with indigna-

1

tion that one of their own needed to provide service to the *humans*. "Though they will be granted to you through a quadruple intermediary, be warned that even so far removed from their source... the words of one that speaks for the Pantheon are not easy for the ears of mortals to bear."

A High Cleric stepped into view, materializing through the quartz walls and trees that composed the buildings of high officials in the Elven Capitol. "The Ascetic sends both praise and pity. Their words are as thus: *Your work both superb, and subpar. The main mission complete, your failures replete. A blessing, a boon, and a trial you earn.*"

The ears and eyes of everyone present, including the Cleric that was speaking, had begun to bleed. The Cleric took several deep breaths, composed himself, then began his own speech. "We have interpreted the words on your behalf. You have completed your main mission, which was to overthrow the Dwarven Oligarchy. For that task alone, all of the rewards that you were due are to be granted. Noble titles, advanced Classes, everything that was promised... is yours."

A few people decided that they wanted to cheer, but the blades pinning them to the ground turned their efforts to wheezing, reminding them that they weren't here to speak, but merely to listen. The Cleric ignored them and continued his ponderous oration. "Here is the blessing that you have earned: you may choose a single target on this Zone in the opposite faction. You will be able to damage this person twenty percent greater, fail to land blows on them fifty percent fewer, and all debuffs you place on them will last thirty percent longer."

"*Yes.*" One person couldn't hold in his glee for a moment longer, letting out a hiss of pleasure. The attention of the Cleric came to rest on him, and the Elf gently lifted a hand to keep a guard from stabbing the human, then paused to take in the odd choice in garb.

"Trench coat, welder's goggles, and *far* too much black leather for the high heat and humidity." The Cleric nodded sagely and took a step closer. "I was told to speak to you directly for this next part... Herr Trigger."

"You have *all* of mine attention." The slight German accent that the man feigned colored his words, and the wide smile on his face brightened the area. "As you know, we are ready to do whatever the Theocracy requires of us. No matter who it is that needs to be... silenced."

The High Cleric tilted his head slightly to the side, as though trying to understand something. "But you *failed*. Why is it that you consider this to be a happy day for you? Your main task was important, but the Ascetic herself had granted you additional tasks as directly as your mind could handle."

"The... side quests? They were labeled as optional." Herr Trigger's brow furrowed, and a slight hint of nervousness touched him for the first time since he had been forced to his knees. "They were also near-impossible, as the little Hamlet was on high alert due to the loss of the Oligarchs. I died trying to achieve my goals!"

"*Everything* in life is optional, is it not?" the Cleric wondered aloud, a hint of a sneer peeking through the calm facade. "We can choose to eat or starve. We can choose to advance or stagnate. We can choose to complete the tasks given to us by the Chosen of the Heavens, or we can give up because... it is too *hard*."

Herr Trigger's eyes narrowed at the obvious mockery, and he clearly forced himself to refrain from saying even one more thing. The Cleric shook his head sadly as he watched the internal struggle. "The Hamlet is lost to us. All memory and recordings of its location have been hidden. Search your own memory; where was this battle? *Where* did the Royal Family die?"

"It was the..." Herr Trigger's mouth lost its wide smile, twisting into an ugly frown. "How is this possible?"

"Who can say," the Cleric stated lightly. "Your trial follows next. You, your team, and our representative are to continue your work as a strike force. The Ascetic has seen that an enemy, whom you know personally, is currently creating a stronghold that is otherwise hidden to us, bringing the refugees to a new, protected land. This man will be in unprotected lands at least three times over the course of this cleanup our opponents call a war. By the time the Bifrost has opened, you must have either captured this man and *ensured* his captivity until the High Clerics take responsibility for him, killed the human enough times to make impossible his timeline of the final mission, which his pride forces upon him. The target must be slain at least three times for this outcome. The final option? Slay a Dwarven Grandmaster that he is attempting to convert to his cause."

"This person is…?" Herr Trigger had a few ideas, but he wanted it to be stated clearly.

"His name is Joe, the Chosen of Occultatum." The Cleric's statement restored the smile to Herr Trigger's face. "To ensure that this task is possible and will be done correctly, allow me to introduce our representative. Mirak, if you will?"

An Elf appeared even more suddenly than the Cleric had, and Herr Trigger realized that the man had been there the entire time; his mind simply hadn't been able to register his presence. "High Cleric."

"Trigger, Mirak has been assigned as your party leader. You will follow his commands, and he will ensure that you are where you need to be." The Cleric once more gave the human an order, something Trigger hated with a passion. "He may choose to aid you in combat, or not."

"My apologies, Cleric, but how can I *not* be in charge and yet still be held accountable if we fail?" Trigger glanced at the Elf, who remained motionless in his kneeling position. "He may be able to hide in broad daylight, but that means nothing to me. How will we find our quarry? What will happen if we fail to find them, and what if they get away? Will *I* have failed?"

"You are being moved across the board based on the orders of the *Ascetic*." The Cleric's emphatic tone carried a clear warning to the bounty hunter. "As a result, you do not need to worry that you will not find them. What you do from there is *your* issue, though I have little doubt that you will have any difficulty tracking them after the first time you locate their trail."

"How so? Is our new party leader a Druid that will have the land whisper into his ear as we search for tracks on broken rocks?" Herr Trigger's mocking tone caused the blade at his back to shift forward slightly, the guard almost ready to ignore the Cleric's attempt to keep things calm.

The Cleric himself appeared to be trying not to laugh. "He is that, and more. If you look to your left, you will understand why you won't lose the trail, and also why you should make sure to be *very* friendly with your new team leader. Meet Ron, the bonded beast of Mirak."

Herr Trigger's head swiveled to the side, and he flinched as his gaze was met with *teeth*. Long and metal, they were clearly razor-sharp and ready to tear flesh. He started to raise his eyes to see how large this beast was, but a wash of hot steam rolled over his face—along with a spattering of mucus as the nose of the beast blew out, then in… savoring the human's unique scent.

Ron the Razorfang Direwolf. Level: 28.

"For now, I…" The Bounty Hunter swallowed and turned back to the Cleric. "Have no further questions."

"You may address me as 'Your Grace'." The High Cleric shook his head sorrowfully, waving at the guards to take the unindoctrinated humans away. Moments later, blades were torn from bodies, and the bleeding humans were tossed out of the courtyard.

CHAPTER ONE

"I don't know what to tell you, Joe. We're focusing on turtling up, and I'm actively against doing anything else." Havoc tapped his cigar on an ashtray, sending the burning cinders to land in the porcelain dish with a too-loud *clunk*—as though rocks had been dropped into the dish. "The Shoe is closed tighter than an Elf's grip on one of their holy books. You're just going to have to stay here and train like I've been pushing ya to do."

"I'm telling *you* that I need to travel to one of the other cities and convince another Grandmaster to come here." Joe's voice was as calm as he could keep it, but several days had already passed, and they'd had this conversation time and again. He practically *threw* the information from the quest at Havoc, who waved it to the side to read later. "Look at that, Havoc. I have a quest that will turn this place into a *hidden* Hamlet. If we combine that with your obfuscation and defensive measures, we'll have a solid position to strike back against the Elves after we build up our forces and prepare. But we *need* that time, which means *I* need to get moving!"

"You can't just be thinking about yourself, being all nice and calm as you go about your business. If I open a door for you, *everyone* is going to run out of it." Havoc nodded into the distance, highlighting various groups that were forming up and preparing to attempt breaking out of the volcano. "All they want to do is get outside and throw themselves into the meat grinder. They want revenge; they want to get straight into combat. Every single one of them is going to get turned into Elves If I let them walk away."

Shouting reached them as someone ran out of a building holding a communication device. "This just in! The Elven armies have invaded en masse! Without cohesive leadership, our people are being *slaughtered* if they haven't retreated to a city! Storm the walls of The Shoe!"

"See?" Havoc shook his head and sighed as he twisted a dial on a board, sending a bolt of lightning to strike the hysterical Dwarf. The ground shifted as the Dwarf was carted away, though there didn't seem to be anything under him. The Ritualist shuddered as he wondered how much of this place had been replaced by golems. "Look, Joe. You don't get to be my age without seeing some crazy things. You also don't get here without an unhealthy dose of paranoia. I locked down the volcano. Sure, this is your town, but I entirely control the space around it. No one gets in, no one gets out. That's the best way that I can guarantee our safety."

"Temperature has risen by *three* heat units!" Lord Checkoff's voice was accusatory and stiff. "This is unacceptable, and *must* be rectified. Even so, this lapse will most certainly be going in my report as a negative mark on the potential Lord's record."

"To *whom*, Lord Checkoff? To whom do you plan to hand over that report?" The familiar voice of Bauen increased as he called into the open. "Has anyone seen Joe? With the volcano sealed, the temperature is increasing too rapidly for the current system to keep up. Joe! Where are you? We need to get the new ritual in place or-"

"Look at that, it seems that you're needed! Maybe you can

go do some actual work or training, instead of bothering me." Havoc turned away, only pausing as Joe's retort reached his ears.

"The new Guildhall is already built, and the teleporter should be active by the end of the day. I'm *telling* you this as a courtesy. We either make a deal soon, or everyone is going to leave anyway." Deciding that he wanted the last word, Joe turned and ran to help the Dwarf with the failing heat containment and redirection system.

He departed too quickly to see Havoc pause and look into the air at the quest information the human had sent along, his eyes flashing blue in the process. The Dwarf stroked his beard as his frown twisted into something ugly. "Yeah... looks like we *might* need to go after this quest. That's a serious buff..."

Joe was sweating as he hurried over to the center of the town, his eyes fixed on the white-hot ceiling of the solidified bubble they lived in. Luckily, the Reductionist had been ready for this task and had prepared a Student-rank heat sink system in advance. It was far more refined than the current version, and most importantly, it was ready to be put into place *immediately*.

There were several critical systems that Joe had been redesigning ever since he had gained deeper insight into his class, specifically since his knowledge of Ritual Lore had reached the Student ranks. He dodged a dollop of molten stone as it *hissed* through the air, landing on the ground to form the start of what was doomed to be a short-lived stalagmite. "I need two high-mana capacity people with me, five in a secondary ring around me, seven in the third, and eleven people at the outermost edge! This is going down faster than we thought, but we can stave off disaster—*together*! Bauen, get someone working on protection detail to intercept those drops of slag!"

He deployed the ritual without another word. Four spell circles sprang into being, and people rushed into the indicated positions without any issues; by now, they were used to jumping into giant magical designs. The ritual began once the last one stepped into place, the first ring spinning like a windmill as it began siphoning off heat and redistributing it into previously-selected locations such as smithies. There were a few moments of great concern, specifically when the previous ritual failed and the ceiling began to sag inward, but luckily everything was already starting to rapidly cool.

Within a few hours, the old ritual had been removed and fully replaced, the ceiling had been reshaped, and the timer on the new ritual was counting down at a normal pace instead of multiple seconds at a time as the failed one had been. Joe understood that this was a sign that the ritual was properly designed to counteract the natural forces degrading it, and announced that the installation had been a success.

Quest update: Student Ritualist. Student rituals designed and deployed: 9/20.

Everyone breathed a sigh of relief as the spiking temperature began lowering to a normal level throughout The Shoe once more, and a cool breeze was released from the vent system. Bauen turned to Joe and waved his hand around the area. "You know, I've been hearing about your shouting matches with Havoc. Being trapped in The Shoe might be a blessing in disguise for you, if you want it to be. I'm only a simple engineer, but if you cared to learn... I could teach you some basic thermodynamics. If you have any kind of fire affinity at all, it's useful for reaching Expert level in new flame spells at an increased pace."

"You know, I just might take you up on that." Joe reached up to wipe away some sweat from his face, only for his Neutrality Aura to take care of it for him. "I'll only be here until the teleport is open, but I'm thinking I should start filling out my repertoire of spells, and if you can help with-"

"I've changed my mind." Havoc barreled into the conversation as though a giant gorilla had thrown him. "I didn't have all of the facts previously, and now that I do, I recognize that you need to get yourself some real life experience. Also, you. Get out. There's a matter that my Apprentice and I need to discuss in private."

"Havoc, Bauen makes a good point… you should know better than anyone that I am severely lacking in terms of offensive and defensive spells. Even worse, my rituals are solely based on spell work to which I have access." Joe found himself in the surprising position of having to argue to stay after he had just been fighting to leave. "Maybe I *should* take a few weeks to brush up on my spells and such. I have a whole affinity that I haven't even touched-"

"Like I said." Havoc glowered at Joe, tapping at a screen and sending it to Joe. "I didn't have all of the *facts*. Expand on that quest you have for saving this place, and keep it quiet."

Deciding to humor the Dwarf, seeing as he had never provided any evidence that he was a jokester, Joe pulled up the quest and took a look.

Quest: Not Lost, but Hidden. Convince at least one more Grandmaster of the Dwarven Society to join your burgeoning settlement. Reward: the location of 'The Shoe' will be lost to the Elves and anyone with positive ties to them. This will greatly aid your efforts to return the Dwarven Oligarchy to its position as a Unified race. Failure: The destruction of this settlement.

"Expand? Additional details?" Joe tried a verbal expansion, earning a chuckle from Bauen, though it did work.

Additional details: Because you are the owner of the settlement, as well as considered to be its main defender, a temporary Divine Ward will be placed on the settlement. Until 75% of Dwarven territory has been lost to the Elves, or until the capital city falls, anyone with negative designs on 'The Shoe' will be unable to remember the location. This will not stop people from finding the location by physical means, nor will it cause someone to lose memory of the location once they have rediscovered it.

"Oh. So, no real time limit, but it does have an expiration." Joe considered this new data, rubbing his chin as he eyed his suddenly-shifty mentor with a dawning realization. "Did you think that your defenses were just so scary that no one was going to bother coming here anymore or something?"

"You watch your mouth, kid. You got lucky. The reality is…

it's less luck, and more ticking time bomb. We're already a Shattered race." Havoc shook his head sadly. "The Dwarves *are* going to fall. Our cities are going to be torn down brick by brick, and our lands turned into something... *way* too natural. Probably a forest or—*ugh*—flowing plains. The point is, as soon as our cities do fall, if you haven't completed this quest, pretty much every Elf in the entire Zone is suddenly going to remember where you are, and they'll seek revenge for what you did to the Royal Family."

"*Me*? What are you saying?" Joe's heart started to race as Havoc's stare bored into him.

"What I'm *saying* should be pretty obvious." Havoc's exhaustion was evident in his tone. "What happens to the *Dwarves* will be very straightforward—as soon as we die, we join *them*. Why would they do anything *other* than kill us immediately? You, though? A human scapegoat they can pin all of their people's crimes on? They'll likely toss you in the deepest, darkest pit they can find and make sure there is no escape. You need to either get this city hidden *properly* by completing this quest, or sneak onto the Bifrost and get out of here as soon as the Dwarves are properly routed."

Joe tried to think of an answer, something that would allow him to finally plant his roots and stay in one spot for a while. He was tired of running. Even so, he knew that his mentor was correct. Right now, escaping from Alfheim or hiding were the only real options. "I'm just so... tired of escaping one bad situation only to sprint to the next problem. Are you going to help me?"

"*Absolutely*, I am!" The Grandmaster Dwarf smiled, showing far too many teeth. "I'm going to stay here and keep building this pretty little town up. I'm also gonna stay *away* from the other Grandmasters, so that you actually have a chance at convincing them to join us in our little social experiment."

"I'll help by joining you on the quest directly!" Jaxon called as he walked in on the intense discussion. "Are we going to hunt down some Elves?"

"No, we're doing a recurring fetch quest," Joe grumbled as he turned toward the rebuilt Guildhall, and soon his bald head was reflecting the green lights that the building had been raised under. "Sure, we're fetching Grandmasters, but that doesn't help. Let's get this teleporter online and get out of here."

CHAPTER TWO

Incoming teleportation request.

"You've gotta be kidding me. I just want to get *going*." Joe growled as he stared at the message that appeared on his city command tab as soon as the teleporter came online. "How long has this person been pinging us for their message to come through as soon as the teleporter goes live? Who even is it?"

Message: Invite me in. I've been waiting to use the Alchemy station, and you're almost out of time.

"Abyss and blast!" Joe yelped as he hurried to slap the 'accept teleport' button, and the enchantment spun to life. In a flash, a familiar foreboding figure appeared: Jake the Alchemist, standing calmly and utterly non-threateningly... in a still-some-how-menacing way.

"I was beginning to believe that you had ignored our deal. When the people I had tasked with watching you completely lost all memory of your location, I thought you may have cut and run," the Alchemist stated without preamble as he took his first step into The Shoe. "That would have been very... *not good* for our future relationship."

"How could I possibly forget you?" Joe plastered a wide

smile onto his face and nodded at the oddly disconcerting man, then briefly recalled Cleocatra as well, since that seemed like an important thing to do for the leader of the Nyandrathals. "I've just been making sure that this location was secure before sending along the invitation. As a side note, if your watchers lost this place, that meant that they had designs that weren't trustworthy. Better make sure not to let them know where you went."

"I have my own methods of assuring loyalty, thank you. Let's see this Alchemy shop, shall we? I'm looking forward to seeing what shack you managed to stuff that cauldron into without making it explode," Jake informed the Reductionist coolly. They left the Guildhall, making their way to the completely unused and currently-unusable alchemy building. "Where are we going? Is this shack behind that eyesore in the center of this sweltering locale?"

"Eyesore?" Joe regarded the pyramid they were approaching. "That?"

"Yes. *That.*" The Alchemist shook his head and muttered under his breath, "No sense of subtlety at all."

"I hate to have to tell you this, but that *is* the Alchemy building." The Reductionist chuckled as the irate man did a double-take, then peered curiously at the shining walls.

"Grand Inspect. Eyes of Truth. Endless Array of Eternal Understanding." Mana washed off the man, but not the unfocused cloud that seemed to follow anyone else that Joe had ever seen using spells. Every *iota* of the mana went into use, swirling out and into the building before boomeranging back, and Jake slowly began to nod. "The Pharaoh's Pyramid of Panaceas, an Artifact-ranked Alchemy building that has not yet chosen a master for its domain. This will do. As soon as I assume control, I will consider your side of our bargain completely fulfilled."

"Glad you like it?" Joe's uncertainty stemmed from the fact that the Alchemist was still speaking in the same calm monotone, though it was right on the *edge* of being infuriated. "Anything the matter?"

"Not at all." Jake walked up to the door, laying a hand on it and letting his mana seep from his fingertips and into the building proper. To his surprise, Joe received a confusing message.

Jake the Alchemist is attempting to bond with a building you have created! Jake the Alchemist is not a part of any faction you belong to and is unlikely to do as you ask without a deal in place. Do you want to allow the bond to complete? If you do, be aware that regaining control without his assistance and acceptance will be nearly impossible.

"Yes… I really have no other choice at this point." Joe was concerned, but the deal had been struck, and going back on it would spell a terrible fate for himself and his Hamlet.

Lava began washing up out of the ground below the pyramid, swirling through the layer of transparent crystal that surrounded the building. Joe took a step forward as the building came to life fully for the first time since its creation, and the door began to creep open. Jake raised a brow at him. "Where do you think *you're* going? Until this building is fully operational, including traps and failsafes, no one other than its master will enter."

"Ah… I just wanted to see it, and I have a ton of Alchemical things that I need from you." The Reductionist chuckled nervously, but the Alchemist shook his head.

"Leave a list and a recipe, if you have one. Is there someone here that can get me the things I need, or do I need to secure my own logistics?" Jake looked around and spotted a Dwarf with a cigar sticking out of his mouth sprinting toward them with a grim expression. "This one at least looks competent. Should I be asking him for things?"

"How is this building functional? Why are you still here and not *sprinting* to the next city over…" Havoc's roar preceded him, fading away even as he slowed to a total stop, his eyes locked on Jake. A long period of awkward silence ate away at them until the Grandmaster flashed into motion.

Joe was sent flying by the sonic boom created by Havoc's fist —somehow three times larger than his body—slamming into a barrier of mushroom spores that appeared around Jake with a flick of his pinky. The Alchemist remained calm, though he lightly blew a stream of smoke at the Dwarf, who laughed in his face. "*Compliance* powder? I *invented* that, and I abyss-well-*better* be immune to it."

"I see. I was unaware that your people had any kind of resistance to Alchemical compounds. Let's try something more your style: overwhelming strength." Jake pulled a small vial from a pocket, scattering the contents into the air and mumbling quietly. In the next moment, a portal appeared in the air, and a finger the size of a house came through and poked Havoc in the chest, sending him rocketing away—streaking along until he hit the far wall and became embedded into it; magma leaking from the cracks around him. "How very interesting. He survived that without incurring a permanent debuff?"

"You're rootin-tootin-right I did," Havoc growled at the man as he thundered back over, though he didn't attack again right away. "How? *How* is something like you here? How'd you get on the *Zone*, let alone into this little Hamlet in the middle of nowhere?"

"I'm a quest reward," Jake stated without a single hint of shame, indulging in a slight smirk as though he had pulled a fast one. "Joe here *contracted* me to provide him with at-cost Alchemy for the next ten years, and I just got the invitation to arrive and begin my service. The time has already started. That means I work for him, so please don't attack again. I won't give you another light warning, which means I'll be forced to take your attack seriously and respond appropriately."

"You *invited* that *thing* into this Hamlet?" Havoc turned on Joe, who couldn't get over the fact that the Dwarf had a ham-sized hole through his chest—his internal organs were on display, each of them apparently having *dodged* the attack that hit him. "Wait... he's working at-cost for ten years... works for you... and you're my Apprentice. Do you know what the transitive property is? Can I give him a list of things to do?"

"I had just specifically requested a liaison to the town," Jake butted into the conversation.

Joe nodded at Havoc, feeling completely helpless to do anything about these two monsters in his midst. "I have a few things I need, but my true need is *training*, so... yeah, whatever you think you need, as long as it doesn't get in my way."

"Well." Havoc looked at Jake and considered him while taking a puff on his cigar. The smoke wafted over, and Jake's nose twitched. A moment later, the Alchemist had materialized fifteen different ingredients in the air. With a turn of his hand, they combined by themselves and dropped into a sachet.

"That should fix the power requirement issue you have with lighting those," Jake stated as if they would just *know* what he meant. Havoc reached out and slowly took the small bag, peering into it curiously.

"Now that's how you make a good first impression." The Dwarf practically *purring* the compliment made Joe roll his eyes. "Okay, he can stay. *You* need to get out of here, and please try to stop making deals with-"

*A-*hem.** Jake lightly coughed into his fist while glaring at the Dwarf.

"-entities you don't understand." Havoc finished lamely.

"I'm... I don't know how to respond to that? I normally don't?" Joe wavered between wanting to ask questions and wanting to immediately commence mass-producing potions and the like. Havoc shook his head and walked away, and Jake turned away to go do his own things, so Joe rapidly wrote down what he needed and handed it over.

Jake skimmed the requested potion and scoffed. "Give me five minutes and three seconds, and I'll get you a binding agent for your weapons. First thing to be made in a cauldron that Alchemical Scions would kill for, and he wants *binding agents*. Wait here. *Celestials*, I work for this-"

Standing alone in front of the pyramid as the door closed in his face, Joe sighed and turned away, looking out over the ramshackle town that was slowly coming together. "It's been a strange morning."

CHAPTER THREE

"That's why we have a completely unknown amount of time to get this taken care of." Joe was wrapping up his mission briefing to Major Cleave and Jaxon, just as Daniella arrived wearing a travel pack. "Off to... somewhere, Daniella?"

"I'm coming with you. I want to get out of this... whatever it is that you want to call it. I'm thinking you should name this Hamlet 'The Gilded Cage'?" Her words soured Joe's mood slightly, and he was a little less receptive than he normally would have been as she stated, "I feel like I was helpful back in the fight against the guardian, so-"

"Not particularly!" Jaxon informed her cheerfully, causing the room to go still. "Though you were *excellent* moral support, you were—in actuality—a large burden on the team. Your combat abilities are geared toward non-lethal, and your survival instincts are questionable at best."

Silence met Daniella as she looked to the others to back her up; both Cleave and Joe had busied themselves with something else as the completely unexpected verbal beatdown sent the young woman reeling. The Dwarf started sharpening an axe completely unnecessarily, and Joe willed AutoMate's huge ebon-steel coffee mug—which he *totally* needed both hands to hold—to appear in his hands. He took a long, slow sip, savoring the flavor of the perfect roast in lieu of paying attention to the conversation.

She cleared her throat and looked to the chiropractor. "Do you not want me to come along and be a member of this party?"

"I have no issue with you coming along! Whatever would give you that idea?" Jaxon's head cocked to the side as he regarded her quizzically. "I was merely mentioning that your previous statement was incorrect, as far as I could tell. Would you mind informing me as to how I am wrong?"

"I...!" Daniella thought back on the fight, then slowly shrugged and offered a sheepish smile. "It was a lot of fun to go out and try new things, even though it was scary a few times. Do you guys mind if I come?"

"Keeping yourself alive is your responsibility. Long as you realize that, I don't care what you do." Cleave nonchalantly shrugged and motioned for the Architect to sit down. Her deep voice made *Joe's* chest vibrate as she patted the human on the arm. "It'll actually be nice to have another lady along for the trip."

Joe merely smiled hesitantly, still unsure of his thoughts regarding Daniella. Being around her always made him doubt himself, and he wasn't sure *why*. That alone was enough reason for him to feel uncertain whether he wanted her around for the long haul, but before he could say a word, she started speaking in her own defense. "I'll be a lot more useful in cities, *that's* for sure. I think that I'll even be able to point out buildings with unique features and special prowess and see if I can manage to convince the owners to give us access to them. Maybe that's what I can do while you're all running around doing whatever it is you need to? I can convince landowners to let you make blue-prints out of their structures?"

That settled it for Joe. He knew for a fact that she was an expert in convincing people to let him scan buildings, and that was certainly something he *wanted*, even if he didn't currently *need* it. He'd eventually want to rebuild a Dwarven city for his friends, if nothing else. "Daniella, of course you're welcome to come along. Like Cleave said, you have to watch out for yourself in combat, but I'm sure your skills will come in handy outside of that."

"Absolutely," was Daniella's only reply, knowing better than to keep trying to sell him on it: any salesman worth their pay knew when to shut their mouth.

"Then, even though I think we're completely unprepared for this, I guess it's time to go." Joe activated the teleporter, choosing to travel to the only available location: the Dwarven Capital.

"A quick question for you, Joe!" Jaxon waved at the energized dais of stone that housed the teleporter. "If we had access to this the last time we went to the capital, why did we travel by bubble?"

"I wanted to test it out." Joe smiled at the fond memory, which had only been slightly spoiled by breaking his neck upon landing. "Never know when we *won't* have access to this sort of system, so it's good to have everything set and ready for when feces hits the fan."

"How's your trainee chiropractor doing?" Daniella questioned Jaxon just as Joe stepped through to the capital, making him miss the assuredly enthusiastic answer.

The Ritualist looked around the area, gulping as he took in dozens of Dwarven guards pointing their weapons at him, suspicion hot in their eyes. "Major General Pyrrhic here, passing through on a mission for the enrichment of the Oligarchy!"

It seemed that his enthusiasm allowed the Dwarves to trust him a small fraction more than they had upon his arrival, and a few of the weapons waved as they scanned him and found that the information matched up. Even so, it was not until Major Cleave appeared that they fully relaxed their ready stance. Joe grumbled about that for a while as they made their way to Grandmaster McPoundy's workshop and delivered the linked teleportation pad.

Knowing that time had been short, Havoc had deigned to assist in the production of the schematic. Joe *wanted* to think that there was another reason, perhaps familial love, but... that didn't seem to play into the Grandmaster's plans at all. He shook his head at the abrasive Dwarf's scoffed assertion: 'These need to be able to expand to allow for large groups of refugees to escape all at once. If I left you to do this, I just *know* you'd figure out a way to accidentally kill everyone that steps through it. Sit back and pay attention. Maybe try to learn something without having it spoon-fed to you?'

Even though he knew that Havoc was correct, it still irked Joe that he wasn't even allowed to have a *minor* part in the creation of such an awesome item. Teleportation had been the dream of humanity for as long as he could remember—same as flight—and he wanted to be one of the pioneers of this kind of magical technology for humanity. He understood, logically, that having someone else do it correctly the first time was going to be the best use of time and resources... still, he wanted his work and expertise to matter.

One of the smiths carried off the large metal-and-jewel encrusted platform, refusing to allow them in to see the Grand-master. The Ritualist wasn't sure if it was on orders, or because he just was not well-liked as a member of humanity at this moment. Either way, Joe was fully immersed in a foul mood as they walked away and into town. It didn't help that most shops wouldn't sell to them as soon as the vendors noted their height, claiming that the goods and services were needed for people they knew for certain would not use them in 'unsavory ways'.

Eventually, Joe simply gave up on trying to complete anything else in the capital and transferred a large amount of reputation over to Cleave. "I hate to ask this, but would you mind getting the supplies that we are going to need for our trip? I have no idea where we are supposed to go or how to get there. So... maybe a map would be an order?"

"I understand. I'll make it happen." Cleave seemed to be in a much better mood, ever since she had managed to take care of the Elven subversive group that had been creating zombies in the sewer. Perhaps it was just the fact that she knew for certain that he was not going to betray them, or maybe it was that she had achieved some hands-on catharsis against their sworn enemy. No matter what it was, Joe was just glad that she was acting more normally toward him. "What are you going to do while I'm-"

She stopped short as Joe held up one of his Ritual Orbs and a bottle that Jake had given him. "I'm going to try binding another attribute to my weapon. I figure I'll just do it in a park or something, then swing over to Tatum's Temple and see if there's anything he can offer for the trip. Advice, spells, you know the drill."

"Havoc *really* knows drills," Jaxon piped up. "How does one go about making a *drill* into their main weapon?"

"Practice," Cleave answered with a grunt as she walked away.

Knowing that the Dwarf would get better deals if she went on her own, all three humans adjourned to the park nearby and waited as Joe set up his ritual. "Really, the only thing that I need to do now is figure out which attribute to bind. I did Intelligence, so perhaps I should add its counterpart in the physical characteristics and bond Strength next?"

"Make sense to me! Just like when you are tightening screws, you want to do one side, then the other, so that everything is sturdy and well-maintained," Jaxon opined as Joe pulled out an inscribing tool and started etching the Ritual Circle on a large section of nearby stonework. "It's always interesting to see you use that stuff; it looks like you're drawing with fire."

"Thanks, Jaxon," Joe muttered as he turned his focus to the Ritual Circle. It was fairly basic, even if it was a Student-ranked ritual. The difficult and dangerous part was the fact that he was assigning something to it—as though the orb was a voodoo doll that controlled his physical strength. As he had learned the first time, it wasn't a pleasant experience; certainly not something to do lightly. Still, he had gained enough control over his weapons that he felt confident using them long-term.

Extremely long-term.

After the circles were complete, he began etching directly on the orb. He had to put down his understanding of Strength in the equivalent equation form, shaping the resultant calculus to have a sympathetic link to his body. In essence, that meant drawing out his body and highlighting muscles that may or may not really be there. "Now all I need is the Alchemical solution, thank you Jake, and I'll... *activate!*"

His bright white robe fluttered in an artificial breeze as the ritual spun up. The orb he had chosen, which was currently bonded with the spell 'Corify', was pulled into the center of the ritual. The fluid from the mixture was sucked directly out of the bottle, spreading evenly over the surface of the ritual before the entire thing collapsed around it as though it were a person who had watched through a spiderweb. As soon as the ritual moved, Joe was completely immobilized as the orb and his body fell into sync.

Quest updated: Student Ritualist. 10/20 rituals activated.

The orb dropped out of the air and into his hand, which moved almost entirely on its own to catch what now felt like an extension of his own body. He let out a deep sigh of relief that he had not messed up and damaged himself in a way that he could not yet fix. "*Whoo.* Oh man, is that nerve-wracking. Let's see what you can do..."

Ritual Orb of Strength (Masterwork). This Ritual Orb has gone through an Alchemic treatment as well as an extra round of enchanting via rituals.

Base Damage: 100 blunt -> shifting in progress.

Characteristic assigned: Strength. Any spell assigned to this Orb will have the primary damage effect slightly altered. Base damage will shift over time to become a damage type associated with the Characteristic.

Automatically grants Orb the 'recall' ability; it will return to you after five minutes if left behind, forgotten, or stolen.

Core assigned: 902/1,112

Spell assigned: Corify (Beginner V, awaiting unbinding for skill upgrade).

Ritual Diagram captured: None.

"It's strange that finding this characteristic has such a different effect, although... is it really? It makes sense that Intelligence would enhance a spell. Or... is something happening each time that makes the effects different? Some small alteration in the ritual itself?" Joe rubbed at his bald head, wanting to do nothing more than study this strange phenomenon and its effects. "Let's just do the next one and find out."

A slew of messages popped up at that moment, startling him enough to make him drop the inscriber that he had just picked up.

Alchemical Rituals has reached Beginner 0! Alchemical side effects created will be 70% easier to understand. This will make it possible to recreate or mitigate them in future rituals!

Ritualistic Alchemy has reached Beginner V!

Caution! You have two characteristics bound to Ritual Orbs. The strain on your being is reaching a breaking point. To continue binding additional weapons, you will need to provide higher-quality energy sources. Recommendation: get a full assessment from a high-ranked Cleric or Alchemist before your next attempt.

"Need a higher-tier ritual and better Alchemical concoctions, but now I'm better at making them. Neat." Joe translated after he had taken in that information for a moment. He could only be thankful that the system had given him a warning instead of just letting him blow parts of his body off unnecessarily by attempting to do the same thing a third time. He packed up his tools, then looked around at his friends and whispered to himself, "Speaking of damaging me unnecessarily...

Cleocatra, I'm thinking of you all the time nowadays. Please don't randomly attack me."

With that out of the way, all they could do was wait until Major Cleave showed up with their supplies. As soon as she located them and they divided up their gear, they started their trek toward the next major Dwarven city, a third of the Zone away.

CHAPTER FOUR

"Remind me again why we are walking instead of tearing apart our atoms and sending them across space so that we can appear directly in the next city over as they all come back together?" Jaxon spoke out loud to no one in particular, but it was Daniella that answered him.

"It is a safety feature built into the teleporters," she informed him with a resigned tone. "In an effort to make it less feasible for spies to gain control of teleportation points and send troops directly into cities, in addition to setting rules and restrictions in place that make it more difficult to send reinforcements during an invasion, major city teleporters are not allowed to connect to each other during a full incursion. It is likely that we could have gotten out to a minor Fortress, similar to how we came in, but the costs associated with that would be astronomical right now."

"She's right," Major Cleave affirmed when the human stopped speaking. "That's something that you should have known, considering the rank that you have. It's general knowledge, and seeing that you are missing that hurts something inside of me. I forget sometimes that you got to your position in no time flat, through achievement rather than through promotion. There's a *whole* lot that you're going to need to get caught up on if you're going to be an effective military leader for my people."

"I don't think that's gonna be an issue for long, Cleave." Joe snorted with unintended callousness. "We have a mission, and I think that the end goal of this chain of events is to escape the Zone entirely, bringing all the Dwarven refugees with me that we can possibly manage."

"But…" Daniella stuttered as she realized that Joe *wasn't* planning to hole up in his hidden Hamlet when the conflict was all over. "What about all your hard work? Your buildings, the town, all of that?"

"Not the first time I've had to start over. I'll do it again." Joe shrugged and continued walking toward the nearest exit of the city. He nearly stumbled as he abruptly remembered a series of rewards that he had gained the last time he had been in the area, and he decided to go and gather them. "Nearly forgot, I have a reward from Tatum to go collect. While I'm at it, I should go gather whatever aspects managed to get collected in the dump."

Jaxon looked at the others in the group and pointed at a small restaurant. "Anyone for lunch? I'll make Joe pay, as he's the one that wasted our time by not remembering to do all of this when we were waiting for our supplies acquisition specialist!"

"Sounds good." Cleave cracked a smile for the first time that day when she saw Joe's narrowed eyes.

"I *am* getting hungry." Daniella led the way, the three of them laughing at Joe as he sputtered out a quick to-go order for himself. He chuckled ruefully as they vanished from sight, deciding to head over to Tatum's Pantheon Temple.

Just like everything else in the city, the roads were planned efficiently and carefully, allowing him to reach the brand-new temple district with only a short few minutes of running as quickly as possible. Soon he was walking past the purple-smoke-releasing Juggernauts that guarded the area, and approached the huge book that represented Tatum's power on the Zone.

"Howdy, friend." The Ritualist tapped the shrine reverently, even though he spoke casually to the deity. "If I remember correctly, I earned a reputation-based reward from you?"

Between one blink and the next, Joe found himself moved to Tatum's *actual* seat of power, facing the incomprehensible being in person. "Good to see you, Joe. I'm glad you came, because we need to discuss what I can actually do for you."

"I seem to recall the last time I got a reward from you; I got a really cool boon...?" Joe stated leadingly, wiggling his eyebrows—some of the only hair he had left on his head.

"Then you'd also recall that I got locked away for over-reaching what I was allowed to do for you?" Tatum shook his head at the Ritualist and showed only a slight hint of a grin. "Between pulling the king back and letting you build that Pathfinder's Hall so far ahead of your ability to actually do so, I got slapped silly by... by the system."

"I understand." Joe looked around the area, noting the fact that thunderstorms seemed to be gathering around the temple. "Everything going okay with you, big guy?"

"Mmm." Tatum shook his enormous head as he too watched the brewing storm. "Just another reason to keep the reward I owe you to something more like a token of appreciation. There's also the fact that I'm not going to be earning a ton of Divine Energy in the coming months, since there's a good chance that the Dwarven populace is ravaged. That means that I'm going to be back to a bare handful of followers."

"Well, yeah, with *that* attitude..." "Joe tried to joke, but Tatum was having none of it.

A document appeared in front of Joe, the inscribed design shining brightly. "I'm just being realistic. Here's what I *can* do for you... an IOU, and a token reward. You're level twenty-three right now, so let's say that when you get to twenty-five, I can give you a spell variation—and I'll make it a *doozy*. I can do that for Extended Family."

"I'll look forward to it. For now, I'll take whatever you're willing to give me." Joe took the paper, realizing as the glow faded that the document was a blueprint. "This looks like... a shrine?"

Lightning struck at the paper from one of the nearby clouds, only to be slapped away with a casual motion by Tatum. "Yeah, not sure if you remember, but you were once warned away from scanning a shrine. It's a monument-class structure, and it's very efficient for what it does and costs. Most of the deities don't like people knowing how to make these, because they can become a real problem. Building them is always risky, because they can be stolen, but that's not the annoying part. If someone can *make and hide one* away in a Zone... then a single pantheon can't get the *utterly massive* bonus that comes with being the *only* pantheon in a Zone."

"I see." Joe nodded as he perused the information on the sheet, noting especially that for such a tiny structure, the shrine used a *lot* of Rare resources. "Probably was used by cults, or something else the leading pantheons declared 'unsavory', right? It sure would be a shame if there was a shrine built somewhere *super* hidden away. Somewhere annoyingly hard to find, so that even if all the main temples were destroyed, some little shrine in a nondescript rabbit hole kept an annoying group from gaining a giant bonus."

Tatum tapped the side of his own nose and winked at Joe. "Sure would."

Reputation Quest generated by yourself and agreed upon with a Deity: Occultatum is 'totally not' requesting that you create at least one well-hidden shrine somewhere on Alfheim in order to prevent the Elven Pantheon from gaining a large bonus to their power bases by being the only pantheon collecting DE on the Zone. Reward: a minor boon for each day that the shrine remains undiscovered by the Elven Theocracy. If at least one shrine remains hidden for a year and a day, Tatum will directly upgrade one of your spells to a higher tier. (Maximum upgrade will allow you to reach Expert 0). Failure: None.

"I can handle this, Tatum. Thanks for the-" Joe blinked and

found himself standing back in the temple, in the same position he had been in before he was pulled up to see the deity. "-stuff and the fun little side mission."

Now that his primary task had been completed, the Reductionist decided to try out the reward he had gotten from clearing out the dump. Focusing his mind on the A.S.P.E.C.T. that he had left down there, he tried to move to it directly. Anyone watching him would have observed the Major General as he stared at a shrine for a few seconds, muttered a few words, and then vanished, leaving behind a tiny clap of thunder and a foul smell.

Upon approaching the building that was hovering nearly a hundred feet above the top layer of garbage, thanks to the four small Ritual of Force disks he had built it on, Joe popped into the structure and deactivated the ritual that continually carried garbage, then pulled out the Aspect Jars that had been collecting the broken-down waste. "Hmm, pretty good haul. So glad I automated this."

Burble?

"No, no. Automate means to do something automatic; you are Auto*Mate*, with the extra emphasis on the last syllable."

Burble.

The Rare aspects were making especially good headway, and Joe decided right then that he would spend some of the bounty on creating a small shrine in the very middle of the dump, buried as far down into the garbage as possible. "Let the hiding of the shrines begin. The Elves are only ever going to know me as the shrine bunny, because whenever they think they've found the last one, there's always going to be one more hidden away, rotting in silence until someone accidentally steps into it."

His eyes shone with excitement as he thought over the next stage of his diabolical plan. "Maybe I'll leave a little surprise for anyone that thinks they can show up and convert it, too."

Two rituals were used in conjunction for the first time that day, the combination of which would eventually become a warning to low-level Elves: their instructors would strongly caution them against ever stepping into an unknown shrine shaped like a book, for fear of becoming trapped in a bubble of force that would rapidly fill with acid.

To Joe, it was just a childish part of him that didn't want anyone to break one of his toys, along with a slightly petty side that wanted anyone impacting his potential quest rewards to pay for it. As soon as the tiny monument was created, the A.S.P.E.C.T. turned back on, and all aspects being collected for later use, Joe exited the dump and found himself only a short distance from the restaurant where his friends had been taking up tablespace.

Feeling good, refreshed, and ready to gain some levels, he happily paid their appetizer-and-dessert inflated tab and led the group out of the city. "Where's the nearest Grandmaster, Major Cleave?"

"Not the closest, but our best bet is going to be Dehur Bethi, the High City of Deep Thought," she answered after a moment of consideration. "You only need *one* more Grandmaster, right?"

"...Right." Joe looked at her questioningly, "Is there a city that's closer?"

"Yes, but the other one..." She hesitated for a moment before waving her hand. "You have a good chance of succeeding in Dehur Bethi. The Grandmaster there likely has a few bonus reasons to join us. As to the location itself, it's a city created for training enchanters and others that have their minds set on pursuing magical classes. It's in the central mountains, away from the rest of the population, mainly so that their experiments and ideas can't get out and corrupt the rest of the monster population."

"In a figurative way, or do they regularly lose experiments that run wild and attack people?" Daniella questioned the Dwarf as their path was slightly altered. When her question went unanswered, the human grumbled, "I knew it was a literal way."

"I wouldn't say it happens *regularly*." Major Cleave coughed into her arm to hide her face slightly. "Not after the upgrades in our containment facilities. Now it's just the strongest or smartest that get out and about."

"How exciting! Do these creatures by chance have abnormal skeletons?" Jaxon rubbed his hands together as he began to generate his own side missions.

"Usually." Major Cleave glanced at Joe, who was smirking as he peered closely into every shadow that they passed. "That won't be an issue for you, right?"

"What? Me? No, ah… no issue," the Reductionist stated distractedly. "Any chance you know some little areas that are never visited or checked up on?"

"Uh…" Major Cleave looked between Joe, who was clearly planning something sneaky, Jaxon, who was obviously preparing to experiment on escaped experiments, and Daniella… who seemed to be lost in thought while sketching out the capital city's walls as they walked away from them. "Am I missing something here?"

"*Nah~h.*" All three of her comrades denied in unison.

CHAPTER FIVE

"I don't particularly like the fact that we're going to be traveling over land for a long period of time, but I also feel that it'll be good for you." Major Cleave shot Joe a pensive look as she took the lead. "There are several things that will be working in our favor for this trip, namely the fact that Dehur Bethi is in the exact center of Alfheim. Wha...? Not Alfheim, *Alfheim*! I... I can't call the Zone by our name for it?"

"One of the curses that comes along with being a Shattered Race." Jaxon patted her back sympathetically, once, twice... then adjusted her, bringing her spine into alignment. "There you go! That should help you get used to reality faster!"

"Never try to touch me again without expecting an axe through the offending hand," Major Cleave growled as she rubbed at her mildly aching spine.

"That soon? I *suppose* I can get you on a regular schedule if you're *this* interested in it." Jaxon replied cheerfully, drawing a chuckle out of Joe. There was something so... non-player-character about the chiropractor when his interactions were impacted by his low Charisma score like this.

"As I was saying, before I was so rudely adjusted by the

system *and* my traveling companion," Major Cleave barked, causing the others to wince at her anger, "the distance from any border is a benefit to us, as is the fact that *getting* there is difficult. You can only be led there by someone that knows the way, and you need to contend with monsters, traps, and enchantments that are attempting to lead you astray the entire time."

"Few active enemies, lots of passive enemies." Joe took out a notebook and started writing down his thoughts, as well as questions that needed answers. "How long will it take to get there? What sort of rituals should I make? Is there anything that you can think of that would be useful? Attack, defense, utility… anything that will give us an edge is good."

"What's all that about?" the Dwarf grumbled at the sudden barrage. "I've never seen you being so proactive."

"I *am* a planner, believe it or not. The problem is that I almost never know ahead of time what sort of trouble I'm going to get into." The Ritualist shrugged off the misplaced suspicion and pondered what she had been explaining. "If we can only find this place by being led there by someone who has prior knowledge, losing you means we can never find this place. To that end, I'm going to design a barrier for you that will keep you alive and send you away if the worst comes to pass."

"You'll do no such thing!" Major Cleave huffed at him threateningly. "I can abyss-well take care of myself."

"There's no reason to be so *rude* about it, Cleave," Daniella shot at the Dwarf. "This is out of character for you. He's just trying to help."

"I can make it and apply it secretly, or I can do so *openly* in order to allow you to get rid of it when you don't need it." Joe glared right back at her through his dazzlingly white half-mask. "There's no coming back for you *alone*, meaning this mission can always continue if we lose someone else. *So*, as I was saying, I'm setting up protection and escape for you, and some more general protections for the rest of us. I'm also planning weapons to take down any overly potent creatures we find, though we can use our standard weapons and spells for the rest of them."

"How far away is this place, anyway?" Jaxon questioned the entire group. "Could we bubble-jump there? Walking is great, but there's that whole 'invasion' thing going on."

Joe lit up at that suggestion, already reaching into his storage ring to pull out one of the prepared ritual tiles he carried, but Major Cleave caught his hand and shook her head. "That's a last resort right now. Don't forget that Elves are powerful mages. We need to *not* be seen, and we also need to *not* have the bubble dispelled while we're zipping through the sky at the speed of sound. Unless you've already figured out a work-around for those particular issues?"

The human ruminated on her points for a few moments, slowly shaking his head after a moment of serious considera-tion. "I can make it move, or I can make it blend in. I don't think that I could make a camouflaged transport with this rank of Ritual Diagram. Maybe at the next rank, but I don't have the needed... *Knowledge*, or Alchemical Lore."

Mana drained out of him, then *into* his brain. His Alchem-ical Lore reached Apprentice four, and the nagging feeling that he had been forgetting something vanished. Major Cleave was staring at him as though he had just set off fireworks, and the others were sending equally confused looks his way. Daniella eventually cleared her throat, inspecting his mana-saturated form. "Did you just interrupt yourself and cast a spell?"

"I had just noticed that it went off cooldown, and I've been trying to make sure that I take full advantage of it." Joe shrugged as the others remained silent. "What? You guys don't have things that you need to do regularly for best effect?"

"Usually we don't *slap* the ambient mana like a dinner bell when we're trying to be stealthy." Major Cleave's voice was more high-pitched than usual, but she noticed that none of the others were exhibiting the same concerns. "None of you have Mana Manipulation at the Journeyman rank, do you? I didn't think so... when you *do*, you'll realize that you can feel powerful spells and skills being used, as well as when *huge* bursts of mana are expelled, like the one our clueless Ritualist just managed.

Have you never wondered *why* incredibly powerful people show up during or just after massive battles?"

"Because they can... sense it?" Joe ventured as he started mentally kicking himself. "Why have I never thought of this? For that matter, why hasn't anyone ever mentioned it?"

"Think about it." Major Cleave hung her head slightly as she once again found herself needing to explain basic world mechanics. "When's the last time you had to be sneaky around high-ranking magic users? For you, Joe, how quickly have you been discovered each time you use a powerful ritual? The point of this is to say, don't use... whatever you just did... unless you're in a safe area, or at least an *enclosed* area where the ripples in the ambient magical fields will rebound to enough of a degree that they scatter."

"I got it," The Reductionist promised her as he worked to pull his Neutrality Aura, Exquisite Shell, and Retaliation of Shadows back to full power. "In case anyone forgot, restart your buffs after leaving the city. They'll deactivate if you don't, but I think the guards were too busy to stop a group of humans that was *leaving*, you know?"

Each of them accordingly activated their various spells or skills. Jaxon wiggled around happily as he pressed against his joints in strategic locations, and Daniella seemed to reflect slightly more of the daylight cascading through her hair after a moment of concentration. Major Cleave rolled her eyes and muttered something about working with amateurs, then shot a glance at Jaxon. "The foothills of Dehur Bethi are approximately five days' travel inland. That's assuming we move at least at regular marching speed for a full twelve hours each day."

"Celestials." Daniella shivered slightly, though she firmed up after the others eyed her with droll amusement. "*What?* Is it so bad that I'm a city girl? Either way, I'm sure it'll be good for boosting our Constitution."

"When you get tired enough that you need to focus on staying upright, it'll help you with your Dexterity as well."

Major Cleave half-grinned as her declaration landed with its intended effect. "Let's get moving."

She started them out at a punishing pace, something that by Earth standards would have been an all-out run. Joe relished the chance to see what his massively-characteristic-enhanced body could do; he had already been mightily pleased during combat in the tunnels that surrounded The Shoe. There was something just... *amazing*, about performing at this level with just his physical body. The wind blowing over his bald head created a pleasing whistling sound, while the pounding of his feet on the dirt road sent small rocks and dust into the air. "Constitution makes it not hurt... Strength sends me forward at higher speeds, Dexterity lets my feet land perfectly every time. I love this."

"Maybe you should look into getting some physical skills!" Daniella called to him over the roaring wind. She was falling behind Major Cleave and Jaxon, just as Joe was, as both of the others were specialized physical-builds. "I know I need some. That reminds me! I heard there was a woman in the capital that mastered 'power walking' to such a high level that you can barely see her move!"

"Yeah... almost ran into her once." Joe chuckled at the memory of *Havoc* needing to dodge the lady who couldn't see where she was going. "She really *is* that fast, but her lack of Perception gives her a lot of issues."

"Is that a problem you have, Joe? Can't see what's right in front of you?" Daniella turned her head to smile at him, and he was about to respond when she slammed into a tree.

The tree had *not* been there a moment before, Joe was sure of it. His concerns were confirmed as a long, undulating war cry rose from a half-dozen Elves erupting from the ground around where she had fallen. Joe skid to a stop and Omni-vaulted back as he simultaneously bellowed, "*Cleave!*"

Jaxon and Major Cleave had already crossed half the meadow that they had been traversing, and he knew it would be a few seconds before they managed to re-enter combat. Whilst airborne, he tossed out his two most-used orbs and sent them spiraling at the same target: a red-haired Elf. As the weapons sped through the air, he noted that the newest Alchemical-enhanced orb resembled a standard dumbbell—two orbs connected by a short bar. The information on the fully shifted weapon appeared in his vision, and he would have whistled appreciatively, were he not entering combat.

Ritual Orb of Strength (Masterwork). Base Damage: 182 Blunt (100 blunt + 50% Strength characteristic).

Characteristic assigned: Strength. Any spell assigned to this Orb will have its primary damage effect slightly altered. Base damage increased by half of your Strength characteristic.

Automatically grants Orb the 'recall' ability; it will return to you after five minutes if left behind, forgotten, or stolen.

Core assigned: 902/1,112

Spell assigned: Corify (Beginner V) -> Corify Deadlift.

Ritual Diagram captured: None.

Surprised that the spell assigned had been shifted, Joe made a note to look at the details later. He knew better than to cast Corify on any intelligent race, such as Elves, and he assumed that the small alteration wouldn't change that. What *did* matter was the fact that his Strength-bound orb was going to hit a *lot* harder than his Intelligence-bound version. The bonded objects slammed into the Elf's face, the first shattering a hastily-cast barrier and then his nose, the second hitting at just the right trajectory to break both cheekbones. Joe winced as he angled himself to land in a stomp on that guy. "It'll be better for you to be unconscious. Yeah."

Damage dealt: 169 piercing, shield absorbed 150!

Damage dealt: 251 blunt!

He realized that his landing on the Elf hadn't counted as damage, so he clapped a hand over the downed Elf's mouth and cast Acid Spray directly down his throat. "I'm sending you on a one-way acid trip, but you aren't gonna like it."

Coup de gras! Instant kill of unconscious Elf to prevent unneeded suffering. (Damage would have accumulated enough to slay him.)

"Now let's take care of these *basic* Fighters." The other Elves had completely stopped as they took in his entrance, and Joe could see that a few of them had shaking hands. "I'm guessing you're not the usual fighters that the Theocracy sends out. Who hit Daniella with a tree? Is one of you a Druid?"

One of the scholarly-looking Elves was pointing at the rapidly vanishing Elf whom Joe had already beaten down. "This one was... Senior Andre was-"

"Ayy!" A blond Elf to his right slapped the trembling hand down and yelled, "Stop talkin' and make with the killin' of the Dwarf sympathizers!"

"In some people's eyes, throwing acid is wrong," Joe was already next to them, sending a wash of corrosive liquid at them both. They flailed back, but their barriers were apparently more well-put together than their compatriots had been, "But ignoring the battle is just an oxidant waiting to happen!"

As the more aggressive of the two tried to dodge to the right, he found that Joe had planned for him to move. The icicle-shaped orb lodged in his shield with a shriek, sending charged energy flying as it tried to tear through the hardened mana. "Dark Lightning Strike!"

The electric current finished off the shield as it struck and ran through the orb, and Joe winced as the weapon lurched forward and came to a stop with a wet *squelch* like a blender trying to pulp an entire mango at once. He hadn't forgotten the other attackers, but he was fairly certain that Major Cleave had joined the battle, based on the sound of rapidly-fading screams behind him. It was nice to know that he had someone watching his back so that he could do things properly.

Joe completed his kill with acid once more, pleased that he didn't need to just keep hitting an opponent until it stopped twitching. It made him miss getting knocked out during high-level battles; he almost hoped that the next boss that got its paws on him would trigger an event like that for him, instead of being forced to endure. His eyes fell on the final Elf, the one that had seemed reluctant to battle. "Why are you here? What's your mission?"

"I-I-I don't-" The Elf fell on his butt as Joe advanced like an avenging angel. "This pathetic one is merely here to be a lookout for any major Legion movement. This one is just a scholar that got dragged along to start cataloging the new territory of the glorious Theocracy. Please don't... acid wash this one."

"There's no need for any of that," Joe assured the fumbling sapient as he crouched down next to him. Major Cleave came to stand next to him, her axe streaked with blood that was just a little too purple to be a human's. "All I need from you is some information, and I'll send you on your way."

"My... I can't... that's not needed!" The Elf stumbled over his words until Major Cleave swung the blade of her axe forward to rest on his throat. "H-here."

The Elf presented a paper covered in Elvish script. "As you can see, these are our orders, and they are written in a fashion that prevents someone without an Elvish affiliation from reading it. You can have it, but it won't do you much good unless-"

"Surely you can help us out with that...?" Joe's grin was wide and as dark as the lightning he could call down.

"Don't trust him, Joe." Major Cleave demanded as the Elf helplessly offered the document. "There's no way someone like him was here by chance, and a *Gold*-haired Elf acting like a servant? This reeks of a trap."

"Let's hear him out." Joe reached out and grabbed the paper, and a fanatic smile blossomed on the Elf's face.

"Fool."

The Elf yanked on the sheet, and a blast of energy shot into Joe—while a column of light raced into the sky and hung there like a flare. "Now there's no escape."

His head fell to the ground with a twitch of Major Cleave's axe, a happy smile painted on his face. Why wouldn't he be happy?

The mission had been a resounding success.

CHAPTER SIX

Joe swept up from the ground like a whirling dervish, ready to tear into the Elf that had launched the sneak attack. "*What* did you—oh, he's dead. What did he do to me?"

"I'm pretty sure he marked you." Daniella pointed at the sky, where the heraldry of the Elven Theocracy floated high above them. "Do you know any dispel rituals, or something that can cancel that out?"

Not exactly wanting to reveal his lack of diversity in spell casting, Joe could only shake his head and point in the direction they had been running. Major Cleave stopped him as he took the first few steps, shaking her head at him incredulously, "Where do you think you're going? Do you really want to point a giant arrow in the direction that you are heading for the next five days? We either go back to the city and get this fixed, find a way to handle it now, or take down anyone that is coming after us."

"We have incoming!" Daniella shouted as she gestured into the distance. Joe glanced in the indicated direction, spotting a wave of golden-haired Elves racing toward them. If Major Cleave's comment about Elves was any indication, the color of their hair likely indicated their position in society, which meant these ones were going to be deadly. "We need to get out of here; we can't fight that!"

"Quick!" Jaxon turned and sprinted along the dirt road. "Back to the city! We need to show all these potential clients where they can come for adjustments! We're going to make a fortune!"

"We need to get there for *reinforcements*, Jaxon." Major Cleave picked up Daniella and began running as the human yelped in surprise. "Joe, I know you can keep up, so start jumping!"

"I think what I do now is technically *vaulting*," Joe countered while posing like he was laying on a couch in midair—hands propped under his chin as his body lazily spun, in order to keep the Dwarf in his line of sight—having activated Omnivault before Major Cleave had finished speaking. "Should I worry that I have the flag of the Elves waving in the air above my head? I feel like the Dwarves aren't going to let us in when they see this attached to me."

"That's a problem for future Joe, right?" Jaxon laughed as the first ranged attack crashed down nearby. A huge shard of glass hit next to the road and shattered, sending slivers of the material through the air and onto the road. It wasn't much of an issue for Joe, as the shards simply bounced off his Exquisite Shell without even sending him a damage notification, but the loose material seemed to have made the ground slippery. At the speed they were traveling, that resulted in treacherous terrain, showcased by Major Cleave slipping and sending Daniella flying.

It just so happened that the human was tossed up into Joe's flight path, or perhaps Major Cleave had purposely aimed her trajectory while falling, but he was able to catch her as he sailed past. As the unexpected force sent them tumbling in the open air, Joe quipped, "We keep meeting in the strangest places."

She rolled her eyes at his forced nonchalance, and he observed hundreds of tiny puncture wounds on her skin that were healing up under the influence of his Neutrality Aura. "Thanks for the rescue, but don't start getting any ideas. I'm married—"

That rattled Joe, even though he *hadn't* been planning on making any moves on the Architect. "O-oh! That's great... I *am* a little surprised that this is the first time-"

"—to my work." Daniella grinned at him, her chin jutting out a little, as though she were proud of something that she had accomplished. "Don't be *too* down about it. I know you're the same, after all. Who knows? Someday after I manage to make a Mythical building design, I might find you to build it for me. At least I know it'll be done to my *exact* specifications."

Joe had Omnivaulted twice during their short conversation, so he shifted his grasp on her in midair, allowing them to land safely and keep running a few dozen feet in front of their other companions. "Is that your goal? Designing the best buildings?"

"Sure is! Eventually, the skyline of an entire city is going to be made *exactly* how I want it," Daniella informed him with a crooked grin. "I just need to study high-rarity structures and blueprints for a few decades while raising my skills up to the Grandmaster rank at the minimum. Then I-*hup*."

Major Cleave had scooped the woman up in passing. "How about you two watch our surroundings and check for threats, instead of making doe eyes at each other like a pair of lovesick Thunder-Skunks?"

"That's not what they were doing!" Jaxon protested with complete certainty. "They were telling each other how they were both too interested in their own goals to pursue any kind of long-term relationship."

"That's how it always starts," Major Cleave guffawed as Daniella protested weakly. "Then they start slowly merging their interests, and *bam*! They're seeking out a five year relationship license."

"You need a *license* for a relationship? That's the most-" Joe was cut off as Jaxon and Major Cleave started laughing at him.

"If it isn't an issue..." The Dwarf met his eyes knowingly, making him blush furiously. "Why are you so interested?"

Joe was saved from needing to answer as another dump truck-sized cone of glass impacted directly below his Vaulting body, the colossal projectile superheated by a flame spell that had been simultaneously cast alongside it. When the slivers began flying, they turned into molten beads that hit Joe's Exquisite Shell like a claymore going off.

Damage taken: 764 combination damage! (Struck 218 times, see breakdown?)

Doing his best not to be even further distracted in combat, the Ritualist instead focused on controlling his descent. The blast had sent him flying away at a strange angle, and only his Dexterity was allowing him to *not* hit the ground face-first. He knew it wouldn't damage him all that much—between his shell and his reduction to fall damage—but it was still an ignoble way to land. Instead, Joe managed to hit in a 'cannonball' position, making his knees crack as his butt bounced off the ground. "Oof. If I were still on earth, that would have shattered my pelvis."

"Also, no one would *ever* believe that you got hurt in that spot from just falling!" Jaxon cackled at him as Joe hurried to catch up. "Whoops, we need to *adjust* our running path, we have incoming! *Port!*"

"Not on a boat here, Jaxon!" Daniella called at him, "You can just say 'they're on the left'!"

"But I think they're attacking with wine bottles!" Jaxon skipped forward and caught a jug just before it hit the ground, whipping it back at the incoming Elves. "You dropped this!"

The attackers scattered with a variety of screams as the jug landed in the center of their group—exploding into a wall of green flames that covered a massive swath of land, strangely shaping itself to flow in a straight line instead of detonating in a sphere as expected. Major Cleave hissed. "Abyss, they have Alchemical Wyvern fire. Don't let that get on you, it's... difficult to run after chopping off whatever limb comes into contact with it. Good catch, Jaxon."

"First off, *loving* the recognition." Jaxon gave her a thumbs-up, then gestured at the people that were in hot pursuit. "Any idea why we aren't charcoal right now, though? They're certainly close enough to be blasting us with more than the disabling spells they've been using up until that jug."

"They must want to capture the group, since we're so small," Major Cleave grumbled as she dove forward and rolled, a perfect disk of glass filled with what looked to be crackling lightning zipping through the area where she had just been standing. "I guess they don't mind losing a few of us to soften the target."

"I *knew* they'd be hunting you almost exclusively." Joe turned and sent an Acid Spray at the road behind them, only for his hands to flash white and the acid to splash ineffectually against the Exquisite Shell protecting his face. "*Abyss!* That Excommunicated title is getting on my nerves."

Anything else he had planned to say was cut off as a fist-sized chunk of metal caught him square in the chest, sending him spiraling backward and bouncing along the ground; he dug a trench with his body before he finally slid to a halt—the metal melted and smoking on his torso.

Damage taken: 8,125 shield buster. (base 2500, 2x Sneak attack multiplier, +30% effectiveness against shields, +25% effectiveness against airborne targets.)

Exquisite Shell: 1,502/10,391.

"Here I thought I wouldn't get another *shot* at you in the open after you turtled up in that little settlement you sneakily hid away," the German-accented voice called from further down the road as Herr Trigger stood, throwing off a dirt-covered blanket that matched the ground nearly perfectly. "How did you enjoy my anti-air mark-one cannon? I feel like it could use a few more features, but how would you rate your first experience? The next version will almost *certainly* be able to go directly through you, as well as any protections you have in place."

"You… suck. Why are you so good at finding and hunting me?" Joe wheezed as he scraped the molten chunk of metal off his Exquisite Shell, where it had remained after it had flattened against him.

Major Cleave appeared next to Herr Trigger in that moment, only for her axe to be deflected by a barrier of stone that appeared the instant she swung down. Herr Trigger barely spared her a glance as he answered Joe. "Why, because I am effective, efficient, and excel at everything I set my mind to doing well. I call it my 'triple E' rating."

"This is bad," the Dwarf stated calmly as she hit the stone twice more, only stopping as she discovered that the damage was being fixed at nearly the same rate that she was generating it. "This is the work of a Druid, likely one doubling as a Cleric for their nature deity."

"Ron. Bring." A new voice cut into the conversation only an instant before Major Cleave was tackled by a dog so large that it would put a Siberian tiger to shame. All Joe could see of his armored companion was a whirl of flesh, metal, and blood. The dog had sunk its teeth into her right arm, practically invalidating the limb, but she fought back stoically, slamming her axe down awkwardly with her left. Even so, the beast was starting to drag the Dwarf to the side of the road, where the ground began *unfolding* to reveal what looked like a naturally-grown iron maiden.

"Bad doggy!" Jaxon landed on the creature's muzzle and shifted his hands into T-rex heads… except his left hand appeared completely different than before. Now, while his right hand remained a single cohesive head, the left had developed a tiny T-rex head at the top of each finger, all digging in with just as much gusto. "Drop it! She's not a chew toy, as far as I'm aware."

His fingers struck like snake heads, one after the other in the same spot, and he managed to *adjust* the muzzle of the beast to pop open. Major Cleave used that moment to boot the massive Direwolf away from her, her gear ravaged. "It's been enhanced with metal! Those teeth have armor-piercing capabilities, so watch out!"

Joe took another round to the chest, dropping his Exquisite Shell by four hundred points. "*Celestials*, Trigger! How do you get those to have so much impact!"

"Every little *bit*," Herr Trigger called in a sing-song tone as he pulled back the bolt of his rifle, "of mine rifle is enchanted to *hit*, at its maximum potential~1."

The Ritualist tossed out his Intelligence-bound orb and sent it zig-zagging through the air at the Bounty Hunter, keeping his strength-infused projectile moving low to the ground in an arc. "You *know* we're going to beat you down, Trigger!"

"I'm not trying to *beat* you, Joe." The man's black goggles automatically telescoped wider as he took aim at Joe once again, his position of using the stone barrier as a rifle stabilizer doing nothing to hide his wide smile. "All I need to do is *stall* you significantly. Then everything you're working on that is contrary to my goals will fail, and my allies coming up behind you will toss you in a hole for a few months before you undergo loyalty training to make you as obedient as this good wolf over here."

Joe was flabbergasted, and he *really* wanted to turn his head to gauge the incoming opponents behind him. He resisted, knowing that as soon as he did, a round would enter his chest. Herr Trigger whipped his hand to the side, a concealed revolver blasting the incoming orb away without causing him to break line of sight on Joe. "Nice try, but a trick only works on me once-*ow*!"

The second orb Joe had been stealthily controlling used that moment of distraction to swoop up at an angle and hit Herr Trigger with the equivalent of an uppercut to the lower mandible. Joe launched himself at Major Cleave, grabbing her and Omnivaulting over the barrier. She struggled against him while he used Lay on Hands to close the shredded flesh of her arm. "Put me *down*! I can slice and dice that Elf-"

"Major Cleave, we're losing this battle." That was all Joe managed to say before they hit the ground on the other side of the stone barrier, and a round took him in the back. His Exquisite Shell shattered, and the round entered his abdominal cavity, where it lit up as though it had been filled with burning phosphorus. Wheezing around it, he shoved the Dwarf at the Capital, sending her stumbling up to a Legion unit racing toward them. "You gotta live, and I'll do my best to get the others outta here. Let's try this again, once we're properly outfitted with safety features."

"Joe-"

"*Retreat*, Cleave," Joe ordered her as he cast Mend on himself and turned to glare at the Bounty Hunter and his team. "Dark Lightning Strike!"

The attack landed on target, causing Herr Trigger's henchmen to lock up, several of them popping off rounds as their muscles spasmed. A grin appeared on Joe's face as he realized that, even though the creator of those weapons knew how to use them, the people with him were amateurs with trigger discipline.

"You can't blast your way out of this one, Joe!" Trigger snarled as he tried to regain control of his hands.

Joe's Ritual Orb of Intelligence swooped above the firing squad, and he cast Cone of Cold on the whole group at once. "Haha, cold people go *brrr*."

"No!" Daniella's scream cut through the noise as she was grabbed by the Elves that had been closing in on them. Jaxon raced toward her, only for a root to burst out of the soil and catch his leg. A moment later, the Direwolf latched onto him, and the Chiropractor was pulled to the ground.

Joe didn't last long either. As he closed in on Herr Trigger, an Elf stepped out of nowhere and slammed a blade into his gut. Another simple move kept Joe pinned to the ground, but he knew that he didn't need to worry about being captured: the Legion was moving in on them too rapidly. The trench coat-wearing contract killer appeared over him, a smile on his face.

"One down, three to go. See you soon, Joe... we've got your scent now. Time to leave, team!"

"One of four *what*-" Joe's question was cut off as the butt of the man's rifle popped a blade out of it and slammed down on his head in the next second.

You have died! Calculating... as you were killed by a player, you lose 7,360 experience!

You have leveled down! Welcome back to level 22!

Combat Ritual Orbs has reached Beginner III!

Mental Manipulation Resistance has reached Apprentice 0!

Battle Meditation has reached Student II!

Dark Lightning Strike has reached Student II!

Lay on Hands has reached Student VI!

As Joe stood in his respawn room, raging against the death or capture of himself and his team, the skill increases were a cold comfort.

CHAPTER SEVEN

As he waited for his death timer to count down, Joe decided that this would be a good opportunity to go over his messages and stats, and plan out what he needed to do to get the situation in his favor once again.

Name: Joe 'Excommunicated' Class: Reductionist
Profession I: Arcanologist (Max)
Profession II: Ritualistic Alchemist (1/20)
Profession III: Grandmaster's Apprentice (14/25)
Profession IV: None.
Character Level: 22 Exp: 274,424 Exp to next level: 1,576
Rituarchitect Level: 10 Exp: 53,700 Exp to next level: 1,300
Reductionist Level: 3 Exp: 8,836 Exp to next level: 1,164
Hit Points: 2,139/2,139
Mana: 7,585/7,585
Mana regen: 63.2/sec
Stamina:1,711/1,711
Stamina regen: 6.57/sec

Characteristic: Raw score

Strength (bound): 164
Dexterity: 166
Constitution: 158
Intelligence (bound): 174
Wisdom: 158
Dark Charisma: 111
Perception: 161
Luck: 96
Karmic Luck: 18

There hadn't been any drastic changes since the last time he had gone over everything, but it was always good to get a baseline for when he wanted to see how much he had grown. "Need to get luck over a hundred; that's likely making things harder for me than they need to be. As always, that and charisma are the most needed stats."

He sighed and turned his attention to his skill pages, trying to consider what he could use more effectively. He was leery of adding his Dark Lightning Strike to an orb, same with his Acid Spray, as that would leave him effectively empty of immediate spell-casting. Resurrection and Retaliation of Shadows both carried such rare and complex requirements that he assumed would make it nearly impossible to translate them over. Wither Plant was a spell that he wanted to get rid of, due to its niche applications, and his healing spells... "Could I channel Lay on Hands through an orb? It's a divine spell, but I feel like it's *natural*, so I *should* be able to do it, right?"

Then his attention landed on Planar Shift, and his eyes lit up. "Now *there's* an idea... it requires Ritual Circles, but I'm currently *vastly* underutilizing all of my orbs—or I'm using them for gimmicks. Makes me wonder how Herr Trigger managed to throw off that Ritual of Insanity."

Joe made a note to look through his book on summoning to find a combat-capable creature. "First one down. The second attempt is going to be Lay on Hands, so I'll research the underpinning spell usage when I get a chance. *Any* other skills? My body and mind skills all require senses, so no... wait."

Essence Cycle practically jumped off the skill list, and he remembered one of the main issues with actually *using* that skill: namely getting lost in the beauty of all the energies that created the framework of this universe. "If I could put that in the orb, all I would need to do is let the mana battery die instead of tasking someone with shaking me out of it."

That would do for now, at least for the orbs, but he was glad that he had a direction for each of them. "Speaking of orbs, didn't Corify change on this?"

He quickly scanned the information panel that appeared when he held the Ritual Orb of Strength, searching for any new details to the spell.

Corify Deadlift: Add 1n% chance that any target creature which dies within five seconds of spell cast will solidify a Core upon dying. Cost: 100 mana. Cooldown: five seconds.

Upgrade (Only usable while assigned to Ritual Orb of Strength): When this spell is cast on a target below 3% of their maximum health, there is a 2% chance that the Core will instantly solidify and be pulled toward the caster, simultaneously killing the affected target.

"Now *that* has some serious potential." Joe grasped the dumbbell-shaped Ritual Orb and curled it a few times, just for old time's sake. He wasn't expecting a notice to appear.

Alert! You cannot train your characteristics while you are dead. You are welcome to practice your form, of course!

"Now that I think about it, using my orbs *would* be excellent training, wouldn't it?" The Rituarchitect pondered the possibility for a moment as he tested how well he could press the orb away with his mind while simultaneously attempting to lift it. As far as he could tell, his mental strength outclassed his physical by a wide margin, and his stats backed that up. "I can use this for resistance training to boost skills and characteristics at the same time? I bet I can."

*Ding!** An unread message appeared on what he was fairly certain was a computer screen, where all his mail accrued while he was alive and not bothering to look over it in safe areas like taverns. He strolled over, welcoming the notice; it was always good to know that someone out there was thinking about him.

Message from Aten: Joe, I'm in the Dwarven Capital, and you should get over here as soon as you can. There's someone that I think you should meet; he has some great information that could be helpful for us. If you can get to the Sticky Chicken eatery by five in the evening tomorrow, it'll be worth your time.

A glance at the clock and some rapid finger-math left Joe nodding, so he sent back a message affirming his planned attendance. Without anything else to do, he sent a few messages to friends, as well as his mother, then decided to start reading through his book on summoning creatures. He slowly paged through it, forced to maintain the reduced pace due to a buildup of pressure as he progressed.

Any Novice summon was easy to read about, and Beginner was *fine*, but at Apprentice, things became slightly harder. He had started as a Student in this skill, which allowed him to read those pages as well. However, when he reached a fresh chapter of the book, which detailed upper-Student and low Journeyman summons, he started to get a serious headache.

There was a definitive point where he simply couldn't push on, the words becoming blurry figures that hurt his head with each attempt to focus, and he knew that he had reached his limit for his current skill level. "Ugh... I know I can't die here, but what's with this feedback? I never had to worry about that out there; the words would just become illegible!"

Some system functions—such as mental pain mitigation—are not available during respawn. Please note that your mind is a fragile construct, and severe pain during a respawn session should be a great time to stop doing whatever you are doing before you break it.

Thoroughly freaked out by the discovery that he actually *could* damage himself in respawn, Joe hurriedly paged back to the low-Student-ranked summons and tried to narrow down what he should be bringing with him. "Jaxon and Major Cleave are melee fighters, Daniella is… not something to take into consideration currently, and I'm mid-range."

His mind went back to the fight against the Hidden Guardian, and he remembered the way that the bird form it had shifted into had been able to firebomb massive sections of the area with barely any fear of retaliation. "I need a long-range creature, but not something that flies. At least not something large and easily spotted… Herr Trigger has a nasty new weapon, and those Elves are surprisingly effective at taking things down in midair."

The Rituarchitect rubbed at his chest, which had taken the brunt of the exploding glass beads. That attack had been crafted by Elves on the move—he didn't even want to think about what they could do to someone when they were attacking from a fortified position. "Fire Elementals can toss fireballs… too likely to hit allies. What's this? Is this a bad idea? I feel like it'll give people the wrong idea about *me* if nothing else."

He was staring at a creature that was apparently only ever summoned to defend stationary positions, as it had no way of getting around on its own. It resembled a human skull, though it had long fangs instead of upper and lower canines. The Ritualist decided to go over the information once more, just to make sure he *didn't* want it. "Pseudo-Lich skull. This creature is the result of a failed union between a corrupted mage seeking immortality and a powerful entity that tried and failed to take control of the mage. The mage's skull becomes immortal, and a small portion of their memories are retained. Pros: it has True Sight, which renders illusions and disguises useless. It can also cast dark-mana bolts of various power levels, reaching the Student Ranks at a maximum."

Curious, Joe read over the cons, then winced. "Cannot move on its own, *highly* likely to attempt to kill its summoner unless they have good compatibility as well as an offer that excites the Pseudo-Lich. Makes for an excellent guard of an area that you expect to be attacked frequently, but if it gets too bored, it will attack *anyone*, including the summoner. Phew... I don't know, it seems like a bad idea."

Even so, something about the image in his head felt right. Being a powerful Mage with a skull-topped staff or something, living in a magical tower, and scaring off random thrill-seekers appealed to him. "Wait, why would I put that on a staff... instead of an orb? Then I could make it fly around. I bet *that* would get a Pseudo-Lich excited to sign a contract."

Ding! Joe walked over to read the new message, noting that he only had a few more minutes to wait before he could leave this place.

Message from Jaxon: Joe, Daniella is here, she respawned just after I did. You don't need to worry that she got captured. She let us know that they killed her when she was struggling and the Legion was closing in! Just thought I'd put your mind at ease!

The portal popped open as Joe frowned in contemplation. "I thought I saw her getting hauled away... how did she get back there before I did?"

CHAPTER EIGHT

"I have a somewhat strange title effect," Daniella admitted as they all sat together drinking cappuccinos. "I'm such a workaholic that I accidentally died of starvation, continued working in my respawn room, and got kicked out of the room... without noticing that I had died. It's called 'Hardworking Ghost', and it decreases my respawn timer by a set amount."

"Not gonna lie, that's a sad story." Jaxon patted her on the hand, earning a simultaneous eye roll from Daniella and Joe. "I hope you get the help you need to feel better."

"I *like* what I do!" Daniella was blushing furiously, setting Major Cleave and Joe to laughing, which only made the color creep higher. "I'm glad you made it back safely, Major."

"Not much choice when you're given a direct order." The Dwarf tried to glare at Joe, but he met her eyes, and she turned away with a quiet grumble.

"I told you; *you* need to live. To that end, I need another couple days here." Joe ignored their collective complaints and merely shook his head. "I need a few failsafes, and I have a few rituals that require advance preparation. Beyond that, I need to try to see if I can find some spells or skills that will be useful on the road."

"Don't bother." Cleave explained her thoughts right away, a nice change from keeping them in the dark all the time, even if it wasn't intentional. "When we get to Dehur Bethi, I'm certain you'll be able to find whatever you need, so long as you convince the Grandmaster to work with you. That's our city of magic, and all centers of magical learning are within its borders."

"All I *need* is a few spell books, but a teacher would be nice." Joe started to say more, but she shook her head.

"You should make a better habit of keeping your secrets safe." She eyed him dubiously from across the table before taking a sip of her drink. "Also, do you really need to be drinking out of an Ebonsteel mug? Someone is going to mug *you*. Do you have any idea what that stuff is worth? It's the only metal under Legendary that completely ignores corrosion."

"I do, Major. I absolutely do need to use this." Joe slurped loudly, causing AutoMate to burble happily as it produced fresh coffee for him to sip on. "Never-ending coffee that tasted good the entire time I was drinking it was only a dream for a long time. Now that it's a reality? No way am I going to ignore it."

"Right. Well, I'm going to go to the practice yard to see if they need any help training people with axes." Major Cleave shoved back from the table and took her leave. That seemed to be the signal for the others to start on their own way, and Daniella excused herself to go and check out some interesting buildings. Joe glimpsed some of the sketches she was making, and realized she was sketching a preliminary blueprint for each one on a separate page as she went.

Jaxon started to depart as well, but Joe caught the Chiro-practor before he could go too far. "Jaxon! That was super neat how your hand did that... I want to say, 'snake shifting'? I didn't know it could convert into multiple forms."

"I suppose we never talked about that!" Jaxon seemed almost surprised and settled into the conversation by rubbing his hands together in excitement. "When you came to this

Zone, I followed a *super* neat Profession and eventually learned that a fully completed Profession can sometimes be used to create a new Specialization. I used that knowledge to upgrade my class to a *Vile Bonecrusher* and managed to earn a reward that allowed me to start slowly draining the essence of a Pond Hydra into Lefty and Terror!"

"That's... a lot to process." Joe separated out all of the pertinent points and looked at Jaxon's wiggling fingers. "Where did you get the essence of a Pond Hydra? That sounds expensive."

"Not at all! I tamed one, and then I drained its essence into a Targeted Assimilation Mutation Egg, or *T.A.M.E.* I tamed it *twice*! Ha! See what I did there?" Jaxon wiped a tear of mirth from his eye and sighed in contentment. "Of course, since I recently died, I'll need to get back to level twenty-five in order to keep absorbing that beast. Eventually, I'll be able to convert *both* of them into full hydras!"

Jaxon abruptly walked away from the conversation, fully lost in his own thoughts. By contrast, Joe remained rooted in place, shocked that his friend had achieved such a high level so far ahead of him. "I just gotta get on top of things and work harder; no point in being jealous."

The Ritualist decided that it was time to start putting a few of his own plans in place. If he couldn't acquire new skills, it was time to rearrange his current ones in such a fashion that he would remember to use them properly. He made his way to the park and dropped a bubble ritual around the rock he planned to be sitting on while he worked. That would keep any accidental misfires contained, as well as affording him some protection while he was focused on his task. Shaking out his hands, Joe started the process of creating an Enchanted Ritual Circle.

He didn't use his Somatic Ritual Casting—as he was still unsure how to add enchantments to a ritual that was hanging in midair—instead using a Field Array to lop off a large section of the boulder to create plenty of space to work on. "It seems counterintuitive that the easiest of the spells to convert to a ritual is the summoning spell. Why is Lay on Hands such a giant sack of bloat?"

Ignoring the fact that the healing spell was able to restore practically any living being that he had encountered, and the fact that Essence Cycle used extrasensory perception at a level he couldn't currently fathom, Joe grumbled under his breath as he set up the diagram. The sun slowly crossed the sky as he *skritched* away at the surface of the stone with his inscription tool, leaving behind complicated formulae as glowing strands of fire. When he had finally completed the ritual to his satisfaction, he huffed out a blast of air as he let the feeling of succeeding suffuse him.

"That was *so* much easier to do than it was back in the Caves of Solitude, even with the enhancements required to contain a Student-ranked spell." Joe chose one of his unbound orbs at random and set it in the center of the Ritual Diagram. "Alrighty… all I'm binding to this is the basic spell portion of Planar Shift in order to generate a Pseudo-Lich; not sure what that'll look like when it's supposed to be a whole ritual."

He strategically placed a couple Mana Batteries to provide energy input to the Student ranked ritual, then stood to the side and began casting. Mana poured out of him, arresting a moment later as the batteries took on the burden. The ritual circles lit up in rapid sequence, until four were swirling around the slightly hovering orb. "Looking good thus far. Here comes the full activation…"

Cast the spell you want to assign to the orb directly onto the orb!

"Huh. I wonder what you're supposed to do if you want to bind a skill." Joe shook his head and snorted at the fact that he could have just as easily set up this Enchanted Ritual Circle to apply either of the other options he had been considering. He had been needlessly building this process up in his head, making a minnow into a whale, instead of just doing the work. "Totally forgot that I just needed to cast the abyssal spell on the orb, because it's a completely different process than binding characteristics. Silly me… *Planar Shift*! Ahhh!"

For one long, terrible moment that seemed to last hours, Joe stood in the void, surrounded by hundreds of seemingly inanimate skulls. He was there just long enough to watch darkness filling their empty eye sockets as they started to turn toward him... and then he was back, standing at the edge of a scorched rock. He surveyed his surroundings in a daze, eventually coming to the realization that he had *physically moved* to a different dimension for a moment, and that the ritual had destabilized and exploded in that time frame.

Planar shift has reached Student IV!

"Wh-what just happened?" Joe's teeth were chattering, and he found that he was *freezing*. He rubbed his arms and hopped in place as he inspected the damage. "Good thing I had that shield in place."

He checked his normally-hidden deeper notifications, the ones he had to really *dig* for, and found an explanation.

Luck is two thresholds below Wisdom! Spell instability drastically increased.

Excommunicated! Your spell has backfired!

Caution! You have been reverse summoned to a different dimension! Your body cannot handle this transition. As you didn't cross Planes of existence correctly by utilizing the Bifrost, all teleportation safety features have been activated. You have two minutes to return to the Plane of origin, else your current body will implode and be returned as energy, and a tiny demon will be summoned in your starting location as a warning to others and will cause mischief!

You have safely returned to your point of origin! Luck +3!

"I *reverse summoned* myself? I came back, though... even the *system* agrees that was some insane luck. Thank goodness that spell only pulls something through for a brief moment unless a contract is made." The Rituarchitect shook his head at the narrow miss as he finally started to warm up. "This title is *unbelievably* inconvenient."

With that restriction hindering his process, there was nothing else to do beyond reshape what was left of the boulder and get back to work. Almost two hours later, he had formed the ritual again and bent slowly to add a few lightly scorched Mana Batteries to their locations. "Here's hoping this works properly."

The ritual activated without issue, but that had never been the question. When he got around to casting the spell, instead of lazily sending it toward the orb as he had the first time, Joe focused entirely on following the path the spell made through his body before being ejected into space and crossing the distance to the orb. With such care devoted to the process, it was no surprise to him that the orb accepted the spell readily, and he felt all of his knowledge on how to cast it slip away.

Magical Matrices has reached Student I!

Enchanted Ritual Circles has reached Beginner VI!

"Urg. That always feels so disgusting." He held his head as the last dregs of the spell faded from his memory and the ritual ended. Grimacing, he inspected the area, where the only signs of his ritual being completed were a few burns in the stone. He inhaled deeply and set up a new Field Array. "Lay on Hands next, then I gotta figure out how to get Essence Cycle bound to one of these bad boys."

CHAPTER NINE

Lay on Hands was surprisingly easy to capture in an orb. That made sense, as the literal instructions were 'cast spell on orb', and the spell was cast by touching something. It made him want to kick himself for thinking he couldn't manage it—getting caught up in the spell's complexity and forgetting the actual process—but he… refrained. He had to focus now that he was at the key moment in the follow-up ritual, attempting to place Essence Cycle.

It was… not going well.

First, he had attempted to cast the spell while holding the orb, hoping that it would be placed properly. Unfortunately, the only result was that he became so caught up in staring at the resulting energy flows that he held still until he ran out of mana and the ritual self-destructed. The blast was contained, helped along by the fact that it had broken down because it was out of energy. There was one small benefit to watching the energy, as well as observing what it looked like as it broke down.

Essence Cycle has reached Apprentice 0!

Joe had taken several deep, calming breaths before starting again—opting to fit the ritual with three Ritual Circles instead of two—and it was evening before he had felt ready to try again. It was growing dark as he stood staring at the orb, knowing better than to activate the spell but finding himself unable to *will* it into the orb.

"Abyssal spell... what are you? A spell, or a skill? Pick one, blast it!" Joe slapped the orb, knowing the strike wouldn't impact anything that he was attempting. "How do I assign a *skill*? Forget this. *Query!*"

What would you like to ask Tatum?

"How do I assign skills to the Ritual Orb?" Joe snapped at the input command, angered that an artificial layer had been created between his deity and himself to *intentionally* make it harder for him to get information.

Processing... response earned: Say 'assign next activated skill to Ritual Orb' before activating skill. Feel free to ask another question tomorrow!

Query has reached Novice VIII!

"When was the last time that doing stuff like this required a verbal component?" Joe grabbed the orb, said the words, and activated the skill. The familiar feeling of loss arose, but then the world faded away into energy, and he watched it for as long as he could. When the real world came back into focus, he worried that he had failed once again... until he saw the message waiting for him.

Ritual Orb (Essence Cycle) energy remaining: 0/1,213

"Celestials, it only ran out of mana?" It suddenly occurred to Joe that he had been standing in a park, at night, staring at energy movements that only he could see. He was lucky that he hadn't been attacked, and even more lucky that the ritual had ended cleanly without exploding him into another world. He shivered at the memory of that void and distracted himself by inspecting his orbs. "This could be a potent weapon... touch it to someone, and they'll get locked down as if I managed to put them in an illusion. Better keep the amount of mana in the battery low, either way. No need to pump it up and starve myself."

He quickly got to the next part of his plan: setting up the

remaining Ritual Circles required for the activation of Planar Shift. Joe needed four in total, and he couldn't count the orb that the spell itself was bound to, as that was needed as the spell focus. "Yikes, that means that five of my six total orbs are going to be devoted to casting the spell. Was that a bad idea? Should I have thought this through more? No... I might as well at least give it a shot, since I've done all of this work. I'll keep one of them as an activation ritual or something."

Once the rituals were set up—which he had generated with Somatic Ritual Casting to make sure they were floating in the air—he opened his orbs and tossed them at the Ritual Circles one at a time. It was strangely fun to watch all of the internal wire twist and bend itself into the shape that he had generated in the air, then suck an orb in and snap closed around it. If he were still back on Earth, he would have made that into a video with the tag 'satisfying' and gotten thousands of views.

With all of the work done, he desperately wanted to try out summoning the... Abomination wasn't the correct word. He didn't want to have to call it a Pseudo-Lich each time it was necessary to explain the thing, so he hoped that whatever creature he brought through would have a name that he could call it instead. The spell had a hefty price attached to it: four thousand, nine hundred and eighty mana would be pulled each time he used it, and the creature would only remain for an hour at maximum.

All of that together meant that he could only cast the spell four times in total before needing to either replace the Mana Battery or recharge it. "I suppose that means I can't just try it out for funsies. Plus, you never know how the guards in this city might react to a *kinda* demon summoning happening in a public setting."

Resolving to only test it out right before a battle, or when he thought he might be in danger, Joe packed away his orbs and started walking away. He quickly came to a stuttering stop as he realized that he still needed to make a deal with the creature that was pulled through, and doing so directly before combat was obviously a terrible idea. Plus, he had to ensure that the spell had been put in place correctly... right? "No! No, I can do this when we are *outside* the city walls."

Very, *very* reluctantly, he managed to gather the willpower necessary to ignore testing out his new pretties, and instead went back to the inn where he and his team had rented rooms for the evening. They would need to spend at least one more day in the city in order to meet with Aten and learn what was going on, but he had a feeling that the time would at least be used productively.

What little remained of the night passed quickly, especially since he only needed a few hours of sleep a day, thanks to his enhanced Constitution. In what felt like no time flat, he was up and sipping his first coffee of the day while he planned out a new training regimen. "I can start with curls and keep boosting my Strength and Intelligence by working them against each other. The great thing is, thanks to feeding ten percent of my Intelligence into it, if my Intelligence does go up in response, that will also slowly increase my Strength! It's a double win for me."

"Ooh! Whatcha got there? That one seems different." Jaxon reached out and poked the orb that Joe had assigned Essence Cycle onto, his jaw going slack as Joe noticed the charge in his orb starting to drop *right* after he had returned it to full power!

"Jaxon!" With a simple mental demand, the orb flew away from the Chiropractor, who swiped his hand in an attempt to catch it. "Leave it, it'll drop you into a trance-"

"*Jo~oe!*" Jaxon whined as he tried to retrieve the orb that kept dancing out of his reach. "It's so pretty in there! Let me see it again!"

Joe thought about it for a moment and decided there was no harm in letting the Chiropractor be entertained while he did his own thing. He narrowed his eyes, and allowed a devious plan to form. "That's fine, but you'll need to recharge the orb with your own mana. Deal?"

"Sure! There's nothing strange about that; of course I'd

happily replace what I use." Jaxon smiled at him so winningly that Joe felt bad for planning to fully drain his mana at least once a day. He was still going to do it, but now he felt *bad* about it. The orb dropped into the Chiropractor's waiting hands, and his pupils dilated as drool instantaneously began dripping from his mouth.

"No wonder I couldn't get anyone to come and shake me without paying them." Joe muttered with slight disgust. "I bet I looked just like this when I was using the skill."

Satisfied that Jaxon was fully occupied, he turned his focus to his other orbs and started applying pressure to push the weapon away while using his muscles to force it back to him. "This is some... intense isometrics!"

If his Neutrality Aura hadn't been in place, he knew for certain that his clothing would have been absolutely soaked with sweat after the first few minutes. Joe put everything he had into lifting the orb just one more time, just one more time. Over and over, he lifted, until, after nearly a full hour, nothing happened. He *almost* gave up, then remembered that he was attempting to train two characteristics at the same time. The training requirement was doubled, and his efforts were likely to require a full one hundred and four minutes to get them both higher.

"I shouldn't complain; thanks to being a Ritualist, I'm managing this four times faster than I would have with any other class," Joe grunted as he continued his intense workout. "There are people that are doing this all day, every day, just to boost their characteristics. Got to... use my... advantages!"

Jaxon had come out of his trance a while ago, saw that Joe was busy, shook the orb twice to make sure there was no more fun-sight juice left in it, and wandered off. Joe could barely think straight by that point, the repetitiveness of the actions nearly driving him crazy. At one hundred and three minutes, he was almost entirely spent, and he used the few remaining seconds in an attempt to lift the weight one more time while also pushing it away. Just before he was about to give up entirely, he was granted a notification that he hadn't seen in *far* too long.

Characteristic point training completed! +1 to intelligence and strength! These stats cannot be increased further by any means other than system rewards, study, or practice for twenty-four hours game time.

Artisan Body has reached Beginner VI.

"Yes!" Joe collapsed onto dry ground; his clothes perfectly cleaned each time he rolled around on the not often-swept surface. "The system works! I can use my own weapons against myself to become better, faster, and stronger!"

He studied his other orbs with excitement, wondering what they would turn into when he managed to bind them to his characteristics. He tried to temper his exhilaration with the fact that there were increasing downsides, which would likely be more noticeable with each new characteristic he tied to the orbs. Not to mention the fact that he currently only had six orbs, and in order to assign every single one of his characteristics to an orb, he needed nine of them—if he could consider Karmic Luck as an assignable skill. "That means I will need a Sage set—also known as a *Mythical* set—if I actually want to use every one of them. I will need to unbind them, and rebind them, and… that's a lot of work that'll eventually need to happen. Better not think about it too much right now."

That, more than anything, allowed him to bring himself back into the present moment. Not only would he have to upgrade the ritual to fully utilize his weapons, but he also needed a greater theoretical understanding of the currently ambiguous characteristics in order to do so. As it stood, he wasn't sure how several of his skills even affected reality, especially the more esoteric ones such as Luck and Karmic Luck. Attaining the Karmic King award while he was fighting the Hidden Guardian had opened his eyes somewhat to the mysteries that lay within, but it was going to be a long road to true understanding.

He took care of a few other minor tasks, though he mostly ended up spinning his wheels while waiting for his meeting with his Guild Commander. Joe wasn't exactly certain what the meeting was going to entail, but the fact that Aten thought it was important normally meant that it would be. Aten hadn't gotten his position by chance, and Joe remembered how well the man had handled the pressure of mediating between two sets of leaders from warring civilizations. Deciding that he would rather be early, he went over to the restaurant that had been designated as the meeting spot and sat down.

Almost immediately, a man wearing dark sunglasses loomed beside his table. "You fit the description. Are you Joe of The Wanderers?"

The Reductionist nodded, keeping his mouth shut as he privately assessed the man. Frankly, *he* fit whatever description could be used for Joe as well, being equally as bald. Likely, the phalacrosis was a choice for this man, though Joe could not fathom why someone would *choose* to have such a hairstyle willingly in a civilization where the quality of your hair dictated your position in society. The man motioned for Joe to follow him, leading him to a private back room in the restaurant.

Aten noticed his arrival and came to greet him, a strange look of sheepishness on his face as he shook Joe's hand. "Glad you can make it. I wanted to give you the chance to meet my father and ask him a few questions; he has a lot of knowledge regarding what is coming, and what we can expect in the next couple of Zones. If you wouldn't mind, I'd really prefer if you would keep his identity between us. There are a lot of people looking for him."

"Is he a criminal?" Joe turned to scan the room, freezing in utter shock when his eyes landed on the only person—thanks to the Guild Commander's preface—that could be Aten's father. "Uh… a pleasure to meet you, President Musk."

"Likewise."

CHAPTER TEN

"*You*... are Aten's father." Joe snorted and glanced at the Guild Commander. "I'm incredibly surprised, yet somehow it makes perfect sense. I hope you aren't worried. I have come to understand that the apocalypse on Earth was not your fault, and you were only trying to give people a fair warning. Also, I got a pod ahead of time and was already a permanent addition, so you *really* have nothing to worry about from me."

"I'm glad that you liked our products, and I appreciate you trying to put me at ease, as unnecessary as it is to do so." The man before him was no longer his president, seeing as the country as a whole had likely been swept away under a tide of monsters. "What can I do for you today? Aten here has filled me in on some of your exploits, and I understand that you are currently being hunted by the Elves. I don't have a large amount of time, since I need to be ready to move along as quickly as possible. The more humans that are in the same Zone as me, the more likely it is that we will have an... incident."

"Not everyone is as understanding as I am about the whole 'planet being overrun' thing?" The Ritualist quipped, his attempt at a joke falling flat as the other people in the room only nodded solemnly. "Okay then. Ah… to use our time as efficiently as possible, I can describe my plans to provide you with the context to offer pertinent advice? I think that would work better than simply trying to delve for random information. If you actually have advance knowledge of the upcoming Zones, it would be incredibly helpful to be able to plan ahead. My present goal is to amass a large group of Dwarves and bring them with me to the next Zone as soon as the Bifrost opens. First question is this: what can we expect in the next Zone, and how can we best prepare for it?"

"That's a good question, but you are ignoring a few of the small details that need to be taken into account before you make a jump like that." The ex-president had always been known as an extremely intense person, and that had not changed in the slightest during his time in the program. The only real difference Joe could spot from the man he used to watch on television was the oversized and extremely well-defined muscles. "First of all, the next Zone is what will come to be known as a watershed Zone, or a bottleneck. Do you remember when you first got to Alfheim, the intense pressure that you had to withstand in order to even walk or breathe?"

"Incredibly clearly," Joe deadpanned, not wanting to get into the fact that he had been exiled to the Zone and had died multiple times before figuring out how to fill his lungs with life-giving air. "Is it going to be like that?"

"Yes and no. It will be easy to breathe, and you will have no physical troubles after learning how to navigate the currents of energy there." The father of his Guild Commander leaned forward and stared into Joe's eyes. "The problem is going to be any skills or spells that you plan to bring along with you. In order to use them, you have to achieve a certain skill level. From this point forward, there is a minimum requirement of Mastery for all of your abilities, or you will simply not be able to access them in the next areas. Just so you know, the Bifrost connects this Zone to Jotunheim, the World of Giants. Anything remaining in the Novice ranks will be completely ineffective, and Beginner ranked skills and spells will drop to the point of being functionally useless."

"How are we expected to learn new skills, in that case? What about the people that have already lived there, or have risen into higher areas?" Joe's brow furrowed as he tried to calculate what the restriction would mean for him. His plan of loading up on spells and skills in the next Dwarven city seemed to be crumbling around him.

"You will still be able to train in whatever you wish, but you will be unable to generate the desired effect until it has reached at *least* the Beginner ranks." Musk sighed and sat back. "It is difficult to describe exactly what it'll be like; it's just something you are going to need to experience for yourself. I would advise you to plan accordingly, with the knowledge that Novice abilities are useless. The second thing, the most important thing, is the knowledge of how to open the Bifrost to the next Zones from there. The reason that you were asked to come to this meeting is because you are likely going to be a key component in making that happen."

Aten joined in on the conversation, addressing Joe directly. "I filled him in on your ability to create buildings rapidly, especially your ability to integrate seemingly any sort of resource that you can get your hands on."

"The Bifrost, the path to the higher realms, has been closed for *centuries*," the president began speaking slowly, "mainly because the only way to open it is to build a proper city. The sheer amount of time that would take has made it nearly impossible for singular persons, small groups, or even a moderate faction of people. Typically, it would require a massive influx of resources equitable to an entire civilization moving in. However, that doesn't take into account the existing denizens of the Zone. On Jotunheim, there will be none of this 'Unified Race' or 'Shattered Race' nonsense. There are only monsters of varying degrees of intelligence, and the most powerful among them either remember or were informed of what happens when the Bifrost opens."

"People travel on it?" Joe guessed, starting to piece together the big picture. "If the entire Zone is only populated by monsters, at one point, it was likely used as some kind of elite big game hunting area, right? Either that, or the monsters themselves are worth something; perhaps they can be made into high-end gear or components?"

"You told me he was a quick learner; I'm glad I took your advice and took a chance on this guy," Musk called casually over to the person that was apparently his *son*. Joe was still having a hard time wrapping his head around that. The powerful man turned back to Joe and steepled his fingers. "Here's what is going to happen. As soon as you make the smallest settlement possible, such as a camp, you are going to have to start dealing with monsters. If you set up shelter for yourself, for your people, they will come in droves. After you pass a Hamlet in size, the monsters will stop coming continually, instead gathering together to attack in waves. You need to be ready for that, or all of the Dwarves that you managed to rescue will be slain in the first few weeks. Remember that as a Shattered Race, even if you get them up there, they will respawn down here as an Elf when they die."

"Well, *that* really throws a wrench in my plans." Joe sighed and started massaging his temples. "I suppose I could start with a wall? Maybe build a fort or something?"

"Just remember that the higher the town ranking, the more numerous and powerful the monsters that come after it will be. If *I* were you," Joe perked up as he prepared to receive the first actual bit of actionable advice the president was about to offer, "I would figure out how to make a building that can defend itself. Perhaps if you can figure out a way to combine golems with-"

"I need to design auto-turrets. Got it. I think that's something I can set my mind to." Joe grinned as plans started swirling in his mind, slowly for the moment, but he knew that they would start churning soon. "Thank you for the heads up. Is there anything else that you think I should know before we get on with our trip?"

"I've explained low-level skills failing, the type of monsters you can expect, and the requirements to get past the next Zone." Musk ticked off each item on one of his fingers as he listed it. "No, I think that should do it. Good luck out there, and never forget that you are *not* alone. You have an entire Guild working hard in the lower Zones, trying to reach the highest heights. I'm pleased to see that there is someone other than Aten who is forging ahead and paving the way for the others."

"Thank you for all of this. I'm sure that it will be incredibly useful knowledge in the future." Joe reached out a hand, and all of the people he now recognized as secret service members stiffened. Musk cracked a smile and took the proffered limb. The Ritualist chuckled with pure giddiness; he had always wanted to meet this guy. "I hope I get to see you again in the future!"

"If you keep doing the things my boy tells me you have been, I think that is more of a guarantee than a mere hope." With a shake and a smile, the meeting was over, and Joe was escorted out of the building.

With his thoughts swirling with information regarding what would be coming, and *finally* getting advance notice of what he would be facing, Joe started to sketch out a new plan. Even so, nothing fundamental about his mission had changed. Knowing that none of his team needed to sleep regularly, he met up with them and exited the capital city as quietly and stealthily as possible under the cover of night.

CHAPTER ELEVEN

They were only a little way outside of the city when Joe handed Cleave a small tile that contained a ritual he had spent a few hours crafting. "This is a Ritual of Bubble Travel. To activate it, all you need to do is put in a little mana right *here*, and it'll send you flying in a straight line toward the capital. It only has a range of a hundred miles or so, but that should get you out of any immediate danger. I need you to *swear* that if we get into too much danger, you will leave immediately."

"No," Major Cleave announced firmly.

All Joe could do was shrug, and he held up another tile. "If you won't do it of your own volition, I'll have to make my best judgment call and send you off whenever *I* feel it is necessary. Let's be realistic. I look at danger a lot differently than you do. If you can't keep yourself safe, I'll make *sure* that you're out of harm's way as soon as I get nervous."

The Dwarf *very* begrudgingly took the original tile he had offered her, sticking it in a pocket where it would be easily accessible. The Ritualist patted her on the shoulder to show that he had meant no harm, then tossed five of his Ritual Orbs into the air. "Now that we have that unpleasantness out of the way, I'm going to try my hand at summoning a… definitely not a demon. I think. Pretty sure. What? I waited until we were out of the city!"

"Is this what you were doing out until the wee hours of the morning?" Daniella crossed her arms and glared at him. "Is this a healthy, or *safe*, way of progressing your power?"

"I'm not sure yet, which is why I'm going to *try* summoning it!" Joe could only chuckle as the others retreated a hefty distance, but when they were out of easy earshot, he swallowed nervously and mumbled under his breath, "I *really* hope this goes well. Kinda need to keep my traveling companions happy."

It was awkward controlling all five of the Ritual Orbs at the same time, especially once he had set them out in what he believed their relative positions should be for the ritual. Even a slight loss of focus would result in an orb dropping to the ground, flying off into the distance, or otherwise making a nuisance of itself. The main problem was that he could still only skillfully control two of them at a time, although he found it surprisingly much easier than he had expected to keep the others under control. He shrugged and whispered, in an attempt at keeping his mind more focused, "Probably has something to do with my Exotic Weapon Mastery increasing."

Deciding that trying to move all five at once was not going to work as well as he needed, he called back the first orb, which had been bound with the summoning spell, and mentally commanded the first circle to pop out of the next orb in line. Once it was extracted, he guided the second one into position and commanded that to open as well. He discovered an unexpected benefit: since the first two circles were meant to interact with each other, he was able to somewhat link them together in his mind's eye, giving him finer control over them as a single unit. He added the third circle, then the fourth, and checked to see how long it had taken. "Abyss. Fifteen minutes is far too long to do this during combat; I'm going to need to practice a *lot*.

With the four open orbs acting as a single ritual, he added

the final one to the center and sent the mental command to activate the spell. The resulting surge demonstrated *exactly* why the orb consumed nearly five thousand mana in a single shot. Power raced out of the central orb, traveling through all four Ritual Circles in a flash.

The ritual sprang to life, and a ghastly visage appeared to surround the main spell focus, which remained firmly planted on the ground. The details of the ghoulish face filled themselves in as the being was summoned through the barrier keeping it separate from this Plane of existence, soon followed by a black fog that was more akin to fire than water. Empty eye sockets peered at Joe, and a strange empathetic link was created between them.

<*Kill. Feed. Taste life.*>

"Now there's a pleasant way to introduce yourself." Joe spoke cheerfully, deciding that he needed to keep his audience from seeing how much that presence in his mind was making him shiver. "I want to make a long-term contract with you in order to use your power in battle and further my own goals. What do you say, want to come and do fun things?"

<*New experiences. Constant stimuli.*>

"I can't promise constant stimulation, as this spell can only summon you for an hour at a time. I plan to summon you just before I enter battle, so you would be able to attack creatures fairly quickly whenever you are brought here. Does that interest you?" There was no answer to Joe's query, so he decided to sweeten the pot a bit. "Unlike anyone who may have summoned you previously, I will not be putting you in one spot to watch others fight from a distance while restricting you to blasting away with your mana. Observe."

Joe took control of the orb that the skull had formed around, sending it into the air to fly around. If a skull surrounded by withered flesh could show absolute shock, this one would have. Joe let it zoom around for a few minutes, then guided it back to complete their contract.

<Flight. Always flight. Sink teeth into flesh from flight. Kill only for you, never kill you.>

"I can only guarantee flight for about half of each time you would be here, since we would be in combat, especially at the start of your summon." Joe was stuck on something else that the Pseudo-Lich had projected at him. "Why would you want to sink your teeth into something? Your main mode of attack is bolts of mana... at least, that's what the book says."

<Teeth main attack. Drain Energy. Life, mana, stamina.>

"That means that... everyone who has ever summoned one of your kind has got it wrong? They have always been used as sentries, beings that could protect a designated space at a distance." Joe's eyes were shining as he considered the ramifications of the new information. "With this knowledge alone, I can contribute to the repository of magical knowledge. I could write an entire paper on this subject and present it to the Mage's College back on Midgard! After my exile is completed, that is. Ah... anyway, back to the main point: do you accept the terms as offered?"

<So much yes.>

It did not escape Joe's attention that the longer they spoke, the more articulate the entity was becoming. He decided he would keep an eye on that, but he felt confident that he would not need to worry about the thing's betrayal, or at least not betraying *him*. Magical contracts were very difficult to break, after all. "Then I accept as well. Would you like to stick around for the rest of your allotted time?"

<Stay. Hunt?>

"No hunting right away, but we can get you up in the air. These are the members of my party; alert me if you see any other creatures moving around us." As an afterthought, Joe added, "Don't attack my party members."

<Lame.>

As Joe set the orb to hover over his left shoulder, slowly rotating, his friends approached him cautiously. Jaxon was glaring at the floating head with severe disappointment evident on his face. "How can you summon something like that? This is *completely* unacceptable."

"Agreed. Summoning demons has to be some kind of-" Daniella was cut off as Jaxon threw his hands in the air, then pointed both of them at the floating head.

"It has no *spine*, Joe! No spine at all! How am I supposed to learn advanced bone structure from creatures I've never interacted with if they don't even have a basic spine? Are you going invertebrate on me, *bro*?"

"That is the most... Jaxon-style argument against demon summoning, I suppose; what else should I expect from you?"

Major Cleave kept her eyes on the floating head, slowly shaking her own head in consternation. "That is very illegal, Joe. Back near the founding of the planes, there was a terrible infestation. You couldn't tell who *was* possessed, and who wasn't... until they tore their way out of the bodies. You're playing a dangerous game by letting something like that out in the open."

"I have an answer for both of those issues." Joe held up two fingers. "I won't pull this guy out in populated areas, at least not in a Dwarven city or town. That's one problem solved. As for you, Jaxon, do you mean to tell me that you can't figure out a way to adjust more than spines? What about the temporomandibular joint? Look at the TMJ on this guy, it's got to be *twice* as tight as coiled steel wire! Also, I know for a fact that you can adjust ears and all sorts of other things! Abyss, look at him! He's immortal, so even if you mess up, all I need to do is resummon him!"

<Wait.> Joe wasn't expecting to hear concern from his summoned being, but he supposed that fear of a maniacal Chiropractor closing in was more universal than he had expected. *<What doing!>*

"You have a good eye for this sort of thing, Joe! Look how tight this is. I'm surprised it could even open its mouth in the first place, let alone try to bite me, like it's trying to do right now. But with just a few small... *adjustments*!" The last word was practically screamed into the Pseudo-Lich's hollow eye socket as the Chiropractor slammed both hands into the sides of the summons's face—three hits in rapid succession. "There you go! *Whew...* I might need to go pour some cold water on my face after an exciting workout like that. I like your new pet, Joe!"

The entity tumbled to the ground, discarded like a half-eaten apple as Jaxon sauntered off. Joe let it lay there for a moment, since it wasn't trying to communicate anything to him, but then gently floated it back up into position over his shoulder. "With that out of the way, let's get back to the mission at hand? We left from a different gate, and I think we should circle around our actual path at least a little bit before-"

"There's no point." Major Cleave shook her head and started marching directly toward their destination. "A Bounty Hunter team is searching specifically for you, and not only do they have a druid, but they also have a Direwolf to assist in tracking you. So long as you are traveling via natural means, the only way to get where we need to go without taking them down is to stay ahead of them the entire time. Otherwise, we will end up walking into an ambush. Forget whatever you are about to say. We are not going to be hiding, we are not going to be circling. We are going to practice the best and most effective movement technique the Legion has to offer."

"You just want us to sprint the entire time, don't you?" Joe snorted at the idea that *running* was her idea of a high-quality movement skill.

"No time like the present to get started." Major Cleave took off at a pace that she knew all of them could keep for a long period of time, even if it wouldn't be comfortable. "Nice night for a run. The moon is beautiful tonight."

CHAPTER TWELVE

"I don't know who they are, but they're gaining on us," Daniella managed to voice amid her huffing and puffing. It was just past noon, and they had been running for over twelve hours. If Joe hadn't been nearly as exhausted as she was, Major Cleave would almost certainly have scooped her up and forced them to continue going. But with *two* humans on her shoulders, even she would be slowed down enough that the people coming after them would start to catch up just as they reached a low point in their ability to fight back.

"Maybe saying this trip would only take five days was a little generous of me," Cleave grumped as she led them up a hill. "We need to find out how many of them are coming after us. If there are more than we can handle, we are going to have to jump in a bubble and hope for the best."

"I vote for doing that right away." Joe raised his hand and looked around at the others, hoping they would get on board. "Oh *come* on, how likely is it that the Elven incursion has been able to get ahead of us and set up anti-air equipment? Plus, I have a whole new setup that I've been wanting to try out!"

"Please don't test new things on us when we are in a life-

and-death situation," Major Cleave replied calmly, pulling out her axe and a whetstone. There was no way that the small rock was going to do anything for the clearly enchanted blade, but it was obvious that the practice was more of a cathartic motion for her than anything else.

"Trust me when I say that this one is a *whole* lot better than my last attempt." Joe rubbed his hands together slowly, the villainous glint in his eye doing nothing to boost his team's confidence in his abilities to get them out of the situation. "Listen, I'll just get to work, and if this isn't a battle we can win... we go the magic route!"

"Is there a reason we waited until now? It's just past noon, so it's going to be kind of hard to hide a giant bubble flying through the sky." Daniella petered off as Joe pointed firmly at the Dwarf who was their guide.

"She wouldn't let me."

Major Cleave swung her axe through the air, glaring at the Ritualist. "You sound like a small child! Are you seriously *tattling* on me? The rules and regulations put in place by the Dwarven Oligarchy are there for a good reason. Just because you don't understand what those reasons *are* does not mean they are not *good* reasons."

"Is it so bad to have a backup?" Joe's voice was filled with exasperation as he waved his hands to the side. "We are on a hill with very little cover, and we're being actively pursued by an unknown force! If that isn't the time to have a solid backup plan, I don't know when is!"

"Fine!" Major Cleave slammed the butt of her weapon onto the ground while angrily staring him down. "When this goes terribly wrong, don't come crying to me! Start setting it up."

"I'm already done, as a matter of fact." Joe chuckled at the frustrated scream that she tried to muffle. He tossed a tile onto the ground, then started setting Mana Batteries in their proper places. "Only thing left to do is charge it, and I know you aren't a huge fan of the mana signature that gets blasted all over the place when I start using my power. In this case, since they already know where we are, we might as well get it out of the way!"

Static electricity crackled in the air as Joe began weaving huge flows of power from both of the stones as well as his body. The resulting circuit released an increasingly high-pitched whine, setting their teeth on edge as the Elven war-party closed in on them. Daniella gulped and turned to look back at the party leader. "About how much longer do you think before we can hit the button? There's got to be at least three dozen of them, possibly more, if some of them are camouflaged."

"Or there are only four of them, and they are using an illusion to mess with us." Cleave growled the words out, flavoring them with excitement. "That's a pretty standard tactic that they use—in fact, it is a tactic we use as well. We just don't use illusions; we send a few people to carry extra torches when we attack at night to make it appear as though we have a force double the size of reality. I think we can take them."

The Elves, apparently coming within firing range, started sending arrows at them. Unfortunately for Joe's team, bow range was almost half a mile for the incredible archers. Another cluster of the attackers shifted off to the side and started simultaneously casting a spell. Jaxon watched them curiously and let out a low whistle. "Interesting! So *very* interesting! I haven't seen Mages working together to cast a single spell since we were back on Midgard. I wonder if that has any special meaning?"

"Abyss! They're casting a *war* spell on a small party? That will alert every Legion force in the surrounding fifty miles to their location!" Cleave waved her axe, slapping a duo of arrows from the air and howling into the distance. "*Cowards!* Come closer so I can kill you!"

"Yeah, see, I don't think that they are going to do that," Joe muttered as his mana inched down to the halfway point. "I've tried that a few times myself, but they never listen. Infuriating, isn't it? Any idea what kind of spell it is going to be?"

Jaxon rubbed at his chin. "Hmm. Elves are all about natural things, right? Well, the way the wind is blowing, and judging by how rapidly your magic generated static in the area, I'm going to go with the idea that they're going to augment what nature is already providing by casting some kind of overcharged lightning bolt at us."

"That was…" Joe paused for a moment and looked at his friend, "surprisingly well reasoned. Good call. If we have an idea of what is going to be coming at us, is there anything that we can do to *not* get hit by the spell?"

"Not be here when it hits?" Daniella offered with a weak chuckle as the wind changed direction and began gusting toward the Elves that were working together. Even with the air blowing against them, she swore that she could still hear the spell weavers chanting in a rhythmic pattern. "Is that an option? I think that they're nearly done…!"

"It's up to the Major." Joe fell back from the ritual, which completed by creating a swirling effect in midair above the anchoring tile on the ground. "She needs to escape first… but if she's not going, I guess we all die here together!"

Ritual Circles has reached Expert V!

Quest update: Student Ritualist. 11/20 Student Ranked rituals activated. -Woa~o~oh! You're more than halfway there!

"Ahh! Ritual Circles went up a level! Celestials, when was the last time… and now I'm going to have that song stuck in my head for the next week." Joe gestured at the strange distortion hovering in the air, unable to keep a smile off his face despite the dire situation. "Major, if you'd be so kind, hop in first? This will take us… I think about one hundred miles straight in that direction? We won't overshoot, will we?"

"What do you mean you *think* it will take us?" Cleave eyed him askance as she slapped down a few more arrows.

"Woo, they *really* want you dead." Jaxon chuckled as an arrow *pinged* off the Major's breastplate. "They haven't even tried to get *me* once! Not that they could; I'm amazing at dodging arrows."

"Spell is reaching completion, everyone! Now or *never!*" Daniella did her best not to shriek, but she was definitely eyeing the ritual and considering using it while the others made up their minds.

Cleave jumped into the distortion with an infuriated snarl, coming out on the other side surrounded by something resembling a massive soap bubble that was roomy enough for her to move fairly comfortably. A quarter of a second later, she shot into the distance as quick as an Elven arrow could fly. Daniella went next, followed by Jaxon, and finally Joe backflipped through.

As his bubble formed, Joe felt the air around him becoming supercharged, crackling with energy as the Elves in the distance were hidden by an intense flash that put the light of the sun to shame. Thinking quickly, he cast Dark Lightning Strike at his ritual just as his bubble shot away.

The soundless pure black bolt contrasted wildly with the thunderous tribulation of lightning that seemed to *crawl* through the air over the hilltop, shattering the Atmo-flat—not an atmosphere, as they were on a disk world—with thunder along its entire path. As far as Joe could tell, the lightning was supposed to impact a designated area and spread out, especially useful for striking an army marching toward a fortified location. However, it had been at least partially mitigated by his own energy hitting the ground and acting as a short-circuit.

Dark Lightning Strike has reached Student V! Now that was using your skills in a new and effective manner!

Luck +1!

Luck has increased to a new threshold! Luck is smiling on you!

Golden lightning converged on the hilltop and coated the ground in luminescence too bright to look at... and the entire hill detonated, sending tons of debris into the air as a mushroom cloud. Rocks whizzed by Joe's bubble, filling him with great concern—these bubbles were built *only* for speed. Practically any damage at all would cause it to pop like the soap bubble it resembled, and either the destruction would catch him, or the Elves would.

"Looks like my Luck increased *just* in time." He laughed

wildly as the explosion settled and the lightning crawled along the ground. "Silly lightning! None of us are on the ground. Ha… woo. What?"

In the distance, the lightning wasn't vanishing. As far as he could tell, it was rearing up and looking around as though it were a living being. "Was that actually an electric eel summoning spell? Huh. Well, either way, I'm happy not to be there right now."

He relaxed back within his bubble and turned his eye to the horizon. His ritual effect was still going, even though the generating ritual had been destroyed. That wasn't a bug; it was a feature. The ritual created bubbles around whatever entered it and sent the intruding object flying. The trade-off to the continued effect was the fact that there was no way to aim the bubble, and it only moved in a straight line. If they encountered terrain, monsters, or anything else, they would just crash into it unless they managed to pop their bubble from inside. "I'm just glad we were at a high point, otherwise that would have been a *really* short trip."

Now that he thought about it, there were secondary benefits to traveling by bubble, as well as a few things that he needed to change in the next version. For instance, it was starting to get hot inside the iridescent sphere , because no air was being exchanged from the inside to the outside. Thankfully, their intended trajectory was going to be a fairly short trip, otherwise he would have been concerned about the others suffocating or having to smash their way out. *He* would be fine, of course, thanks to his Neutrality Aura keeping things fresh.

One of the advantages was that they were neither touching the ground, nor were their scents able to escape the thin membranes. He could only hope that such obfuscation would throw off their pursuers, at least long enough for them to get into an advantageous position. Joe surveyed the terrain that he was soaring over and tried to calculate exactly how fast they were moving. "We are definitely above sprinting speed, even for the Dwarves in the capital. Eh… no real way to figure it out.

What can I do for the next few minutes while… right! *Knowledge, Alchemical Lore!*"

As his mana drained into his skull, Joe felt the faintest pulse in the surrounding world. "Shoot… forgot that was a noticeable thing. I guess I can only hope that the war spell that just went off is making it hard for anyone to sense any small disturbance I just caused."

Alchemical Lore has reached Apprentice V!

Knowledge has reached Apprentice IX!

"Oh yeah…" Joe's eyes closed in pleasure as he perused the new information that had been shoved into his skull. "That's the stuff."

CHAPTER THIRTEEN

A quarter of an hour later, Joe was starting to get a little bit bored. He browsed his skill list and decided to try out something that he had practically never used: the spell 'Message'. "It's at Novice one. All that means to me is that it should level up real quick. Also that... it probably has a super high chance of back-firing, thanks to me being Excommunicated, but I have no idea what that would look like. Let's give it a shot!"

He chuckled evilly as he targeted Jaxon, whose bubble was just ahead of him. "Message to Jaxon; 'How are you enjoying the ride?'"

It cost him six mana to send the message—one per word—but that was such a blip on the radar that it had already regenerated by the time he could have checked to see if it was gone. He watched Jaxon looking around warily, apparently trying to spot whoever was messing with him. To be fair, Joe *was* messing with him, but there was a good reason for it!

Skill grinding!

There was supposed to be a 'return message' function, but the spell faded away before Jaxon took advantage of it, so Joe tried again. "Message to Jaxon: 'This is Joe. Try sending a message back.'"

As soon as he tried to send it off, Joe's ears were ravaged by a scream of feedback that lasted four entire seconds. When he pulled his hand away from his sensory organs, several spots of blood stained his fingers for a moment before they were whisked away, thanks to his Neutrality Aura. "Ah. *That's* what the spell failing is going to look like. Great. That's just *lovely*."

Message has reached Novice II!

"Oh good, it reached the next level. Now it only costs point-*nine* mana instead of one *whole* mana to send." Joe rolled his eyes as he repeated his message to his buddy ahead of him. This time he got a reply, but it was a stream of gibberish. It took him a while to parse what had happened, and another long minute to piece the response together to a comprehensible degree. "Message to Jaxon: 'Did you send a message back to me using only your thoughts? It wasn't something I could understand; also, I didn't know that was possible. Try speaking the words aloud next time?'"

The larger amount of mana required to cast such a long message zipped out of him, creating a flow between the two men, and soon Joe received a reply.

//This is a very disturbing experience! I hear your words as written text, and the cognitive dissonance is driving me insane. Please stop immediately.//

"Alright, sending my words as written text. Got it. Can't tell if that's the spell failing in a strange way, or if that's just how this thing works." Joe had intended to continue testing the spell, but he spotted something in the distance that concerned him greatly: a cliff wall. "We all need to get out... and of course they don't know that we'll need to bust these ourselves. They're gonna smash into the wall; that's a rough way to go. I'll send flowers. No, wait! I can warn them!"

He prepared himself and tried to keep one eye on his mana, working to condense it down into the proper channels so that his Excommunicated title would be able to work against him a little less. "Message Major Cleave: 'This is Joe. You need to pop the bubble or you'll hit that wall. No steering or built-in avoidance!'"

The message sent, and with a flash of steel, Major Cleave began falling to the ground. Joe was unable to watch how well that went for her, instead focusing on sending the same message to Daniella. He knew it went through, because he got a reply that greatly concerned him.

{*I can't make it break! I don't have anything sharp!*} Daniella's voice reached Joe's head, along with a strange feeling of walls being built up and closing in.

Message has reached Novice VII.

Unable to do anything for her at the moment, he sent the message along to Jaxon as well. The Chiropractor quickly popped his bubble, falling out of Joe's line of sight. The Ritualist pulled out his Ritual Orb of Intelligence, aiming it carefully at his trapped companion, knowing that he only had one chance at keeping her from hitting the wall at full speed. "*Omnivault!*"

Since the skill was almost purely physical, the fact that he shouted it was entirely to psych himself up. He kept his orb directly in front of him, focusing on it along with his target in the distance. As soon as he began moving forward, leaping off of the bubble, the icicle tip of his weapon shot forward, destroying his own mode of transportation. Unlike the others, he continued forward for a few long moments, allowing him to keep his aim perfect as he sent his projectile at the rapidly receding bubble. It struck true, turning like a boomerang and zipping back toward him. That was all Joe saw before he hit the ground at an awkward angle, having forgotten to prepare for his own landing.

Damage taken: 210 Terrain.

"Nothing like half fall damage." He wheezed with contentment as he hopped up and headed toward where he assumed Daniella had fallen. He hoped that his other teammates were doing the same thing, since they had fallen so far back from where Joe had landed. He glanced to the side, and all of his levity vanished. "Hooray, a reminder that this is monster territory."

Several boulders had been scored deeply with claw marks, a few of them even shattered, and all of them had been shifted out of place from where they should have naturally landed. Joe started running toward Daniella, *definitely* not out of concern for her, but knowing that the best thing that he could accomplish in that moment was being together. There was safety in numbers, or at least the *perception* of safety. Joe knew that he only needed to travel in a straight line, as it was unlikely that she had moved far off the path yet. He breathed a sigh of relief as he found her, sitting up and trying to clean out some blood that was starting to congeal in her hair.

"Hit pretty hard. Help a gal out?" She smiled weakly at him, and the blood smudging her lips made Joe feel terrible. A quick Mend fixed up the minor damage she had accrued, and his aura took care of the rest.

"My apologies. I had no idea that we would have such a rough landing." He could only offer a lame regret. Frankly, he had known *exactly* how his bubbles were designed; Joe just hadn't expected anyone to take serious damage coming out of them, certainly not in this Zone. High Constitution was the name of the game, as well as lifesaving skills designed to miti-gate damage. The fact that she was broken in several places was not a good sign for her long-term success.

Daniella stood up and looked down at the small imprint that she had left from landing so hard. "Maybe I'm really *not* cut out for all of this travel. I bet none of you even got a scratch."

"Hey, that was a totally unexpected fall, right? Not exactly ideal circumstances…" Joe trailed off, saved from having to try to play off her previous injury by the arrival of his other party members.

Major Cleave grabbed his shoulder roughly. "This sort of garbage is *exactly* the reason why I don't want you testing out brand new rituals on us! Find animals or something; there are no activists in this world that care what happens to monsters!"

"Can confirm!" Jaxon called over, reminding Joe that the Chiropractor had been working hard to become capable of adjusting any xenofauna in this universe. That made him wonder if his comrade had been doing anything some people might consider... unethical. He immediately let that thought go. Someone who was summoning creatures from some kind of abyss was *probably* not the person to be giving off moral advice. Not without having had terrible incidents and changing their ways, and *that* didn't sound like anything he was going to do.

He needed to make progress, after all.

"*I'm* certainly not going to be changing my ways," The Ritualist muttered under his breath, earning a strange look from the others. "That is... Major Cleave, are we on the correct path for reaching the city?"

"We are, and if my guess is correct, you saved us perhaps... two days of travel?" The Dwarf spoke begrudgingly, clearly not wanting to give him any accolades after their recent mishap. "We are also firmly in the foothills, which means we are going to start needing to be cautious of natural monsters, as well as the very *unnatural* monsters that have been released or have escaped. Keep your eye holes peeled like potatoes, as you humans say."

"None of us say that." Daniella piped up before anyone else could, a smile cracking the stern face she had been maintaining. "You should stop trying to pick up idioms from Havoc."

Joe was about to answer, but his vision shifted, and he found himself approaching the ground at high speed. His face was slammed into the earth, and he was crushed back down as he bounced.

Damage taken: 92 terrain!

Exquisite Shell: 10,801/10,893

"What's going on-" His confused inquiry was cut off by a screech as he was repeatedly whipped into the ground, finally getting chucked into the distance when it was apparent that he wasn't taking any health damage; as well as the fact that what-ever had a hold of him was getting continuously slapped by his Retaliation of Shadows. As he tumbled through the air, he looked back to find a swarm of creatures charging at the group, screaming with excitement at the prospect of an easy meal.

They looked like… he tried to put the picture together in his head, but it was so far from natural that his mind was resisting categorizing them. Each one consisted of a round body that had split in the middle to reveal a huge, lamprey-style mouth, which opened so wide that the body looked like it was about to invert. Coming off the body were only two limbs that seemed to function as both its arms and legs, raising the beast up to nearly thrice Joe's height. Two tiny square eyes on eye stalks peeked up over the mouth, allowing the creature to use its entire being to swallow its prey without needing to make allowances for sensory organs.

Joe bounced a few times, recognizing that he had taken a total of about two hundred damage to his shield after the first impact. Frankly, it was completely negligible, which perhaps gave him a skewed representation of the sort of damage these things could inflict. Namely, by the time he stood back up, the only part of Daniella that remained were her feet and ankles, the rest having been chomped off and swallowed by the time the others were able to respond to the threat that had come out of practically *nowhere*.

Major Cleave's axe was exceptionally effective against the threat, perhaps due to the fact that the creatures had no sense of self-preservation in the slightest. Joe wasn't entirely certain if it was because they were constantly starving, but their only modes of attack were grabbing something with their hand-feet and slamming it back and forth or chomping down on anything that could fit into their oversized maws. The Dwarf expertly cut through the limbs flailing at her, felling a handful of the crea-tures before they resorted to trying to get her in their mouths instead of grabbing at her.

Jaxon was dancing around the creatures, feeling their legs

with practiced ease. He didn't start fighting for a few seconds, until he suddenly crowed, "Initial patient examination has been completed! Proceeding to a more *thorough* anatomy check!"

The monster he had been touching was abruptly *twisted* and dropped to the ground, where Jaxon had easier access to its body. "Let's get all this boring *flesh* out of the way. *Living Weapons!*"

The Chiropractor was drenched in a shower of green ichor as his hands shifted into a T-rex head and five tiny T-rex heads, which tore into the body of the beast. Joe shook off his shock and got to work sending shocks back at them, starting with a Dark Lightning Strike. As the small cluster of beasts seized up, he sent his Ritual Orbs into the fray, using them to beat one of the beasts down, then driving his sharp orb through it and into the ground.

"One down, a swarm to go." Joe did a double-take as his current target hopped back up and started running at him. "Scratch that. None down. *Cone of Cold!*"

CHAPTER FOURTEEN

Joe was on his third Omnivault of the fight, and the constant dodging was starting to wear on his patience. "Cleave! How are you killing them? This. One. Won't. *Die!*"

He punctuated his statement by driving his Ritual Orbs one after another into the beast that was lunging at him, its mouth snapping closed on the location he had vacated only a moment ago. "Seriously, what are these things supposed to be? Snapping turtles mixed snails and leeches? Rocks with legs and teeth? *Angry* rocks with teeth?"

"If you want them to stay down, you have to outpace their natural healing factor," Major Cleave informed him while engaged in combat with yet another of the beasts. "At a certain level, all monsters are able to heal extremely efficiently, so you have to burst down their total health, or inflict such terrible debuffs on them that their flesh is unable to heal it in any kind of reasonable fashion. Take Jaxon, for example: he's doing both at the same time. Severe skeletal damage, in conjunction with shredding the flesh so that it cannot pull together at the same rate as it is being torn apart."

"Right, well, I don't have anything that can do that," Joe

grumbled as he slid under a snapping maw. "Time to try my backup plan."

Plan determined, he hastened over to an outcropping that he didn't think the creatures could easily ascend, jumping up to spring off an adjacent wall and onto the exposed rock with a double Omnivault. Once he landed, he took a moment to attempt to center himself, then threw his Ritual Orbs into the air one at a time, unfurling them into the enchanted ritual diagram necessary for Planar Shift. It was significantly easier now that he was familiar with the process, and he felt pleased at his success in reducing the total amount of time connecting everything to about thirty seconds.

"That is *way* better than fifteen minutes." Joe shook off the feeling of smugness that tried to settle in. He was no Elf; he wasn't about to become an unrepentant narcissist after such a tiny win. As soon as it was up and operational, he ordered his Ritual Orb to cast its assigned spell, and the veil between dimensions was ripped asunder as the Pseudo-Lich was pulled through. The gaunt visage formed around the orb, exactly as it was supposed to, and Joe only took a moment to coax the other orbs to snap back into their normal formation before rejoining combat.

"Do you have a name? Or can I give you a name? Referring to you by your summoning articles is a little strange for me," Joe stated as he directed his orbs back at the creature that he was mentally calling a Serrated Maw. He hadn't had a moment to check his notifications or combat log yet, so he did not yet have its proper name, but he thought the label fit pretty well.

<Mo~orsum.>

"Morsum?" Joe watched the floating skull zip at the Serrated Maw in confusion, "The opposite of less subtraction? What does that mean?"

Morsum didn't answer, too focused on acquiring a new taste in its mouth for the first time in centuries. The teeth of the floating skull latched on the left side of the massive mouth, piercing through the lower lip with its elongated canines. A strange flow of energy initiated, which Joe could just barely see, and he received a message that was not only unexpected, but seemed to be going against the very definition of what the spell itself could achieve.

Pseudo-Lich (Morsum) summon time remaining: 1:01:43.

"It can self-sustain by consuming energy coming off of the creatures that it bites? That's not good... or it's really good? No wonder it wanted to make a contract with me as soon as possible; using its main attack allows it to continue living on this plane of existence longer, and no one ever gave it that opportunity before." Joe was curious about what would happen to the creature being attacked, but after a few seconds of contact, Morsum had fully drained the creature, and it collapsed. Only then did his mental command for the orb to fly away come into effect, and the Lich released its prey in preparation for a fresher meal.

"Oh no... that means that by the terms of our contract, I could end up needing to focus on keeping its orb flying around for a *huge* amount of time if I'm not careful. Double oh no; I still don't know how to *unsummon* something!" Even as he fretted about what he would need to do at the end of combat, he sent the skull flying at the next of the creatures, managing to get Morsum attached to its leg. That particular creature had not yet taken much damage, so the draining effect seemed to work at a slower pace.

Joe didn't hesitate to start sending spells and orbs after the Maw, though he pondered what it meant for his new creature to be draining an opponent more slowly. "Most likely, it has an ability to pull a portion of health and mana from a creature, based on how much they have already lost. That would make sense for a necrotic or demonic ability... both of those are reputed to be magics that latch onto someone or something that is already weakened, and this squarely confirms that folklore."

Indeed, as his attacks beat against the oversized creature's flesh, the draining effect noticeably picked up speed. Joe wasn't able to get much data before the Maw used its other limb to grab the skull and chuck it away, having figured out that the floating annoyance was dealing more damage than expected. The Ritualist sent his Ritual Orb of Intelligence flying directly into its open mouth, casting Cone of Cold before the projectile hit the flesh on the back of its throat. The spell filled the beast with an arctic blast, sending the orb shattering its way out instead of simply slicing a neat hole.

Damage dealt: 888 (179 Piercing + 268 cold + 441 lifedrain)

Mana drained: 441. Summoning duration increased by 8 minutes and 48 seconds.

"All right, I'm going to have to make sure to come back to this portion of the combat log and figure out exactly how much damage this bad boy is doing. Looks like about fifty damage in a second or so, but that was before I started dealing damage as well... no, do this later!" Joe had completely lost track of where Morsum had landed, and since it had not been bonded to one of his characteristics, he knew that he needed to find it. It would not yet automatically recall after five minutes. On the plus side, the Lich was making it easy to locate his discarded head.

Clack, clack, clack!

Joe simply needed to track where the chomping noises were coming from, and a moment later, his mind was able to latch on to the Ritual Orb and send the creature back into orbit around his body.

Combat has concluded! 10 total 'Mobile Starvation' defeated. Experience gained: 1,958.

You have returned to level 23! Yay, you! Try to stop dying!

Exquisite Shell has reached Student VII.

Combat Ritual Orbs has reached Beginner V.

Battle Meditation has reached Student III.

Retaliation of Shadows has reached Expert 0!

"Well, that was a horrifying and wonderful battle! It's been too long since I worked my old bones. It was rather refreshing," Jaxon stated cheerfully as he stretched his limbs. "Too bad about Daniella, but I suppose she was a sacrifice we were all willing to make."

"No, she wasn't, and that is definitely not how we should be thinking of her." Joe rolled his eyes as he picked his way over to the last remaining bits of his slain companion. Targeting the blood-soaked right foot that she had left behind, he took a deep breath and began channeling his mana. "Sorry if this alerts our enemies to our location, Major, but I think it is much more important to have our entire group together than it is to worry about what-ifs. *Resurrection.*"

Having performed the entirety of the necessary motions, mana channeling, and spoken commands, Joe cast the spell as carefully as possible. As he had been doing ever since the fall of the Dwarven Oligarchy, he winced as the spell finished, expecting some form of backlash for using it. He knew that there was only a ten percent chance that it would rebound on him, but he had no idea what that would look like for a resurrection spell. Planar Shift had been an unpleasant surprise, and this spell was a *substantially* higher Rarity and tier.

Blzzt

The respawn portal opened directly above the remains of her previous body, and Daniella stepped through it into the world once more. She peered around the area, which had become a quagmire of churned blood, flesh, and gore. "What in the abyss happened while I was gone? I didn't even get a chance to see what took me out!"

"Instant death is always better than suffering!" Jaxon called over to her from his reclining position. He was holding a set of bones connected together by a joint, bending them back and forth in an attempt to test how resilient they were. "Shall we proceed right away, or would you rather stay here and wait for whatever monsters will be drawn by the commotion, or perhaps you wish to wait for whatever Elves will be on their way after feeling that level of mana disturbance?"

Joe wasn't currently listening, too excited about a notification he had been hoping to get for far too long.

Resurrection has reached Beginner 0! Congratulations! Now that you have surpassed the Novice ranks, certain restrictions on this spell have been lifted! You are now able to resurrect a targeted being that is up to 2n+L higher than you, where n=skill level bounded by the Beginner tier and L=your current Level! Current maximum level of being you can Resurrect: 23. The skill can now be increased like any other spell, through study and devoted use.

"Alright, that makes sense... I am level twenty-three, and my skill level at this tier is technically zero." Joe slowly bobbed his head in thought. "Good... yeah. That math works out."

"Obviously we need to get moving, Jaxon, but there is no need to be snippy about it." Major Cleave made no effort to hide her weariness. "Joe, how often can you use that spell? If I get taken out, can you use it on me and keep me from becoming an Elf?"

The Ritualist shook his head, having been expecting that very question. "Currently, I can only bring back people that are my same level or lower, and there's no way someone with something like a century of experience in combat is that low."

"You might be surprised. Most Elves and Dwarves tend to have lower general levels, with much higher skill or spell levels. Combat is great for increasing our skills, but the fact of the matter is that most of us have died repeatedly, sometimes for centuries." Major Cleave started leading them toward the cliff, which they would need to go *over* instead of around. "You are correct that I am not quite low enough, but perhaps you will get plenty of opportunities to use your spell in the coming months."

"I'm glad to hear that you're not looking at this as a one-way trip." Joe chuckled as he observed the others climbing the rock wall. After taking a few moments to map out all the protrusions that he could find, he ran toward it and jumped. "See you all at the top!"

Being able to perfectly visualize where he was going, Joe scaled the entire cliff face with only five total jumps, doing a little flip at the top just for fun. "I'm *so* glad I glitched into this skill; it's about as close to perfect for me as anything I can think of."

Only about two seconds after Joe reached the top, Major

Cleave was over the edge and standing by him. Daniella came into view next, a slight surprise since Jaxon had started before her. Perhaps it was a bonus that somehow had something to do with buildings, such as climbing scaffolding, or needing to get to a certain height to examine them for damage? Before he could inquire into the specifics of whether or not she had a skill that boosted her climbing speed, Jaxon had heaved himself over the top, and they were all running again.

"If we are where I *think* we are," Major Cleave called over her shoulder, "then we have a few hot spots coming up that we are going to have to keep an eye on. The monsters tend to migrate, rather than holding too much to a single territory, but in general, I believe that this territory is devoted to turning debuffs into monsters."

"What does that even mean?" Jaxon questioned on behalf of the group at large. "Are we going to bleed or something? Perhaps getting slowed? Other than that, I can't think of a single one of these 'debuffs,' as you call them."

"Are you being serious right now?" Daniella didn't wait for him to answer, instead turning the query to Joe. "He *is* being serious right now, isn't he? Jaxon... you are practically the *incarnation* of a Charisma debuff. The things that you do, the ways that you seem to interact with the world and the system? That's not natural."

"Awww. You sweetie, go on. No, really, go on! I love it." Jaxon blushed and playfully batted his hand at her. Daniella kept her confused gaze on Joe, who could merely reply to her wordless befuddlement with a helpless gesture.

"You literally cannot get through to him on this sort of thing. The system just won't let it happen." Joe looked at his good friend, and found himself smiling. "I think it finds it funny to do stuff like that? I've gotten used to it, and you know what? I would have to agree with the universe. Jaxon's oddity makes life a lot of fun."

CHAPTER FIFTEEN

"What are these ones supposed to represent?" Joe tried and failed to understand what exactly his team was fighting right now. The creature had an incredible Constitution, making it incredibly difficult for any damage that they managed to inflict to permanently damage the beast. If there had been more than one, it was unlikely that they would have been able to fight them, instead needing to rely on agility to escape or get around it in a different manner.

"This is an Elite creature called 'The Wooze'," Major Cleave explained as she wielded her axe akin to a lumberjack. Back and forth went the blade, chopping in a rhythmic motion. "It is entirely unable to understand its intuition, which is supposed to be comparable to a threshold differentiation between Constitution and Wisdom. That's why it isn't bothering to dodge any of our attacks, only reacting after we have already struck."

"I've never heard of these 'threshold' issues, and for some reason, hearing about them now makes me grumpy," Jaxon confided in them quietly. "Perhaps we should only worry about destroying the monster, instead of talking about whatever it is supposed to represent. I don't need that information!"

Daniella swept up next to him and gave him a side hug. "Perhaps *you* just don't worry about that information, and we can have the conversations that we want? I really enjoy learning all of these things, as there is no written guide that I have been able to find."

"That would be because he is not the only sort of person who gets uncomfortable when they hear about these things." Major Cleave's swings accelerated as her chopping finally started to bear fruit. "Anyone who has threshold debuff issues and doesn't understand what they are, or that they are being affected by them, tends to go a little manic around these sorts of conversations."

"*I* know! I just won't pay attention while you guys have your talks on this disconcerting topic." Jaxon immediately started humming to himself, his expression growing distant as he dug into a twitching muscle on the side of The Wooze.

Joe was having a good time, since he did not have to worry overmuch about this creature dealing damage to him. It was almost pure Constitution, and the only reason they had bothered to take the time to take it down was that it had been following them relentlessly. It was a persistence hunter; even if they managed to get away, it would eventually show up to fight.

Summoning Morsum would have made this fight a cakewalk by draining the health from the beast for however long it would stay alive, but even though that would have been beneficial in the short term, the facts remained that Joe had no way currently to recharge the required Mana Batteries at a sustainable rate while out in the open. Not unless he wanted to stop and create a charging array for them, and he was starting to run low on cores that he could use so casually. Even those, he had begun wanting to save for activating rituals.

The Wooze went down with a mournful cry—like a whale being harpooned, knowing that it would soon be harvested for its oil. Joe's contribution only netted him two hundred and thirty-six experience points, barely worth stopping to fight, if they'd had any other choice. He scanned the horizon, noticing that the elevation had taken a drastic upward pitch. "How long until we get into the mountains proper, do you think? Wait, do you think this creature has anything in it that is worth harvesting?"

"I suppose this would be a Rare or better monster." Major Cleave replied guardedly, not quite certain where the conversation was going.

"Give me five minutes to harvest it, if you wouldn't mind?" Joe didn't wait for an answer before setting up his Field Array around the difficult-to-define corpse. He supplied the mana required, and with a burst of light, the entire body disintegrated, reduced into various rarities of aspects. As he straightened, a portion of the remaining energy cloud dissipated, and a core dropped to the ground. "A good selection of Rare aspects *and* a core? Nice!"

Jaxon eagerly scooped it up, and the core vanished in a flash of light. "Hooray! I am that much closer to regaining level twenty-five!"

For a moment, Joe had to force himself to stop from lashing out, reminding himself that he wasn't automatically entitled to every resource that came into the group. In fact, he began feeling guilty about all of the cores he had appropriated in the past without considering his teammates, and resolved to be a better sharer. His preschool teacher would be proud of him.

"We should get there tomorrow and be able to see the mountains by first light." Major Cleave's assertion earned her a rough cheer from the others, and they all began their ascending hike once again. "Keep an eye out for small creatures, and remember that if you see something cute or cuddly, there must be a reason that it has survived this long in such a harsh environment. Creatures like The Wooze are very solitary, but they are also extremely resistant to status effects. That tends to allow them to ignore Charisma-heavy creatures or at least the influences those have on most every other entity."

"What would they be able to do? Is there something specific that we should watch out for?" Joe had his notebook out in a flash, ready to start taking notes and perhaps gathering material for his eventual research papers for the Mage's College, or perhaps the Scholar's Society, if they stopped hunting him like a rabid dog sometime in the future.

"It's pretty simple. Anything that is a Charisma-based hunter tends to lure you into a false sense of security, and some can even deal damage to you while preventing you from reacting in a negative way. For instance, if we run into a discrepancy creature that is based on having a threshold of Charisma that is significantly higher than Strength, it will *appear* to be very strong. That means that it will bluff us, and if we fall for the intimidation, it might achieve something to the effect of... chasing us off of a cliff, or into the jaws of a creature it has developed a symbiotic relationship with." Major Cleave looked at her team to make sure that everyone was understanding what she was saying. Both Joe and Daniella nodded along in comprehension, but Jaxon's eyes were glassy and he was humming a soft tune.

They had a few encounters over the course of the day, but most of the time, they were not with creatures that had been magically or 'scientifically' altered. They were simply monsters that were in the wrong place at the wrong time, looking for an easy meal rather than a battle with this group. Evening ended quickly as the party drew closer to the mountains. The light cut off, leaving them in a long shadow that stretched to the horizon and turned into darkest night.

"Daniella, as far as I can tell, you have much higher Perception than the others," Major Cleave asserted as the stars in the sky burned clearly. "I need you up here with me to watch for threats. Joe, you should be fine going as you are, but Jaxon... I need you to keep your eyes on me unless a fight breaks out. That means get as close as you can and run with me while bumping into me as infrequently as possible, if you please."

"It's the new beard and haircut, isn't it?" Jaxon winked at

her, even though she was facing forward and trying to pick out the best path in the darkness. "My Cultural Understanding skill is tingling!"

"Bump into me too often, and I will slice off your arm. Then we'll see what *tingles*," Cleave threatened vaguely, too distracted at the moment to come up with a better warning.

All of them were expecting that the monsters that hunted at night would be bigger, meaner, stealthier, and harder to kill than those they had been running into intermittently throughout the day. It wasn't a great feeling, and the fact that their ability to see incoming threats had been reduced was putting *most* of them on edge.

Contrary to what he had been told to do, Joe went to the front and ran alongside the Dwarf. She scowled at him and was clearly going to say something to put him in his place, but he pointed at his face. "I have Darkvision. I am likely more useful at night than I am during the day, at least in terms of scouting."

"See, to me, your usefulness is still up for debate." Major Cleave's retort could have been taken as insulting, but Joe understood that she was merely trying to make a joke to lighten a very stressful situation. The night began to pass, seeming to last forever while also vanishing in a blink. By that point, they had been traveling for several days without rest, even eating their food and drinking their water on the move. All of them were getting tired, and perhaps a little snippier than they would otherwise have been.

Contrary to expectation, the various fights throughout the night were easily resolved, with most of the creatures running off as soon as they got a taste of the firepower that could be brought to bear against them. Daylight began to dawn, and they crested one final ridge before sighting the mountain range that was their destination. Joe immediately understood how it would be nearly impossible to find where they were going if they didn't have a guide, as the entire mountain range looming in front of them was shrouded from tree line to summit in a thick cloud bank.

"Which one are we going to?" Jaxon clapped his hands in excitement as they started forward again. "Not going to tell us? Excellent! I love surprises!"

Major Cleave mimed zipping her mouth closed before she clarified, "Until we are in a protected area, we never gesture or say aloud where we are going. You never know who is listening, or what kind of devices—magical or otherwise—might be used to record what we say, or where we go. Simply follow, and trust that anyone who is tracking us at this moment is going to have a very difficult time piercing the enchantments and formations that have been put in place to stop them. Stay close. It would be a great shame to lose you all so close to our destination."

CHAPTER SIXTEEN

Contrary to Joe's expectations, they were not led to a secret tunnel. There was no entrance hidden behind a bush, no waterfall guarding a secret path to a magical city. Instead, they simply began their trek into the mountains, following a narrow path that could fit only a single Dwarf at a time. If it were not for the fact that he knew of the existence of magical storage devices which would allow for the rapid transit of huge amounts of resources and everything else that a thriving city needed, he would never have believed that roads of this quality would be sufficient for their needs.

"I'm just checking, are we on a goat path right now?" Jaxon peered around in excitement. "I love those fluffy little guys and their square eyes! Basically the cutest things I've ever seen in my life! Beyond any random snake sunning itself by the side of the road, of course!"

"This is actually known as *the* G.O.A.T. path." Major Cleave favored the Chiropractor with a rare smile; clearly she was feeling more secure as they got closer to the city proper. "According to every magically inclined Dwarf that has come from this place, it is the path to true enlightenment and understanding. The 'greatest of all time path', or the 'G.O.A.T. path'. At the end lies a repository of knowledge, secrets of the Oligarchy, and opportunities for advancement both in careers and society. That is what Dehur Bethi, the High City of Deep Thought, represents to my people."

"That's pretty grandiose... in that case, the capital has to be even more amazing, right? A symbol of prosperity and wealth, perhaps?" The Chiropractor questioned with unbridled enthusiasm. "Also, is it just me, or is it starting to get bitterly cold?"

"The Capital is merely the center of trade. It's home to the Oligarchs, as well as the citizens that want to climb the social ladder. You will always find the highest ranks of military, nobility, and merchants in that city. It is not designed for innovation or anything else beyond functioning as a central hub for the rules and regulations of our civilization." Major Cleave blushed slightly at the words coming out of her mouth, which almost sounded treasonous. "That's the reason *I* was there, for sure. Clearly, it worked out for me, since I reached the rank of Major in only a few decades, instead of a century and a half, as is custom."

"Right, and the *cold?*" Jaxon gestured at the air as he pulled out a large parka and shimmied into it.

"Yes, this mountain range is frozen in an eternal winter below the cloud layer." Major Cleave could only shake her head and continue on as the others began to bombard her with questions.

"Are there going to be more monsters up ahead?" Daniella's voice was quivering slightly, and Joe tried to feel sympathetic to her plight. As far as he knew, she had always been able to gain levels through her profession instead of through direct, dirty, painful combat. Or, it could have been the fact that it really was getting pretty cold. "That is, how much further do we have to go until we get to the city?"

"Now that we are on the path, which is protected from eavesdropping, both magical and physical, I can give you a better idea." Major Cleave pointed directly up, and a smug smirk graced her face. "Straight up. All we need to do is follow the path until we get there. We're already on the mountain that the city is built on."

"Wait, it's the *first* mountain? The very first mountain in the whole range? The easiest one to get to out of all of them?" Joe started to scoff, but it turned into a tiny laugh as he thought about it. "That's *tricky*! Put a city inside of a massive mountain range, lead on that it is going to be very difficult to find the city, but it's actually just... right here?"

"You know it." Major Cleave's words floated back to him on the wind, as she was facing forward to scan for threats, as well as to ensure her footing. "It is still going to take us a day and a half to get there at this pace, more if we run into any monsters."

That put a damper on Joe's spirits. "So long? Why? Don't we just have to go up?"

"We need to circle the entire Mountain several times, due to the necessity of staying on the path or in the larger rest areas attached to it," Major Cleave explained easily. "Normally, of course, people that are coming to the city would simply teleport in, never knowing the difficulty in reaching the city by foot. However, with that option unavailable to us, the only thing that we can do is follow the ancient way. On the plus side, this is also the path that any magically inclined Dwarf would need to follow to even be considered for training. If they teleported in, it would show a lack of resolve."

She gathered her thoughts, then continued in a considering tone. "The path is magically guarded, with various effusive and misleading enchantments woven into the stone over the last millennia. Leaving the path, even for a moment, will result in you finding yourself back at the bottom of the mountain, nowhere near the entrance path at all. *If* you are lucky."

"That means taking this route will give us an easier chance of getting access to the people we need to talk to in the city above?" Joe voiced his hopes carefully. "If we combine that with my military rank, what do you think the likelihood of meeting with a Grandmaster is going to be?"

Major Cleave pondered the answer she wanted to give him as they continued to hike. "Back in your world, if I remember correctly, you had something called a lottery? I believe the odds of getting to speak to a Grandmaster so easily has similar odds to winning the grand prize on that game of chance, if for no other reason than you are a human, and to them, an unknown factor. With a bounty on the heads of the Grandmasters, that is the best odds I could possibly give you."

With the newfound awareness that all they had to do was climb, the blistering pace that they set for themselves was more easily accepted by everyone in the group. All the way until they made it to the first rest area. Upon encountering magically comfortable tents, enchanted perpetual flames that would easily remove the chill from their bones, and a large pot of soup that was stirring itself... all of the humans started to build a slight amount of resentment in their hearts as their Dwarven escort rushed them past.

"But there was *soup!*" Jaxon pouted as he waved sadly behind them. "It looked like *hot* soup, and this place is chilly."

Cleave shook her head and handed him a small bar of travel rations. "*Trap* soup. When have you ever seen my people —at a level where they are seeking higher understanding—act excited about mere creature comforts? You are in the Legion; you should have a good understanding of what my society thinks of people who are just seeking handouts. If we would have stopped at the first rest station, the way forward would have been barred to us."

"You Dwarves and all your little *tests*." Jaxon spat to the side in consternation. "Why can't you just give people soup when you make it *look* like you are going to give them soup? Soup, soup, soup."

"Reaching the highest heights requires an iron will. It requires doing whatever needs to be done, to advance yourself as far as you can." The Dwarf's voice was tinged with nostalgia as she said these words, which had clearly been passed down to her. "The G.O.A.T. path is narrow for a reason; there is not room for everyone to walk it. It is a hard path, full of tests for your mental, physical, and emotional being. Only those that can continue to put one foot in front of the other and stay on the path, no matter how long it takes them to arrive, can reach the summit."

"Ugh, these *metaphors!*" Jaxon broke the solemnity of the moment. "What's so bad about resting every once in a while? Taking breaks? When you have *forever*, why not allow people to advance at their own pace?"

"A flawed argument." Major Cleave shook her head, completely disregarding his griping. "That is definitely what an Elf would think, but we know better than to give in to the lure of hedonism on our march toward eternity. When you stagnate, that does not mean you stay the same. It means that you'll need to work twice as hard, *three* times as hard, and you still may never catch up to those who simply continued walking the path… no matter how sedate their pace."

The group lapsed into pensive silence, each of them mulling her words and taking their own meaning from it. Joe nodded along, thinking that he understood exactly what his companion had been getting at. Jaxon was shaking his head, clearly disagreeing with something in her arguments, and Daniella… seemed contemplative, but her jaw firmed up as she reached a conclusion of some kind.

Joe had always loved how the wisdom of the ages could affect people in so many different ways. It made for rich conversation and a deeper overall understanding as their individual points were expressed and examined. He sank into deeper thought, trying to figure out what it was exactly that his friends may be agreeing or disagreeing with, and attempting to consider what Cleave had said from a new light, a light where he didn't agree with her completely. It was difficult, but he *could*, perhaps, see how someone could take this message as 'always be working'.

The Ritualist knew, or at least believed, that this was not the actual counsel that was supposed to be taken to heart. Following the path was not about grinding until it simply wasn't possible anymore; it was about doing the work consistently, taking breaks as needed, but not every possible break available. It was also about not seeking comfort at the first opportunity. He believed, at that moment, that he understood why it was known as the G.O.A.T. path. He had a lot to learn still, and he was loving every moment of it.

Wisdom +3!

"The greatest of all time, indeed," Joe murmured to himself, pleased at the fact that he was achieving such great results from this adventure. "I'm looking forward to what other lessons reaching the pinnacle of Dwarven success will bring to us."

CHAPTER SEVENTEEN

"I think—mind you I don't know for sure, but I *think*," Major Cleave reassured them as they reached the third rest area on the path, "that we can stop here for some rest and recuperation."

"*Finally!*" Jaxon dove into the roughly one hundred by one hundred foot space, pulling out a bedroll in midair and pushing his face into it. By the time he hit the ground, he was fully ensconced in the sleeping bag and resting comfortably. "One of the drawbacks to having Living Weapons as a large part of my combat utility is that I accumulate their fatigue! Wake me up if you need something to die, otherwise be warned that you most likely shouldn't rouse me until I get up on my own."

Joe had never seen this side of his friend before, but then again, he was generally only around Jaxon during travel or combat. "We should have a board game night or something soon, just to sit back, relax, get to know each other better?"

There was no answer from the already-snoring Chiropractor, but Joe knew he would be excited to play a game. Each of the others set up their own area in rapid succession; the Dwarf pulled a chair out of nowhere and sat on it while sharpening her weapon, Daniella set up a tent and disappeared inside for some privacy, while Joe simply sat in a far corner and began tinkering with his rituals and skills.

"The bubble travel was good, but I think I underestimated how dangerous straight-line travel would actually turn out to be." The ritual clearly needed to allow for some form of control, even if it was simply object avoidance, or the ability to bring them to a safe landing after going the maximum distance that they could have traveled. He played with it for a while, as the dark night that his friends were sleeping through slowly passed. Unfortunately, he could not find a solution to the problem that he was having due to his Student rank in rituals.

Normally that wouldn't have been an issue: he was an Expert in the field, after all, and quickly closing in on true Mastery. However, his current class quest dictated that he could only produce Student rituals, and it would be a waste for him to put together something so much higher without the secondary benefit. Yes, safe landings would be nice, but rewards... *that* was where his passion lay. "I could always try to make it a linked ritual, and also use a few different circles to help control the main circle, but something tells me that is going to be more difficult than I think it is. Abyss, I blew myself up just trying to set multiple rituals to discharge at the same time. Having them actually interact? Forget about *that* for now."

As any engineer, scientist, or research and development team would confirm, just because a person has an idea for something does *not* mean that it will always come to fruition. Knowing that he needed to get some sleep to maintain his health and mental acuity, Joe made sure someone else was on watch and passed out.

"Everybody up!" Major Cleave's commanding tone shook everyone out of whatever stage of REM sleep they had been in. Luckily, Joe had managed to get a few good hours of sleep—all he needed with his current bodily capabilities. "We slept here without issue, but if we stay here, by the time daylight touches this site, all of us will be booted off the mountain."

"Taking a rest is fine, so long as you get back to walking the path immediately, I assume is the lesson here?" Daniella cheerfully tossed the question at their guide, who nodded with a pleased expression.

"I'm glad to see that the lessons which our ancient masters have tried to impart to their own people are more universal than I had hoped for." Breaking camp was an easy process when everything could be swooped up into a storage device. There was no need to break down tents, as they could be stored fully erected. That meant that within moments of waking up, they were on their way once more. "We are halfway up; that means the path is going to be growing wider to accommodate more people, as well as the enemies that we will find in our way."

"Hold on, I thought you said that the monsters and creatures that we would see around here were accidentally loosed experiments. Are you now telling me that anything we fight against is something that was specifically put in our way?" Joe didn't mind the fact that he would be needing to fight stuff, he just wanted to make sure he was absorbing all the information he could glean from this strange journey to the high city.

"If you want to understand why, put it in perspective of your own path to mastery." Major Cleave slowed down slightly in order to walk side-by-side with Joe, which the path now easily allowed for. "Tell me, why do you think this change has happened?"

The Reductionist ran along silently for a while, trying to spot the trick that she was trying to catch him in. Eventually, he just decided to hazard a guess, "The enemies make more sense. I think it is a common idea that when you are going the right way, you are going to run into enemies. That's certainly video game logic, but I can see how it applies to real-world events as well. Either people will see that we are doing well, and be afraid that we will replace them as the best or most profitable... or we will have detractors telling us that there is no way that we possibly *could* be as good as those who walked the path before us. Something like that?"

"Certainly something to take into consideration." Major Cleave deflected easily, truly enjoying her opportunity to teach people. That made sense, as that was her end goal with her military career. "Would anyone else like to expand on that, or why the path has opened up?"

"I would think that the path started narrow, because anyone starting their own journey begins as a Novice and needs to take the time to collect the skills they need, learn what they need to do, and understand that it is unlikely that the people who are the best at that craft are unlikely to offer advice." Daniella slowly offered her own insights. "Most likely because those same Masters have seen hundreds, if not thousands, of Novices over the years who are looking for an *easy* path. But how many of those Novices are going to step off that same path, or fall prey to the easy comforts that they could have? My guess is... most of them?"

"You're not wrong." Cleave then gestured at Jaxon. "You always have a fairly unique perspective, and it is almost always an attempt at seeing the side of humanity that other people do not. The good side, the positive side, things that most people will avoid even hoping for. So can you answer... why do *you* think the path widens?"

"You had mentioned that we are halfway up the mountain," Jaxon began without hesitation, clearly having been waiting to explain his own line of thinking. "If we are looking at the halfway point between Novice and Master, right now, we would be a Student of the craft. At this point, it is expected that a person has some serious dedication to the craft. They will find peers—other people to walk the path with them, and likely stay with them all the way, or as close to the peak of Mastery as possible. So, walking beside them at this point makes sense, and I am betting that it will widen again as we move into the Journeymen area, then narrow when we get to Expert, and shrink even further when we are near the peak, or the correlating Master status in terms of this life lesson?"

"Correct-" Major Cleave began, only to get cut off as Jaxon got back into it.

"But that lesson is *wrong!*" The Chiropractor shook his head and gestured at the mountain ahead of them. "It doesn't *need* to be a competition! The path through life doesn't have to be something that we walk alone. We can keep those friends with us, prop them up when they fail, knowing that they will do the same for us when the time comes. If we do what we can, motivating each other and offering our skills and advice, it doesn't *have* to be a narrow path to becoming a Master. We can all get there. We can travel *together*."

To Jaxon's surprise, the Dwarf didn't immediately try to shut him down. "Perhaps. Maybe you *can* find a group of people you can trust implicitly, someone you can share your hard-earned resources, skills, and secrets with. If so, I wish you all the best. Something to keep in mind... there *is* a point where there is no room for anyone else. Only one person can stand at the very highest peak of the mountain. In this analogy, that would be the *Sage*. There can only be one Sage of a particular class or skill. You could become a Sage of Chiropractic services, while someone else only became a Sage of Acupuncture. Yet, if you are the Sage of Chiropractic services, they could not attain that same level."

"But they could get close, and I could help them make that final step!" Jaxon attempted to refute her logic.

"No. You *can't*." Major Cleave decided not to keep him waiting any longer. "To become a Sage, you must have your skill —or *all* of your class skills if you are attempting to become a Class Sage—at the very peak of Grandmaster status. Then, you need a Mythical core in order to bind yourself and those skills together with the ideal that you are attempting to become a Sage of. There are twenty-one total Mythical cores available at any given time."

"How do you *know* that is the truth?" Jaxon pressed; his eyes full of suspicion.

"I could even tell you where seven of those could be found

right now." Major Cleave kept her cool. "It's simple. In order to earn a Mythical core, you need to defeat a World Boss. There are seven known Bosses, one per plane of existence, that you can defeat in order to gain the right to become a Sage. The other fourteen come from hidden World Bosses, who travel the various Planes at their leisure, in no pattern that anyone has ever been able to determine."

"Does that mean there can only ever be twenty-one Sages?" Joe felt his heart sink at that information, though it lifted back up as soon as he heard the answer.

"No. As soon as a core is used for that purpose, the World Boss it had been taken from is respawned. However, it becomes impossible for anyone *else* to become a Sage in either the class or the skill that was bound. What makes it even harder is the fact that several of these cores have been found and now sit in a vault—waiting for the moment when their owner can step forward and become a Sage themselves."

"I can see why it is difficult to become a Sage…" Daniella muttered under her breath, but not quietly enough.

"In a literal way, it's worth killing entire civilizations for." Cleave shook her head ruefully. "Why do you think the Dwarves and the Elves have been going back and forth for so long? Both of them are holding a Mythic core in their most hidden locations."

"Why doesn't one of them just use it to become a Sage, then go beat the other civilization until they give theirs up?" Jaxon scoffed at the idea. "Abyss, why don't they just use it and then go defeat the World Boss again?"

"As soon as one of them would use it for personal gain," Cleave's eyes came to rest on Joe, "the other side would use their core to unleash a Sage-rank superweapon. For centuries, it has been a question of who would use it to empower one person, versus who would use it to destroy the other race entirely."

"All of that would be solved if one group simply had both of them, wouldn't it?" It was a sad revelation for Joe. Once again, thousands were dying because the leaders on opposing sides wanted the resources their enemy had. "I guess we should at least be happy that they didn't decide to just go ahead and sacrifice all of their citizens."

"Yeah, that would have been bad." Jaxon agreed as they raced up the incline.

CHAPTER EIGHTEEN

It wasn't too terribly long before they found the first enemies along their path. The small group of cat-like creatures made Joe think nervously about Queen Cleocatra, although these were definitely monstrous Lynx. While they may have been as intelligent as normal cats, they certainly were not a shape-shifting race of hidden beings. He didn't even need to ask; Cleave simply announced what they were up against.

"I don't remember the name of these things, but I know what they do. These are another type of Threshold monster, which is a Dexterity disparity to Strength." Cleave cracked her neck and limbered up her axe. "Expect them to be fast and hard to hit, but easy to kill when you do! The damage they do mostly inflicts debuffs, so watch out for bleeding. Joe, do your best to keep on top of that."

"Too easy." The Ritualist calmly tossed his orbs in the air and set them to moving in randomized patterns so that he could have a clear shot at any enemies that got past the front line, currently consisting of the Dwarf and Chiropractor. Daniella was standing next to Joe, perhaps a couple of inches behind him, and shifted into a ready stance.

"If I throw them off the path, do they stay out, or can they come back?" she questioned Cleave.

The Dwarf sliced the first of the monsters in half with an easy backhand before she managed to reply. "If someone or something is off the path, they are off for a long time. Creatures like this are allowed to re-enter at a lower area, but it will take them a fair bit of work to get back to us. If you toss them away, expect that they are out of combat. Unless they can fly. Pretty sure these can't fly."

"Between my own Perception and Dexterity, I have a pretty good feeling about this fight," Daniella stated confidently to Joe, and he nodded along while pretending not to notice the trickle of nervous sweat dripping down her right temple. His Neutrality Aura caused it to summarily vanish and would have made him doubt his own eyes if he hadn't seen it so clearly.

"I'm always nervous during fights, but at least I have a barrier. It's pretty impressive that you're just standing here, no weapon in hand, no magical defenses, ready to take on the world. You're pretty cool." His casual compliment made her blush slightly, and she turned her head away to avoid meeting his eyes. Instead of dwelling on the odd response, Joe studied the cats that were swarming their front line, and decided to get involved. "Cone of Cold!"

The blast of Arctic air swept over the kitties from the side, dealing a little less than their standard damage. He wasn't terribly surprised, as they were thickly furred and likely adapted to the cold environment. He found more luck with sending in his Ritual Orb of Strength, managing to smack one of the animals in the side of the head hard enough to send it sliding off the path, where it promptly vanished as if it had never been. "Great call on throwing them away, Daniella!"

"Son of the *abyss*, that stings!" Major Cleave had taken a paw swipe to the face, shaving off the tip of her mustache and opening a wide laceration on her left cheek. "You overgrown pests; be happy I don't have time to waste on you!"

She turned to the side, putting all of her force behind her

metal-clad foot and punting the animal that had sliced her out into the open air next to the mountain. It yowled its rage as it flew, vanishing without a trace as soon as its head crossed the boundary of the enchanted path. Jaxon turned toward her, catching one of the animals midair as it tried to leave a matching slice on the Dwarf's other cheek. "A long time ago, I found the best way to skin a cat! Would you like me to keep a few for the road?"

Daniella stepped forward and grabbed the Lynx, tossing it over the edge without waiting to hear Major Cleave's reply. "Either slay them or just get rid of them. Please don't make strange plans that a normal person would get squeamish about."

"But I wanted a new set of boots!" Jaxon wailed as his hands darted at another pair of incoming monsters. "I *need* another pair. I've gotten a great amount of mileage out of these custom baby seal leather boots, but they are starting to get a little worn! Obviously, I need to throw them away immediately."

Even Joe stuttered to a stop at that line, frowning down at the cloth wrappings that kept Jaxon's feet protected. He breathed a sigh of relief. "I'm going to go ahead and chalk that one up to a Charisma-based filter that made us hear something really... yeah, I think we can go ahead and ignore what he just said. Dark Lightning Strike!"

The timely spell landed just as a dozen more of the beasts joined the growing clowder, managing to stun a large number of them, which in turn kept the vast majority alive as they were swept to the side instead of forcing the group to take the time to slay each one. There were a few inevitable casualties, as monsters did not back down or run away. Even so, within five minutes of combat starting, the group was able to start picking up the pace once more.

Experience gained: 715

"Is anyone else surprised at how much experience these creatures are worth?" Joe wasn't complaining, but normally his experience bar barely budged from defeating individual monsters.

"Those were a base level of level twenty-three each. If I was not here, you would have been in serious trouble," Major Cleave informed him sternly. "Remember that this path is meant for people that are on their way to seek high-tier magical skills. That means that they must have completed their stint in the Legion in order to go and pursue their own goals in life."

That made sense to him, so he stopped asking questions. Clearly someone that had served the entire stint of time required in an active war world was going to have the combat prowess necessary to scoot a few kittens out of their way. Combat continued in a similar manner for the rest of their journey, all the way until they reached the portion of the path that was supposed to represent the first steps as an Expert.

Having taken the time to sleep the night before, they had no need to reduce their speed, pause at a rest area, or even fight monsters if they were too slow to keep up. A small issue was that walking side-by-side was becoming treacherous, with the path too narrow to safely traverse two by two. The Dwarven guide took the lead once more, and the rest followed in single file.

Those factors made it seem strange to Joe that, only a half an hour of travel later, the path widened out once more into a comfortably large area. Or, in his mind, he considered it an *uncomfortably* open space. "I don't like the look of this; why would there be so much space if we weren't going to need it in the next few minutes?"

"Yeah, sometimes the random encounters in your path just aren't enough, so they make sure to put in a few places to test your resolve." Major Cleave kept her head on a swivel, but no matter where they looked, there was no sign of a monster waiting for them. That made Joe even more suspicious, and he decided to send his Ritual Orbs forward to test the snow ahead of them.

"I hear a sound…" The Ritualist knew what it was, a manifestation of his Hidden Sense skill. The only question was, what was it that was hiding from him? "It's got to be something in here, so can we all please stay back for a moment while I try this out?"

The icicle-shaped orb darted into various snowdrifts, while his strength-bound weapon bounced across the ground at set intervals. As the blunt weapon came down for the third time, it impacted with a terrible *crack*. The entire path began to crumble, slowly shifting and slumping into open air on the side of the mountain. Major Cleave gaped in horror, one hand reaching out as if to grab what was being lost. "You destroyed the path! *Why* would you cause an avalanche here?"

"It *wasn't* the path. Look." Joe gestured to the ground that was falling away, over half of the open area that they had been about to step into. "That was a thin ice shelf, something that only looked like the path. If we would have tried to cross, not only would we have been booted from continuing to advance, but we would have been caught in an avalanche and likely crushed, or at least taking a severe amount of terrain damage."

Jaxon waved his hand in the air like a schoolboy, "Oh, I know! I know! This was to show that while some people continue on the path to Mastery, other people take the incorrect path, falling through the thin ice that they were trying to-"

"No, stop it. That's not supposed to be here." Major Cleave twirled her weapon nervously. "Anyone can step off of the path at any time, but no Dwarf would intentionally offer someone the wrong path. This reeks of Elves."

"How could there possibly be Elves here?" Joe rubbed at his head in annoyance. "Let's go over the facts. We are in the center of the Dwarves' seat of power. We are about as far from the border as you can get. We are on an enchanted mountain that has hundreds, if not thousands, of devices meant to keep this place hidden."

The Dwarf ignored his logic, as she had more information about this subject than he could bring to bear. "They must be setting up their attuners already... I thought we would have more time. The issue that we are running into right now, humans, is the fact that the Elves have won. With most of our population moving away from rural areas, including major and minor forts, into the more well-protected cities, the Elven infiltrators must have started working to change the flow of mana in the Zone."

Joe wanted to roll his eyes and call it a conspiracy theory, but there was an easy way to check if the power flowing in the world around them was changing somehow. He sent a Ritual Orb floating out of his bandolier to hover over his hand, specifically the one bound with Essence Cycle. "Slap this out of my hand in a few seconds, would you?"

"What did he say?"

Having expected that he would be heard properly, Joe had already cut connection to the orb, and it dropped into his hand. Before he could curse at the fact that he should have spoken up, the way he saw the world shifted into a spectrum of energy normally invisible to the naked eye.

"Abyss."

CHAPTER NINETEEN

He was frozen in the moment, staring at the strange, creeping... the only word he could think of to describe what was happening to the essence of the world at this moment was 'influence'. The energy that undergirded reality, that seemed to make up everything, was having something added to it. Anything that was free-floating seemed to be impacted by it, including the mana that he was regenerating, and what he was expelling by using the orb in his hand.

Joe wasn't entirely *certain* what it was, but he had to hand it to his Dwarven companion; she had understood simply by shifts in the terrain that the Elves were up to no good. His eyes traversed the area, and he saw a strange dead spot just-

Slap.

"Snap out of it!" Daniella demanded with concern in her voice. "You can't just zone out in the middle of a conversation like this. It isn't safe or healthy!"

"Cleave, you were right." Those were the first words Joe was able to eke out as soon as he regained his bearings. Going from seeing the world as energy and... had those been *equations*? Was he seeing base level physics as they interacted with the world directly?

Essence Cycle has reached Apprentice III!

"Always good to hear." Major Cleave didn't bother to look at him, too focused on the fact that something was amiss in the area. "Anything else to report?"

"They are changing the mana. It's becoming... different. How can I explain this?" Joe cast about for any sort of analogy that he could use. "It's like adding artificial sweeteners to a drink instead of sugar. Sure, it might make it better in one way, like not storing fat, but it's ten times worse for your kidneys because it's not natural and your body doesn't know how to process it."

"Not quite what I was asking, but a good observation." Cleave shivered slightly, and Joe was almost certain that it was not from the cold. "Because they own the area, they can spread the influence of their Pantheon across the entire Zone. Anyone who is a follower of those deities will experience a significant boost in how easily they will be able to cast spells. Anyone who is not... well, you already have the Excommunicated title. It's just more of that. Making things unstable. Now, answer the question. Did you see what is waiting for us out there?"

"Fifth snowdrift to the left-"

Wham.

The Dwarf blinked across the space and slammed her axe directly into the snowbank. The cloud of snow was sent flying away, followed quickly by a rain of blood and viscera. "Anything else?"

Daniella's face went a little green. "How did you-"

"Sneak attack, critical, based on instant movements and a full power attack." The Dwarf was getting truly short with them and ignored any further attempts at conversation as she hustled them along the path. "If the mana is already being corrupted, we have even less time than we originally thought. There is a chance that the fortifications of the city are already being worn down, since the enchantments are drawing in ambient mana in order to function. Soon enough, it will be the wrong type of mana. The enchantment will either fail completely... or possibly self-destruct."

With that dire pronouncement, the team turned and ran along the true path. They were nearing the summit and knew that it was only a matter of time before they needed to get off the path. Exploding enchantments were one thing, but there was also the likelihood of getting trapped on the path, or getting blown off the path and sent to the base of the mountain. None of the options were good, except getting to their destination as quickly as possible.

Circling the mountain three or four more times brought them right up to the end of the path, and they could see the walls of the Hidden City as they broke through a frozen cloud layer. While the rest of the team exclaimed excitedly, Major Cleave reached up and pulled on her mustache in consternation. "The bridge is gone! How in the abyss are we supposed to cross?"

That brought quiet back to the group, as each of them examined the treacherous drop they had not even noticed. They were just barely above the clouds, and it still swirled around their feet as fog. Joe knew that he would have been the first among them to fall, as he had already begun walking toward the open gates. "There's supposed to be a bridge?"

"It is so heavily enchanted that it should never have fallen," Major Cleave confirmed distractedly, "unless... since it was the most heavily magical space along this entire path, it could have fallen first, or the magic's failed and brought the whole thing down. I have no idea how we are going to get across now, as trying to climb across will count as us going off of the path and send us back to the base of the mountain."

"I could set up bubble travel!" Joe whipped out a ritual tile and started the process of setting it up, only to be stopped nearly right away by their traveling companion and guide.

Cleave pointed at the entrance to Dehur Bethi. "Just like every major settlement, an anti-magic enchantment protects the threshold to the city. Unless we were starting on that side, there would be no way to get into the city. We would fall prey to the defenses, and the bubble would pop as we tried to get close. Only something coming from the city will allow us to cross over safely."

That stumped all of them for a long moment, and each of them tried to calculate a way across. Joe knew what he wanted to do: he wanted to test out Omnivault. He had no idea if it would count as a failure, or even how he was supposed to know where the safe path across would be. "Cleave, do you think that I could jump it? I *think* that I could make it, but how am I supposed to know if I am getting too close to leaving the path?"

"That would never... no, it might work." The Dwarf gave him a considering look and slowly nodded. "That might work, indeed. The only issue is that a corridor of power connects the gates to the path. With the bridge gone, all that is left is the residual mana, and I have no idea how to describe what it looks like. I suppose I could try to sketch it out, but you are going to be flying blind."

That sparked an idea in the Ritualist's head, and he fished out one of his orbs. "Knock this out of my hand in a moment, would one of you?"

This time, he waited for confirmation before grabbing the orb, and with a touch, the world shifted into a kaleidoscope of colors, mathematical formations, and interesting implications that were just out of his mind's reach. Most notably, he could see waving tendrils of energy in the air, clearly demarcating where the enchantment had been affecting the space. It appeared to have been torn asunder and was slowly dissolving as the attunement of mana broke it down. The vision abruptly ended as his hand was slapped. "I saw it! I think that I can get through there, so I'm going to go for it."

"Joe, broken enchantments always leave distortions; were you able to see them?" Cleave let out a sigh of relief as he nodded, then shook her head at the thought of him jumping through that. "If you touch one of those, one of three things is going to happen. It will short-circuit what remains of the enchantment—dumping all remaining energy directly into your body—or it will boot you off the path."

Joe counted the listed possibilities on his fingers, raising an eyebrow at her. "That's two; what is the third?"

"That would be both options happening simultaneously." Her mouth tightened grimly. "By the time we could get back down there, to the start of all of this, we would find your charred corpse while you waited in respawn."

"If I can't touch them, I'll just have to be able to know where they are the entire time." Joe reached for his orb once again. "All I need to do is make sure that I am not completely entranced and force myself to see the world, and the energy, all at the same time."

"Right. You've never done that before, have you?" Jaxon inquired as he bobbed an eyebrow at his friend. "You let me take a peek at that, and even *I* couldn't escape! Let's be real here, my willpower is so much higher than yours that there is practically no comparison."

Everyone on the team stared at the Chiropractor strangely, and the only reason an orchestra of crickets didn't start up was that any that could have been near enough were frozen solid. Joe painted a smile on his face and patted his friend on the arm woodenly. "Of course yours is. Still, I need to try!"

He checked to verify the consensus with the group, but the fact of the matter was that no one else had an actionable plan, let alone a better idea. Steeling himself against the numerous possibilities for the attempt to go awry, he walked to the end of the path and stared straight ahead. "Okay, here's what I need to do. Orb goes on my palm with my hand facing down. That way, as I jump, I will lose sight of the energy and be able to focus."

"Nope!" Major Cleave called at him. "The energy is going to be shifting and flowing the entire time. You need to be able to avoid it directly! You need to see it the *entire* way."

"That makes things harder," Joe continued in the monotone he hadn't thought his team would be able to hear. "Still, I believe in myself. Only one shot, or I am likely on my way to respawn."

Trying to psych himself up without psyching himself out was difficult, but he felt that he was more than up to the task. He canceled all of his normal passive spells, such as Retaliation of Shadows, Exquisite Shell, and Neutrality Aura. Joe wanted as much of his mana available as possible, just in case he found the opportunity to activate his Omnivault a few times in a row.

Gearing himself up, he took a deep breath, got into the best position possible, and Omnivaulted forward just before grasping his Ritual Orb, which remained in his bandolier to ensure he did not drop it. Essence Cycle overwhelmed his senses, and Joe watched in awe as the air-attuned mana rushed past his flesh-imbued face.

Seeing the Essence of things could make for a pretty wild experience.

CHAPTER TWENTY

The colors shifted from moment to moment, energy never staying in a single place for more than an instant. Everything was in flux, and the fact that he was moving made the visualization so disorienting that he could fervently describe it as nauseating. As he flew forward, the contents of his stomach erupted into the air, and he was able to see how a combination of coffee, elemental mana, and stomach acid appeared when represented as purest energy.

It looked *nasty*.

Even so, there were some constants—or at least more constant—in the form of the destroyed pathway into the High City of Deep Thought. The fraying enchantments trailed structured mana from their unraveling ends, and it spoke to the level of craftsmanship that they were failing so slowly. Most of the streams of energy undulated through the air in a set pattern, following their woven energy as it was released. A few, however, had reached the point that they were self-destructing quickly. The resulting dissolution made for dangerous barriers, and at the speed he was moving, Joe didn't have many options for avoiding them.

Spotting an issue that was coming for him, Joe forced his hand to unclench and release the orb with Essence Cycle bound to it, shifting his attention to the Ritual Orb of Strength. The form that this orb had taken—as a dumbbell—gave him a perfect foothold if he stepped on the crossbar. Utilizing the practice he had been developing, namely of using his Intelligence to force the Ritual Orb upward, he stepped down and pushed off to launch himself continuously forward, but at a slightly different angle.

Unable to maintain contact with the orb that he had kicked off from, it fell away and vanished. On the plus side, he knew that it would reappear in his bandolier in the next five minutes. Still, it left him one fewer option to use, and he was only halfway across the chasm. "That's already two Omnivaults; not even going to worry about my mana right now."

The world faded away once more as he lightly rested a finger on his Essence Cycle orb, noticing that he was no longer in the path of any waving tendrils of energy, but the angle he had propelled himself into was sending him closer and closer to the edge. He was going to need to kick off again soon, or he was going to be banished. Pushing his mind to the absolute limit, he simultaneously found the path forward and forced himself to let go of his orb.

"Orb of Intelligence, go!" Sometimes, the Ritualist liked to pretend he was in an anime, and that shouting the description of what he was doing would evoke additional power. It may not have been true, but as he kicked off with the third Omnivault, there was certainly more power behind his jump. Unfortunately, he had not contained his energy correctly, and the mana-using skill backfired. Instead of launching himself forward directly and true, he booted the orb and sent it zipping away off the path.

His course had corrected slightly, but now he was out of bound orbs, and anything that he tried to kick off would likely be permanently lost. That put him in a serious conundrum, as having a full set was imperative to his future success, but reaching the city was far more important. Still, he hesitated a moment too long, and by the time he decided to give up an orb, he had fallen too close to the bottom of the path to get it in position in time. "Abyss! *No!*"

Suddenly, his eyes registered that he was about to land atop a strange type of energy field. It wasn't the path, and it wasn't loose mana; it was something that—while shifting—was far more stable than he had been expecting. "The ground? There's *ground* right here! I can kick off of that!"

With a split second to go, the Reductionist glanced forward and calculated the path he needed once more, pressing down with his energy-coated foot and activating Omnivault with the conviction that it *would* work perfectly. His foot landed on the plain, and he pushed up and forward, launching himself into the gates of Dehur Bethi. "I made it!"

As he landed, he bounced and jostled himself out of his energy-viewing state. His intent had been to immediately turn around and figure out a way to bring his team over, but a message appeared in his vision that he was utterly unable to ignore. In his mind, trumpets blared and fireworks went off. He gaped in confusion as the world seemed to pause around him.

Omnivault has reached Master 0! Congratulations! You have reached the Master rank in your first skill, and this time, you actually earned it! As a benefit for reaching the Master rank, the task that you completed which put you over the edge will become a permanent feature.

Since you were able to Omnivault off of a cloud to achieve true Mastery, you will be able to use any water source—no matter what state—as a platform for your $n+1$ Omnivault, where $n =$ any activation of Omnivault after the first. You should try jumping through a column of steam and bouncing around in the clouds! It's fun!

Guild alert! A member of The Wanderer's Guild has achieved Mastery over one of their skills! The royal court of Midgard has taken notice and grants an additional $+1,000$ reputation to your Guild on Midgard! (Lost if player leaves Guild.)

The Theocracy has noted your Guild's devotion to bettering themselves, therefore all positions offered within the Theocracy will start one rank higher than they would have originally for all Guild members.

Except for the final line of the last notification, Joe was ecstatic to have finally returned to Master status. There was something poetic about achieving it just as he finished the G.O.A.T. path to Mastery, a symbolic tradition for what was now a Shattered Race. Finally able to clear the screen from his vision, he hurried back to the edge and pulled out his Ritual Tile. "Okay... what I need to do here is figure out a way to send the bubble there and bring it back. Send it there, bring it back... how do I alter this design to make that happen?"

A few minutes of tinkering later, he realized that attempting to change the entire function of the ritual was a foolish move, especially when his teammates were slowly freezing in the cloud layer just below him. It wasn't terribly far away, obviously, since it was within Expert-rank jumping distance. He chuckled at his internal joke, but the thought still sparked an idea.

"Instead of trying to change the function of the ritual, what if I just alter the position where the bubble itself is created?" Joe sketched out a few numbers, and the formula looked like it would work. "If I simply set the manifestation point down there, and set the movement as a slope instead of a straight line... got it!"

Magical Matrices has reached Student VI!

He activated the ritual, and bit back a cheer as a slight distortion appeared in the air in front of his group. "Get in the bubble!"

"Who said that?" Jaxon shouted in surprise. "You can't be an echo; echoes need to come from a source, and I haven't said anything!"

Major Cleave had apparently dealt with enough of the Chiropractor's malarkey and gave him a brisk shove into the distortion. He let out a yelp as the bubble formed around him, but it was extremely muted, thanks to the thin membrane of force surrounding him. He screamed the entire way, but soon he was floating in front of Joe, and the bubble burst. Joe, having expected that result due to the placement of the anti-magic enchantment protecting the gates directly behind him, reached out and grabbed Jaxon, pulling his friend to safety.

"I *severely* disliked that," Jaxon informed Joe shakily. "Bubbles have no bones. How can you trust them to bring you somewhere safely?"

"Um." Joe decided to try and answer in as wacky a fashion as the issue presented itself. "Once you get in the bubble, the bubble has *your* bones in it, right?"

"I... I never thought of it that way." Jaxon collapsed to the ground, staring at his hands. "There are so many places where I can apply this logic..."

Joe left the mumbling Chiropractor to himself, allowing him to muddle through his existential crisis in peace. Daniella was already on the way up, and Joe's hand was extended in preparation—perhaps a *little* more enthusiastically—to catch her as the bubble popped. He felt very 'hero of the story' as she pulled herself into his embrace and was deposited safely in the city.

"I'm starting to get the hang of that. Those things are pretty fun!" Daniella smiled at Joe shyly as she peered out over the cloud layer. "I bet if you set one of those up at this altitude, you could travel so far... what if we just do that, instead of keeping on with this mission? What if we just try to find the most beautiful sights in the universe, and tour them via bubble?"

"We're already here!" Joe dismissed her strange daydreams with a small laugh. "I think the lack of oxygen is getting to you. No more monsters up here, and all we're going to be facing now is a bunch of magical titans in the form of Dwarfs. Nothing to worry about here."

He winked at her and caught Major Cleave just as she started to fall, and the Dwarf noticed. "Not cool, human. If I would have fallen off of this mountain because you were acting all coquettish, I would have come back to destroy you, even if I had to do it as an Elf."

"Give it a rest, Cleave," Joe grumped as they turned to take in the wondrous sights of Dehur Bethi. "Look at how amazing those buildings are. They've got to be spatially expanded, as well as enchanted for all sorts of inclement weather and attacks. It's amazing."

"The architecture alone is phenomenal." Daniella breathed in the sight, letting it fill her mind completely. "The sheer amount of detail that has been put into even the least of them is amazing. It must be a trait of the undying, that they want to surround themselves with beauty and give themselves tasks to keep their minds and hands as busy as possible."

"That's cool and all," Jaxon pointed forward at chest level, "but am I the only person noticing the entire battalion of angry Dwarves walking toward us? That doesn't seem right. You see them too, don't you, Cleave?"

"Yes, Jaxon." The Dwarf put up her hand in greeting and walked to the front of the group, rolling her eyes in annoyance the entire time. "I see them. We *all* see them, but only the *two* of us are paying attention to our surroundings."

CHAPTER TWENTY-ONE

Happily, the presence of Major Cleave made the welcoming party actually welcoming, instead of an angry mob out for their blood. It was with a collective sigh of relief that they were welcomed into the city, which apparently had been expecting to be besieged, rather than visited. Even with their story checking out, their Dwarven companion vouching for them, and Joe's high rank in the Legion, they were still assigned a high-level guard as their escort-slash-executioner.

The guard had been told to play nice with them, and happily, he seemed to take that aspect of the job seriously. No matter what question they threw at him, he did his best to answer it in a clear and concise manner. If he was allowed to speak on the subject, that is. The magical city, as it turned out, was governed by a Council of Masters, with a Grandmaster acting as the tiebreaker in any instances when it was required. Technically, the Grandmaster was in charge of the city as a whole and had the right to veto anything the Masters proposed.

That gave Joe the feeling that the entire mountaintop was one giant university, similar to the Mage's College, though with a tremendous difference in scale. Thanks to spatially enhanced buildings, as well as what had previously been easy access to the city with any teleporter, the municipality was brimming with highly specialized Dwarves. There were very few merchants, farmers, or laborers of any kind. Any of such classes that *were* present tended to be instructors in their field, instead of actively practicing their class skills.

Altogether, this meant that the city was soon going to be facing a resource crisis, and the Council was exceedingly busy. According to the guard, it would be practically impossible to meet the Grandmaster directly, and even getting an audience with one of the Masters would be a huge undertaking. Joe found the restriction completely unacceptable, as he knew that his settlement had only a short amount of time remaining before it would be discovered. The invasion was moving faster than any of them had expected, and as soon as seventy-five percent of the land was claimed by the Elves, the location of The Shoe would return to the memory of his enemies and be in danger.

"Please tell me if there is a way to expedite the process? Can I bribe someone? I have a ton of Reputation that I am willing to fork over." The Ritualist groaned as he rubbed at his bald head. The guard was utterly shocked at the blatant violation of the law that this human had just casually offered, and was reaching for his weapon by the time Joe started to wave him down. "I'm joking, joking! I meant that as a symbol of the lengths that I am willing to go to, not as something that *should* happen. Funny, right? Right?"

The guard didn't seem to think so. "There are multiple options for meeting with the Council. All of them must be good, *valid* reasons. Wanting to have a talk with the ruler of our city for personal gain is not a good, valid reason."

"Can you believe they say *I* get snippy during conversations!" Jaxon stage-whispered to Daniella, elbowing her in the side in a joking manner but sending her tumbling across the street from using too much force. "Whoops! I forget I'm in such a young, *virile* body every once in a while."

"Right…" The guard motioned to the center of the city. "You could either meet one of them by chance in public, as all of them enjoy tea houses—"

Joe shuddered and made a face at the mention of hot leaf juice.

"—or perhaps you could contribute to the safety or overall well-being of the city so much that you will be brought forward to be honored." He was about to say something else, but the Dwarven guard paused, seemingly biting his tongue.

That was enough to clue Joe in that there was a third— likely more viable—option for him. "What were you going to say? Spit it out. You've already started, so now you've got to tell us."

"I… fine, I suppose there is no harm in you knowing about it." The guard regarded the human with a small smirk. "You could always attempt to join the Council of Masters by challenging one of them to a display of Mastery. Of course, you would need to have your own Mastered skill or spell, and be able to teach it to more people, faster, than the current Masters can. This would give you automatic rights to enter the Council, and I'm sure you would be able to figure out a method of speaking to the Grandmaster from there."

Charisma +2!

"Well, that settles it." Jaxon shook his head at the guard knowingly. "You laid down a challenge after a slight hesitation. That means that we must take that option and follow it to the bitter end, succeeding beyond your wildest dreams and proving that we have what it takes to be better than anyone else. Because that is what we do."

Joe didn't want to admit that Jaxon had his number and tried to accept one of the other options. "No, we don't… that's not something we have to do. Come on."

"My friend, you have a lot to learn about the hero's journey." Jaxon shook his head knowingly. "Something like that is an obvious Chekhov's gun. Someone can't just bring it up so pseudo-casually and expect us *not* to do it. At this point, everyone is *expecting* you to do it. So why flail around and try all those other things, when we know what you are going to do?"

At that moment, Joe wanted to strangle the man he had been traveling with for far too long. He reached out with both hands, making the motion in the air, before forcibly relaxing and setting his palms to his sides. The Ritualist then turned to the guard with as broad of a smile as he could manage, "Is there any detriment to challenging a Master? If I fail to prove my ability, are we going to get chucked out of the city or anything?"

"No, nothing like that." The Dwarf was smirking over the interplay between party members. "Although whichever Master you challenge may have a lower opinion of you, as every Master who is challenged is called out specifically. That means if you put it forward, it is the same as telling them that you think they are the least skilled among their peers. It's a surefire recipe to get someone mad at you, but it is part of the regulations of the city, and they will honor that."

"Fair enough." Joe sent a side-eye glare at his team, who were all snickering at him. "How does one make a challenge to one of the Masters?"

"You speak with someone of high enough rank to get the ball rolling." The guard was beaming with anticipation. "That would be me. Thanks for doing this; we've all been aching for some entertainment. Do you mind if I choose which Master you are going to go up against?"

"That is a hard no from me." Joe scowled at the guard, who was clearly trying to set him up.

"Perfect! I will make the arrangements right away." The guard vanished, and Joe realized too late exactly what he had just agreed to.

"I meant that I don't want you to pick for me!" Joe howled into the empty air, but the Dwarf was either too far away or ignoring him for the sake of entertainment. "I meant *no*, I didn't want you to choose for me!"

"I *was* surprised when you allowed him to make the choice."

Major Cleave ushered them along, pushing the group closer to the center of the city.

"I said no!"

"Right, when he asked you if you would mind if he did it." The Dwarf looked at him without a trace of humor in her eyes. "You clearly said you didn't mind; a 'hard no,' in fact. That's on you."

Joe internally lamented the fact that the Dwarven race regarded a few things so differently. "We can almost always get along and understand each other, but as soon as it really matters, they make a joke out of it. I swear…"

"What would you all like to do while we wait for the challenge to go through?" Daniella was gazing around longingly. "Any chance someone would want to go and take a look at that sewage treatment plant? It is put together in a way I've never seen before, and I think that-"

"Pass." Jaxon and Major Cleave both held up a hand to forestall any further details at the same moment.

Daniella turned to Joe pleadingly, but he was so sick of dumps and sewers that the thought of going to a new one made him physically tired. "I can't do it right now. If you want to go talk to them, I would be happy to make you a blueprint later, if they allow it."

"That's fair, and more than I can normally ask for. Where will I be able to find you?" The young lady was barely in the moment with them, her eyes traveling the boxy structure of the distant building, her nose twitching as if to see if she could get a whiff of stench in the air. "Do you think it is magically contained? It must be, right? Oh… sorry, did you say something?"

"I didn't, and I guess you can go ahead? Our escort left us, not the other way around, so… I assume it's fine for us to do whatever it is we want to do?" Joe pointed at a uniquely shaped structure in the distance. "We can meet up under that, or just look for the largest crowd you can find. We'll either be at one, or the center of the commotion."

"Plan to look for commotion." Jaxon winked at the Architect, and she nodded in return. As she ran off to investigate the rustic, yet charming architecture, the Chiropractor turned his attention on Joe. "I've got to know, when are you going to make your move?"

"Right away," Joe told him firmly, receiving a tiny smattering of applause from his remaining companions. "After all, he said that another path forward would be meeting a Master by random chance or contributing to the city. What if I contribute to the city in such a way that it draws as many people as possible? If they are in imminent danger of having a food crisis, I know a building that would be extremely beneficial to the city."

"He's pretty thick, isn't he?" Major Cleave nudged Jaxon as she shook her head in disgust at Joe's obliviousness.

Jaxon couldn't help but agree with her assessment. "I feel like Daniella is interested in his thickness. It's too bad he can't see that."

"What?" Cleave frowned at the Chiropractor in confusion.

"Hmm?" Jaxon met her eyes innocently and extended a hand. "Did you say something? Hello, I'm Jaxon. And you are?"

"Get out of my way. I already warned you that I'd cut off any hand you tried to touch me with."

"Now *that* doesn't sound familiar at all."

CHAPTER TWENTY-TWO

"Pardon my intrusion. I was simply wondering if the impending lack of food in this area is going to be an issue for the city?" Joe had asked the same question dozens of times already, each time earning an unintelligible grunt, glance of disdain, or occasionally a wordless shake of the head in reply. "Anyone? This is an issue that I am very concerned about! With the teleporters down and the bridge from the goat path destroyed, so few opportunities for gathering food exist!"

At this point in his speech, a few guards drifted into the area, their focus honing in on what appeared to be a rabble-rouser. Joe took note of them, but only in passing. He had nothing to fear, as he was not trying to start a riot or incite the people to go against the local governance. In fact, all he was trying to do was find a way to gain approval to build another structure within the city. "I have a solution to this, but I need your help! I need nothing from you, except for you to sign on that you would like a self-sustaining source of food available to the city! If you wouldn't mind putting your name on this petition, which you can see is clearly non-magical, I will take it before the Council of Masters and do what I can to ensure that this city never needs to fear hunger in the future!"

"What kind of snake oil salesmen are you?" Major Cleave hissed into his ear, her hair standing on end in the Dwarven equivalent of blushing from embarrassment. It was quite the sight to see her bushy mustache. "You don't have a way to guarantee food supplies for them!"

"He does, actually." Jaxon came to Joe's defense, slapping his friend on the back like a car salesman informing a buyer about how many potatoes the trunk of a car could hold. "Then again, it wouldn't be Joe if the boon didn't come with a significant bane as well. You're talking about the building that turns into a dungeon if it is left unchecked, right, Joe?"

"Certainly that is something that we could bring up *later*, when we are *not* trying to get people interested in it." Joe attempted to chastise his friend in a soft tone while keeping a smile plastered on his face. He waved at the guards, who were playing some form of rock paper scissors to see which one of them would be hauling him away. "Guaranteed food source, sign right here so that I can make sure the city won't go hungry! Get your food source right here! All for the price of signing your name to show that you think it's a good idea."

"How interesting of an idea you are presenting." A Dwarf in incredibly simple clothing stepped out of the crowd. He wore only brown travelers robes, and as far as Joe could see, the Dwarf carried no weapons and had no adornment on his gear whatsoever. There was nothing like someone with no distinguishing features to put the human on edge. This had to be some kind of hidden powerhouse, and Joe knew better than to be rude or disingenuous. "What kind of food are we talkin' about here... bro?"

The fact that the Dwarf was well-versed in modern Legion lingo—meaning he knew Joe's rank and thought it was... *cute*— was concerning enough to make the Ritualist start sweating to the point of activating his Neutrality Aura almost subconsciously. His clothes smoothed out, the small amount of grime that he had accumulated vanished, and his confidence soared. "Whatever you can plant! Fruits, vegetables; anything can grow in my greenhouse. If you have animals, you can introduce them into the greenhouse as well, in order to generate an unending food supply, so long as they have something inside to eat for themselves."

"You expect us to willingly place a dungeon within our city limits?" The condescending smile on the Dwarf's face wrinkled and shifted into a scowl, and Joe cursed at Jaxon's blabbermouth. "It seems that your rank and companions truly *are* a facade, and that you intend our people harm."

"That is a bold claim, and one that I would be happy to refute." Joe met the other man's stare easily, knowing that he had nothing to hide. "I am more than happy to discuss all of the plans in front of the Council of Masters, and I would expect nothing less than their scrutiny on a project of this seriousness and magnitude."

The easy smile returned to the Dwarf's face, and he shrugged while turning to walk back into the crowd. "Well, I hope you are able to attain what you are seeking, and that you are willing to pay whatever the price is for your failure or falsehoods."

"No falsehoods here!" Jaxon called as he lifted the back of his traveling robes over his head. "As you can see, all we have are real, hand-stitched hoods! Not for sale, of course. This one is mine. Back off."

An hour went by, and Joe still only had his own signature and Jaxon's to show for his efforts. Major Cleave decided against adding her own, not wanting to leave any written proof that she was a part of his team if he got thrown off the mountain. While he *understood* her concern, the human was a little rankled by her lack of faith. Still, it wouldn't be fair for him to demand that she do something she clearly did not want to. Only Jaxon seemed to be along for the ride with him; everyone else always seemed to have their own plans and schemes.

"I met a Master, by chance, and it did not go well." Joe

grumbled over his third cup of espresso in the last five minutes. Perhaps rage-sipping coffee so potent that it would show up on a drug test wasn't the healthiest of activities to pursue, but he was going to do it anyway. "The skills that I have to offer in terms of quick advancement of the city are locked, due to being unable to build somewhere I don't own without permission. I guess... my only hope of getting to the Council of Masters is defeating one of them in a trial. But who knows when that is going to happen?"

"I do!" A passing Dwarf stared at Joe in confusion, and he seemed oddly familiar. "Your trial time is already set; how do you not know when it is going to occur? It's on you to put forward the challenge, and that means you pick the time."

"A guard I was with did it on my behalf...?" Joe answered with mounting excitement. "Good fellow, would you mind letting me know when I-"

"Nah, it's more fun to make you figure it out on your own." The Dwarf's face bore an evil grin. "I'm going to follow you around for a while and see how long it takes you to figure this out."

A part of Joe was not even surprised that this was the reception he was getting in a new city. Their race was shattered, which had to be at least partly his fault, and simply by killing a large group of them, he could expunge his negative title and easily join the Elves. It was unlikely that the Dwarves here had as much exposure to humans as the capital city had, which had its own pros and cons. On the positive side, no one knew that he'd had a part in the Oligarchs being dropped into lava and torn apart by a World Boss. That was a *big* pro.

On the negative side, all of the achievements and reputation that he had built had not preceded him, so his claims to fame were practically ignored without question. Added to that was the fact that most Dwarves had a negative view of all humans in general, and it made sense why no one was willing to put themselves out for a stranger like him. "You would think that being a Major General would afford me a few more benefits."

"Yeah, if you went to a Legion *outpost.*" The snarky Dwarf snorted as he continued following Joe around. "Then you could walk in and order people around, all the way up until someone with a higher rank came along and kicked you out again."

The Ritualist scowled at the random detractor that had decided to tag along just to be annoying, and he tried to just walk away. To his consternation, the Dwarf easily kept pace, taunting him the entire time and beginning to draw a crowd. Soon Joe was jogging through the streets, and unfortunately, the entire throng was coming along for the ride. The laughing and taunting increased to a near-untenable level, and before long, the roads were so packed with bodies that Joe would have needed to abandon his teammates in order to Omnivault over the crowd and be on his way.

"That's enough, that's enough!" the original taunting Dwarf shouted, his voice echoing above the entirety of the crowd and bringing them to near-silent in an instant. "I'm glad everyone was able to gather so quickly, and I think it is time to show this human what happens when you come to a place that isn't happy to see you!"

"Yeah!" The crowd cheered in response to the Dwarf's declaration, many of them pulling out weapons or sending mana to dance over their fingertips. Joe slowly backed up, getting close to his fellow human so that they could protect each other.

"I saw this going another way in my head," Joe grumbled as he sent a couple orbs into the air. Against what felt like the entirety of the city's population, the small silvery weapons looked like toys.

"People *hate* petitions, Joe," Jaxon told him sadly, "Didn't I mention that to you? The only thing that annoys people more than bothering them when they are just trying to go about their day is trying to get them to sign a random document. You may as well have held up a sign that said 'Spying for the Elves, right here!', and then had an arrow pointed down at your face."

"Helpful."

"Anyway, let's get on with this!" The Dwarf stepped forward and tossed off his outermost layer of robes, and Joe recognized him in that same instant. He was the unassuming Dwarf that Joe had assumed was a Master, and had nearly brought the guards down on him. "I need twenty volunteers who want to take lessons from a Master! Ten of you will be learning from him, the others from me! The winner of this competition gets the seat on the Council!"

"*What?*" Joe involuntarily started, taking another look at his strange opponent. "I knew it. But why do all this? If you're one of the Masters-"

"The first thing you need to do is prove your Mastery," The Dwarf informed him coolly. "Are you going to be presenting a skill or spell?"

"It's a skill, but it uses mana and stamina to function," Joe babbled, unable to get over the fact that this person had been messing with him for nearly half an hour before revealing himself. "Again, why did you-"

"Look, human. *Nobody* likes being challenged." The Master's face hadn't changed from the apparently ever-present scowl he wore. "Originally, I was going to beat you down in a nice and quiet fashion, but then it turned out that not only did you *not* know who I was, you hadn't even bothered to propose the challenge yourself! Now I don't even know who to go and *throttle* when I'm done with you!"

"Then..." Joe could only throw his hands up in the air and wish for a do-over. "Look, can't we just-"

"The crowd is here, and *we* are here, so unless you are going to retract your challenge and publicly apologize for wasting our time, let's get to it." The Dwarf was obviously expecting him to continue, because he made no move to leave the small arena that had formed around them.

All Joe could do was scratch at his head. "I don't know what this challenge consists of. What am I supposed to do?"

With a grandiose sigh, the Dwarf scanned the crowd and

shook his head theatrically. "He doesn't even know what he's doing! Let's give him some proper Dwarven hospitality and show him why only the best of the Masters sit on the Council!"

There was a roar of approval as the Dwarf began to glow.

CHAPTER TWENTY-THREE

"I am a known Master of the Council." The as-yet-unnamed Dwarf called to the crowd at large. "Today we had a *human* walk into our city, and one of the first things that he did was challenge me directly!"

Booo!

"That's right, Boo! Boo for this ridiculous, over-entitled smear that came in here to cozy up with the leadership of our city!" The Dwarf turned and glared directly at Joe. "I don't know about the rest of you, but I think that he has other plans. Sinister plans."

You are being affected by a Master-rank speech skill!

Joe took the message without flinching. He wasn't entirely sure what the speech skill was going to do to him, but the Dwarf would not have gone first so easily if it was nothing. He decided to interrupt the flow of the Master, hoping that it would break whatever compounding affect the words were having. "In human society, it is considered polite to introduce yourself. Especially before you start going off on someone with no justification."

His casual rejoinder had a profound effect on the people

around them, and the rowdy crowd started to settle a bit. It took a few moments for Joe to understand why the onlookers seemed so very confused. Then, one Dwarf called out and his words made everything click into place. "Hold on, how could he have challenged you directly if he doesn't even know your name?"

"My apologies, I was challenged directly, but through a proxy on his behalf." The fact that this Dwarf apologized and told the truth so publicly meant that his skill had something to do with believability, and Joe figured that was something he could work with. "As for you, human, my name is Stu Sarcasm, Master of Sarcasm. I am the first Bard in Dwarven society to reach the Master ranks with one of my skills, and I am by *far* the most difficult to unseat from the Council."

"Because of course you are." Joe muttered under his breath. Then, in a regular volume, "My name is Joe, the Excommunicated. It is... *somewhat* pleasant to meet you."

Ooooh. The crowd started chuckling at Joe's attempt at a joke. It seemed that his ploy was working. By mentioning his title, he informed everyone around him that he was wearing the mandatory title with pride. It served to indicate that he had no intention to switch over to the Elven side in this war. By downplaying his reaction to meeting the Master, he hoped to put the Dwarf on the back foot.

"Why don't you go ahead and tell us what skill you have mastered and intend to teach faster than I can teach someone to be sarcastic?" Stu, as a Bard, was certainly not going to allow Joe to take over the crowd without a fight.

"Are you teaching them to be sarcastic, or are you teaching them a sarcasm skill?" Joe grinned as he responded, getting into the rhythm of this strange type of battle. More than anything, it felt like a slam session, and his time in the military had been filled with people listening to unending rap battles and diss tracks—while not wearing headphones. Even if begrudgingly, he had picked up some techniques. "I am going to be teaching people the skill 'Jump', which I recently evolved to a new Tier, Omnivault, and upgraded to Master status."

Stu's eye twitched, and Joe wondered if the fact that he was going to be teaching a purely physical skill was going to help him in this public arena. "Why don't you go ahead and prove your you-totally-have-a Mastery?"

"Certainly." Joe looked around the area, realizing that they were surrounded on all sides by buildings. That was perfect for what he intended to do, so he crouched down, chose his target, and launched into a perfect Omnivault, only to fall flat on his face. "...What?"

"That certainly doesn't look like jumping to me!" Master Stu started laughing, and the crowd had begun laughing with him.

The Master skill that you are being impacted by has added another stack!

That message made Joe's mind spin, and he thought he had figured out what was going on. This Dwarf was a Master of Sarcasm. In order for it to become an external skill, it had to have some sort of effect on the people it was used on. By the fact that he had just fallen on his face and received no message that it was due to his Excommunicated title, he had to assume that Sarcasm impacted his ability to use skills. Joe stood up and grinned at the Dwarf; who began to scowl immediately. "What a fun skill *you* have! Too bad for you; now that I know what's going on, it's not going to be a problem for me anymore."

He had plenty of experience using his skills in negative conditions, and he knew that the best way to get around the limitations was by focusing all of his mentality on using them correctly. Before he activated Omnivault again, Joe sent a small amount of power flowing through his body and into the skill. Feeling out the pathways, he focused on compressing his mana into *only* where it should be going. *"Omnivault!"*

From a complete standstill, Joe was able to leap forward with one-tenth of his strength multiplied by three. In an instant, he soared forward forty-nine and a half feet, his shoes easily touching down on a building a dozen feet above the Dwarves' heads. With barely a pause, he activated the skill again, burning one hundred and fifty-two mana and seventeen Stamina to flip back over the street and bounce off the opposite wall.

He was able to activate the skill a total of seven times, including his first usage. By the time he pressed off of the wall the seventh time and aimed to land in the exact spot he had started, Joe had burned three thousand, one hundred and ninety-seven mana, as well as three hundred and fifty-eight stamina. Even with that expenditure, he still had a comfortable amount of both resources remaining, but not enough Mana to reactivate the skill an eighth time. When he landed in front of Master Stu once more, and did not seem to be in any sort of distress, the Dwarf didn't seem to know how to handle himself.

"Interesting," he gruffly grunted, "you can prance around all fancy-foot-like. Not exactly sure what good that is, but no one ever said a Master skill had to be *useful* in order for it to be mastered."

A few people in the crowd laughed, and the Dwarf's smile grew fractionally.

The Master skill that you are being impacted by has added another stack!

"There's a crowd requirement, huh?" As he was hit by the skill once more, Joe found yet another potential weakness. In a loud voice, he casually fired a reply back at the Dwarf. "*Clearly* you're correct. It *doesn't* need to be a useful skill, otherwise... how would *you* be on the Council?"

The Master skill that you are being impacted by has lost a stack!

"Gotcha." Joe's eyes practically glowed as he was able to throw off the skill that had been weighing on him. Master Stu was practically snarling at him, but he composed himself as quickly as he could in front of the audience that he needed to keep on his side.

"That is good enough for me, I suppose. Proof of Mastery... *accepted*." The words were obviously meant to be ceremonial, because the ten people that had volunteered to train under Joe and the Dwarf stepped forward as soon as he voiced them. "Now we can get to the parts of the challenge that actually betters all of our people, and I'll win and get back to my normal seat in the Council halls."

"I think you mean to say, 'Winner gets the seat on the Council'." Joe shot back instantly.

Stu tugged on his beard, pretending not to understand what Joe was saying. "What did I say? Pretty sure I said it correctly; what do you all think?"

A roar of approval met his query, including the people that had volunteered to be trained. That made Joe nervous, as it was possible that these prospective students were plants in the crowd, and his odds of winning had just dropped even further. Stu called out, "We will have ten minutes to bring all ten people to the highest skill level we can, potentially jump-starting their path toward Mastery! Two... one... begin!"

"*Jump* starting is my specialty." Joe considered the Dwarves in front of him doubtfully. "Okay, so I have only taught the skill once before, and it was in the middle of a dungeon. It should be fairly straightforward to learn. Here's what I want you all to do."

He parted his lips to give the same instructions he once had given to his party as they had worked to escape a burning building, but what came out of his mouth was nowhere near that minimalistic explanation. "Jumping is all about achieving the highest heights that you can. Something to remember is that if you are moving forward and you 'jump', that is actually *leaping*. They go hand-in-hand, and as far as I can tell, the system does not make any distinctions. I *do*."

After waiting to get confirmation that they were listening, Joe charged along. "That means, what we are going to attempt right now is a vertical jump. In order to jump as high as possible, drop into an imaginary chair and use the power of both your legs to push off the ground. Be careful that your knees don't point inwards, as that can result in a 'knee-lock'. Short version: keep your knees as straight as possible, ideally positioned vertically over your toes."

With that, Joe guided them to practice using his instructions.

It was a strange feeling to be teaching other people something so physical, as in his own mind, he was a pure Mage. If he had only raised his Ritual Magic to Mastery first! All of the Dwarves were able to jump, as they were not elephants, but the height that they could achieve began slowly increasing as he continued to give them instructions.

"Hold on; I see a small issue in your form. You! You're flailing your arms as you push off. Do what you can to keep your arms at your sides and your back straight. Better... good." Joe moved to the next Dwarf and tapped on the man's thigh. "You are using your abdominals too much. Push your body with your legs. Spring off the balls of your feet and swing your hands up into the air for additional momentum. Better."

By this point, over half of the time in the competition had passed. Joe began searching his mind for any other information he could give them to generate a competitive edge. The biggest issue was that he did not have a teaching skill or anything equivalent to it. His opponent clearly did, and was using it in conjunction with his skill training. "Properly done, your feet should roll forward, from your heels to your toes as you jump off. You should feel pressure on your heels; guide that force upward towards your toes as you come back to a standing position. Practice that a couple of times, then do the same thing much more quickly in a proper jump. Wait, no, you're pushing off oddly. You've gotta *roll* all the way to your toes."

Joe had never felt ten minutes pass so quickly, and he was starting to lose his composure as the other group started laughing at something their instructor had said. His instructions became slightly more frantic and demanding. "Keep your arms parallel to each other and move them just behind your rear! Swing your arms forward while straightening your whole body! Land on the balls of your feet and roll back onto your heels. When you land, you should take care to land in such a way as to keep the kinematic chain going in a single plane from the ball of your foot through your ankle into your knee and finally through your hip joint-"

"*Time!*"

In only ten minutes, the Dwarves that he had been working with had more than doubled the height that they could reach from a standing position. Joe didn't know if it would be enough, and as they had an appraiser walk down the line, the human's bald head became ever shinier from sweat. Neutrality Aura activated, and light stopped reflecting so intensely from his follicle-free pate after a moment.

The appraiser finished and turned to the crowd. "On average, Master Joe was able to bring the skill level of his trainees to Beginner three! Master Stu was able to bring his trainees to Beginner seven! We have a winner!"

As the crowd cheered for the incumbent Master of the Council, Stu crossed his arms and smirked at Joe. "Looks like the only chasm you *can't* jump… is sarcasm!"

CHAPTER TWENTY-FOUR

"I never cared about getting on the Council," Joe grumbled as the Master celebrated with his people around them. A piece of rotten fruit bounced off of the Ritualist's face, and the human whipped his head up with fury in his eyes, daring someone to try that again. A few of them appeared as if they were willing to take that dare, so he kept the smirk off his face and activated Exquisite Shell and Retaliation of Shadows. His protective spells sprang up into place, and as a walnut bounced off the barrier that was now in front of his eye, a crisp *slap* rang out.

The Dwarf that had been hit by the slap of Joe's shadowy doppelganger had been completely unprepared for the retaliation and was directly knocked off his feet. As the bearded individual hit the ground, all sounds of jubilation stopped. In an instant, the crowd turned hostile, and a few began to advance on the human, seeing this as proof of his treachery. Suddenly, an arresting chuckle rang out. It started low, but each time it echoed off the surrounding buildings, it seemed to gain in strength and volume.

Soon, dozens of the people were holding their ears as blood trickled from the canals. The laugh stopped all at once, and a white-mustachioed Dwarf stepped forward, using an intricate cane to methodically approach. All the fight went out of the crowd as soon as they saw her, and a good number of them even saluted by slamming their fists over their hearts.

"*Grandmaster!*"

The Dwarf didn't bother to acknowledge the show of respect from the crowd, moving forward far more smoothly than someone using a cane had any right to do. Her eyes never left Joe, and he could feel the tell-tale prickle of a skill being activated on him. He saluted, just as he had learned to do in the Legion, and nodded his head at the leader of the city. His voice was low, but he knew that anyone of her status would be able to hear him clearly, no matter how quietly he spoke. "Grandmaster."

"What's all this, then?" The ancient Dwarf was smiling gently, seeming to be no more dangerous than any elderly grandmother. As Master Stu began his tale, the Grandmaster's expression turned ever more ominous. When he finished, she heaved a long sigh and shook her head solemnly. "Let me get this straight... this man arrived here via the goat path. He offered to solve any issue we had with our food supply, which would allow us to maintain our independence and remain a bastion fortress against the invading Elven forces. He was assigned a guard, who went out of his way to bend the rules, and then he was subsequently humiliated in a competition which he had not been provided the rules for. Rules which you, Stu, twisted almost to the point of breaking."

"But only *almost*, Grandmaster," Stu agreed with her irreverently. "I certainly didn't *break* any of the rules."

The white-haired Dwarf appeared next to Stu, crossing the distance so instantaneously that it could have easily been a teleportation skill. She briskly bopped the Master on the head with her cane, shaking her own in disappointment. "The rules clearly dictate that the challenger is allowed to make the challenge properly. *They* get to set the time and place. They get to choose which Master they challenge, and they *certainly* get to choose how many people they train at a time. Let's have a little test, shall we? One where *you* don't get to choose the perfect amount of people for *you* to train?"

"Grandmaster…" Stu looked around the area pleadingly.

"We are going to restart the training challenge!" the Grandmaster called, and by contrast to the previous event, no one cheered or said a word. "As the challenger does not know the rules, I will act as the arbitrator on his behalf. If anyone finds that this is unfair, feel free to speak up at any time. We will engage in two competing rounds, where each Master trains while the other attempts to throw them off their game. Whoever can train more Dwarves faster, to a higher level of skill, will walk away the winner of the seat on the Council. *Major-General* Master Joe, as the Challenger, how many people would you like to train in a skill at a time?"

"I would prefer…" Joe was still reeling from the unexpected turnaround, but he quickly regained his bearings. "Give me a hundred?"

The crowd murmured, some in excitement, some in disbelief over his Elf-like arrogance. The Grandmaster raised one of her eyebrows but didn't ask any further questions. "I need a hundred volunteers, those who would like to train under a Master in a physical skill."

In an instant, there was an uproar as people attempted to be the first to volunteer for the Grandmaster. She smiled and waved them down. "Now, now… I see all of the people from Master Stu's faction among you. Feel free to step back and away. We don't want a repeat of this last attempt."

"I *knew* it," Joe muttered as quietly as he was able, even still earning an amused glance from the Grandmaster.

"I certainly hope your teaching skill is up to the task. One hundred people learning from you at a time is no mean feat," she cautioned him, her voice reaching his ears directly. No one else seemed to have noticed that she was speaking.

"Will I have a surprise for *you* when this competition ends." Joe chuckled as her look shifted to one of minor confusion. The fact of the matter was, he didn't currently have a teaching skill. The entire process was all going to be hands-on learning and an info-dump for the trainees.

"You have ten minutes and the undivided attention of the people who want to learn how to jump properly." The Grand-master waved her hand, and a timer appeared in the air over-head. Joe thought that was a nice touch, as it had felt like he had not been given a full ten minutes previously.

The human turned his complete attention to the Dwarves and began teaching them. As he spoke and demonstrated the motions required, it felt akin to being back in basic training once more, having to explain the most simplistic movements to people that had never needed to learn a skill in their life before this moment. It was an interesting memory, and it certainly impacted the way that he taught them. Then, the fly in the oint-ment appeared.

"You're *such* a great teacher!" Stu's voice overflowed with sarcasm, and Joe felt the skill activate against him as though it were a physical blow. "That's right, only focus on your best students! The other ones don't need this training at all!"

You are being affected by a Master rank speech skill!

You are receiving guidance in a Teaching skill from an Expert teacher! This skill will increase quickly under the tutelage!

The first message had been expected, but the second one almost made Joe burst into laughter. However inadvertently, it seemed that the Master was teaching him the teaching skill and giving him pointers on how to do it better. Joe let the sarcasm flow around him but began paying attention to what was actu-ally being said.

The time passed rapidly, and he adjusted his efforts the entire time, based on the heckling that he was receiving. It didn't matter so much if he himself were unable to use the skill, which the sarcasm seemed to be targeting. Or, Joe mused to himself, it could be that the Dwarf was actively targeting his usage *of* the teaching skill, which would explain why he was constantly going on about better ways of instructing his students. The only issue was, since he didn't have the teaching skill currently... there was nothing to impede.

"Time!" The Grandmaster called, her eyes regarding Joe questioningly even as a smile tugged at her lips. "It is time for the next round. Joe, feel free to attempt to impede your opponent with your skill in whatever way you wish, so long as you do not stop him from instructing those around him or touch him."

You have received instruction from a Master! You have successfully taught one hundred people at one time to use a skill, bringing 21% to the Novice rank, and 79% to the Beginner ranks as you learned how to properly teach.

Skill gained: Teaching (Student 0). You have shown an innate talent for this skill, gained instruction from an Expert Teacher, and learned the skill while bringing a century of people to new heights, literally! Uses: You are able to impart $(n\text{-}iT\text{-}s/2)\%$ of your skill level in a skill to those that you are attempting to teach, where n = skill level, iT = the inverse Tier of skill knowledge, and s = the number of students. When used in a public setting, others may be able to learn the skill as well at a rate of $n/2\text{-}iT$, so use caution when teaching skills you don't want to let out! Cost: $1n*T$ mana per second.

The human nodded to indicate his understanding to the Grandmaster while he tried to simultaneously parse the new skill's information. Deciding he could do that later; he got his head in the game and tried to figure out how he could use his Omnivaulting skill best. Could he jump on the Dwarf's head? Could he grab him and jump to the top of a building? The *way* the Grandmaster had set the parameters seemed to be a hint, and he got the sense that using any other skill to interrupt would not be a viable way of creating the interruption. The timer started, and the Dwarf began frantically attempting to teach all one hundred people under him.

Joe decided that there was really only one way he could use the skill, and he jumped to land directly in front of the Dwarf. Stu sputtered to a stop as Joe appeared a fraction of an inch in front of him, recoiling as if he expected to be attacked. The Ritualist simply smirked at him, then jumped over him and landed directly behind him, breathing down his neck as he tried to resume teaching.

Every once in a while, when it looked like a student was about to have a breakthrough, Joe would jump and land heavily directly in front of them, breaking their concentration and ruining whatever enlightenment they were about to attain. With one hundred students, Stu was unable to accomplish the same level of engagement that he had with the reduced number of his handpicked pupils, especially as Joe continuously distracted them and interrupted his ability to pull the crowd into the zone.

"Time!" the Grandmaster called, even though thirty-two seconds remained on the clock.

"*What!*" Stu shouted, completely frazzled by the attempt to teach so many people, the constant interruptions, and ultimately the fact that he did not receive the full amount of time.

"You were given exactly as much time as you allotted in the previous challenge." The Grandmaster smiled coyly, and all the Master could do was clench his fists and drop his gaze in shame. "Humans are not *all* that bad. Well then, let's take a look at the results."

Joe already knew that he was going to rock the challenge, since his skill gain had shown him a percentage. Within the one hundred trainees, he knew exactly what the breakdown had been. The appraiser came around, calculated skill levels, and concluded their passage in front of the Grandmaster. "During this competition, Master Stu was able to bring his students' average level in the skill 'Sarcasm' to Beginner seven!"

This revelation caused no small amount of cheering, as he had performed nearly as well with one hundred students as he had with only ten. The Dwarf raised his hand in premature victory as the appraiser continued, "Master Joe was able to bring the average level of his students in the skill 'Jump' to Beginner *eight!*"

"Welcome to the Council," the Grandmaster stated without any preamble. Before she could say anything further, Joe shook his head and walked over to Master Stu.

Raising his voice, he addressed not only the master, but the crowd as a whole. "My intent was never to join the Council, and so long as I am able to use one of the rights for a short while, I am more than happy to leave this Master in his position."

The Dwarf looked up, hope filling his eyes at Joe's proclamation. Continuing on, the Ritualist explained. "All I needed was a few minutes of the Grandmaster's time in order to propose a plan to help the Dwarven Oligarchy. I cannot stay here, and I certainly cannot be a ruler in this city, when I am needed elsewhere. Grandmaster, could I please have a few minutes of your time?"

"I will allow it. After all, I didn't expect the Apprentice of Grandmaster Havoc to stick around." She snorted as she took in Stu's shocked appearance. "What? You think I would just assist a stranger to overturn our Council so easily? I was merely ensuring fairness, which is something our people are *supposed* to be known for."

Stu shamefacedly nodded, saluting the Grandmaster and turning soberly to Joe. "My apologies for my actions. Please seek me out for recompense at another time."

"All I want is a fair shot." Joe shrugged and offered his hand to the Dwarf, who clasped it with a firm grip. "There is no need for hardships between us, not when this nation is undergoing such a trial. Think nothing of it."

The Grandmaster tapped her cane on the ground, the echo shaking the air of the city. "Masters of the Council, I hereby call an emergency meeting."

Then, dropping her voice to a normal tone, she winked at Joe and gestured for him and Stu to follow her. "Shall we go have that conversation?"

CHAPTER TWENTY-FIVE

Following the Grandmaster into the Council room caused all sorts of murmuring to break out among the other participants. Six Masters were seated around the table, seven when Stu took his place. The guards that attempted to enter, clearly to keep an eye on the human, were waved away by the white-haired leader of the city. "Hello, everyone, lovely day to finally share the secrets of the Sage's Summit with someone else, isn't it?"

Silence met her words, as Joe had no idea what she was talking about, and the Dwarves were far too horrified to comment. Finally, one of the Masters, apparently attempting to keep his temper in check, was able to choke out a response. "Grandmaster, I believe that it is not in the best interests of our people to pursue this line of conversation any further."

"That's where you are *wrong*, bucko!" She slapped her cane on the table, generating a resounding **thwack** that quieted the dissenters. "Do you know what this human just did, and has done, for our people? He may be the only option for unlocking the secrets of our past. I know none of you were there, since you have not bothered to leave your luxurious state houses in over a month, no doubt indulging in as much hedonism as possible before our people get wiped out-"

Several of the Masters flinched at the accusation, the simple motion doing more to confirm her words than if she had brought in a team of investigators. "Joe, Master Joe, Major General, defeated Master Stu by claiming his right to one of the seats on the Council. Yes, yes, get your shocked murmuring out of the way. Listen up: he *refused* the seat. Now, I had already begun looking into his background as soon as he arrived from the goat path, achieving Mastery of one of his skills in the process. This is the Apprentice of Grandmaster Havoc, and the skill that he mastered by traveling here—and defeated Stu with —is merely a fun mode of transportation for him. *It is not even his main skill set!*"

She shouted the final retort, and the room remained deathly silent as rage seemed to waft off of her in a physical mist. "Would you all like to know who he is? *What* he is?"

"I would!" One of the younger-looking Masters raised their hand, causing the Grandmaster to deflate slightly and rub at her forehead.

"Still haven't reached the Novice ranks in reading a room, I see. What are we going to do with you, Master Don Punchy? You're so *dopey* sometimes." She muttered the complaint so quietly that only Joe could hear her. Sighing, she waved at the human and stated for all of the Masters present, "This man is a twice-specialized Ritualist."

All of the eyes in the room turned to Joe, sizing him up and attempting to verify whether the Grandmaster's words were true. He smiled nervously, not entirely certain where this was going, even if he did have a vague idea. A Dwarf at the table slowly stood. "You cannot possibly be thinking of *bringing* him to the—*achoo*—Sage's Summit?"

"Of course I am, and it is not a question of 'if,' but 'when'. This is happening now." The Grandmaster gestured around the room. "This is a direct order: get off your lazy butts and open the way."

"You... he... this is our history as a nation we are talking about!" The Master didn't back down as the glaring intent on him increased, though he did break out in a cold sweat. "We can't just show him... the... *achoo!*"

"There has got to be something in here that you are allergic to, Master Northwind. You need to figure that out. There is *no* reason you should be so sneezy with your ranks in wind magic; it's dangerous to everyone around you. As to Joe..." The Grandmaster sighed, clearly trying to figure out how to explain herself. "What you should know..."

The Dwarf was obviously using circumlocution to avoid directly stating what he was hinting at, and that was all the indication Joe needed to be certain of the topic they were discussing. "If this is about your Ritual Hall, that's not what I came here for, but it would be very cool to see it."

Utterly flabbergasted, the sneezy Dwarf flung his arms to the side and flopped down into his chair. "You *told* him? That is a national secret!"

"No, in fact I did not even mention that we were going to travel to a building." Now even the Grandmaster was looking at him searchingly. "How *did* you know about that?"

"I built one back on Midgard." Joe casually shrugged as one of the Masters' eyes rolled up in his head and passed out. "When it was completed, the lore of the building informed me that the Dwarves had built a better one that they had hidden away from the world. To be fair, if you hadn't been so excited about my class, I likely wouldn't have been able to figure out what you were talking about."

"Remarkable." The Grandmaster waved at everyone, then pointed at the fallen member. "Somebody shake Mr. Sleepy awake. We have no time to lose."

"At least have some decorum in front of the outsider, Grandmaster!" Stu begged of the city leader. "There is no reason to deride Master Dreamstrider like that."

She didn't acknowledge any of them, simply gripping Joe by

the shoulder and walking away. At that moment, the Ritualist realized that his team members hadn't been allowed inside. "Pardon me, Grandmaster, but where did my friends go?"

"They were given rooms in which to recover and will be attending a small banquet shortly." She eyed him with a sober expression. "I fear that you will most likely be too busy for guests in the near future. Friends or otherwise."

He wasn't sure how to respond to that, so he simply allowed himself to be led over to a large teleportation pad. "Wait, where are we going? Also, I need-"

"Grandmaster McPoundy already reached out and explained your situation," the Grandmaster countered with a warm smile. "I let him know that if you managed to get here, I would accept your proposal without any hesitation. Here, transfer the teleportation pad to my storage and consider your quest complete."

Moments later, as the exchange of goods occurred, Joe received the official notification of his success.

Quest complete: Not Lost, but Hidden. Convince at least one more Grandmaster of the Dwarven Society to join your burgeoning settlement. Reward: the location of 'The Shoe' will be lost to the Elves and anyone with positive ties to them. Anyone who had stumbled upon this settlement's location since the start of the quest will also be affected by this Quest reward! Settlement 'The Shoe' has been removed from all memories of your enemies!

As you are aligned with a Hidden Deity, you gain a secondary reward for this massive accomplishment: Anytime in the next month, you can designate one Skill, Spell, or Ability with triple experience gain during active use. That boon will last for up to one week. Simply say 'activate skill growth boon' followed by the specific characteristic you would like to enhance.

"Awesome," Joe whispered as the enchantment on the floor began to glow. "Where are we going?"

"That is classified, but since you are going anyway," the Grandmaster winked at him, "there was no location on the Zone that we felt was secure enough to keep this portion of our people's history hidden from the Elves and the Ritualist hunters. Until now, we had assumed that we protected the final Ritual Hall in existence, and the fact that you have created another one has been quite the blow to our collective ego."

"Sorry about that." Joe chuckled, not actually caring overmuch about their wounded pride.

"As to the physical location, since there was nowhere *on* the Zone we felt was secure enough, we moved the entire true Summit of this mountain *above* the Zone." The Grandmaster gestured at the teleportation enchantment. "You have likely seen similar constructs all over the place, as enchanted elevators are highly sought-after no matter where you go. This one upgraded the design further, introducing a straight-line teleportation that allows us to pass through hundreds of miles of open air, as well as hundreds of tons of stone. I warn you, it does... tickle."

"The path to the Sage's Summit is..." Stu glared at Joe as the human stepped into the center of the magical elevator, "...is open for *whoever* wants to use it, I guess."

"Stop being so *grumpy*, Stu." Joe chuckled as the Dwarf squinted at him with narrow, suspicious eyes. "All I need to do is jump, right? Well, at least I have *that* part figured out."

"Yeah, yeah. Rub it in," Stu rumbled as he adjusted something on the teleportation device. "Setting to self-sustaining; collection team inbound at minus five."

"Excellent. If we are correct, artifacts of a far-gone age will have been stored within that building. Designs, crafts, perhaps even something we can use to turn the tide of this war." The Grandmaster didn't sound as excited as her anticipation should have made her. "Hard to know what was left behind over a thousand years ago. While we can dream, let's not get our hopes up too high."

"Only way to know for sure is to check it out!" Joe crouched down and jumped, instantly vanishing from the pad as the other Masters began arguing about whose fault it was that he got to go first.

"Looks like we desperately needed someone to come along and shake the hornet's nest." The Grandmaster rolled her eyes at the bickering over traveling order, jumping slightly and vanishing from sight.

CHAPTER TWENTY-SIX

Unlike every other time that he had accessed a teleportation field or an elevator, the trip was not instantaneous. In fact, it felt much more like riding the Bifrost than it did teleporting from one location to another instantly. Also, what might have felt 'ticklish' to a Grandmaster Dwarf certainly felt like having his top layer of skin flayed off and kosher sea salt rubbed in.

Even so, he was able to fully enjoy the transportation. The sights that grew visible as the Zone receded below him were absolutely wondrous to behold. When he glanced up, he saw only the black, empty sky above. He burst through the final bit of atmosphere, traveling toward a dark spot hidden among a multitude of dark spots. As he flew closer, he pierced through what must have been an illusion, and finally the sun could be seen reflecting off what could only be the top portion of a mountain.

His physical form acted as a stream of energy, blasting through the stone itself and forcing his mind to go blank in order to protect him from the sensation. When he came to, he was standing alone atop the mountain, staring at the most glorious building he had ever borne witness to in his life.

Grand Ritual Hall (Legendary)(Unclaimed).

Joe wasn't entirely certain how he knew exactly what the building was, or why the system would give him the notification so freely, but he felt that it had to do with the unique combination of the building being unclaimed, and him being a perfect fit to open it up for the first time in a millennia. Like a snail inevitably drawn toward a rich man, Joe drifted forward, his eyes unable to see anything else on the Sage's Summit. Other Dwarves were appearing behind him, but all held their tongue in reverence for the structure and the history that it represented.

The Ritualist drew near to the grand Ritual Hall, and his hand extended out on its own as he approached the door. The Grandmaster, along with all of the Masters, held their breath. This was the moment of truth, the moment when they would know if they would be the ones to see beyond the doorway for the first time in a thousand years. Joe's palm pressed flat against the door, and a tiny ritual flared to life. It was the first time he had ever seen this particular ritual, but a single circle Novice ritual hid no secrets from him.

"They can even be used like this?" He shook his head at the wonders he had yet to discover, filing away the inscription with his near-perfect memory. All the ritual had done was to compare data. It verified what class was allowed to enter the building and cross-referenced it against his base class. "This is *spectacular.* I could use that on so many different things... what am I doing? Activate skill growth boon, Ritual Magic!"

Ooh! Good choice! That selection will grant a lesser impact on all subskills of Ritual Magic! However, it will only last five days instead of seven. Do you accept?

"Absolutely, I do."

A second circle summarily appeared around the first, and Joe realized that the building wasn't finished testing whether he held the necessary requirements. It was strange to him, though; he had never seen a ritual that allowed for additional circles to activate if specific conditions were met. "I thought that rituals were all or nothing... I don't know if this changes everything, but it is certainly something to look into."

The door to the building hadn't even opened, and he had already gleaned information that would be incredibly beneficial down the road. Finding applications for it would be a challenge —or perhaps not, depending on what he discovered within these mysterious walls. Joe's eyes scrutinized the new ritual that had been activated, widening slightly as he realized that the addition of the second circle had shifted the purpose of the first. Now the linked ritual was not only checking against his class, but it was also checking against his class *skills*. "First qualifier: class, second qualifier: my mastery of rituals? The way it shifts the language, the vectors, the quotients based on the input from the previous circle is extraordinary..."

Magical Matrices has reached Student VII!
Ritual Magic has reached Expert VI!
Ritual Circles has reached Expert V!

The three skill increases all at once felt more shocking, but the fact that he had gained the increase from what was currently appearing as a Beginner-tier ritual was mind-boggling. The only cause he could think of was that perhaps obtaining this information, especially how these rituals were interacting, was filling in a gap in his foundational knowledge that would become incredibly important in the future. He was already making plans for altering some of his rituals, such as those he used for area protection, to test whether he could designate affiliation and class as his white list instead of the crude methodology he had been using: a drop of blood from each person who needed access to the area. "The level of sophistication this has reached... I had no idea it was possible."

The ritual vanished, and he felt a sense of *presence* wash over him. Even without needing to confirm it, he knew that the building itself was judging him. It had been explained to him time and again, pounded into his head, that enchanted objects were alive, even if only a little. As they aged, they gained more intelligence and more ability to act upon that intelligence. A

Legendary building, over a millennia old—who knows how long it had been around before that—it was entirely possible that this place was smarter than any person attempting to enter it.

The feeling swept away from him, leaving him with a faint sense of loss. However, three emotions had been implanted before it had gone. Amusement, excitement, and a bitter loneliness. If he had to guess, the third of the emotions was the only reason that the door slowly began to creak open.

You have been granted limited access to the Grand Ritual Hall! As this is a Legendary building, only a Grandmaster of Ritual Magic(s) has the credentials necessary in order to attain ownership of it.

"He did it!" The excitement rolling off the Grandmaster Dwarf was palpable, yet she kept her voice pitched low so as not to startle anyone or anything that might be within earshot. "How much were you able to access?"

"Limited," Joe admitted with a shrug, "but I can tell you that just watching as the door opened brought me up a skill level, and I am only three away from attaining Master status. I'm certain that if I achieve that, I would be able to do more with this building."

She nodded, more than happy to agree with his assessment. "Absolutely correct, and let's make that happen. Whatever you need from us, consider it done. The treasury is open to you, as is access to whatever perks this building can give you, so long as we are able to secure our history from within."

"Awesome." Joe forced himself not to jump up and down with joy—the resources that would be available to the ruling faction of the city, Masters and Grandmasters alike, was certain to be far more beneficial to him than repeated trips to the dump in the hopes of finding a diamond among the turds. Oftentimes literally.

The Council walked into the building reverently and began searching around. Joe had expected the Ritual Hall to appear similar to the one that he had built, but he spotted a major difference right away: this building did not bear any dedication to the deities, and therefore no temple portion awaited before entering into the ritual area proper. If he'd had no prior experience with such a building, he would have assumed it was just a giant empty room, just as the Dwarves did.

The sheer disappointment rolling off of them was *hilarious* to Joe, especially as they did not understand what they were looking at. "If I am correct, the ritual area of this building isn't going to be hidden like mine needed to be, which means that this is a false room. Let's see…"

He connected to the building, slowly guiding his mana to flow out of him and into the floor. Typically, such an attempt would cause an explosion as the material absorbing the raw mana would reject it and detonate violently. Here, he was able to feel the strange material that reacted to willpower and smiled as he confirmed that he had been correct. Raising his hand for pure theatrics, Joe brought his palm down as he commanded all of the ritual material to collapse into a large orb to hover above the ground.

The 'room' that they had entered, which had been as large as a warehouse, instantly vanished. Several of the Masters gasped in shock as the *actual* building was revealed. Just as it was on Midgard, the Ritual Hall seemed to hang weightlessly in space. Stars and galaxies surrounded them, pinpricks of light that moved and flowed as the universe itself. Meteors, asteroids, solar flares… every celestial body was captured in the space that surrounded them. Only the huge orb of ritual-stuff that floated in the center of the room gave the lie to the idea that they were striding through the universe unassisted.

"Right, so, if the ritual is intended to be compiled in the open room—thank goodness for plenty of space, finally—that means that the other portions are likely being used for storage instead of secret ritual creation areas." Joe walked to the left portion of the huge space, tapping on the floor as he went. Obviously, there was no way to tell where the entrance lay, but he tried to give the impression that he could hear something the Dwarves could not. He figured it would rankle them. "Sounds like this is the spot!"

"What is he going on about?" Master Stu grumbled just as Joe waved his hand upward, and the floor followed. A staircase leading down appeared, and Joe waved his fellows toward it. "I think this is the storage area, if one of you wants to go and check, I'm sure there is going to be stuff down there that you don't want me to see."

His nonchalance earned him a confused glance, and one of the Masters that hadn't spoken yet voiced the question on all of their minds. "You are just... fine with not knowing what is down there? It could be riches and treasures that would be incredibly beneficial to your class. Something that has been left just for you, the inheritor to the previous owner of this building."

"I want to make my own way," was the human's simple answer. "Of course, if you find something protected by rituals, let me know, and maybe if you find some Ritual Diagrams or grimoires, I would appreciate having access to them. But a deal is a deal. I never bargained for access to those things in advance, so demanding them now would not be fair."

"A human with *honor*!" The Grandmaster crowed, elbowing Stu hard enough to make him gasp for air. "I told you it could be done!"

CHAPTER TWENTY-SEVEN

The Ritualist did his best to concentrate on the changes that he was enacting, but it was very difficult to concentrate with a swarm of Dwarves ransacking the building behind him. Clearly whatever they had been finding was extremely exciting, because the shouting had not reduced for the last hour at the minimum. Even so, Joe found it *wonderful* to be back in a Ritual Hall.

Taking notes and putting his thoughts in order were so much easier now that he was connected to the... goo? "Never did figure out what this stuff actually is. It's part of the building, and it works, but the building would probably not let me reduce it into aspects..."

An ominous rumble came from the structure around him, the Legendary building informing him that *no*, destruction of even a small part of its matter would not be tolerated. He amiably took that in stride and continued working. Mathematical formulae, circles of varying sizes, compass roses, geometric shapes; anything in his head was perfectly matched by the malleable substance.

"This would be so useful if I were an artist." An evil smile crossed his face as he recalled all of the times other people had wished they could create exactly what they saw in their mind's eye. For him, that was presently a reality. It went without saying that the material couldn't come with him, but just the simple fact that he could perfectly replicate anything he could think of… it was intoxicating. Ideas for rituals, the new enhancements that he had learned, all of it soared into the air around him, and he started plotting his new path forward.

"The real issue with this circle combination is figuring out *why* it shifted in the way that it did." While he waited on the Council, he was attempting to replicate the whitelisting ritual which the door had used to grant him entry. It was only a Beginner ritual, which meant he should be able to create the exact same thing in no time flat. The problem was, it wasn't behaving how he expected a Ritual Circle to behave. "If anything, this is acting like an enchantment, in that it can make determinations based on new information, instead of *preset* information the way a ritual does."

Enchanted Ritual Circles has reached Beginner VII!
Enchanting Lore has reached Student I!

"If that doesn't confirm it, nothing else would." Instead of feeling excited about the breakthrough, it slightly aggravated him. A double skill-up was extremely beneficial, but he was not entirely certain what he was missing. Taking a break for the first time in… it could have been a couple hours, he was uncertain… Joe wrestled his focus back to the physical room and found that he was not alone. He had been aware that other people were moving around, but once he shifted and met the knowing eyes of the Grandmaster, he somehow knew that she had just been waiting for him to require assistance. "Was it so obvious that I wouldn't know what I was doing?"

"It is the burden of a Grandmaster to be a guide for Masters," she told him simply, moving closer to take a look at what he was working on. "Oftentimes, people will forget that although they may be treading on a path most others have not walked, it is very unlikely that the path is entirely parallel in all ways. There will almost always be intersections, places where our knowledge meets. It is at these nodes of understanding that we can discuss and ease the burden of walking alone."

That brought a question to Joe's mind, and while he truly wanted the answer, he didn't know if asking it was going to be rude. "You are only called Grandmaster, whereas the other Masters are called by what they are masters of. Like Master Stu Sarcasm, for instance. What are you a Grandmaster of?"

"My name is Snow-on-the-Mountain, at least translated into the modern common tongue." When Joe didn't comment, she seemed relieved, though he was uncertain why. "Most people only call me Grandmaster, because of the difficulty of saying the entire title, name, and skill. If we went by the same conventions as the others, I would be 'Grandmaster Snow-on-the-Mountain Mana Manipulation'."

That got Joe's attention, and his interest in her opinion on things instantly tripled. "Havoc told me that particular skill is absolutely crucial for supporting almost all other forms of higher skills; anything using mana is going to be impacted by it. Is that why you chose the skill to specialize in?"

"It just worked out that way." She humbly waved off his questions. "I can tell you that at my skill level, there is very little I cannot replicate when it comes to skills and talents under the Master ranks. Even there, I can usually outperform the Masters when it comes to Mana circuitry or efficiency. So tell me, young Master, what is it that has you looking so bleak?"

Understanding the evasion of his query for what it was, Joe decided to use the proffered help as much as possible to advance himself. "The issue boils down to the fact that I am trying to replicate the magic that allowed us into this building, and as an Expert in Ritual Circles, and a Student in Ritual Lore—one moment... Knowledge, Alchemical Lore."

Alchemical Lore has reached Apprentice VI!

"What in blazes was *that?*" the Grandmaster grumbled as

the ambient mana in the room was impacted as though a depth charge had been dropped into it. Before Joe could proudly explain his skill, he deflated under her barrage of complaints. "It was so *inefficient...* created so much akashic noise... *ugh.*"

"That was a skill from my deity." Joe only answered after she paused in clear expectation of an actual answer instead of spouting rhetorical questions. "It allows me to increase a lore skill that I have access to."

"Of course it was." She blinked a few times, then shook her head. "Well, I certainly am not going to tell you not to use such a generous gift. I can warn you, however, that if you do not figure out how to use it more quietly, someone is going to throw you into a dungeon and force you to write technical manuals for a few centuries."

"*I knew it.*" Joe whispered harshly to himself as his daydreaming fears were spoken aloud by someone else. "I'll... try to figure that out."

"See that you do." The Grandmaster seemed to settle herself down, then motioned for Joe to continue.

"As I was saying, I am an Expert at these circles." Joe turned his attention back to the ritual circles and matrices he had left hovering in the air behind him. "This is a variant circle, and it uses just a *hint* of enchantment, but somehow, that aligns it with a totally different branch of magic? I feel like I should be able to look at this and understand it without any issue, and yet it is eluding me."

"You say you are an Expert in Ritual Circles." The Grandmaster was waiting for him as he turned back, a coy smile on her face. "Do you think that you could create an enchantment at the Expert ranks right now?"

"Well, no-"

"Do you have any spells that you cast which could be said to be in the Expert or Master ranks?"

"Only my Omnivault-"

"Hush. That is not a spell." Grandmaster Snow took in a

deep breath and shifted into a warm teaching tone. "It is clear to me that you have figured out one of the keys to advancing your base class further. There is no *single* class skill. By explaining that you have a lesser understanding of one portion of your class, do you feel that you will be ridiculed?"

"No, and even if I was, I wouldn't care." Joe tapped the floor with his foot, and a small table generated in front of them, where he placed two cups that were filled with coffee in an instant, thanks to AutoMate. "The issue I am having is that I don't understand why it is so slow to progress, even though I feel it *should* be faster."

"I see." Snow accepted the coffee with good grace, taking an appreciative sip. "The fact of the matter is that you only have half of the convergence that you need in order to achieve a rapid-growth skill."

"Oh. So... you mean that if I had raised enchanting to Expert ranks, as well as my Ritual Circles, then the combination skill 'Enchanted Ritual Circles' would increase much faster?" Joe rubbed at his chin as he stared at the swirling galaxies in the walls. He didn't miss the fact that the Grandmaster was nodding, keeping silent in an obvious attempt to have him explain further. "I also admittedly haven't put a ton of effort into increasing what I have considered as side skills up until this point. I know these spawned off of my main Ritual Magic skill, but... I suppose it is true that I have not really been looking at them as class skills."

"I can tell you this..." Snow set her coffee cup down on the table with an audible *clink*. "You can become a Master of a single skill within your skill set. But *mastery* is not being a Master. Tell me if I have this correct: Ritual Magic contains a small criteria informing you that no other sub-skills can be higher than it is. Correct?"

"That is true." In fact, it had been an issue for him as he had increased his Ritual Circle skill almost instantly whenever he managed to raise the governing skill to a higher level. "It is getting in the way of my progression-"

"Stop right there. No, it is *not* getting in the way, it is telling you that your foundation of Knowledge is patchy at best." The Grandmaster muttered something to the effect of 'every time' under her breath, then started to clarify. "You can reach the low Master ranks off of one of your skills. However, you will absolutely stagnate at that point, unless you also bring your other skills up to an acceptable level. Early in that tier, it would make sense if you left some of your skills lower-tier. Yet, who would believe that a high-ranked Master is still a Beginner, or even a *Novice*, in some of the supporting skills?"

"Ah. That makes... yeah, that makes sense." It appeared that he would need to spend a few more chapters of his life working on improving his skills. He certainly wasn't opposed to that, but it had taken him this long for just one; what would it look like to raise all five to where they needed to be? "Follow-up question: would it be faster for me to train these skills specifically, or should I attempt to boost the main skills, such as enchanting and alchemy, to a higher skill rank? If my general knowledge is higher-"

"I think you know the answer." Snow gave him a look that told him she wasn't just going to blurt out every solution, though she did seem willing to give him a nudge. "Think about it this way: while specializing will allow you to climb to higher heights quickly, if you place your ladder on a low ledge, how far can you climb before it becomes too dangerous or difficult to move higher?"

"General knowledge is still going to be pertinent for achieving the higher ranks." Joe wasn't super happy about that, as it likely meant learning for decades before he... the Ritualist cut off that line of thinking before it could take root. It was important for him to walk the path to completion, and surface knowledge just wouldn't cut it. "All right, I will take that under advisement, for certain. While I have you here... any tips on Mana Manipulation?"

"Ha!" The Grandmaster didn't seem to mind his audacity.

"Certainly. Let's discuss what you have been doing to progress it, and…"

For the next several hours, she put him through the wringer to test his current abilities, as well as giving him tips and strengthening exercises that he could use as he reached higher ranks. Thankfully, it was an enlightening experience, proved by his resulting increases in theory and skill level.

CHAPTER TWENTY-EIGHT

You have benefited greatly from training under a Grandmaster!
Mana Manipulation has reached Student IX!

"You are already a Journeyman in Coalescence? You got there *before* you did so with Mana Manipulation?" For some reason, this seemed to intrigue the Dwarf greatly. "That is backward from nearly anyone else I have ever had the pleasure of discussing this skill with. Typically, that means you would have been using a large amount of power and not overly concerning yourself with its efficiency or functionality. Seeing what you have built... that does make sense. How have you been progressing since reaching that tier?"

"Not at all," Joe told her straightforwardly, if somewhat sheepishly. "I can't seem to find anything that the skill counts as training with it, either."

"A common complaint. Also, it is the answer to some of the issues that I have seen with your skills." The Grandmaster reached out and tapped him on the forehead, right in the center of the golden eye tattoo. "Remember how I mentioned that your recent spell was 'loud'? How do you think you could make it less so?"

"That would be... Mana Manipulation, would it not? Keeping it contained within the pathways that the spell is supposed to be using, and not allowing overflow?" Joe felt that this was the correct answer, even though it seemed like she was trying to get him to say that it was coalescence. He just could not fathom how it would fit.

"It is, in part." Power swirled up from her hands, and he could see that she was directly altering the ambient mana to create a small illusion. "Imagine that the power flowing within you is like a river, and every time you are using a spell, it is equated to a flood."

The illusion sent its water splashing over the boundaries and onto dry land, destroying tiny homes and drowning several people that had been within them. He could practically hear their screams as they were sucked underwater. "Do you need to make it so dark?"

"There are always consequences for failing to use power correctly." There was unmistakable steel in Snow's tone, so Joe decided to stop complaining and just listen. "You will also remember it better this way."

New objects appeared in the illusion, large barriers that rose up along the riverbanks. Before he could start to question her, the Grandmaster continued to narrate softly. "Mana Manipulation can guide what is there, to a point. It can direct mana, it can keep mana within the channels as best as possible... but what happens when the flood is no longer contained within the scope it once was? In our example, that means a spell that has increased a tier in power."

"It floods again? It goes right over the barriers that used to contain it?" Joe had an idea of where she was going with this, but he wanted to *know* instead of simply guessing.

"Indeed it does." The image shifted to demonstrate the principle, and once more, tiny houses—these ones grander than the first—were washed away. "This is where the two skills work in tandem. The river needs guidance, but it does not always need to be a straight path."

In response to her commentary, the flat river lifted into the air, and the image became much more three-dimensional. The river, once a simple stream, was being guided in a new direction. Instead of a straight line, it coiled like a spring. The water surged just as powerfully as before, but no matter how much it tried to overflow and wash away the homes, it simply did not have the ability to escape the banks anymore. "This is not a perfect example, as water does not act in this way without incredible pressure or magic to guide it. Take the lesson; ignore the rest. When we look at the river from the perspective of the people living next to it, all they see is a trickle of water moving past. They do not see the lake's worth of water that is confined within every single step of the waterway."

Joe's eyes were shining, but the lesson that he had learned was not exactly what she had been trying to teach him. "Do you mean to tell me… Coalescence isn't just about crushing and compressing? If I start to purposefully shape the mana within me, will that work?"

"Well, doing so within your core-"

"I don't have a core; I have free-floating mana." Joe rubbed his hands together and turned his attention to the energy flowing inside of him. "Yes… I think that'll work *perfectly*."

His internal mana structures had been a concern for him ever since he had broken away from the standard usage of an internal core for holding his power. Rather, it suffused him like a gas, constantly being refreshed by the ambient mana and filling him up like a water bottle. He had assumed, apparently incorrectly, that in order for his coalescence skill to reach higher ranks, he would need to convince his body to act more like an air compressor. Simply force the air molecules closer together, and bam! More air per square inch—though of course, this was mana.

But now, with the information he had just gleaned from the Grandmaster, he realized that perhaps he could give his mana *some* structure. He would just need to make sure that he did so in a way that continued to feel 'free' to him. "Start small, advance from there."

He was not expecting huge increases in the skill. Not only did he not have someone actively teaching it to him, but it was already at the Journeyman rank. All increases from here on out would require a huge amount of time, and he needed to ensure that the power flowing through him was ideally arranged, head to toe, through every molecule in his body.

Thinking about his actual body gave him an idea of how to shape his mana. "Human bodies are used to double helixes, right? It's literally in our DNA…"

Using his Mana Manipulation to grab the smallest possible unit of mana within him, he attempted to twist them into threads and wind them together. Didn't work; at least, it did not stay the way that he wanted it to. As soon as his attention was off of it, all of the work was undone, unraveling in an instant. "Okay, that makes sense. Even DNA contains a ladder structure, but I don't think that would work for my 'free' influenced mana."

Deciding not to overthink it, he simply grabbed a third chunk of mana and produced a braid instead of winding it. When he let it go, it stayed in place. At first, he thought he had discovered the solution, but then a notice popped up.

15 mana reserved for 'mana braid'.

"Drat. That was supposed to bind it together, not make it impossible to use." Just before he undid the process and started over, he was startled as a hand clamped down on his shoulder. Opening his eyes, he found the Grandmaster nose-to-nose with him.

"What did you just do?"

"I am trying to generate a pattern that my mana will accept, but all I succeeded in doing was putting the mana to the side in a reserved state." Joe pointed at his chest. "I was just about to let it go-"

"Wait. I think you are onto something." Once more, she

lifted a hand and created an illusion in the air. "Describe to me exactly how you made it."

It was extremely simple to explain, so she made a model of it without difficulty. Then, inspecting it, she pointed out a few glaring issues. "Of course this is considered unusable as it stands. Once it is contained in a braid like this, it has no more input and nowhere to output. If you instead used it like *this*, I think it would function."

In her image, the tiny braid turned into a huge weave that expanded until it shaped a man. An instant later, it zoomed out slightly and Joe was looking at himself from the outside. The Grandmaster was mumbling under her breath, and markings appeared in the air around him, mathematical equations that were created and destroyed in the blink of an eye. "I think I've got it. This is a doozy. I don't think you will be able to accomplish this in an area like Alfheim. In order for you to use this style of pattern, you will need to practically give up the use of mana until it is functionally complete."

"Sounds like I'm going to go ahead and give up on making that in favor of something else, then," Joe informed her smoothly, "There has to be something that will allow me to retain access to my power while simultaneously increasing the skill."

"Hold on… this may look simple because I demonstrated it so rapidly, but remember that I am a Grandmaster." Snow tapped on the image, and it *clinked* as though she were tapping on glass. He had no idea how she had solidified an energy source, but he kind of wanted that ability for himself. "If you were able to complete this, it would catapult *both* your Coalescence *and* Mana Manipulation into the Master Ranks."

Silence reigned for a long moment as Joe wrestled with how willing he was to give up his power, even for a short time. The end benefit sounded good, but what would he need to do to reach it? "How long would it take to put this in place, do you think?"

She tapped at her mustache, thinking through her answer. "You will not lose access to all of your mana at once, only what is reserved. Until you reach a certain point, you will simply have an incrementally smaller pool to draw upon. The first step would be creating a weave just like this at skin level. Upon completion of that initial layer, any mana in your system would be trapped within, unable to escape. I believe that you would still be able to pull ambient mana in, but you would simply have no way to access it. Pressure would build up, and eventually it would kill you-"

"I'm liking this less and less. How about-"

"I haven't finished," the Grandmaster chastised him, her flashing eyes leaving no doubt that another interruption would be the end of the conversation entirely. "As soon as you've finished the external weave, you would be racing a time limit to complete the inner one. You would not need to worry about ambient influences anymore, and you would have gained plenty of experience in creating the first layer. Everything after that would only move exponentially faster, until you saved yourself from yourself."

Snow's face broke into a wide smile, "By my estimates, if you managed to bring your Mana Manipulation to the Expert rank before you fully closed yourself off, you would be able to complete the rest of the weave within three months. You would be cutting it close... but I think you could do it. The rewards... would be amazing."

"All of this from a braid?" He wouldn't lie, he was intrigued by what she was describing. "It's a simple structure..."

"*Profoundly* simple," she concurred as the pattern was imprinted into a piece of enchantment paper; carved there by her incredibly precise manipulation. "Here, I made it into a guide book that you can study. If you choose to follow this path, know that I will someday wish to analyze the results."

Joe stared in amazement at the book that had been handed to him so casually, its cover shining with power that seemed to be barely contained.

Grandmaster Snow's Guide to Mastery of Mana. (Legendary). This is a skill book designed specifically for Joe the Excommunicated as a reward for not attempting to lay claim to various artifacts and historical relics stored within the Sage's Summit. While it is not a soul-bound item, no one else may make use of this particular set of instructions. Don't lose it!

"If this is a gift, it is... way too much." Joe looked up from the tome, forced to tear his eyes from the cover. "I have no idea when I'm going to be able to use this, or when it will be safe to do so."

"So save it for later." She waved away his thanks dismissively. "Rent a room in a hotel on a higher world where no one knows you, and lock yourself away until you can make the time to complete it. In the meantime, at least practice with it. It's going to do you no good trying to jump straight into a final product. You will need to weave, tear apart, and weave again, until it is so instinctual that you can do it at even the smallest level within you."

"It'll be good training for my skills... even if I never use it the way you intend." Joe sent the book into his codpiece, thanked the Grandmaster, and turned back to his study of rituals as she shrugged, winked, and withdrew to rejoin the historians and various members of her city who were trying to catalog what items ought to leave their history and step into the present age.

CHAPTER TWENTY-NINE

"To get the most out of my Lore, I need to bring my Magical Matrices to a higher tier. If I can bring it to the Journeyman rank, I will gain at least a forty percent bonus to putting concepts into actual practice." Joe was doing a quick rundown of his class abilities and trying to figure out ways to improve them as rapidly as possible. Unfortunately for him, the only way that he could think to train this particular skill was by utter *grinding*. It was unfortunately imperative for all applications of magical crafting, from Alchemy to Zombification, and thus could not be neglected.

"How did enchanted Ritual Circles and Ritualistic Alchemy fall so far behind?" Joe knew the answer, even if he wanted to grumble about it. They were entire professions, as well as classes, on their own. Some of the best smiths that he had encountered in the Dwarven Capital had been some of the most reluctant to teach someone else their craft. He would eventually be able to convince Grandmaster McPoundy to teach him, but that would occur after the fall of his entire race, and Joe was not entirely certain how willing he would be to help someone from the race that had made it happen.

He also had ten years during which he could receive training from Jake, the Alchemist, but that came with its own set of concerns. Havoc had not called Jake a person, a human, an Elf, or anything like it. He had warned Joe about making deals with *entities* like Jake, and that did not bode well for the future. Still, they had a deal, and he knew that as soon as he was able to make it back to The Shoe, he would experience a crash course in the skill that would make the things Havoc put him through seem like fun little games. Abyss, the first time he had met the Alchemist, the man had blasted him with the equivalent of magical bear mace and tried to entice him into creating a human zombie apocalypse.

"Whatever. Eventually, I will have teachers and a secure way to increase these skills. So what can I tackle on my own? What can I boost without outside influence?" He already knew the answer, and that was why he was procrastinating. It was down to either Magical Matrices or Ritual Circles. Even *then*, he was almost certain that he would gain boosts to his Ritual Circles as soon as he got better at using alchemy and enchanting when he was creating them. That meant, to his chagrin, it was all back to skill grinding.

He was fine with that, in no small part because he keenly felt the need to replace his arsenal. Almost everything that he had been able to use against the Elven Theocracy when they were coming after him had been utility rituals, whose main usefulness had been to help him escape. The main present obstacle was the fact that an entire race of people was too much to plan against. He did have one particular group of enemies that he knew was going to be after him, and decided to begin working to counter them.

"Herr Trigger wants to use something as unsportsmanlike as *guns* in a magical world?" Joe scoffed at that thought, thinking back to the self-righteous, entitled Bounty Hunter that was hunting him. "I have no idea why a Luddite like that would be good at enchanting, but it is clear that he is never going to adapt to this world properly unless he is forced to do it. That works for me; makes him easy to counter. If I plan properly and keep what I need on hand."

The Ritualist ultimately decided to design a set of protective rituals that should allow him to practically ignore normal caliber bullets. "He is always blasting with his revolvers, hitting me at a distance with his rifles, and focusing on heavy penetration of shields and the like. What if I don't even bother to set something up to stop bullets? What if I set something up to stop stinging flies?"

A hint of dark mana seeped from his eyes as he smiled wildly, his Dark Charisma goading him towards violence. "Bullets that he is using in regular combat are small, single-target, but fast. I will need a triple layer of protection in order to make this viable. The first will be a field that extends as far as possible, sensing anything passing through it extremely rapidly. The second will be activated by the first, sensing if the incoming item is biological or not. The third will create a series of tiny shields, almost a cylinder of panels, that will each fractionally deflect the projectile until it hits the ground. It's going to be really difficult to test it out, but on the plus side, I probably won't have to wait long."

He got to work, and soon had a basic concept idea drawn up. Without the knowledge he had gained from the conditional ritual, there was no way he would have been able to put something like this into practice. Even so, it seemed that it was going to end up being a Journeyman ritual at the minimum, because there was just no way he could calculate each of the triggers without the additional supporting framework. It was inefficient and clunky, but he was fairly certain it would do the job.

Joe spent several hours squeezing as much as possible out of his Lore skill, as well as simplifying as many equations as possible with his Magical Matrices, but in the end, he only managed to reduce it from the equivalent of a Journeyman level eight ritual to a Journeyman level three ritual. It didn't sound like much, but that small adjustment allowed him to save hundreds of Unique-rank aspects. Finally, he was ready to create the first prototype.

Back when he had still been allowed to use ink in order to create rituals, he would have simply used the room to create the overall circle, then filled it with ink or slapped it onto a paper. Unfortunately, that would no longer work for... Joe paused, remembering how he had created each layer in his A.S.P.E.C.T. tower. He recalled his ability to use Somatic Ritual Casting and decided to go for it. Pulling out his inscribing tool, he set the ritual up by using the strange material provided by the building itself.

Mentally willing it to slowly rotate, he began at the inner-most circle, the Novice circle, and accustomed himself with feeling how the strange fire would hang in the air. Thanks to Somatic Ritual Casting, he was able to force the drawn-out aspects to also spin, keeping them rotating in tandem with the goo. As he wrote, the goo faded away, allowing him to trace without fear of destroying the building's precious resources. It took a little bit of doing, but it eliminated the need to maintain a mental image of the entire Ritual Circle, which made the proposition all the more doable.

He continued on, completing the Beginner, Apprentice, and Student Circles without issue. Then, for the first time, he crafted a Journeyman-rank ritual while using the skill that allowed him to draw in midair. He had initiated a large barrier around himself, but there was still a good chance that he was going to fry.

Somehow, he didn't.

Joe pressed on, driven nearly to distraction as he constantly braced for the imminent explosion, but a few hours after start-ing, the Circle was completed. He stared at it, completely dumbfounded, barely aware of the skill increase notifications that appeared. "How? How did that happen?"

You have created a triple condition ritual for the first time! Bonus expe-rience gained: 500.

Ritual Magic has reached Expert VII!

Ritual Circles has reached Expert VI!
Enchanted Ritual Circles has reached Beginner VIII!
Magical Matrices has reached Student IX!
Somatic Ritual Casting has reached Apprentice III!
Quest update: Student Ritualist. 12/20.

Increasing his skills wasn't enough for him. He wanted to know *why* he had been able to succeed. "Come on, system. We both know that should have blown up in my face and left me with a single shoe, if I was *lucky*. The fact that I got through the Student Circle was already impressive. Speaking of, that was a *Journeyman* ritual; why did I get a quest update?"

He dug into it further, finally locating what he was looking for under the information about the building. Only now that he had somehow used the benefits that it provided without fully understanding them did it reveal what they were.

Grand Ritual Hall (Legendary) accessible benefits.

1) Ritual stability increased by 100% per tier under Legendary.

2) All rituals Legendary-tier or below may be created using materials one rank lower than required. The resulting ritual will be considered one rank lower than its design suggests.

3) Not yet discovered.

4) Access not granted.

5) Access not granted.

Joe stared at the new information, trying to decide how he should be reacting. On one hand, he was very grateful that the ritual was three hundred percent more stable than he had expected it to be, and that he was seeing progression for his class Quest. He clapped nervously and took in a breath through his nose, "On the other hand, there are *complaints*, so we will just wash that off and move on. I didn't explode, and the ritual was successful. The whole thing used Rare aspects; of course the building considered that I was trying to make it a tier lower than it actually was. The real question is... how can I exploit that?"

All at once, a major issue with his latest accomplishment clicked into place. Joe stared up at the swirling, entrancing ritual with a forlorn sigh. "Welp. I have no way to transport this. Probably should have burned it into a Ritual Tile instead of creating a giant eyesore in the middle of the room."

Carefully not looking at the ritual that he was leaving in place, Joe stepped about twenty feet away and started his next project. "Prototype number two: something to fend off that wolf that has a chainsaw instead of a mouth. For some reason, bear mace is coming to mind, and I think I know how I can replicate it."

CHAPTER THIRTY

It took some doing, but Joe believed that he had managed a working version on only the second attempt. The first one wouldn't even start up—for some reason, any mana he put into it was continually removed—until he located a set of variables that would have probably fried his brain if he *had* managed to get it working. As soon as he had caught the error, he called over a large mass of the ritual goo, formed it into a teddy bear, and gave it a giant hug. "Thanks for not letting me short circuit my brain, Grand Ritual Hall."

Benefit discovered!

Grand Ritual Hall (Legendary) accessible benefits.

1) Ritual stability increased by 100% per tier under Legendary.

2) All rituals Legendary tier or below may be created using materials one rank lower than required. The resulting ritual will be considered one rank lower than its design suggests.

3) NEW! When a ritual under Legendary tier is activated, the structure will be checked by the Grand Ritual Hall. If the resulting ritual would kill the activator, the ritual will be forcefully de-energized.

4) Access not granted.

5) Access not granted.

It made perfect sense to him that a Legendary building designed for Ritualists would set multiple safety features in place to keep them alive. Most likely, it had been a center of training for low-level Ritualists—or at least, that's what Joe would have used it for. Either that, or it would have been reserved for *elite* Ritualists that were working to perfect their craft. "If I am reading that list correctly, the benefits are rank-dependent. If I can become a Master of Ritual Magic, I bet I'll be able to access whatever the fourth one is."

Tearing his loving gaze away from the incredible building, he studied the prototype and tried to decide if he should test it out, or if he should just put it away and hope for the best. The only downside to using it within the building was the loss of resources, and of course the time that he had put into creating it. If it worked, it would be much easier to replicate, cheaper in terms of time sunk into it, and he would have more confidence in the final product. There was also the hidden benefit of just grinding out as many rituals as he could manage.

Quest update: Apprentice Reductionist. 8,216/10,000 Rare aspects used! 10,000/10,000 gathered.

"If I can finish this class quest off, that's a direct addition of five levels to any of my crafting skills. That could be huge…" Checking over his skill list revealed that most of his Ritual Magic sub-skills counted as crafting-based. "I could even bring Ritual Magic directly into the Master ranks, if I'm willing to throw away a couple of the bonus skill levels. Just getting access to the next set of benefits from this place would be worth it."

He decided to go ahead and activate the ritual, and when it was up and running… he felt no change whatsoever. "Perfect. That means that it is not impacting me at all; now let's try it out and see what would happen if a dog were running at me."

Quest update: Student Ritualist. 13/20.

The only problem was, quite obviously, the small truth that there was no dog here. There was only one thing to be done: he had to get down on all fours and run at the center of the ritual while barking. He waited until he was pretty sure no Dwarves would be coming into the room, and he was immediately glad that he did. The ritual registered him as a dangerous animal, due to running on at least four limbs and displaying hostile intent, the first two triggers for activating the effect. As soon as it initiated, Joe knew that it was highly unlikely that any animal would be able to function within its range.

All of his senses were enhanced to a massive degree, likely two or three thresholds above his current stats. In other words, it caused a sensory overload that his mind could barely withstand without taking damage. His nose, well... it wasn't as exactly that something in the area smelled *bad*, he could just distinguish every molecule of scent in the air. His eyes, while nothing had changed around him, allowed in light and colors that he couldn't see naturally. His ears registered exactly where every person was located in the building, as well as where they had been, based on the swirling air. Luckily, his sense of taste was unaffected, thanks to his Neutrality Aura keeping his mouth perfectly clean.

His sense of touch was by far the most devastating. Every inch of his skin felt like it had been exposed to third degree burns, then dipped in lemon salt. His silk clothing felt like sandpaper, but thankfully, his Codpiece of Holding did its job and protected his valuables. He forced himself to stand upright and utter a few words, which canceled the ritual's impact on his senses by letting it know he wasn't a beast. Immediately afterward, he fell to the ground, sweating bullets and panting as though he had just run a marathon. "That sucked so bad that I am *absolutely* going to need six of them. No, ten."

"What are you doing on the floor?" a Dwarf called from the doorway as he carried a large box out.

"Science!" Joe pointed at the ceiling and shouted. His arm involuntarily went limp, and he forced himself to his feet. "Magic, actually. Right; no idea how long I get to be here, so I need to use as much as I can."

He replicated the prototype sensory overload ritual, crafting a few copies and storing them away before he was interrupted once more. This time it was Master Stu, who for some reason seemed to be the Master of the Council that had been put in charge of conversing with the human. Joe didn't really get it, because he felt that literally any other Master would have been a better fit than this grumpy representative with a penchant for sneering at humans. "We found something that requires your expertise."

"As a Ritualist," Joe blatantly sized up the Dwarf with his eyes, "or as a Master jumper that can reach high shelves?"

"Listen *here*, you little-"

Joe chuckled, holding up a hand to mark where Stu measured up to his own chest. "Clearly 'little' is the issue here."

"Just get down here and get these swirling circles out of their faces." Stu's grumble came from deep within as he tugged on his beard in consternation. Joe followed the Dwarf at a leisurely pace down the ramp and into what appeared to be a hastily cleared storage facility. The only indication of recent use was the dust that clearly demarcated the spaces where boxes and various bits and bobs had been. Even *that* was whisked away as he passed by, his aura cleaning the place thoroughly.

"What are we looking at?" Joe wondered as he was led to a closed door with at least a dozen Dwarves gathered around it. They parted and motioned him toward the entryway.

"Can't get this open, and all attempts to smash through it have resulted in us getting blasted down the hallway." Wisps of smoke were still rising from the answering Dwarf's beard, which had clearly been recently shortened. "Figured we should ask you about it."

The human couldn't believe what he was hearing, so gave the Dwarf a hard stare. "Are you seriously telling me that you tried to *break down a door* in a Legendary building? A place so magical and so intelligent that it likely held back instead of just outright killing you for the affront? Do you know you're *impossibly* lucky that it chose to show such restraint, likely only because of how lonely it has been over the last few hundred years?"

"Yeah, couldn't get it open." The Dwarf nodded along with Joe's questions. "Anyway, tried to bust it down by hitting here, and we think the hinges-"

"Someone please tell me this guy is not in charge of cleaning this place out. Half of you are going to die otherwise." Joe scanned the group, only getting a few shrugs in response.

"No one else wanted the job of having to touch things first." the gradually less smoky Dwarf told Joe proudly. "That means I get to choose how we go about doing things!"

"You're a canary? No wonder people are letting you go wild in here." The Dwarf didn't understand Joe's reference, but he did understand when Joe simply motioned to him out of the way with a chest-deep sigh. "Let's take a look."

He reached out to the door, and a thin bolt of static electricity zapped at his fingertips. It could easily have been misconstrued as a buildup of friction, but Joe knew that it was a warning. Pitching his voice to a comforting tone, the Ritualist began speaking to the door itself. "Hey there, little guy. I'm not going to try to smash you open. Sorry about that mean old Dwarf."

"Hey!"

"Silence from the peanut gallery, please," Joe called over his shoulder without looking. "Anyway, can you tell me what conditions are needed so you can be opened?"

He waited out a momentary pause, until eventually he felt something looking at him. There were no eyes carved into the door, so he wasn't sure how it was doing that. It had to be something to do with the mana stored within the door itself. A moment later, a Ritual Circle appeared on the surface of the door, and Joe stumbled back and away, falling to his rear and crab-walking as rapidly as possible to get distance between himself and the iron-banded barrier. "*Feces!*"

"See, I told you he wouldn't be able to help." The canary, as Joe had taken to thinking of him, grabbed a door-breaching iron and held it back as though he were about to attack the barrier again. Joe Omnivaulted from his half-standing position, tackling the man and sending them both tumbling. "Oy! Are you out of your mind, *bro*?"

"Are you out of *yours*? Where are the Masters? Stu! Get over here!" Joe bellowed into the open air. "You need to get some people in here that are trained to handle dangerous artifacts, or your team is going to kill us all!"

"Listen, just because you are the teacher's pet right now, you don't get to talk to us like that." Stu stalked into the room, his posture indicating that he was ready to go on the attack. "If you think I'm going to be allowing myself to be talked to like a child, you have another thing coming."

"Oh, I guess that's fine then." Joe stood upright, brushed himself off and pretended like he was going to leave the room. "Before I go, just for kicks and giggles, how about you take a look at what's on that door over there. The one that they are trying to *smash open*?"

Out of fury more than any intent to do what he had been asked, the Master Dwarf barreled over and took a look at the door he had asked Joe to open for them. He hadn't inspected it himself previously and had only been assigned to get the human because he was passing through to the main area. The blood drained from his face at the sight of the seven-circle ritual that was etched on the otherwise plain door, parts of it fading in and out of reality as he watched. "Black-hearted abyssal Elven trogladonkeys! You were trying to *smash* this door open?"

"Well, yeah. That human was no help at all." The Dwarf that Joe had tackled brushed himself off—obviously offended that no one had come to his aid—and picked up his personal battering ram. "So anyway, I'm going to go ahead and-"

"Get out of here." Stu's eyes were practically bulging out of their sockets, and even as Joe watched, one of the capillaries burst and created a pool of blood in the sclera. "Using such a crude method in a place like this? Do you think this is some kind of Trash-ranked *slum*?"

As the entire team left the building, grumbling amongst

themselves, Stu eventually shook off his angst and turned to Joe. "What do you think this is?"

"I literally can't even tell what that circle, or *that* circle, does." Joe shook his head and waved his hands in a surrendering motion. "All I know is that the first two circles check your identity, the third circle attempts to warn off anyone who does not pass the check, the fourth circle I believe just outright kills anyone who tries to get in without the proper credentials, and I can make a very good guess about the fifth Expert-rank circle… but I couldn't tell you for certain."

"I'm betting it has something to do with killing them even harder than the last one?"

A grin flashed across Joe's face. "Took the words right out of my mouth. I think the difference is in the scale of the event it would create. If the first person was killed off and someone else was still trying to breach it, I'm pretty sure it's programmed to fill the entire area with Expert-ranked death of some kind. Could be poison, could just cause brain aneurysms for anyone in range. Either way, it's not something I want to test out for myself."

"This is most likely just a protected area," Stu muttered to himself as he used his hands to try and gauge the antechamber. "It couldn't be the Master of the building's seat of power; it's too close to the entrance. That has to be behind at least a few more layers of security."

Joe didn't have any comment on that, knowing that he wouldn't be much help in finding the most secret areas of this structure until he was at least a Grandmaster. Now knowing that there were rooms that would hold on to their secrets until he was strong enough to find them for himself, the human decided to go back to his experiments.

"Someday, I'm going to be able to walk through that door like it isn't even there," He promised himself before getting down on all fours and running at a new version of his sensory overload ritual to see if it was more effective than the last.

To his great excitement and pain: it was.

CHAPTER THIRTY-ONE

Joe received two notifications nearly back-to-back, quest completions that he had been running toward since he had first gotten access to this building. In fact, he had completed the quest requiring him to use Rare aspects first, but he didn't look at the rewards until he had activated the twentieth Student-ranked ritual. Once that criteria had been satisfied, he settled in to experience both of them at the same time... and was met by a wall of text that made him rethink his future schedule. Specifically, he decided then and there that he needed to work on his Constitution until he reached the point where he never needed to sleep again.

That was the only way that he was ever going to be able to keep up with the constantly branching quests for his class.

Quest completed: Student Ritualist. Congratulations! You have completed a step that all Students of the path of rituals must walk upon! 20/20 Student rituals drawn out and activated.

Reward: Access to Journeyman Ritualist Class quest. Tome of Lore (Beginner).

Record breaker reward: Access to quest: Student Ritualist II!

Quest completed: Apprentice Reductionist. Collected and used 10,000 Rare aspects!

Reward: +5 skill levels to any crafting skill under the Master rank. Access to quest: Student Reductionist!

First ever completion reward: Congratulations! You are the first person to ever complete this quest! As such, the base reward will be doubled, and you will gain access to quest: Apprentice Reductionist II!

Quest gained: Student Ritualist II. You aren't the typical student, are you? You are the teacher's pet, or you want to be! Nothing makes a teacher as happy as laughter, and what is Slaughter but laughter with an 's'? Kill 100 creatures with Student-ranked rituals of any type. 0/100. Reward: access to Student Ritualist III, and a template for a stationary Ritual of Slaughter (Student).

Quest gained: Journeyman Ritualist. It is the task of a Journeyman to go out and gain experience, finding new ways to enhance and practice their craft. It is also their duty to bring people onto the path behind them. To that end, establish a coven of Ritualists with at least 5 members, and guide one of them into the Student ranks with at least one Ritualist skill. Coven Established: 1/1. Student-ranked Ritualist: 0/1. Reward: Knowledge that you have brought others on the path, as well as a Journeyman-ranked utility item that will be customized to your needs.

Quest gained: Apprentice Reductionist II. How exciting! You are the first to walk this path. Just remember, being unique does not guarantee being useful! It certainly doesn't guarantee success or getting paid for doing what you enjoy. In fact, sometimes it can act as a reverse barometer, and is a direct detriment… like now! Reduce 5 items you have created that are at least Apprentice-ranked back into aspects. Reward: Access to Apprentice Reductionist III, and a permanent 10% boost to the speed of reducing items.

Quest gained: Student Reductionist. Making the system -work- today, aren't you? That's fine, it's not like we have to go and make coffee and take a cake out of the oven. Go collect Special aspects or something. 0/5,000 Special aspects collected. Reward: Special aspect usage pamphlet.

Item gained: Tome of Lore (Beginner). Gain a lore skill for the class skill or sub-skill of your choice. The selected lore skill will start halfway through the Beginner ranks.

"Wow." Joe had to read over the information a full three

times in order to fully understand everything that he had earned. "I'm gonna ask for clarification. When it says that I have doubled the reward, does that make it ten levels, or two five-level bumps that I can use?"

No answer was forthcoming, but this wasn't something that he was going to leave up to chance. He would be okay with sacrificing a couple of levels to reach the Master ranks, but he would *not* be okay with sacrificing seven. Luckily, he had a work-around that he was able to use. "Query! The thing I just tried to ask the system!"

Calculating response... answer granted! 'Reward doubled' means two different skills may increase by 5 skill levels.

Query has reached Beginner 0! Cooldown set to 18 hours! More complicated Queries may be answered!

"I've got my answer, and it was *exactly* the one that I was hoping for!" Joe literally jumped up and down, bouncing off the walls with Omnivault and screaming for joy at the top of his lungs. When he finally landed, he took a few deep breaths and decided to hold off on assigning the skill levels for just a moment. "I would like to use the Tome of Lore to gain a lore skill for... is there a lore skill for Magical Matrices?"

Tome assigned! Lore skill gained.

Calculus And Number Theory (C.A.N.T)(Beginner V): Study of calculus and number theory is extremely useful in nearly all fields of magical crafting, Ritual work, blueprints, and template design. There are very few areas within crafting untouched by this type of lore, and it will help to improve the rate of skill increase by $1n +- T\%$, where $n = lore$ skill level and $T = Tier$ difference.

"Oh, *no*. I can't *C.A.N.T.* I just can't." That was all he could get out before every instance of learning calculus and any associated skills were dredged up through his memory, highlighted, and given new meaning. A ton of new material was populated into his mind, due to adding mana and various energies as variables within the equations. There were even several 'impossible' formulas which were instantly and easily solved thanks to the new equations that had formed. Luckily, the torture stopped after only a few moments. Beginner meant *Beginner*, even if a beginner in calculus was incredibly advanced compared to the average math skills of the general population.

Drinking a large cup of coffee to calm his nerves, he checked the timer he had set for his Knowledge skill to determine how long he had been locked within the building. It was just about off of cooldown, which made perfect sense to him. "I have spent nearly eighteen hours setting up the requirements for two rituals. Kind of crazy how long it takes to make the design, versus just making the actual ritual. No *wonder* research and development teams were so highly paid back on Earth."

The timer ticked over, and the skill was available again. Not wanting to waste a moment, he activated it, bringing Alchemical Lore up to Apprentice seven. "While my cooldown is running again, let's think about that Calculus And Number Theory Lore. It looks like the positive side of this is that I'll be able to bring skills up from lower tiers into higher ones extremely quickly if I put a lot of effort into raising them. The negative is that I'm betting my head will be absolutely crawling with numbers every time I set the process in motion. I guess the only question I have to answer is… is it *worth* increasing that skill?"

Even though he was complaining, it was only reluctant grumbling. Joe knew that there was no way he could ignore this skill; it was simply too useful. As an honorary Omni-crafter thanks to his Reductionist class, having a lore skill that touched on practically everything he intended to do in the future was incredibly useful and desperately needed. Still, it *hurt* to have numbers shoved into his head like that. Hopefully it would never be so intense again. In all fairness, he *had* just gained a tier and a half of knowledge in a single go.

"Finally on to the fun part." He skimmed through his skill list, practically shivering in anticipation. "Assign five skill points to Ritual Magic, as well as to Ritual Circles."

Caution! Assigning the skill points to Ritual Magic will result in reaching Master 0, losing 2 free skill points in the process. Proceed?

Caution! Assigning the skill points to Ritual Circles will result in reaching Master 0, losing 1 free skill point in the process. Proceed?

"Yes to both." He had been working at those skills for the entire duration of his existence in this world, nearly to the exclusion of everything else, and he had only been able to break through whatever wall had been blocking him by encountering a *door,* of all things. "Yup, I am absolutely ready to skip a couple of steps."

Ritual Magic has reached Master 0! Congratulations! All of your hard work in studying every aspect of your class, going the extra mile to bring your sub-skills to a high level, and dedication to your craft over what has likely been decades has come to fruition: you have become a Master at Ritual Magic! As this is the governing class skill for all class sub-skills, all class sub-skills will experience a 10% increase in growth rate until they have reached the Master Rank. We hope that this will benefit you at least slightly in your journey toward Grandmaster!

Ritual Circles has reached Master 0! Congratulations! Your dedication to pretty shapes, painful and expensive experiments, as well as destroying your enemies and sending them fleeing before you has brought you to the first true point of success! There is a great benefit to being a Master of Ritual Circles: you can now create any ritual circle in the Novice, Beginner, or Apprentice rank instantly if you are able to maintain a perfect mental image of the circle and provide the required materials.

Caution! Losing control of the mental image may cause side-effects. Not recommended during combat.

You have reached Master rank in three different skills! As one of the first 10 Travelers to do so, you have earned a title: Skill Ace!

Skill Ace: This is a cosmetic title that shows you have mastered three different skills! Wear it proudly to inform others of your success. Caution: accepting this title will require you giving up one of your other titles, as you are at the current maximum of ten!

"Excellent, I needed a title that I could throw away. Pass." Joe rolled his eyes at the thought of actually equipping such a braggadocious title. "I mean, if it actually *did* something, yeah. But like this? I would be the laughingstock of any other Masters. I bet they keep an eye out for anyone bold enough to get caught wearing something like this, just to tease them for getting too big for their britches. I know I would."

He was absolutely giddy, and couldn't wait to see how the changes would impact his ability to function as a Ritualist. Completely unable to wait, he called up the simplest ritual that he knew, a Ritual of Glimmering, and held out his inscribing tool. He tapped the air, and the Novice-ranked ritual appeared. After inspecting it for a moment, he started dancing in place. "It still cost the same amount in aspects, but just on that Circle alone, I got back a solid ten seconds of drawing out an image. When I get to the next circles... how much time is this going to save me? *Hours*, in some instances."

Sure, he'd have to factor in the small detail that he would need to either have an image reference in front of him, or have memorized every single twist and turn of the circle he was trying to create, but he understood in an instant how useful the application would be. "This makes combat rituals even more viable, even with that warning. When I'm trying to explain Ritual Circles to my students, I'm going to be able to make them appear with a thought, which will drive them to practice even harder in hopes of being able to do that themselves... not to mention how mind-bogglingly cool I'm going to look doing it."

It was the last part that excited him the most, and he was just fine with that.

CHAPTER THIRTY-TWO

As there is no current owner to the Grand Ritual Hall, you have been granted moderator access! As this is a Legendary building, only a Grand-master of Ritual Magic(s) has the credentials necessary in order to attain ownership, but you are now allowed to enter more areas, access additional information, and control certain portions of the building, such as defenses.

"Moderator access?" That was all Joe was able to get out before the benefits list appeared in his face again, but he removed most of it so that he could focus on the important new line.

Benefit discovered!

Grand Ritual Hall (Legendary) accessible benefits.

4) NEW! Access granted. You are now able to grant access to any person, group, class, or anyone with an identifying feature in a singular or wide-scale manner. Any person not granted access will need to defeat the entire range of defenses and durability in order to force entrance.

5) Access not granted.

"Okay, that's interesting. Is there a list of what sort of defenses this building has? Or am I supposed to build up some myself?" Once again, there was no answer to his inquiry, but he hadn't particularly been expecting one. It was likely that only the owner of the building would be able to discover all of the weapons and traps at its disposal. Otherwise, even someone who was a moderator like him could plan against those protections and gain entry to the building by force, if it came down to that.

Joe decided that he needed to inform the Grandmaster about his improved Master status, certainly not to brag, but to grant them access to deeper areas. If the fact that he was a Master three times over came off a little bit cocky, that was just how things went sometimes. He had not expected to find her in a room full of Dwarves who were all stone-faced and furious. "What's going on?"

"I'm not sure yet, but we may have an issue very soon," Grandmaster Snow informed him evasively. "What can we do for you right now, Joe?"

"*Human.*" Stu growled out a low rumble. "The only newcomers to the city, and the only people with a reason to-"

"Enough of that, *Master* Stu," Snow stated frostily. "Joe?"

The Ritualist looked around at the hard faces, well-aware that something was up. Something had gone wrong, and they weren't sure who to blame yet, so it was best to just pass along what he needed to tell them and get back to work, unless he wanted to get more involved. He didn't. That was what a policing force was for, and he hoped it was an issue that could be taken care of by them. "I wanted to let you know that I achieved Master status for my governing class skill, as well as one of the sub-skills."

He had decided to keep it vague given the audience; there was no benefit in telling people exactly what he could do, especially when they were acting in such a hostile manner toward him. Snow clapped excitedly, a single time, then looked at the space above his head. "Decided against using the Ace title, did you?"

Joe knew that this was likely a test to ensure that he actually had achieved new mastery, so called out the *actual* title. "I rejected the title 'Skill Ace', as I am already filled up on titles, and because it is… gaudy."

Out of the corner of his eye, he saw one of the Masters sigh and hand a thick gem to one of his fellows. Joe hoped that had been a standing bet, and not something directed at him specifically. Stu butted in once more. "Does that mean you can open up more of this place? Did you get higher access?"

"Moderator access," Joe admitted without a hint of hesitation. There was no reason to hide his cards here, since he was only allowed in this location by remaining in their good favor. "Right now, I can grant access to anyone that you would like to allow within these walls."

Calculating smiles broke out around the table, and Grandmaster Snow raised a white eyebrow. "If I asked you to grant access to any member of our Council, even to make them a moderator, which you should have the privilege of doing, then asked you to leave… what would you say?"

He wanted to say that there was no chance of that happening, that they would need him the entire time if he was going to let them continue searching through the building. It was only a flash of greed, and he managed to contain himself before he said anything foolish. "I would say, if that is what you truly want, I will be disappointed… but I will act according to your instructions."

"Please grant me moderator access immediately," Snow ordered him without hesitation. Joe had been expecting that, but it still rankled to have to give up such a nifty level of power. Even so, he was a man of his word and would not impinge his honor over something that was not his to begin with. Joe searched through the options and found the method required to grant moderator access to another. Selecting Grandmaster Snow, he gave her as much authority over the building as he had.

Instantly, she relaxed. Her smile melted from bitter to true and warm. "It wasn't him; no enemy of the High City of Deep Thought would act against his own interests so easily."

The other Dwarves nodded, but they didn't relax as much as the Grandmaster had. However, their wariness and hostility had vanished without a trace. Joe decided that he wanted to know more, even if he didn't want to be directly involved. "Can someone please explain to me what has happened? When I walked in here, you all looked like someone had just asked you to test how hard you had to bite a core before it exploded in your mouth."

His attempt at making a new reference fell flat, but they evidently chalked it up to cultural differences. A Master—the one that had passed out when Joe had explained that he had built his own Ritual Hall—cleared his throat and answered him directly. "I am Master Dreamstrider. I work as the head of intelligence-gathering and predictive force for the Council. During my most recent astral projection, I walked through the realm of Alfheim and discovered that a massive invasion force was surrounding the base of the mountain that our city is built upon."

There was a pregnant pause as all of the Dwarves in the room watched Joe's expression carefully. Luckily, he didn't need to feign his horror. *"Abyss.* How did they know? How did they find this mountain out of the entire range? Did they breach the path upward, or are they-"

"The attack has already begun," Master Dreamstrider informed him heavily. "The goat path is being erased as we speak, as the Elves set up shrines to their Pantheon that influence the very energy of the world around them. They don't need to exhaust themselves; all they need to do now is wait for our first line of defense to fall on its own."

"How much time do we have? What can we do… should we attack preemptively, or defend the city?" Unbeknownst to Joe, the fact that he said 'we' in reference to the defense of the people was doing more to get the Council on his side than anything he had done to this point.

"No…" Grandmaster Snow stated softly. "All we can do is begin preparations for evacuation. The city was never meant to withstand a sustained siege, and you have given us the mechanism for our survival. We will escape with you to your town, hauling all the resources we can carry as we plan our resistance to our new Elven overlords."

The Ritualist fell silent for a few seconds as he tried to think of anything he could do to ease the pain they must be feeling at this moment. As far as he could tell, the city had stood for hundreds of years, perhaps thousands. Yet, they were abandoning it at the drop of a hat. If it was shocking to *him*, he had no idea how dumbfounded *they* must be. "I don't know what to say."

"The worst part is that we will not be able to bring the vast majority of our resources with us. There is simply no way to expand the portal device you brought beyond what Havoc intended without damaging it and reducing the amount of time we will be able to use it for. Any Enchanter could open it wide for a few minutes, but after that, it would snap closed and become scrap." Snow turned back to her conversation with the Dwarves. "Fill every spatial container to the brim, prepare everyone for evacuation, and set the defenses in place to ensure we will have enough time once the goat path has been turned into an invasion superhighway."

"Wait, what about the Grand Ritual Hall?" Joe questioned suddenly. "What is going to become of this building?"

"We will remove the Keystone from the teleportation device." A surprisingly sweet voice came from one of the mustachioed Masters. "Without that, the teleportation pad will send whoever attempts to use it to a random location, but certainly not here. We have no fear that the Elves will destroy the enchantment, but they will hunt our people for the Keystone until the end of our race, then turn their eyes towards any human that might have run off with it."

That was better, and worse, than Joe had been hoping for. In his mind, he had expected that they would be able to take the entire teleportation array with them and jump to the Sage's Summit from anywhere. That was a foolish hope, and he knew it had been, as the physical location of the teleportation entrance was just as important as the magic required to empower it. Then again, what if they never needed the teleportation array? "I might have a solution…"

Silence filled the space as the Dwarves waited for him to finish his thought.

"What would you think if I said we might be able to take the Grand Ritual Hall with us?"

CHAPTER THIRTY-THREE

His thoughts required further clarification to the Council, but once he had answered to their satisfaction, they had flown into action. There was only a slim chance of his plan working—and he made sure they knew that—but Joe had gained a ritual from leveling up his class that he just *might* be able to create, thanks to this building. The Ritual of the Traveling Civilization was a Grandmaster-ranked ritual, and under normal circumstances, he would have no hope whatsoever of bringing the final circle to completion. Not with his current understanding and power level.

But now, with the additional stability provided by the building, as well as the fact that he would be able to craft the Grandmaster circle as though it were a Master circle—therefore only requiring Artifact-ranked aspects for the final two circles—there was a chance of it succeeding. In terms of supplying the necessary mana and resources, he would have the entire city at his disposal, as per the order of the Grandmaster.

Putting the idea into practice meant that he would have plenty of people donating their personal energy, and since the city was expected to fall, he would be able to acquire and use as many resources as possible in the intervening time. To start things off, Joe began creating Rituals of Raze ceaselessly, until he reached the point where he could have instantly created the first three circles in his sleep.

As he used Somatic Ritual Casting the entire time, he was able to bring that skill to the cusp of the Apprentice ranks. He handed the rituals out to the Masters, who distributed them to areas with high-power Mages so that *they* could knock down any building not deemed necessary for the next few days of survival.

The benefit provided by this ritual was something that the Dwarves normally did not achieve. Usually when a building was destroyed, for whatever reason, the materials that went into creating it were completely lost. At best, they could expect one-fifth of the input materials to remain in a usable condition by the time they were done. With his ritual, over ninety percent of the materials were stacked neatly and carted into a huge ware-house, where Joe was waiting with a Field Array to convert those materials into aspects. Beyond simply collecting what he needed, he was able to complete one of his quests in a literal record time.

Quest complete: Student Reductionist. Special aspects collected 5,000/5,000.

Reward: Special aspect usage pamphlet.

Record breaker reward: Access to Student Reductionist II!

Quest gained: Student Reductionist II. Now that you have collected a large amount of special aspects, try them out by using them to create at least five Unique crafted items. Reward: A forging blueprint useful to your class.

Item gained: Special aspect usage pamphlet. This pamphlet contains a list of the most common special aspects you are likely to encounter! It is not exhaustive, but it should give you a good idea on how aspects can be used and combined to add interesting new final touches to your crafts!

Not having time to peruse interesting little tidbits like the pamphlet, Joe worked tirelessly for the next several days as the Elven incursion slowly but steadily pushed their way toward the top of the mountain. Only the fact that the pointy-eared invaders knew they didn't need to hurry was keeping the

Dwarves alive for the time being. It was also greatly working in their favor and increasing their odds of survival by leaps and bounds, as any people deemed non-essential were evacuated to The Shoe.

Once Joe stopped converting materials into aspects, he had already accrued at least twenty percent more than he needed, including a good amount of Artifact-ranked aspects. Even so, he only had twenty-five Legendary aspects at his disposal, which he had been holding on to for months. It was his hope that he would not need to use them for any reason, as he intended to slowly build up a store of them to create an aspect jar. In fact, that was his plan for all of his extras. If he could manage to create the Natural Aspect Jar, he would never have to consider deconstructing nearly an entire city to fund a single ritual again.

That would be nice.

Returning to the Sage's Summit after checking in on his friends and making sure they were being treated well, Joe settled in to work on the Ritual Diagram, the most intense and important ritual he had created yet. He had more than one chance to succeed, but if he was forced to go back and gather more aspects, he didn't know if he would be able to escape with the rest of the population. He would be happy to remain trapped on the Sage's Summit, but something told him that would not work out very well for him. The lack of food was telling, and there was only enough space on the meteor floating in geosynchronous orbit around the Zone to hold a single building.

The fact remained: once he used up everything he had brought with him, there would be no additional influx of resources to use. "Gotta get the job done, then get outta here."

Not wanting to waste a moment, he dove in straightaway. As per usual, when generating a new ritual for the first time, everything took longer than it needed to. While the first three circles didn't appear instantly, it was still pretty quick to shape the diagram burned into his mind thanks to the ritual goo. With the knowledge placed directly in his brain, he knew that he *could* attempt to instantly make the circles, but the idea that even tiny discrepancies might exist made Joe sweat. He wasn't going to take any chances. Everything was going to be triple checked.

The fourth circle, the Student Circle, was a breeze due to the enhanced stability granted by the Grand Ritual Hall. The same could be said of the Journeyman Circle, but the real trouble began at the start of the Expert Circle. Joe was carving the circle into a specially prepared Enchantment Stone that Snow had given him, which would allow him to draw length and width, as *well* as depth. But he quickly found that doing so was nearly the same as attempting to draw directly in the air.

Even with the enhanced stability, the aspects flowing out of him were a massive pain to control properly. They were mentally heavy, and every scratch of his inscribing tool—which left a streak of burning light that was captured by the stone— felt like he was hoisting a twenty-five pound kettlebell into the air by *staring* at it really hard. Giving it everything that he had, he was only barely able to put the final marks in place, completing the Expert circle.

Somatic Ritual Casting has reached Student 0. Congratulations on becoming a Student of super-magical jazz hands. Skill information has been updated: When creating Student ritual circles, the stability of the circle is set at 100% for the first three portions, and $60+n\%$ where $n =$ skill level in the Student rank. Each rank of ritual circle above Apprentice will be calculated at $60+n-25T$ where T is each tier above Student.

Mana Manipulation has reached Journeyman 0! To be a Journeyman is to go out and influence the world around you. You get to do that in a more literal sense! You are now able to manipulate the ambient mana around you in a $n/10$ foot radius. Current range: 4 foot radius.

Immediately, Joe felt much refreshed, as his governing skills for creating rituals in midair broke through the bottlenecks that had been holding them back. A good portion of the strain he had been feeling vanished, and he decided that it was time to take a break. With the Expert circle completed, he had at least a short while before the overall ritual would start degrading, and he needed to verify whether there was anything he could do to make the next two circles more manageable.

Several of the Masters were lounging around, keeping an eye on him as he worked. Frankly, he felt like he should be charging them rent for allowing them to observe a Master at work, seeing as they would have if they were in his shoes. But before he could make a snarky comment, one of them noticed that he was no longer working and decided to speak up. "Looks like you were getting to the edge of your limits. What are you going to do? By the looks of the goo circles still floating around the fiery ones there, you're nowhere near done."

"I know that I *can* do the next one," Joe stated grimly, "But you are correct to say that the one after that, the Grandmaster circle, is going to be touch and go the entire time. I just don't have any experience with that level of circle. Abyss, I'm only Master zero in making these blasted things. In fact... blast is probably a good descriptor of what is coming. I know this is interesting to watch, but you all might want to make a run for it while you can."

"Think you're going to melt down?" another of the Masters chimed in, smiling knowingly. "Let me tell you something; if you think it's going to happen, it *will*. Now, I'm going to offer some help. Let me be clear, this is not coming from a place of altruism—it is coming from a desire to do everything to survive and get into position to drop a turd in the Elves' cereal-"

"*What?*"

"-making sure they get *nothing* from us if possible. What, you've never heard that before? It's just another way of saying 'force a Pyrrhic victory', so I would have thought *you* of all people would get it." The Dwarf chuckled at the range of emotion contorting the human's face. "Why do you think we have a Council of Masters, as well as a governing Grandmaster? We can all help each other and lend our expertise where possible. I don't know what she's going to say—most likely yes—but it looks like your biggest hurdle is fine control over the mana and energy that is being siphoned into those circles... so why not ask whether the Grandmaster will help keep it from... imploding?"

Another among the group muttered, "I'd help just so he doesn't accidentally take me out while I'm just sitting here. If those Elves want my head, I want them to have to work for it."

"I can impact stability," yet another claimed.

"If you are all willing to work with me to make this happen," a few more assenting noises confirmed the offers, and Joe started to feel hope that this ritual might actually reach completion, "let's snatch this prize away right from under the Elves' pointy noses!"

CHAPTER THIRTY-FOUR

"Have you ever worked with a group to cast a spell before?" Grandmaster Snow questioned Joe intently as she stared at the ritual. They needed to get back to it soon, or it would start to unravel in a fashion most glorious.

The Ritualist bobbed his head in acknowledgment. "Very often. I have sometimes guided more than a dozen people through participating in one of my rituals."

The Grandmaster waved off his excitement, even as a couple of the less savory Masters snickered at his statement. "That's not what I mean. Injecting mana is not the same as delicately sharing control of the power you are wielding. Let me give an example: to cast a war spell, an artillery spell, or simply a higher-tier spell than a single person could manage on their own, a group can work together to cast in tandem. There could be a single person shaping the spell while the others simply provide mana, but that is a completely different experience than what I am describing."

"No, then." Joe was starting to feel anxious. The Dwarves had made this sound like it was going to be a sure-fire thing, but what if his lack of ability to work in a group came back to haunt him, just as it had in his attempts at higher education; or when he had accidentally killed the Archmage in a particularly horrific manner, or-

"That shouldn't be too much of an issue, though it would have been nice to practice when the stakes were not so high." The Grandmaster regarded the circle and seemed to be considering all of the information that Joe had given her over the last few days. "One last question before we get started. You mentioned that this Legendary building will allow you to create rituals with materials from a tier lower. Does that apply only to the final circle, or can you substitute lower-tier material throughout? That would help to reduce the strain tremendously."

Joe stared at her for a long moment, shifted his gaze to the circle floating in mid-air, and cursed softly. "Abyss."

"I take it to mean that it is the latter." Snow couldn't hide her smile as the other Masters laughed uproariously. "Take this as an incredibly expensive lesson that all of us have had to learn. The rules *as written* are to be used as such. You can interpret the rules however you like, but always be on the lookout for technicalities. In a very real way, this circle right here could have the same basic price as one of these Master's workshops. It might have once *been* one of their workshops, in fact."

Nothing could have stopped the laughter coming from the Masters faster than being hit with the memory that Joe was *not* personally funding this venture—like *they* had been when they made the similar mistake earlier in their careers. A few of them even tugged on their beards or mustaches in a show of barely-contained frustration, but their nonchalant reaction to the egregious error certainly helped to put Joe more at ease. The greedy, hoarding raccoon portion of his brain was also squealing in delight and rubbing its hands at the realization that he would likely walk away with enough Artifact aspects to create a high-quality aspect jar.

"Begin the process, attempt to listen to my instructions, and let my control of Mana Manipulation guide you. No, let me help you lift the burden; *you* must guide the process." Grand-master Snow heaved a weary sigh as she realized how long it had been since she could not be the guide for someone of a lower rank. "Make sure that you are using discolored fire of a lower rank than needed."

"I don't think I would make that same mistake twice." Joe pulled out his inscribing tool, following along with the ritual goo that vanished as he wrote in the same spot it had previously occupied.

"I still thought I ought to say it once more," Grandmaster Snow mentioned lightly. "Judging by your incredulous expression, I think it might be difficult for you to understand just how often something like that has occurred over the years. When you have students, you will see *exactly* what sort of mischief they can get up to, and how often they will repeat mistakes that you warn them away from."

The smile dropped from Joe's face as he remembered what had happened the last time he gave instructions to students and expected them to be followed. He had been exiled from Midgard, hundreds of thousands had died, and he was likely being put into songs as the newest boogeyman of that plane. "I will make sure to… keep that in mind."

Then the time for conversation was over, as all of his attention was concentrated on not blowing up the Dwarven Council around him. Or the building. Or himself. In that order.

Over the next several hours, as a fresh circle of indigo fire was sketched around the previous one, various Masters spoke up to guide Joe's hand. Depending on their skill set, the advice was sometimes extremely helpful, while in other cases it only eased his movements a little. Ultimately, the fact of the matter was that everyone brought something to the table. If the Grand-master decided to speak up, she was offering a cornucopia of goodies. Sometimes, one of the Master's comments would only be a slice of bread in comparison; but to a starving man, even that much was a precious gift.

Hours later, the Master-rank circle was completed using

Expert-rank aspects, and Joe fell to the ground, panting for breath. "That was an *amazing* rush."

Each of the Masters offered their own cheerful comments. Even for them, getting the opportunity to work on a Master-rank craft was somewhat of a rarity. Seeing the intricate diagram being built in person lit a fire of passion in all of their hearts; one that wouldn't leave them a charred husk, like the ritual would if it failed. Snow inspected his work, and Joe watched anxiously as she went over each layer.

This Dwarf had more experience with magic than he could even imagine, Joe was sure of it. That fact made it deeply satisfying for him to catch a slight wrinkle of confusion on her forehead when she was studying the ritual from certain angles, or when she opened her mouth to voice a concern, only to close it as she partially solved her question without uttering a sound. The best part came when she was closely scrutinizing one section of the Ritual Circle, only for it to phase out of reality in front of her eyes and vanish entirely.

That was the best part, because she let out a small scream of terror and fell on her butt, only to be caught by the ritual goo as Joe created a chair under her. "Is there an issue, Grandmaster?"

She glared in his direction momentarily, but couldn't hold the expression. Relief flooded her entire demeanor as she took a deep breath. "I thought the ritual was beginning to fall apart, and standing so close would have meant that the resulting damage would blast directly through my defenses, no matter how prepared I was. If I might ask... what happened to the circle there?"

Joe could only shrug. "Your guess is as good as mine, but based on what my class is whispering in my ear, when a ritual reaches the Master rank, it is no longer only impacting the physical world. This ritual in particular is designed to move entire *cities* at a time, if we can figure out how to supply enough mana and space to accomplish it. My best guess is that the ritual is bonding not only to the other circles, but to a slightly out-of-phase dimension. I could be wrong, but that is what it looked like when I accidentally chucked myself into the abyss."

That admission made her pause, but she shook her head and continued with her line of questioning, instead of allowing her curiosity to derail the entire conversation to delve into an off-topic inquiry like Joe would have done. "What a strange and impressive design. I can't wait to see what the next circle will look like when it reaches completion."

"Frankly, I have no idea." Joe shivered slightly as he accessed the Grandmaster portion of the ritual in his mind. He had no idea what the completed circle actually looked like; his conscious thoughts unable to grasp the slippery concepts embodied in the design. "That is a whole tier above me, and I would have never *thought* of trying to build this ritual without the assistance of the Grand Ritual Hall. Somehow, it simplifies the equations and false realities created by such a high-tier circle, and... my concern is that those simplifications will make the final product come out much weaker than it would have otherwise."

Snow reached over and grasped his elbow, the highest point she could easily reach to offer physical comfort. "All of us understood that this was a long shot, don't worry. If worse comes to worst, we will follow through with what we had planned all along. We'll remove the keystone and make a run for it. Someday, we can only hope that we will be able to come back here, either by force or by stealth, and reclaim our heritage. I hope at that time that you will take on a few students that I recommend. I truly believe that our civilization will be greatly benefited by following this path of magic and developing it in our own way."

"Nothing would make me happier than to be able to share knowledge with you and people you trust." Joe stared at the dull black circle surrounding the other multi-hued, iridescent ones. "I think we should get back to it while we are still fresh. I have no idea how long this is going to take, or what sort of effort we will need to put into it... but I am ready to go if you all are."

"Not like we can let some wet-behind-the-ears human upstage our Constitution," Stu called sarcastically, which Joe knew was his forte. "After all, the real Masters here are Dwarves!"

"I think Joe is a Dwarf where it counts," Grandmaster Snow commented, tapping Joe on the chest. "In his heart."

"Oh, his *heart*. Sure. Why not be a Dwarf where no one can test the authenticity of that claim? I thought you meant somewhere else," Stu sniped with a salacious grin and wink, eliciting a few catcalls from the other bearded Masters, as well as eyerolls from the mustachioed ones. Joe chuckled appreciatively; it was nice to see that some things transcended species. "Want to show us, human? Like a length of rebar holding a pentagon, am I right?"

"Too far, Stu," Snow warned the Dwarf as she tied his lips shut with a rapid stitching of mana.

Joe wasn't even concerned about the joke going too far; he was cringing too hard at the mental image of what Dwarven anatomy must be like for a comment like that to roll off the tongue so easily. "Let's... how about we just get back to it?"

Before anyone could nay-say him or continue on with a side conversation, Joe created an inscribing tool at the Master rank for the first time ever. Just as before, he bent his mind to the task, creating a wholly unique item that resembled a wildly impressive writing utensil. He settled on a steampunk-style base, designing whirling gears and small dials that indicated things like total pressure on the nib of the inscriber, the time, or the flow rate of aspects.

Generally speaking, something so complex wouldn't be possible without high levels of proficiency in mechanical or golemancy professions. The only reason he could get away with it was that the entire item was formed out of a single aspect, and was a self-contained unit that had a singular purpose. None of the functions particularly mattered; it simply needed to be considered 'Artifact quality' in order for Artifact aspects to run through it. It was a strange requirement, but one that he was not opposed to in the slightest. It certainly made him *look* like he had fancy tools and knew what he was doing.

No one in any world needed to know that he was flying by the seat of his pants ninety-five percent of the time.

With his tools ready, the Grandmaster ritual-circle-but-actually-a-stencil in place, and a troop of incredibly powerful Dwarves to ease his way forward, Joe reached forward and touched his inscribing tool to the diagram, and began rewriting the physics of the world.

CHAPTER THIRTY-FIVE

"What just happened?" Joe blinked as his senses came back to him, his head swimming with fatigue and questioning his very existence. Something about him felt... stretched. As though he had overexerted himself in a way that left his muscles over-worked, strained, and on the verge of snapping—but not quite broken. "Did it explode?"

"No, we all lived through the experience." Grandmaster Snow's voice was hushed, and Joe truly appreciated that fact. Even with her taking care to keep her voice down, Joe's mind was in *incredible* pain. Even his sensory overload ritual had not been able to impact his wellbeing to such an agonizing extent. He was so tired that he wanted to throw up and pass out in the puddle, in the hopes that he might drown in the bile and sleep forever. "We made it happen. You completed it."

"Auto... Mate..." Joe managed to squeak out the words, earning both a confused glance and a stream of crystallized caffeine that penetrated his neck and was injected directly into his veins. It hit his heart in the next instant, spreading through his body and passing the blood-brain barrier within five seconds. He tilted his head back and roared at the ceiling, finally having the energy to explode with jubilation. "*We did it!*"

The other Masters—more used to this level of exertion and fine control for what felt like days on end—were also cheerful, but nowhere near his level. A small notification symbol kept flashing in the corner of Joe's vision, and he eagerly pulled up the screen to learn exactly what had transpired.

As this is the first time you have created a ~~Grandmaster~~ ... created a degraded Grandmaster ritual, counted as Master-rank for all purposes, an instant skill level and experience have been gained.

You have gained 1,600 Reductionist class experience.

You have gained 2,000 experience.

Level up! You have reached Reductionist level 4! Congratulations, you have taken a huge step toward being able to transmute anything... into anything else! There is no bonus other than a wink and a nod to boost your excitement for what is coming at level 5!

Ritual Magic has reached Master 1! All characteristics except Karmic Luck have been increased by 5!

Ritual Circles has reached Master 1! All characteristics except Karmic Luck have been increased by 5!

Somatic Ritual Casting has reached Student VIII!

Mana Manipulation has reached Journeyman I!

Coalescence has reached Journeyman I!

Magical Matrices has reached Journeyman 0! Your ability to impact the world is based on understanding the world around you. The barrier between your mind and the understanding of the potential of Karmic Luck has thinned slightly.

You have successfully created a Ritual of the Traveling Civilization (Master).

- *This ritual must be assigned to an item at least 10 feet long by 10 feet wide. It is highly recommended to use a material that is difficult to damage.*
- *Once the ritual has been assigned, it will spawn sub-rituals that can be attached to any building that is owned by the user of the ritual, has permission from the owner, or has no owner.*

- *Upon the sub-ritual being assigned, the parent ritual can be activated to relocate the assigned building and any necessary attached land anywhere there is space for it within range of the parent ritual.*
- *As this ritual is a degraded version of the Grandmaster design, it can only be used to relocate buildings up to Artifact rarity. The cost of relocation will be based exclusively on the size and rarity of the building.*
- *If the parent ritual, or the item it is assigned to, reaches 0 durability or time remaining, both will be destroyed. As this is a Master ritual, the length of time it can continue to run can be increased by sacrificing cores. Higher Rarity cores will increase the amount of remaining time significantly.*

As he perused the messages, Joe felt a phantom strangling his neck at the thought of increasing Ritual Magic any further. Now that it had reached Master one, there was a nearly *tangible* bottleneck that had sprung up to stop any further progression, and only the previous advice from the Grandmaster allowed him to keep from panicking. "All I gotta do is get all of my other sub-skills up to a decent level, and this issue should fix itself. Celestial feces, no wonder people are excited about increasing their levels to the Master ranks and beyond. Five characteristic points per skill level? That was *insane*, even if the level of effort could easily be compared to training for weeks or months at a time... or decades, if you're following something that doesn't fit, I suppose."

Finally his attention dropped down to the completed ritual, and his heart fell into his stomach. All of the plans they had made, all of the effort that had gone into making it, and it was all for nothing. He turned to the Grandmaster, his head hanging in shame. "I am sorry to report... the ritual cannot take this building. Because it is considered to be only of the Master rank, it can only move Artifact rank or lesser buildings."

All voices in the area stopped, and each Dwarf had their own internal reaction. The Grandmaster took it with good grace, though he could see that she was deeply troubled. "I understand… this was always a possibility, but I had certainly hoped for a different outcome. We will proceed with removing the Keystone. On a positive note, I am pleased to announce that my moderator privileges have allowed us to strip the Grand Ritual Hall of all items that we believe will be useful to us in the coming months. Thanks to you, we will be able to retain our history, as well as bring a greater arsenal to all remaining battles for the survival of our species."

Joe somberly stowed the ritual in his codpiece, knowing that even though it wouldn't work for what he had intended, there was a good shot it would be useful in the future. Along with all the others, he filed over to the teleportation array, and waited for his turn to return to the High City of Deep Thought. While he waited for the transport to be activated, he decided to browse his character sheet and inspect the changes.

Name: Joe 'Excommunicated' Class: Reductionist
Profession I: Arcanologist (Max)
Profession II: Ritualistic Alchemist (1/20)
Profession III: Grandmaster's Apprentice (14/25)
Profession IV: None.
Character Level: 23 Exp: 279,833 Exp to next level: 20,167
Rituarchitect Level: 10 Exp: 53,700 Exp to next level: 1,300
Reductionist Level: 4 Exp: 10,436 Exp to next level: 4,564
Hit Points: 2,327/2,327
Mana: 8,160/8,160
Mana regen: 67.83/sec
Stamina: 1,837/1,837
Stamina regen: 6.64/sec

Characteristic: Raw score

Strength (bound): 176
Dexterity: 177
Constitution: 169

Intelligence (bound): 185
Wisdom: 168
Dark Charisma: 123
Perception: 173
Luck: 110
Karmic Luck: 14

It was an impressive change, even more so because Joe realized he hadn't looked over it in quite a while. As he grew stronger, his small increments seemed less impressive, even though he knew that each increase was wildly important. After all, research and application during the minutes and hours of active work seemed to take forever, but real progress was only measured in months and years—and those were seeming to fly by far too quickly.

A quiet *hum*, as well as a strange tingling sensation across the surface of his body, drew Joe from his introspection as he looked up at the teleportation array. The sensation it had created was not something he had ever felt before, but the slight ringing in his ears indicated that the feeling certainly had something to do with a powerful magical object being activated nearby. "This must be the effect of bringing Mana Manipulation to Journeyman. Since I can impact nearby ambient mana, I must be able to feel when it is being shifted. Now I understand what Cleave was warning me about when I was using my high-tier skills. That's going to take some getting used to-"

His musing was cut off as he was dropped without warning through thousands of tons of stone, cast into the void surrounding the Zone, and rapidly approached the city far below. He expected his bones to shatter from the force as he hit the ground, but the only noticeable sensation was one of rapid deceleration, and not pain. Grandmaster Snow gave him a small hug, then shooed him out the door. "We will see each other again soon. Why don't you go on ahead and find your friends? They should be waiting for you, and we are going to head straight for evacuation. I have to tell you, I'm looking forward to seeing Havoc again after all this time. He always has the most *fun* ideas, and now that there is no one to stop him from putting them into practice... well. I'm looking forward to it."

"The words that just came out of your mouth were terrifying." Joe didn't wait any longer, aware that she was chuckling instead of nodding along seriously. As he made his way from the Council holdings to the general evacuation site, he could spot spells arcing up over the walls of the city, only to be snuffed out as they either hit a barrier or met an enchantment that was protecting the people within the city. "Looks like the Elves are close enough to not be so passive anymore. I hope I can find-"

"I'm *so* glad we're back together, Joe! I got stuck in a little room, and they just kept *feeding* me!" Jaxon wailed as he threw himself at his party leader, seemingly materializing from nowhere. "It was like attending a convention full of grandmas in a mega-kitchen where the door gets barred behind you. Then they suddenly got *mean* because the Elves found this place right after we got here! But they knew where I was the entire time, so they stopped being angry and just started feeding me again. Eventually I had to bring out Lefty, Lefty, Lefty, Lefty, Lefty, and Terror just so that I could tunnel my way out of there in time to escape with you."

"I thought they were having a food shortage here, or something like that?" Major Cleave joined the conversation as she arrived to travel through the portal with them. Joe spotted Daniella hurrying toward them as well. "How would they... was it just that they were getting rid of all of their excess food, and you wouldn't get out of the way? Did, *no*, it can't be... Jaxon, is there any chance that you spent the last several days in a dumpster?"

"Little of this, little of that." Jaxon waved off the question. "Sometimes you just need a nap in an enclosed space to feel safe in a new area."

As happy as he was to see his team, Joe had no idea how they were all arriving at the same time. "Did you guys get directed toward me or something? Is there some kind of a beacon above me that tells you where I am?"

"Ah… kinda." Daniella had drawn close enough to hear his question, and she blushed cutely as she pointed to her own head, then his. "It's just about noon right now, and no one else's head reflects light *quite* like yours does. I don't know if you realize this, but you also, um, glitter."

Her explanation stopped Joe in his tracks, and he faced-palmed as he remembered that he had never figured out a way to mitigate the refraction of his Exquisite Shell. That, combined with his bald head once-curse-now-trait—which made all light reflecting off of him seem much brighter than normal—probably made his skull look like a disco ball. "I should put some effort into manipulating the functionality of that spell. I bet I could make it perfectly transparent if I work with it hard enough."

"*I* like it," Jaxon told him resolutely. "It helps me find you when it gets foggy. You're like Rudolph the red-nosed reindeer."

"Always looking at the bright side; thanks, Jaxon." Joe heaved a sigh, but he couldn't keep himself from grinning.

"Around you? There's no other choice!"

"…*Thanks*, Jaxon."

CHAPTER THIRTY-SIX

Explosions, as well as various natural and magical phenomena, were being generated by the increasingly brutal attacks on the city walls. The line for the portal into The Shoe was moving quickly, but Havoc had only been able to alter the structural integrity of the portal enough to allow two people to go through side by side. Even with as quickly as the Dwarves were moving, running an entire city through took time, especially when they all wanted to bring everything they could carry with them.

The delays created some serious tension, and when a meteor hit one of the walls, knocking off the top quarter and clearly penetrating the magical defenses of the city, people started to panic. The Dwarves began pushing, and the humans that were waiting for their turn—they were last, since they could respawn—became ever grimmer. It was practically a reversal of how similar interactions had normally occurred, and it was strange to be in the mix of it.

Even so, there was nothing to be done at that moment. Knowing that there was a chance that they wouldn't be able to get through the portal, Joe started setting up a secondary option. Bubble travel was a tried-and-true method, and his newly enhanced version would allow for a much safer landing than before. The main issue was that they were surrounded on all sides, and unless some kind of major distraction pulled the Elves' attention, anyone trying to escape would likely get blasted out of the sky without being able to put up a fight.

Still, it was good to have options, even if they were bad ones. "Maybe I should work up some shields or something so that I can protect anyone else still in line...?"

Joe's thoughts were all over the place as the sounds of battle grew louder and louder. He tried to eyeball the distance, wondering whether he could just start setting up barriers and not run into any issues. Before he could make a move, a call rang out from behind his team. "Make way for the Council! Make way!"

He had to give them credit; the Dwarves fully understood that the Masters and Grandmaster were utterly necessary to their people's survival. Even with their own panic and increasing sense of impending doom, the line split to prioritize the people that could train the next generation—if they were lucky enough to produce another generation. Major Cleave watched the seven Masters and Grandmaster pass at a fairly quick speed, elbowing Joe. "That's who you were hanging out with instead of us for the last few days? Find anything fun?"

Weighing the pros and cons of blurting out national secrets aloud, Joe decided to come down on the side of keeping his mouth shut. "Nothing I can tell you about, other than it was a very good training opportunity for me."

"You do look healthier, I'll give you that," the Dwarf grumbled, her annoyance at not getting a straight answer poking through. "What do you think happened to this place? How do you think the Elves found it and managed to get an army here so quickly?"

Joe could only toss his hands up, "I really hope it had nothing to do with that Direwolf tracking us. I would feel like a *giant* tool if it is our fault that an entire city was about to be overrun."

"It's not *your* fault, Joe," Daniella told him firmly while she patted his arm soothingly. "Sometimes things just happen, and we can't beat ourselves up for doing what we need to do. No one could blame you for taking care of yourself and completing a quest that's super important to your future, right?"

"Yeah... I suppose it's not like we had a lot of other options. We had to get here, we had to warn them, and at least we are providing an escape." Joe could only hope that if any of this was his fault, then his guilt could be mollified by knowing he had done everything he could to help them on the other side. As the Council started filing past him, Grandmaster Snow paused to speak with him for a moment.

"Thank you for bringing our history back to our people. It will help more than you can know." She gripped his hand, and a notification appeared that she was trying to transfer something from her inventory to his. Recognizing that she was trying to be as stealthy as possible, Joe simply smiled, nodded, and accepted. She patted his hand once more and continued to the portal.

Item gained: Teleportation Keystone. There is no further information available, such as which teleportation array this Keystone will work for, or where you can use it. By placing it in the correct position, in the correct enchantment, you will be able to teleport to a certain location. Somewhere.

It took everything the Ritualist had in him to keep his face straight as he realized what he had just been given. He didn't know why it had been given to him, other than the fact that there would likely be no one else that would become a Grandmaster Ritualist before he could. He had proved his loyalty to them, as well as promising to train some of the Dwarven people if the option ever came around. Actually, now that he had thought it through, it made a *lot* of sense to give it to him. He just didn't know why they hadn't kept it on hand, allowing him access at a later date.

Unless... unless they thought they wouldn't be *able* to give it to him another time. He had a firm belief that he would be able to do something to help them, to keep them alive, and this result of even a Grandmaster seeming to give up formed a solid ball of concern in the pit of his stomach. Before he could reach out to let them know he would do anything for his adopted people, someone stepped in front of him.

The motion was confusing, because it seemed so casual. Because of this, it took a moment to recognize that a blade had just been shoved into Grandmaster Snow's back, and a torrent of blood was spurting out from around the metal that was still embedded into her flesh. As his eyes went wide, the gem slotted into the pommel of the blade flashed once, twice, then exploded, the shockwave sending Joe flying away.

He hit the wall of a nearby building, dismissing the damage notifications and loss of integrity for his Exquisite Shell. There were only two images in his mind, and the dichotomy between them was causing him all sorts of cognitive dissonance. The first was the blade that had been slammed into the Grandmaster. The second was the terrified face of the person who had put it there.

Daniella.

"What...?" Dozens of tiny memories suddenly surfaced, and he saw them in a new light. Daniella practically forcing herself to join them on this mission. How she had been shaking in terror every time she had joined combat. The look in her eyes after she was resurrected, when a monster had bitten her in half. How she had continually tried to comfort him when he messed up, citing the fact that sometimes things 'just had to be done'. Even upon their arrival to this city, she had gone off to 'inspect buildings', then made a beeline directly for the sanitation area. Joe knew better than anyone how little oversight there was in an area like that, and how easily she could have placed a beacon, or even opened a path directly into the city for the Elves. No one would have come to check.

Finally, the most notable memory was back when he had first let her join his team, and they had faced off against the Hidden Guardian.

"It was trying to give me a warning..." Joe whispered in

horror as he gazed numbly at the devastation and the people that were reacting violently to it. Dozens of 'Dwarves' had dropped the illusions around themselves, and the revealed Elves were tearing into the civilians that had been attempting to escape. "The Guardian told me that every one of my allies *it had seen* were good people with no foul intentions towards the Dwarves. She was still down in the garbage tunnel, and she waited there until it was fully defeated. How did I miss all of this?"

Horror-struck, he remembered how every time he had been around her, especially when they had been alone, he had been questioning himself over and over. Something about her had always been shouting at him to be careful, but he just hadn't realized what it was saying. "That had to be my Mental Manipulation Resistance... but why? Why all of this effort, just to throw it all away when we were about to win?"

He was hoping someone would pop out of the woodwork and monologue at him, giving him a chance to gear himself up and get answers at the same time, but anyone in the attacking force was focused on killing and not dying. He sprinted forward, pulling out his Ritual Orbs with a thought. The Intelligence-bound one shot forward ahead of him, burrowing into one of the Elves just before they could cut down a group of Students. "Everyone get to the portal! Stop playing nice, and *run!*"

The very few combat-oriented Dwarves remaining in the area were forming up and holding back the traitors, but there was no way to be sure if all of the illusions had been put aside. They were forced to watch their own backs, and it was causing them to make mistakes. Mistakes that might only leave a single cut, one bloody line across their face, or might cause them to lose their head entirely. The population had descended into chaos, and Joe didn't know what to do about it, other than killing anyone with pointed ears.

But, more than that, he wanted to find his traitorous teammate and get a direct answer as to *why* she had done this. That was the only thought occupying his mind as he battered the illusion-focused Elves with his Ritual Orbs. Most of the Dwarves knew that they would be dying quickly, since they weren't combat-focused, but for each Elf they managed to slay, at least five Dwarves had been killed as well. That meant *six* Elves would come back from respawn, and the Dwarven population had been permanently reduced by five.

As the last of the Elves that had revealed themselves were brought down, Joe scanned the crowd with furious eyes and released a bellow that brought all eyes on him. "You're going to pay for this, *Daniella!*"

CHAPTER THIRTY-SEVEN

As far as Joe could tell, the attackers had been stopped in their tracks. Thankfully, he had a good lead on where more would be coming from, as well as where Daniella had likely run off to. Joe scanned the crowd, noticing that his other teammates were also trying to figure out what was going on. "Major Cleave, I need you to provide security to the people escaping; make sure to get out of here when you can. Jaxon, we're going after Daniella."

For the first time, Cleave didn't complain as Joe left her behind and ran off into danger. She had done her duty, more than was needed with the chain of command gone, and she knew that Joe would likely be throwing himself at the most dangerous area in the city. "Be safe. I expect a full report when you return!"

Jaxon ran alongside Joe, his face still stretched out in the wild smile that he always wore, though this time the corners were pointed down. It took a moment for Joe to realize that the man was frowning, in his own way. "I should have seen it coming, but I just thought she was really into you or something. The way the light reflects off your head, the *severe* slouch you always stand in while working, your crippling addiction to coffee… what's not to love?"

The Ritualist nodded, for the first time admitting that he had been taken in by it as well. "I'm not going to lie; on paper she seems like she would be a good match for me. Part of the reason I am so angry about this betrayal is most certainly because I am emotionally compromised over it. There was one thing… the way she looked when she stabbed the Grandmaster? She didn't look smug, or pleased. She looked scared. If I'm being honest, that's the only reason I'm not using her blood to send a nasty curse ritual her way right now."

"How did you get her blood?" Jaxon's slow question had a very large note of concern in it, but Joe knew he had done nothing wrong, and he explained himself as the sewage treatment plant came into view.

"I was taking a sip of coffee when we were ambushed once, and some of her blood splashed in the cup." Joe pulled a face, smacking his lips in disgust. "AutoMate takes any liquid that comes into his Ebonsteel mug and stores it for a later time. I don't need much to destroy her from a distance, but… I would rather have an answer as to why this is happening."

His anger was cooling quickly, but the shame of being tricked for so long was coalescing into a white-hot core of rage over the betrayal of the team, the Dwarves, and—he had to admit it, even if only internally—himself. They slowed down as they reached the doors to the sanitation facility, which lay wide open, almost as though whoever was inside was inviting them to enter. Joe wasn't about to fall for that and pulled out one of the spare Rituals of Raze that had not been used up in his unrepentant aspect grab. With a twitch of his wrist, the ritual was assigned to the building, and he began powering it himself.

The building imploded in slow motion. From the outside, it was almost like watching a black hole that appeared in the center of the building, except for the strange geyser of usable materials that shot into the air, only to be gently piled in neat rows alongside it. A dozen people ran out of the crumbling building, the fury written deeply on their faces confirming that some kind of trap or ploy had just been foiled. There were two notable faces among them: Daniella, who couldn't meet his eyes, and Herr Trigger, who wouldn't look away.

"Why do I even bother with refined methods of trying to take you down?" Trigger inquired fairly casually, though he did speak with a slight edge to his tone. "Traps, subtleties, multiple angles that you might attempt to use against me... none of it matters. All you do is charge straight in. I could use a cannon, and you would put your head down and run at the rapidly accelerating ball of metal, wouldn't you? At least if it was in front of you and your destination, that is. I will file this away for later use-"

"Stop talking," Joe shouted harshly, pointing at the trench coat-clad man. Then his accusatory finger shifted to point at Daniella. "*Start* talking."

"You need to *run*," she whispered, her voice barely reaching his ears. "They want you specifically."

"No, no. No need for that anymore." Herr Trigger snorted; every aspect of his bearing confidently casual. "Everyone saw the Grandmaster get blown to bits. That was one of the alternate paths I could take to complete my quest. Hunting you down now? *Well...* that is just the stroopwafel after the meal. You just aggravate me, so I'll take the bonus that comes from putting you in the ground."

Joe's attention did not shift away from the traitor, even as the other people slowly started to encircle him and Jaxon. "*Why,* Daniella?"

"I made a deal." She finally lifted her eyes to meet his. They were filled with worry, but their depths also contained a steel that proved she would have done it, no matter what he had done or said. "I am an *Architect*. I'm not cut out for living on the wrong side of the law, the ruler of this entire world. I need access to materials, information, and people with high positions in society if I want to be able to live the sort of life that I have always dreamed of. You are... *dangerous*, and you live an exciting life. Everyone knows that. I can also tell you that I died more often from being in your party than I did the *entire time* that I've been in Eternium. At a certain point, it just became... it was too much. Then there is-"

"You are glaring at a person that is practically a High Noble!" Herr Trigger crowed on her behalf, exulting in the fact that Joe appeared to be nearing a breakdown. "All she needed to do was bring us to the goat path, and any extra assistance would bring her additional rewards that someone like you could only dream of! She opened the path directly here, dropping mana-influencing devices along the entire thing, then smuggled in saboteurs and assassins! A fun fact for you, oh bald one: somewhere in this city is a Legendary building, and *she* is going to be given exclusive access to creating blueprints for it. She will be a Grandmaster—no! A Sage! In no time flat. As for you... you will just be on the run with the discarded remains of a Shattered race."

Confident that his words had hit their target, Herr Trigger didn't wait a moment longer, signaling his men to attack by opening fire. The Ritualist didn't flinch, didn't even bother to move, as he processed what he had just heard. He had spent so much effort attempting to get the Council to allow his team up to the Grand Ritual Hall, in order for the four of them to be able to work together to fix issues and bounce ideas off each other. Now their paranoia seemed far more reasonable, and he felt like a fool.

On the other hand, Jaxon was flinching wildly, screaming in anticipation of being poked full of dozens of holes. A moment after the attack started, it stopped, and Jaxon lowered his hands from his eyes. "Did you beat them all *already*, Joe? That's fast, even for you—wait, never mind. They just stopped attacking. That makes more sense."

"How are you doing that?" Herr Trigger snarled at the collection of glowing metal that was suddenly gracing the cobblestone road beneath their feet. "What an incredible waste! Do you have any idea-"

"You seem like someone who likes to play the victim." Joe finally turned his attention to the bounty hunter. "Every time I meet you, you monologue like a villain, going on and *on* about how hard you have it. The reality? You just want to live in the past. Well, guess *what?* The reason warfare changes over time is because new concepts are introduced. I'm going to make sure that everyone knows how to set up this anti-bullet ritual, just to guarantee that you are going to be chucked in the useless pile by the people who have been giving you new quests. People who most likely can barely stand you as it is. What's going to happen to you then? Hopefully a wake-up call, but I won't be around to see it. I'll be walking, head held high, into the future... knowing that I did the right thing, and the best I could."

Joe had activated the ritual even before his attack on the sewage treatment plant, certain that the most likely assailants were going to be the group that had been chasing him across the entire Zone. He had also put out the anti-canine ritual, but it seemed he had overestimated the quality of opponents that would be coming for him. The major downside to having used these prototypes at the start of combat was that they were stationary once activated; if he needed to run away... it would be while dodging superheated, enchanted metal.

But Herr Trigger didn't need to know that.

Daniella froze as the others attacked. As Joe waded in to fight, he heard a pained yelp from the side. A grin touched his face even through the terrible situation, as he realized that the ritual hadn't been so much of a waste after all. The Direwolf howled in pain at such an ear-shattering volume that it made it nearly impossible for the assassins to coordinate their attacks. "Where's the Druid...?"

Joe needed to get some distance to be an effective participant in combat, but his immediate goal was not to win. In fact, his mission was already complete. All he had needed to do was prevent further reinforcements from coming directly into the city from a hidden location. With the sewage treatment plant crumbling, it was extremely unlikely that the delicate teleportation magics would be able to function within a few moments, if they were even still active.

He had his completed goal and answer, as filled with feces as both were, and it was time to make a run for it. "Jaxon! Retreat!"

"Eat treats? You got it!" Jaxon's hands shifted; his left hand once more shifting into a miniature Hydra. His fingers stretched into long necks with tiny T-Rex facsimiles on the ends, while his right once again morphed into a large, single dinosaur head. His left hand darted forward, clamping around the neck of one of the assailants as each of the miniature mouths chomped down. Black lines erupted under the man's skin, tracing his veins upward. He collapsed in an instant, and Jaxon looked at that hand in wonder. "They grow up so fast! Look! They already have Hydra venom glands! I didn't think they'd be able to grow those until-"

"Jaxon!" Joe shouted as his friend was tackled to the ground by a trio of fighters. An instant later, he was trussed up in a net of vines that appeared out of nowhere and pulled away from the combat zone faster than a Dwarf could run. In the distance, a solemn Druidic Elf glared at Joe, daring him to come after his captured friend. "*Jaxon!*"

Joe wanted to go after him, but the others were closing in on him in the same formation that the first team had used to capture his teammate. With one last fury-filled glare directed at Daniella, the Ritualist turned and Omnivaulted away.

As he rushed to make good on his escape, Herr Trigger's scathing laughter followed him the entire way.

CHAPTER THIRTY-EIGHT

As Joe soared over the heads of the few people still attempting to protect the refugees, his heart ached for their loss.

"The walls have been breached!"

"Guard companies three, eight, and fourteen have been entirely wiped out." One Legionnaire defender in full plate armor was shouting directions to a few others nearby. "Get two and seven to try and close those holes!"

"Yes, sir!" The enlisted Legionnaires took off at a run, and Joe glanced back just in time to see the officer put his head in his hands.

"All they're doing is buying time. Poor bast-" Then Joe was too far away to hear any more. The Ritualist continued Omnivaulting toward the escape portal, keeping an eye out for any attackers that he could strike at a distance, or any defenders he might be able to help escape. Fortunately, or unfortunately, depending on how he looked at it, there wasn't a single visible person that he could vent his fury on.

Before long, he was close enough to see the last of the Dwarves waiting to make it through the portal proper. During one of his higher jumps, when he pushed off a building, he was greeted by the sight of the northern portion of the defensive encirclement falling, and even at such a distance, he could see a wave of Elves, humans, and summoned elementals swarming over the struggling line of defense. "We don't have much longer... we need to get these people out of here."

But the harsh fact of the matter was, they had already been moving as quickly as possible. Joe decided that he needed to do something to help, even if it was just to take his mind off the loss of his best friend to the Elven scourge. Straight-line barrier rituals were incredibly easy for him to create, and even the most complex of them was only a three-circle ritual. Inscribing tool in hand, Joe progressed up and down the lines of Dwarves, instantly creating the rituals and activating them with a touch of mana. Since they were under the Rare rank, he didn't even need to use his small supply of cores in order to activate them. In no time flat, he had a last-ditch line of defense up and running.

When the final barrier had been activated, he inspected his work and was pleased with what he saw. "Or should I say, what I *don't* see?"

The rituals created reflective barriers, each one angled down, just as those he had created once upon a time in the dump at the Capitol. Anyone casually observing this area would only see a slightly warped road, and whatever was beyond it. Even knowing that the barrier was mere feet from him, and that there were Dwarves packed within its confines on the other side, there was no visible indication that was the case.

"Protection is up; now I need to figure out a way to make the attackers pay for this." Joe's eyes glowed black as he convinced himself to make something *particularly* nasty. At that moment, he was both glad and sad, that he didn't have any of Endgame's blood on hand. If he did, he would have been far too tempted to use it. Under his breath, he started to sing in a darkly ominous tone, "War crimes, war cri~imes."

Since that wasn't a possibility, which was probably for the best, Joe decided to work with what he had on hand. Currently, he had various rituals that could independently attack, but there were too many Dwarves remaining in the area to use them. Each of his stored rituals that could damage someone else were designed to hit as an area of effect, and would also attack indiscriminately. "But I have some new toys, don't I?"

With barely a thought, he was able to create the Ritual of Proximity (Wind Blades), and use it as a reference. "I can exchange this proximity portion and substitute in the whitelisting effect I learned at the Grand Ritual Hall. If I can key-in Dwarves as the only thing to *not* attack, and activate it with a drop of my blood to include me as well... I think that will work as is. Now, I get rid of the Wind Blade portion, and let's see... here it is. Since I've already created a ritual that casts Dark Lightning Strike continuously, I'll use the spell portion of that here..."

Once he was finished altering the ritual, the fighting had been going on for quite a long time, and the screams of tortured metal and weapons clashing with armor were closing in on his location. He studied the ritual one more time, trying to ensure that it was not going to blow up in his face, then activated it, flinching away as it sputtered to life. It didn't explode, and it didn't attack him: that was good enough for now. "I've got to think of a good name for this later, since I'm going to use this again for *sure.*"

It had ended up becoming a Student-ranked ritual, and he was hopeful that it would give some progress to his class quest when the Elves got closer. With his alterations, each lightning bolt would deal nearly four hundred damage per strike, and over two hundred to anything else within ten feet of the hit. Each ritual was good for one hundred charges, but he could only set up a few of them if he worked all the way up until he was in active combat. The singular bottleneck for his ability to produce more was that he only had one core that he was willing to use on these rituals, as anything else in his inventory was Unique or better.

"All I gotta do is hold out for a little while and help any stragglers through the portal." Joe psyched himself up, doing some stretches that Jaxon had taught him once upon a time. "I can get... let's try to make maybe three more of these before the attacking forces arrive?"

With a new personal goal in mind, Joe got to work. As each ritual was completed, he was able to move faster, make the ritual more efficient... but then came the time to test them out.

The first sign that the Elves were almost upon him was a spray of Dwarven blood washing around the corner and painting the cobblestones a sickly purple-red. Then a foot appeared, still attached to the Elf that was rounding the bend. An instant after the humanoid came into view, three bolts of lightning—each from a different ritual—speared the intensely shocked Elf. Nearly twelve hundred dark damage slammed into the assailant, stripping his shields away and leaving him vulnerable to the follow-up blasts of energy.

Seeing that threat easily taken care of, Joe let his eyes roam the street, searching closely for any distortion, shimmer, or Elf walking out in the open. He took a moment to let out a silent thanks that his Exquisite Shell was such a powerful defensive spell—it was woven not only from a divine gift, but also his own Arcane understandings—before they came into view. It wasn't a trickle, but a veritable *flood* of bodies charging toward him.

He silently cursed as he realized that he was not being rushed by Elves, who apparently had gotten the message from the first defensive ritual, but their Earth Elemental summons. Lightning lanced out to strike them, but it was not nearly as effective as it would have been against flesh. Earth Elementals were fairly neutral against Dark Affinity Magic, and they were quite strong indeed against any form of lightning.

It was time to go.

Leaving his rituals in place, Joe ran away from where he had hidden the portal, sprinting back to the only entrance he had left available. He skidded through a doorway, hanging a hard left and running back the way he had come on the inside of the reflective barrier. He could see through it, but he knew that no one should be able to see where he was. In fact, it was quite hilarious to see the Earth Elementals running past him, chasing in the direction he had gone… but the smile dropped from his face when they suddenly came to a halt and turned to stare directly at him.

"Abyss, they can feel the tremors from my feet on the ground." He tried to take care of that the only way he knew how, Omnivaulting down the open path. It seemed that only the ones he had been close to were able to guess where he had gone, because once he was in the air, the elementals that he passed didn't slow or look in his direction. Unfortunately, the ones that had sensed him had found the barrier, and were doing their best to smash it.

He had no concerns over those rituals, as they would hold out for a good long while, but as soon as they realized that the energy wasn't getting out of their way, the elementals sank into the ground, then popped up inside of the tunnel proper. "Faster, faster, *faster!*"

Now that the first few were inside the barrier, more and more Elementals were popping under it, emerging far closer to Joe than he was comfortable with. Earthen spikes shot up, slamming into the ritual from the inside and applying pressure. The stony barriers were no impediment to the Elementals, as they phased directly through the ritual-sapping attacks. One by one, and far faster than Joe was happy with, the barriers snapped.

Quest update: Student Ritualist II. Kill 100 creatures with Student-ranked rituals of any type. 8/100.

Experience gained: 1,920!

"Eight kills? That's *it?* This is a target-rich environment! That is not *nearly* enough to justify the expense of creating you!" Joe shouted at his lightning rituals as he finally sprinted past them. The end of the tunnel was in sight, and he could see the last vestiges of the civilian population pushing their way through.

Needless to say, that was when things went sideways.

Practically literally, as an artillery spell somehow missed all of the buildings it could have hit, arcing over the distant wall and slowly drifting to the ground like a falling star... aimed directly at the tunnel Joe had created. It impacted behind him, the force of the unleashed magics obliterating dozens of elementals, popping his barrier rituals as if they were not even there, and shattering his unprotected lightning rituals. Flame, stone, and crackling electricity filled the air, catching Joe and tossing him along the tunnel. Surprisingly, the blast actually ended up depositing him closer to the portal that would lead to his ultimate escape.

Exquisite Shell: 0/11,669.

Health: 561/2,327

His face was charred, his bones visible in several places as blood gushed out of him, but he was alive and able to force himself to move. "Ha, suckers. Made it."

Only a few feet from the crackling portal, which was somehow still active, the human shambled as quickly as he could manage in order to get through it. A moment later, he stepped from a war zone into a sauna, and the heat of the volcanic Shoe had never felt so pleasant. The area was packed, standing-room-only, and even then, there were at least a few hundred Dwarves that were on top of each other. "Looks like The Shoe is getting a little tight; we must have gone through a growth spurt."

No one laughed at his joke, but that was fine with him. He turned and took in all of the people that had survived the escape, relieved to spot Major Cleave forcing her way toward him. "Joe, there's a whole bunch we need to talk about, right away! Get your wounds taken care of. We need to close this portal."

The pain came back as his adrenaline wore off, and Joe

reached to touch his torn-up face. "I can take care of that, give me just-"

Ffft. FfftFfftFfft.

Joe's health bottomed out as a barrage of enchanted metal passed through the portal into his unprotected and fully relaxed body. No sound came through the shimmering barrier... but as Joe went to respawn, he could have sworn he heard Trigger laughing at him one last time.

CHAPTER THIRTY-NINE

Being stuck in respawn had given him plenty of time to cool down, even though he had raged loudly for at least half an hour upon arrival. There wasn't much else to do except wait, so he took out the *Grandmaster Snow's Guide to Mastery of Mana* and started to read over it. Seeing as it was a Legendary item, as well as something that he could lose, he only ever wanted to bring it out in the safest of areas, and what was safer than a room only he could access, and only when he was dead?

The most interesting thing about reading over the volume was that it had been laid out as though it were a skill book from Midgard. It felt like something that could be absorbed, granting the skill immediately, but he instinctively knew that would be incredibly wasteful. "I'm pretty sure that if I tried to absorb this, I would get maybe a *fraction* of the possible information out of it. It's a Legendary item, so I need to be sure to treat it carefully and learn as much from it as possible. That means assiduous study, a profusion of practice, and an infusion of time."

Reading for the next few hours was fairly soothing, and it allowed him to settle back into a good place mentally. By the time the portal opened, he was confident and calm, ready to dive back into whatever his people needed. He serenely stepped out of the room and into the dry sauna that was The Shoe. His sense of calm and collection was gone instantly, as he took in all of the people that were waiting for him; specifically, a few faces that he had not expected to ever see again. "Master Stu? *Grandmaster?* But you… exploded."

Snow nodded at him gravely. "Joe."

"How-"

"We knew that there was a traitor, we merely did not know who it was." Stu explained succinctly, clearly in a rush and in no mood to mince words. "What you saw was a decoy. We were some of the first people through the portal, transporting as soon as you left our company. The Council has been protecting it from this side ever since we left the Sage's Summit."

That caused a pain in Joe's heart as he recalled that it was he who had brought the traitor into their city and caused it to fall. Intentionally not bringing that fact up, he moved the conversation along. "Did we get almost everyone out? How is the Hamlet doing?"

"It's *full.*" Havoc's gravelly and characteristically grumpy voice broke into the conversation, as the Dwarf himself stomped into the room. "The heat is going up, water levels are dropping, and there's no room to do practically anything. That means we're going to have to accelerate our plans, but we also need a few things from *you* before we get started, or all of us get roasted."

"Why… *hello* there, Havoc." Grandmaster Snow winked at the scruffy, somehow singed Dwarf. "I was wondering when I was going to get the pleasure of your company again."

"Yeah, yeah. Good to see you," Havoc grumbled under his breath, keeping his eyes trained on Joe. "By the way, not sure if you heard, but Francine's back."

The teasing smile on Snow's face fell away, and she dipped her head at the crusty Grandmaster. "She came to visit me soon after she was brought back. Good work on that. She will be an asset to our people going forward."

"You know Francine?" Joe butted into the conversation. "Is that why you were so willing to accept my invitation to The Shoe?"

"I can tell you that saving my daughter certainly gave me a good impression of you," Snow told him casually. "Of course, it wasn't the *only* reason that I agreed to come with you—obviously a good idea in retrospect—but you also had a plan and the ability to carry it out. That mattered."

Joe was still stuck on the first part of what she had just said. He looked between Snow and Havoc, the latter of whom was fidgeting and obviously in great discomfort. "Hold on one moment... you mean to tell me that you two... you're Francine's mother, and Havoc-"

"We don't need a biology lesson, Joe," Havoc cut him off with a snarl. "Sure, four hundred years ago, she was a catch, but nowadays-"

"Do be *careful*, Havoc." Snow had regained the teasing expression on her face, although her eyes had abruptly become as cold as her namesake. "After all, I am right here. Within arm's reach of you... with no one to stop me from making an honest Dwarf of you."

Unexpectedly, a tiny smile cracked the ever-present scowl Havoc normally wore. "You know what? Maybe this whole society crumbling and world falling apart around us thing actually *does* have a lining of silver ore."

This was not what Joe had been expecting to come back to, but he had heard what he needed to hear. "You need a few rituals set up? Please tell me what they are, so I can leave the room at high speed."

"Minimum safe distance is three hundred yards; there's no way you can make it in time," Snow called as she trailed a finger up Havoc's chest.

Havoc started to chuckle, and Joe and Stu fled together as the room became a free-for all of screaming Dwarves. The human actually managed to keep up with the Master, and even get ahead, by using an unlucky Dwarf as a springboard for

Omnivault. As soon as he was outside, he noted all of the innocent bystanders, shaking his head sadly as he left them to whatever fate that being too close to two Grandmasters being 'playful' would earn them. "What did he say before he went all... no, focus on the task at hand. He said that heat and water were becoming a concern? That makes sense; the overhead ritual was designed to encapsulate the area and pull heat from the lava away and back into the surroundings. It's not designed as much to deal with the increasing heat generated by thousands of people rubbing together... ugh, that didn't help my mental image."

The heat was a simple matter to take care of, since he could use his current design and merely shift the parameters to include a different output area. In fact, it would be cheaper than normal, as he wouldn't need to put in a redundancy circle. He hurried to the center of town, jumped atop the guildhall, and pulled out his inscribing tool. Having spent a huge amount of time on this ritual previously, the first three circles were done near-instantly, and the fourth was completed extremely quickly. "Now I just need to line this puppy up with the output areas that the main heat reduction ritual uses... then I can channel the outflow, describe the area, *and*... activate!"

The ritual pulled at his mana, but quickly activated and began sucking in heat from the surroundings. It wasn't nearly as dramatic as it could have been, simply creating a cool breeze that started at the center of town and flowed outward to create a convection current that constantly sent cold air away and drew hotter air into the center. It was nowhere as efficient of a cold air delivery system as the vents that the Dwarves had set up, but it would be extremely beneficial to the town overall.

Eventually.

"I have no idea why water would be an issue... this is a closed system. Any water brought in stays here, no matter what form it takes. It should all be getting re-collected at the water collection rituals, but... perhaps people were filling canteens or something and took it out when the guildhall opened?" Joe proceeded to the water collection sites, trying to suss out the issue, only to find that the issue was far, *far* more basic than he had expected.

Two hours later, he finally resorted to threatening the people that had been hoarding water in giant containers. "Look, that water is for *everyone*, and no, you *can't* try to sell it at a profit right now. There's no more water coming in-"

"Which drives up the price!" the Oligarch-in-the-making tried to argue.

The human had enough at that point, and used his Ritual Orb to puncture the side of the container, driving it straight through one side and out the other. When the Dwarf moved to fight back, Joe stared him dead in the eye and growled, "This is *my* water. I brought all of it into this settlement. You can either take the currency that you have accrued to this point and go away, or you can pay a huge fine, *still* not have access to the water, and get tossed out of The Shoe. Make your choice."

After three additional, far-too-similar conversations, the dry air in the volcanic bubble started to moisten. "I will never understand people that try to become war profiteers by with-holding basic necessities. This is getting ridiculous."

"It's never a war crime the *first* time. Remember that." Havoc chose that exact moment to show up, looking much the worse for wear. "There you are. I'm glad to see that you are taking care of business, but I think it is time for us to talk about our next step. We have the people we need, we are now in a divinely hidden space, and the sheer amount of raw power we can bring to bear is frankly ridiculous, if we can pull off the surprise attack."

"A surprise attack? I don't think that's a very good idea, Havoc." Joe was completely taken aback by the suggestion. "Anything that we do to attack the Elves is going to reveal us, so we should focus on putting together some additional housing, or upgrading what we currently have so that more people can fit within them."

"I wasn't asking a question, Joe." Havoc fiddled with something in his hands, and the entire volcano around them shuddered as though it was about to erupt. "I came to find you so that we could talk about the sneak attack that is *going* to happen."

"Havoc... are we *sinking*?" Joe recognized the sensation from the last time he had taken an elevator on Earth. They were definitely descending, dropping deeper into the lava. "What's happening? How did you do this?"

"I told you that we were turtling up; what did you think I meant? The engineers and I converted the entire shell of The Shoe into a golem. Right now, we're sealed inside of a giant lava turtle that is going to swim through the mantle of Alfheim and bring us up directly under the Elven capital city." Havoc barked out a deep laugh as madness filled his eyes. "We're either going to deal a devastating blow and get our people out on the Bifrost as soon as it opens—or go out in a blaze of glory!"

CHAPTER FORTY

"There have been quite a few ups and downs over the last couple days…" Joe grumbled to himself as he worked on yet *another* ritual of heat reduction in order to keep The Shoe from melting into slag. "Jaxon was captured, Daniella betrayed an entire race—as well as her own team—*but…* Grandmaster Snow and the other Masters are alive. Made it back to The Shoe, only for Havoc to plunge it into deeper, hotter magma. Now an entire city of non-combatants are on their way to war. Apparently. Can't even kill Havoc to stop him; he's the only one that can control the 'turtle' he created."

Joe's complaints trailed off just as he finished the altered ritual that he had been working on. His mentor had known that the Ritualist wouldn't simply let the town fend for itself, but it was the 'requests' that he had passed on to Joe that made the human grind his teeth. His Ritual of Cooling had been altered to collect all of the expelled heat in a single point above The Shoe. According to Havoc, if they could concentrate enough, when they started to erupt out of the ground, they would cut through the stone above them like a hot knife through butter. Then, any remaining flame would be used to set off a volcanic eruption of legendary proportions, hopefully wiping out any defenders in the area as the Dwarves raced toward the freedom of the next Zone.

"I made twenty-five barriers, each one maintaining inward pressure, followed by a triple layer on the outside that keeps the lava from disrupting what's being maintained," Joe explained to Havoc when the Dwarf studied him with a raised brow. He hadn't seen Joe take a break in quite a while, and that usually meant it was time for a new task. "Listen, if we are going to be trying to escape to the Jotunheim, I need to go set up a particular ritual on a couple of the buildings. Especially the Pyramid of Panacea. There's no way we can abandon an Artifact Alchemy shop to our enemies, right?"

Havoc simply gave a theatrical shrug, "If you think *that's* the best use of your time, who am I to stop you? Losing that amount of time will probably only cost a hundred or so lives; a small price to pay for keeping your fancy building, right?"

Joe glared at his mentor, once again trying to decide if meeting the Dwarf had been a benefit or the start of a downward spiral into engaging in war crimes on the regular. "Havoc, let's be realistic. If we come up in the middle of the city, we're going to be dropping this lava on their citizens, not on an army. You know as well as I do that I'm going to do whatever I can to give us the best chance of success, but if you think that I'm going to unleash everything that I possibly can on a civilian population, you're out of your mind."

"Better chuck me in the loony bin, then." Havoc stood up and met Joe's eyes. "Every one of those Elves is a stolen Dwarf. You know as well as I do that they can come back, and they *will* come back, which means everything that we do is only a delaying tactic. If the enemy needs to sift through hundreds of *thousands* of civilians to find their fighters, that'll slow down reinforcements. That's all I'm looking for at this point."

"That's pretty messed up, and I'm going to go grab my building now." Joe marched away, doing everything he could to ignore the taunts that Havoc fired his way. Eventually, he stood next to the pyramid, seething, as he tried to wrestle his mind into a good place for running forward into the unknown. Forcing himself to focus, he continued past its steeply angled walls into the crafting area, where he knew he could work on forging some materials.

Joe marched up to an Expert that was busy at one of the forges, and made him an offer he couldn't refuse. "I'm going to start making Ebonsteel mugs, a whole ton of them. If I hand them over to you, can you remove any additional features that appear and smelt the mugs into ingots for me?"

"Ebonsteel...? Why would you turn them into mugs and then back into ingots?" The Dwarf looked like he was about ready to ignore the rest of whatever Joe had to say, when he recognized the extremely bright, glittery light bouncing off of the human's head. "Wait a second... you're that human that owns this place. I've heard about you. Yeah, *absolutely* I'm your Dwarf! As a matter of payment-"

"I'll let you keep one out of every twenty ingots. But it's important that we get started now." Joe wasn't about to haggle; he knew that Ebonsteel was practically unseen on Alfheim, and the Dwarf could be easily replaced if needed. He got right to work, pulling out his forging template and creating mug after mug. Every time he completed one, he carelessly tossed it to the side, only for the Dwarf to shout and dive for it before it hit the ground, as if the Ebonsteel would somehow get damaged. Eventually, Joe couldn't go any further, and he fell asleep right next to the forge he was using.

When he woke up, he repeated the pattern, until he had generated a stack of ingots eleven feet long and wide. He had used up so many aspects to create them that he was *nearly* out of Common and Uncommon and completely out of Rare, once again. Luckily, he knew they would regenerate over time, since he now had a Natural Aspect Jar for everything up to the Unique rank. At seven aspects gained per hour, in just a few days, he would have regained plenty to make any necessary rituals under the Expert rank.

If he needed more than that, he would be forced to go out and collect them. It would be two months before the jars were full, if he left them alone, but he had no intention of doing that. His eyes snapped to the Expert smith that had been working alongside him the entire time, even waiting patiently while the human got two or three hours of sleep per night. "Now I need to turn this into a solid block. Is that something you can help me with?"

"Yer telling me this *now?*" the Dwarf grumped, motioning for Joe to help him shovel the ingots into a furnace. "I could have smelted it as a single piece from the get-go."

"How would you have been paid?" the human countered, earning a surprised look and chuckle from the smith. After that, it was only a matter of waiting until they could pour the molten metal into a cast and let it cool.

While he waited, Joe used the time to transfer everything from his codpiece of holding to his storage ring. Luckily, aspects didn't seem to take up any space, or if they did, it was such a minimal amount that when he stored the fully cooled block of Ebonsteel in his codpiece, then took it out again to inspect for damage, there was none. Fist-bumping the smith—who clearly wanted to get working on making himself an Ebonsteel item— Joe ran over to his workshop to slap his degraded Ritual of the Traveling Civilization onto the metal. "Now I won't have any concerns about this breaking, and it *should* take to holding the ritual extremely well, since it's designed to be filled with magic."

Having made the block exactly to the specifications of the ritual's requirements, it was no surprise that it fit perfectly. In a few minutes, he was gazing down at a topographical map of the area, with the block at the center. He was surprised by the sheer amount of range that it could cover, but he supposed that as the ritual was meant to move around a city—that was certainly no small amount of space. Even so, he was even more surprised to learn that out of all of the buildings listed that he could move, the pyramid was *not* one of them. "Oh no... did I mess this up somehow? I can't let the Elves take that. I'll have to destroy it first. But then Jake will probably figure out a way to eat me. At least he would do it daintily, with a knife and fork, instead of just tearing my flesh off—wait! Jake! That's right; technically he is the owner of that building right now."

Joe waited until the ritual spat out a child ritual, which he could use to assign the building to be moved. Then he ran over to the pyramid and knocked on the front door. To his great pleasure, no powders puffed out into his face, the door did not turn into needles under his skin just before he could rap on it, and he didn't somehow get dropped into the lava below them. Instead, after a few minutes, Jake the Alchemist simply swung the door open and waved him in.

"Wow." It was Joe's first time getting to see the interior of the Artifact-level building, and he was suitably impressed. It looked like a stereotypical steampunk mad scientist's lab, a huge building that was connected by various piping, spinning gears, diodes, and numerous areas filled with flashing electricity. It was also *much* darker than he was expecting, most of the space cast in perpetual twilight, while the areas that seemed to be specifically for mixing, measuring, or usage all seemed to have spotlights of various colors beaming down on them. "This is amazing. What's up with the light?"

"The light is exactly as it needs to be. There are some concoctions that are sensitive to light, which means it can degrade the final product." Jake raised a perfectly sculpted eyebrow at Joe, "You certainly don't mean to tell me that you'll just work cheerfully under any conditions, correct? If you've been inside one of your class buildings, you should be able to know by now what the optimal conditions are for you to be working."

"Not particularly? I've been inside my Ritual Hall, but it only looks like I am standing into space." Joe was going to go on, but Jake seemed to think that was important.

"Think that through… if you are in a field of stars, galaxies, nebulae… would you not think that perhaps their locations have some form of impact upon the success of your rituals?" Jake's casual observation made Joe freeze as a few things clicked into place.

Ritual Lore has reached Student I!

"It's also practically pitch-black in there, but I've never had any issue with my... oh feces, Darkvision is a class skill."

Ritual Lore has reached Student II!

Joe could only bow his head in shame as so many things became clearer all at once. "Thank you for your guidance, I want to say... Grandmaster?"

"The only rank that has ever mattered is *Sage*." Jake deflected the question without answering it. "What can I help you with today?"

"One moment. First thing: a skill of mine just came off cooldown. I've been really good at using it the last couple of days, and I think I'm... one moment." Joe took a breath, and focused on collecting his mana into the most cohesive pattern that he could visualize, pushing in from the outside by using his fledgling control over the ambient mana. "Knowledge, Alchemical Lore."

Since he had made sure to use it even while focusing on forging his Ebonsteel cube, the Apprentice-rank lore skill finally picked up and tipped over the threshold.

Alchemical Lore has reached Student 0! Having great knowledge on a subject without the experience of the subject itself is the opposite of danger-ous. You now have a 2% chance while creating any Alchemical Recipe to boost the duration of the effect by 100%.

Knowledge has reached Student 0! You are now able to use this skill on two different Lore skills upon activation, so long as only one of them is at the same rank as the skill itself.

"Well, that is pretty nifty," Joe muttered to himself, then turned back to the nonplussed Alchemist. "As I was saying, I was coming here to hopefully get your permission to move this building to Jotunheim after I cross the Bifrost."

"Jotunheim?" The tiniest flicker of emotion, which could potentially have been surprise, excitement, or *fury*, darted across Jake's eyes. "You will have the opportunity to bring me plenty of reagents that I cannot get access to on this plane while we are there. This is fine with me. Also, ensure that you are here every third day for training. Those are the only times I have available for you to learn this craft, unless you are open to attempting to survive while I am working with the... mildly irritating reagents that I am using currently."

Hearing someone who had smacked around Havoc without issue speak about something being 'irritating' was enough to clue Joe in to the fact that there was no way he would survive whatever Jake was offering. "Every third day sounds great."

"Good. Also... whatever that skill was that allowed you to pull information on Alchemy directly into your head from the Akashic records?" Jake paused meaningfully as Joe worked to keep a straight face. "Make sure you never use that in front of a deity, or a champion of one. You wouldn't want to have a crusade called against you to tear it out of your skull."

"Ahh. Say what now?" Joe waited for more explanation, but apparently it wasn't forthcoming. Jake wordlessly waved him toward the door and trundled off to tinker with some tincture in the distance. Joe swallowed, trying to hydrate his suddenly dry throat, and walked over to the wall to install the ritual as he had come here to do.

CHAPTER FORTY-ONE

Since this was the first time Joe had activated a ritual like this—both an assigning version, as well as a ritual spawned by another ritual—he was extremely excited to not only use it, but study it as it propagated throughout the building.

Choosing a fairly hidden alcove, he pressed the Ritual Diagram against the wall, and added a touch of mana in order to begin the process. It was both incredibly exciting, as well as wildly disappointing. If he had solely been watching the ritual with his regular eyes, all he would have seen was a bunch of circles and mathematical formulas getting sucked into the wall like water that was dropped on the sand of a beach.

But he had expected something like this and laid his hand on his Ritual Orb of Essence Cycle. By watching the flows of energy, he discovered that the ritual did *far* more than slip into the wall to stay out of sight. He watched in wonder as the circles expanded and dissipated, absorbing into the very foundation of the building, similar to a virus replicating itself and replacing human DNA. It became an intrinsic part of the building, an identifier that could be used to find it anywhere in a multiverse. A lock that could be opened from anywhere, so long as the key continued to exist.

Magically speaking, it was intensely beautiful to observe something becoming a vastly different item while maintaining all usage and appearance. To Joe, with his limited understanding of what was happening, it was *indescribably* impressive. But he still tried, writing every impression and revelation down as quickly as he could so that he would not forget them. "All of this goes right into the notebook. If I ever figure out a way to teach someone to become a Rituarchitect, this is going to go straight into the lore book that I hand to them."

The process was completed after only a few moments of adjustment, but he was still able to fill out several pages with what he had observed. When he was done—at least, done with everything he could remember—he sighed in wonder and closed the book. Seeing that Jake was otherwise occupied, Joe let himself out and hurried over to his workshop. Just as he had hoped, when he inspected the metal block the ritual was assigned to, the pyramid was now available for him to transfer. "With that out of the way, now I can focus on…"

His eyes gleamed as they fell on several small discs that had appeared next to the iron block. "I guess I can focus on assigning all the other buildings in The Shoe?"

Before he could run down that path of grabbing everything he could get his grubby little mitts on, Major Cleave knocked on the door to his workshop, and he begrudgingly forced himself away from the small rituals to see what she wanted. "Cleave, good to see you. What can I do for you today?"

"As you might have been expecting, I'm hoping that you might be able to offer us some additional protections." Cleave seemed exhausted, more so than he had ever seen her before. "There's barely a platoon of Legionnaires here, and besides you and Havoc, I'm the highest-ranking member of the military that made it back. That makes me the de facto commanding officer, and we are trying to put together some way to keep our

270

people alive, even if Havoc is apparently doing everything he can to kill us all."

"Yeah, going straight to the capital…" Joe interlocked his fingers behind his head and grimaced as he stretched. "Not sure how that is going to work out, but I have to give him points for audacity. Pretty sure they won't expect us to pop up underneath them with a city's worth of Dwarves, with the only warning that precedes us being a super volcano."

"That's what I'm here to talk to you about." Major Cleave straightened into her military bearing and waved grandly at the people behind her. "The lava is going to be an issue, as is keeping the civilians alive, both short and long-term. I was hoping for a three-pronged assist from you. Firstly priority is to give us a secure way of transporting people to the Bifrost from the exit point. Secondly, I need you to advance to the next Zone and secure our landing point. Third, we are going to need defenses against the flora and fauna of the next realm until we establish a proper foothold."

"Make a bridge across the lava, kill anything that moves except the things that move in the way we like, build a city." Joe summed it up so casually that Major Cleave's expression shifted to slightly angry, though she was gradually mollified as he continued. "I can do even better than that. As soon as we exit, I'll set up a bubble travel point. All I will need is someone who can gauge the distance for us, and it will take them directly to the Bifrost. Then, all we need to do is keep attacks off that area. Hate to say it, but if we *do* lose a couple of people to various spells or whatever, it is better than losing everyone at the same time."

"I am most certain that this will not be an easy task. However… I will admit that you planning to work it out is something that puts my mind at ease," Cleave told him stiffly, giving him a sharp nod and turning to leave.

"Aww… thanks for trusting me! You are so *sweet*. I think we should all go and sing around a campfire-" Joe trailed off as she sprinted away as fast as she could go, but not fast enough to keep him from catching the embarrassed bristling of her mustache. "Heh. Got her. Now all I need to do is figure out large-group bubble travel in a safe and rapid manner."

He thought over the issues that Major Cleave had presented to him as he gathered the transporting ritual discs and made his way around to each of the other buildings in The Shoe. He still took notes, but none of the rituals binding to the buildings were as impressive as what had occurred with the Artifact-ranked pyramid. Still, he dutifully recorded his observations, then set back to planning as he hurried to his workshop once more.

Once they reached the Elven capital, evacuation was absolutely going to need to take priority, since there was going to be a nearly-guaranteed rapid response to the escape attempt. Getting as many Dwarves across the Bifrost as possible was the most important thing, even more so than him surviving the attempt. But without knowing the distance they would need to travel, or what kind of resistance they could expect, it was going to be hard to get everything prepared. Then he remembered how Grandmaster Snow and the Council of Masters had managed to survive.

"Maybe the best idea is *not* trying to hide them... maybe the best idea is sending out so many decoys that anyone that *does* attack the bubbles is going to be missing more times than they hit." Joe was reminded of bubble-making toys from his original world, some of which had been shaped like gatling guns and released huge streams of thousands of bubbles at a time. "I can do that... yeah, I will set up a twenty-one Ritual Grid, and set them to constantly send bubbles, whether or not they have people inside. If I make the bubbles highly reflective, no one will be able to tell the difference."

With his plan firmly in mind, Joe dove into designing the ritual. It was a fairly simple addition to his current bubble travel; he would set it up so that the bubbles didn't travel in a perfectly straight line, most of them moving randomly—but within a certain range—so long as they reached the goal at the end. "If I do this right, we might not lose anyone... I can only hope."

Then he found the first major issue. If he simply allowed the bubbles to travel aimlessly, they would crash into each other, possibly causing catastrophic failure. If he wanted to put so many of the delicate spheres all next to each other and make sure that they did not interfere with the movement of the other bubbles, they needed to be linked to a central controller. At first, Joe thought that was going to kill his plan immediately, but then he was struck by inspiration.

His hands seem to move on their own as he sketched out a two-circle ritual, the simplest control panel he could come up with. All the first circle did was to check whether a bubble was going to impact something else, and if so, the second circle would slightly alter the course of the vehicle. The most difficult part was going to be linking both of the circles together and creating the sympathetic links that would have them working together 2 move only a single bubble, instead of shoving both bubbles into a new direction, likely in tandem, causing more confusion and issues.

At first, his thought was to place the small circle in among the nine others, but he found that it would be easier to simply draw the double circle around the other nine. He wasn't going to lie: that made it look pretty fancy. "This basically looks like an anti-air cannon now, except the inner rituals aren't spinning around each other. Should they...? No, that would cause too many issues with getting people through, if we had to continuously account for angular momentum as well."

Each of the four Circle Rituals needed to be created in advance, and he sketched them out on a tile. One of the largest benefits of becoming a Master at Ritual Circles was that he no longer needed to worry about completing multiple circles in time; he was comfortably certain that he could bring both circles up around the other nine and link them nearly instantaneously. Gauging the requirements that he would need to assign, such as distance to travel and the vector of movement, followed by actual activation and sympathetic linking… "I think that after I've made it to the entrance, it should take something like one full minute to get everything ready?"

In his mind, that was too much time. At the speed that residents of this Zone could move and think, one minute was practically an eternity. The only other thing that he could possibly do to lower the time requirement was know *exactly* where they were going to be leaving from, as he would be able to place the rituals and stack them accordingly. Unfortunately, that just wasn't an option. When the volcanic eruption happened, the exit was most likely going to be created right then.

At a loss for how to continue pursuing this particular task, Joe simply had to hope that it would be enough, and moved on to the next task that needed to be done. "Let's start setting up some rituals of attack so that we can clear the area we land on and defend it as soon as we get across the Bifrost. I'm going to need lightning, wind… maybe I can do one that sends out sprays of acid? Actually, with how much experience I have in using acid in rituals, that would make perfect sense…"

Joe got to tinkering, slowly losing himself in the process, but as he was drawing out his first ritual of lightning, he paused and looked at the *Special aspect usage pamphlet* that he had gained from one of his class quests. "You know… I've only ever used special aspects in rituals that were for buildings, or that one time I needed to escape from this volcano, and it nearly killed me. Could it be that I just don't understand exactly what they are supposed to do? I gotta wonder if it's possible to enhance these rituals further, without having to delve too deeply into enchanting or Alchemy right now."

He opened the pamphlet and decided to skim over the top aspects that were listed. Luckily for him, everything was in alphabetical order, making it very easy to move through which common aspects he could use. As it stood, he had five different special aspects stored, and a fairly large number of them to boot. Since he had needed to collect ten thousand in total, he had assumed—apparently incorrectly—that the next stage in that quest was going to be using those special aspects in rituals. Instead, he had been directed to craft actual items out of them.

"No time for that right now; let's see if the system counts rituals as crafts, perhaps?" The Ritualist steepled his hands and tapped the pads of his fingers together as he thought through the options. "Right now I have Anima, Arcane, Molten, Scattering, and Zombified as special aspects. According to the pamphlet, Anima boosts... meat? What does that mean, 'boosts meat'? Is that healing? Or damage against meaty creatures, or flesh? What a glorious quest reward, a pamphlet that isn't super descriptive, I love light overviews instead of direct assistance. Guess I can only hope that I get a better version, or can I upgrade this one?"

He shook off the strange, intrusive complaining that was filling his skull, deciding to keep going. "Boosting 'meat' isn't really what I am looking for regardless, since I highly doubt that the next area is going to require a ton of healing the monsters. I guess that means move on? Arcane 'boosts magical conductivity', but is that something I want on my rituals? Only way to find out is to try it, but I think it is probably going to be more effective on physical items I want to enchant. Molten 'adds malleability', which is not particularly something I need, but Scattering looks great."

Someone jostled him, and Joe growled lightly as the pamphlet was knocked out of his hand. As soon as his door had opened, dozens of people had swarmed inside, happy to get a little bit of breathing room. The only reason he hadn't kicked them out immediately was that they were doing their best to give him all of the room that he needed to work. Even so, no one was perfect. Joe gestured at the fallen document, and at the Dwarf that had bumped him. "Bro?"

"Sup, bro?" The Dwarf followed Joe's eyes and saw the sad little quest reward.

"Can you hand me that pamphlet?"

"Brochure." The scraggly-bearded Dwarf deposited it in his

hand and tried to wiggle away as the human got right back to work.

"Thanks." Joe's eyes traveled over the description, "What was I...? Scattering, right. Bonus damage against magical protections. Now, it still means that the attack against the creature it hits will be less effective than something without magical defenses, but at least some of the damage might get through? I bet those Earth Elementals had some serious resistances at play."

He glanced over his final option, Zombified, noting that it was described as 'eats heat and life', which aligned with his expectations perfectly. At first, he reached out mentally for the Scattering aspects, which he was fairly certain he had gained by breaking down so many weapons that the Dwarves had designed for penetrating Elven shielding, but he paused and decided to go with the Zombified aspects for his first test. He had more of those available than any other, and he thought that eating heat and life would be a benefit to his Dark Lightning Strike if he could make it work.

"Ritual of Zombified Lightning, prototype test number one, begin."

CHAPTER FORTY-TWO

Joe blew on his fingers, trying to warm them up. Never before had he been so happy that he was heavily resistant to dark magic, while simultaneously so frustrated that he couldn't turn off the magical penetration that his dark magic was equipped with. "Better this than with fire or earth, I suppose."

He eyed his failed experiments, pleased that even though the floor and walls of his workshop were scarred and pitted, there was no damage that a simple Ritual of Structural Repair couldn't fix in a few seconds. On the *extremely* happy side, his shield had held out against all of the damage that had been dealt to him, even though the lingering effect of the Special aspects was something that seemed to ignore his defenses. Even though he wasn't physically damaged, it still numbed his arms, seeming to pull all of the heat away from his bones and towards his skin—draining it away until it finally ran its course.

It may have been a purely psychological effect, since Joe didn't have someone else present to test the veracity of his assumptions, and he also didn't have any basic scientific equipment, such as a thermometer. "I guess all I can do is start taking down enemies with this and see how warm their bodies are afterward."

Even though he hadn't managed to put together a working version of the ritual yet, it was showing great promise. He was fairly certain that he had worked out most of the kinks, and he'd found that the number of aspects added needed to be within a certain range of the total *other* aspects added to the final ritual. If he added too few, there was no noticeable effect on the ritual. If he added too many, the ritual would destabilize, twisting and detonating only moments later.

"I think it's eighteen and a half percent of the total amount, to hit the sweet spot." Joe had been taking meticulous notes, and he was fairly certain that this next ritual would be a success. As he poured in aspects to the circles, a little less than one in five being Zombified aspects, he held his breath in excitement as the ritual tried to stabilize. If it did-

Bwamp

The Reductionist was blasted off his feet as the ritual catastrophically failed, sending him thudding into the wall and scattering his notes. He popped up to his feet, gathered the fluttering sheets with the efficiency of clearly having to do so before, and crossed out the test case hypothesis before writing a new one. "Ritual of Zombified Lightning, prototype test number eighteen, now reducing overall additional aspects from eighteen point five percent to eighteen percent. First circle going up... complete second circle, complete third circle-"

This attempt took slightly longer, as he had not perfectly memorized what was required. He had to draw it out by hand more carefully than usual in an effort to engrave it not only on the tile, but in his mind for the next attempt. "-complete. Beginning fourth... now."

He didn't have an accurate way to measure time yet, but he was able to use his various ritual countdowns to track how quickly time was elapsing. Even those weren't always perfect, as they sometimes took more mana than usual, making the estimated time remaining drop faster than one second per second.

Even so, it was better than nothing, and he was able to estimate that he had knocked another thirty seconds off completing the fourth circle.

"Getting better all the time." Joe hummed to himself as he worked. As the circle finished, he stepped back and waited for the completion or explosion. As a man on a time limit, he would be happier with completing the ritual, but as a magical scientist... he would be happy to shift variables until it was perfect. To his relief, the ritual stabilized, and he was able to count the final product as a success—even though it hadn't yet been combat-tested. That was going to be pretty difficult to do in an area where he was surrounded by friendlies, but he knew he would get his chance all too soon.

"Now the real question is..." Joe glanced at the other aspects, as well as the other rituals that he had planned, "Is eighteen percent a standard for this ritual, or this *aspect*? On that note, will it be repeatable on the same ritual?"

Deciding to run that test before any other factor, he recreated the ritual on yet another tile, where it once more stabilized. As soon as he successfully created it a third time, he was confident that he had found the correct aspect ratio for this particular ritual. "Now it's time to try out another aspect. Let's go with Scattering, since that was my first choice anyway."

The ritual went up as usual, but instead of something that would sap life and heat, he was creating lightning that should deal extra damage to magical protections. Joe was extremely happy that he had used Zombified to create the first benchmarks, because he had a much more limited supply of Scattered aspects. As the strange energy was poured in, he waited until the end and watched curiously as the ritual became firmly set in the tile. "Excellent! It looks like eighteen percent is the standard for at least this ritual, now we can test-"

Bzzap!

The ritual detonated, sending black lightning—with white sub-arcs highlighting it—scattering around the room. His Exquisite Shell, having already taken a beating, was completely *shredded* by the release. He was rooted in place as the remaining lightning attempted to wreak havoc within his body, only to be mostly shunted off, thanks to his resistances. Even so, "That abyssal *hurt!*"

Even though the ritual had seemingly failed at the last moment, Joe recreated it in exactly the same way. There was no way to know if it was a failure in the aspect ratio, or if it was a different factor such as the fact that the mana in the atmosphere around them was becoming more heavily tinged with the Elven Pantheon's influence the closer they got to the capital city. Seeing as the ritual had initially *seemed* stable, he was betting on the latter.

Less than ten minutes later, he was proven correct as the ritual stabilized into a cohesive travel form. Even so, he was cautious with it, as the first one had originally seemed like it wasn't going to blow up. It was only after he stored the ritual away in his ring that he was able to breathe a sigh of relief... and then he made another one to verify that the diagram was correct.

Hours passed in this manner, as he designed protections both for attacking and defending. Before he knew it, he had a huge stack of ritual tiles filed away carefully in his storage ring, and he was forced to create some more of the thin stones by carefully slicing the ground with his Field Array.

Rejoice, all those associated with the Elven Theocracy! A second Dwarven city has fallen, and all that remains is the Capital itself! March on the final stronghold of the Shattered race of Alfheim, and finish what you've started!

With the fall of the Second City, the Bifrost is beginning to open in the Capital city of the Elven Theocracy! Prepare yourself for monsters, monsters, and monsters!

Jotunheim awaits!

Reading the notification while cheerfully slicing fresh rocks, Joe found that it was a very good thing he was crouching. It gave him the stability that he needed to not bash his head on the ground as the entirety of The Shoe shifted suddenly, dropping a few feet before beginning to drive upward at a frankly concerning pace. "What's going on? Are we at the Elven capital already? There's no way!"

Joe knew that if they had been approaching, all of the population *should* have been lining up outside of the buildings in preparation to flee to the Bifrost as quickly as possible. That was when the shouting began, as dozens of mouths opened across every building in the area and shouted in Havoc's voice. "I sure hope everyone is ready to kick some Elven behind! We have begun our ascent into the Capital of the Theocracy, so I highly recommend for everyone to get ready! At this speed, we have anywhere from thirty minutes to an hour before we start breaching the city's lower defensive wards, and if you're not ready to go, you are going to be left here!"

"Oh good, *there's* the warning," Joe growled as he picked himself up and joined the crowd in filtering into any space that could be considered an open area. With the countless thousands of people packed into the open Shoe, there had been very little space for anyone to have any kind of privacy at all. Even Joe had only been given his space after his rituals started to explode. The fact that he had instantly jumped back to his feet to make even *more* powerful versions had sent people scampering out of his workshop, finally giving him the necessary breathing room that he had needed to succeed at his efforts.

"We have been circling under the Capital city for a few hours. With the Bifrost starting its initial opening, it's go time!" Joe followed the sound of Havoc's voice through the streets, his eyes eventually coming to rest on the Grandmaster, who was in a small circle with the Council that they had managed to rescue from the High City of Deep Thought. All of them clustered near the Guardian, who was scanning the crowd with his flood-light-like eyes. The Dwarf was screaming at everyone to assemble, and begin directing them in an orderly fashion. "If you don't get scanned by the Guardian, you do *not* get to leave this place alive!"

Fighting broke out in an instant as various people clad in

illusion—or hiding their affiliation to the Elves—began rampaging. Each of them knew that they were going to die here, but they did their best to take as many Dwarves with them to respawn. Havoc refused to let that happen; anytime someone was revealed to be a spy, the ground itself reached up and clapped manacles around their limbs, then pulled them to the ground in a spread-eagle fashion. Once secured, they zipped along the stone, until they were hanging on the wall like a starfish in a dentist's lounge.

"That's eighteen, twenty-two, forty-seven, one hundred and fifty-eight in total." Havoc's counting and muttering was loud enough for everyone to hear it, as though it were being amplified in the sudden silence. "Not bad! Not bad at all. Out of ninety-eight thousand, seven hundred and twenty-six Dwarves and humans rescued from the city or having already been relocated here, there were less than two hundred total spies. Great work, everyone! Stay on your toes; those Elves are tricky!"

A round of cheering broke out, and Joe realized that the last minute call to assemble and gather for the assault on the Capital was a tactic that must have been spawned among the devious minds of the Council of Masters. By not telling anyone when they would be arriving, no spies were able to send a message out to warn their superiors. By capturing them instead of sending them off to the afterlife, there would be no changes in the Ledger of Souls in the city above them to tip the Elves off.

In other words, they were about to hit a completely unprepared populace from below, and Joe just needed to be okay with that. He was just coming to grips with the situation when Havoc started singing his signature song, and soon the walls were vibrating from all of the voices joining in.

"Are ya *ready*, Dwarves?" Havoc's excitement was palpable as he started the chant that activated his title; it infected all of the Dwarves within hearing range with his large group buff.

You have entered a raid area! All experience gain has been paused and will only be calculated at the end of the raid, or upon leaving the raid area.

The Lord of Slaughter stands with you! -30% sensation of pain.

+25% damage dealt with melee weapons. 10% reduced damage taken from all sources.

For the vast majority of the assembled people, no one had ever been able to partake in an attack on the scale they were about to attempt. Beyond that, only a handful of people had actively participated in Havoc's war chant. That didn't stop every single person that could hear him from responding perfectly. "Aye, aye, Major General!"

"I can't *hear* you!" Havoc howled animalistically as smoke poured from his mouth.

The excitement was returned in full. *"Aye, aye, Major General!"*

"Ohhh!" The ground underneath them lurched as the mountain started moving faster, and the entire room began to spin as though the tip of the volcano were going to act as a drill to penetrate the crust of Alfheim above them. "Elves in the city, suck on this rock!"

"War crimes, war crimes!"

"What will we do when we get out up *top*?" Havoc bellowed as the mountain made its first impact, sending dust, rocks, and people flying everywhere.

"War crimes, war crimes!"

"Is bloodshed and slaughter something you *wish*?"

"War crimes, war crimes!"

"Then get out of here, and serve them a fist!"

"War crimes, war crimes!"

"Ready?" Havoc didn't need to hear the answer, which was good, as almost nothing could be heard above the screeching and grinding of metal and stone as the superheated peak of the volcano melted through the crust, and the angular momentum of the object propelled them ever upward in a rising plume of gas, magma, and vengeance. "War crimes, war crimes…"

"War crimes, war crimes!"

"War cri~imes…! Here we go~o!"

CHAPTER FORTY-THREE

The top of the mountain breached the surface of the world, which was only noticeable due to the sudden lack of screeching rock, followed by the detonation of the super-volcano on a scale that left everyone's ears bleeding. In the next moment, anyone or anything not bolted to the ground was slammed to the floor as they accelerated upward by the escaping gasses, then became weightless and drifted in the air as they entered free-fall.

Having healed his ears near-instantly with his Neutrality Aura's passive effect, Joe was able to catch the orders that Grandmaster Havoc was issuing. "Deploy legs! Activate stabilizers, fire boosters as needed, spare no mana even if it burns out the components. Brace for impact!"

Attention! Your Hamlet has revealed itself to the world! The Divine Ward protecting it has been broken! It can no longer be considered 'Hidden'.

It took a few moments for Joe to realize that the Grandmaster was not shouting at anyone in particular, but at the volcano around them as a whole. Somehow, it still hadn't quite registered that he had converted the entirety of the mountain around them into a golem, and had prepared it with this exact situation in mind. Now that he factored in Havoc's preferred method of attacking, he was certain that the volcano had not just *acted* like a drill… it almost certainly *was* a drill.

Now that the outer crust was no longer needed, portions of the exterior walls began tearing themselves off and leaving gaps that people could see through… or fall out of. Some hapless residents were pulled toward the openings as the surrounding space explosively decompressed, only to be grabbed at the last moment by… nothing that the naked eye could see. Joe touched the Essence orb on his bandolier and instantly was able to observe the effects of mana actualized in the world. Lines of power were strung from everyone who had been about to be ejected, leading all the way back to Grandmaster Snow, who was holding them in place with threads of mana that she was manipulating.

"I'm going to be able to do that someday," Joe promised himself, watching in admiration as she directed the fall of tens of thousands of people without breaking a sweat. Moments later, a sort of net ejected from her, falling over the assembled masses and keeping them securely fastened to the ground. "Nothing quite like magical seat belts; don't know how much that is going—*ugh*!"

They had struck the ground, and while Havoc's design had kept the volcano from being completely eradicated, the walls had undeniably sustained heavy damage. Large chunks of rock fell, only to be caught by either Grandmaster Snow or another Dwarf who was at minimum an Expert earth-based mage of some kind. The rubble didn't stay in place; instead, it grew small legs and crawled back up into position, seamlessly melting into its surroundings and repairing the damage.

When everyone was certain that they had survived, and the Grandmasters agreed that there was no more movement to be wary of, the secured people were released and encouraged to get to their feet. Joe suddenly found himself being pulled through the air, landing inside the encirclement of Masters and Grandmasters. Havoc gave him a once-over, shaking his head at the fact that Joe was still pristinely clean, his all-white gear free from even a smudge of ash. Everyone else looked like they had been living in a chimney, though that was rapidly changed for those within the range of Joe's aura. "Alright kid, I'm going to open a path so you can do your thing. What do you need?"

"For the evacuation?" Joe's question popped out of his mouth before his rattled mind caught up, only realizing how clueless he sounded when his mentor rolled his eyes at him.

"*No*, I meant what sort of *creamer* did you want in your *coffee*. Yes, the evacuation, you snollygoster!"

The Ritualist shook off his fugue state and focused on the issue at hand. "Got it! I need nine different entrances, and the ritual can take the Dwarves as fast as they can pass through it. First, though, I need an estimation of the distance it is going to need to take them, and what sort of conditions we will need to avoid. I need to account for all variables, if possible."

Havoc gestured at the wall, which slid open to reveal a beautiful city engulfed in flames.

"Looks like total travel distance is about five kilometers, and there are some buildings in the way." The Dwarf smirked, watching as a few of those buildings started to topple, lava washing over their foundations and sending the structures tumbling. "Although it seems like the issue is resolving itself, so I don't know how long you'll need to watch out for those."

"Plan for the worst, and all that," Joe muttered distractedly, already tweaking the distance variables of his bubbles. Surrounded by people that he could absolutely trust, he didn't have any concern about watching his back or protecting himself as he worked. The security of his surroundings allowed him to get everything in place with incredible efficiency, and at his nod, they all floated through the air at high speed to the opening that Havoc had made.

Joe set out the ritual tiles, activating them as he placed them, and soon nine perfectly round distortions were hanging in the air—each separated by a couple of feet on either side. Once they were stable, he pulled up the double circle that he had designed specifically for this formation of rituals, sending it into the air and pulling the sympathetic links from the encapsulating circles to the inner active ones. As expected, and as his research had promised, the nine circles integrated the additional instructions without complaint or strain. "Can anyone set up nine tunnels running to this so that we can get people moving through them right away?"

The ground itself shifted, breaking apart into innumerable thousands of fragments resembling beetles, which grabbed each other and reverted into what appeared to be only stone, but was functionally a honeycomb of tunnels long enough for everyone to start moving through them. Platforms extended, as did ramps, and people began choosing their lines immediately. Joe couldn't encourage them enough, and as the very first of them reached the distortions and stepped through, the rituals burst into full swing.

"Line up! I need three Dwarves per second per line!" A voice Joe hadn't been expecting broke in and took charge of the situation. His eyes flicked over to where Lord Checkoff was ordering people around and getting the chaotic lines to move in a semblance of order. "That's not good enough! You! Two inches to the right! You! Your carry-on must be stowed in a spatial bag, there's no room for that in the tunnels, and you'll hold up the lines! *You-*"

Joe tuned out the Noble Dwarf as he watched the spectacle of fleeing refugees. Dozens of bubbles per second blasted out of the hole in the side of the mountain, resulting in hundreds of empty ones shrouding those in use. Even with as fast as the Dwarves and enhanced humans could move through the lines, at least four to five bubbles floated between any that held a person. Joe watched with pure excitement, barely even managing to whisper softly to himself, "Bubblebeam is super effective!"

The total travel time from the mountain to the shining light reaching into the sky—the Bifrost—was only about two minutes and nineteen seconds, which meant that the bubbles were rocketing along at just over eighty miles per hour. As the first of them reached the light bridge rising into the sky, a notification popped up that infuriated Joe to no end.

A large number of The Shattered Race: Dwarven Oligarchy, is attempting to flee from this Zone! The first of them have already started to escape upon the Bifrost! An emergency quest has been issued to all Elves and Elven-affiliated humans on the Zone Alfheim.

"Abyss, I really thought we were going to have more time before the notification went out." Snow shook her head sadly. "If only our ancestors hadn't chosen the path of violence when they first arrived on this world, we could have avoided all of this."

"Well, we won last time." Havoc also sounded tired, making Joe wonder what he had needed to sacrifice in order to orchestrate this escape attempt. Judging by the sheer amount and strength of the golems that had replaced an entire mountain, he likely had invested *everything* that he had managed to save and build over his centuries on this Zone. "Why would we have chosen to be pacifists when we were the victor? *Now* that seems foolish, but at the time, it was the best move to secure the greatest number of resources and highest chance of success for our people."

"Conflict breeds creativity," Joe interjected before they could sink into a downward spiral. "The problem with a Utopia is that if you have no reason to progress, you *won't*. I think perhaps your ancestors knew that if they allowed themselves to become complacent, they would devolve into something they didn't want to be. Look at us now! We just rode a volcanic eruption into salvation. How cool is *that*?"

The Grandmasters looked at each other, a ghost of a smile appearing on their faces. It was Snow who answered, since Havoc merely harrumphed and lit his cigar. "Pretty 'cool' indeed."

"I don't suppose you mentioned to your Alchemist worker that he needed to get out of here, did you?" Havoc had barely gotten the question out when Joe's face went pale, and the human turned and sprinted toward the center of the hamlet.

"Guess not. Alright, Snow. Let's get to Jotunheim. It's been *far* too long."

"Lifetimes," she agreed in a wistful tone. The entire Council blurred and vanished, moments later shrouded among the thousands of bubbles that were streaming toward the Bifrost.

Joe saw none of that, keeping his attention on his Omnivaulting so that he didn't accidentally crush anyone when he landed. Only a few minutes later, he was pounding on the door of the Pyramid of Panacea, which opened instantly as the Alchemist emerged. Joe had to stumble away, the bloodlust and killing intent rolling so densely off the person in front of him that he touched his Essence Cycle bound orb to see if there was an actual effect in the ambient world around the man.

There was.

A massive cloud of rage-tinted mana generated a ghastly, horrific form around the man, as though a skyscraper-sized monster was contained within the deceptively frail human vessel. "I am going to assume my experiment was ruined due to Havoc's actions, and not yours. Otherwise, I must hold *you* responsible for the damage to my garments, as well as the reagents that were lost in the attempt."

Unsure how to answer without putting his mentor at risk, Joe gestured into the distance, where the bubble beam was sending hundreds of Dwarves toward the Bifrost every second. "We are escaping to Jotunheim. I think you should come with us, and I will make it a priority to bring the building shortly thereafter."

"Is that an invitation to join you in the next Zone?"

"Does it need to be?" Joe narrowed his eyes as he considered the man... no, the entity in front of him. When Jake remained motionless and waited without speaking, Joe slowly nodded. "Jake, I'd be honored if you would join me in the next Zone to continue your work as an alchemist."

"That's more like it. Now, in all fairness... if I had been working in anything other than the cauldron that you created the building around, I would tell you that leaving right now would be *literally* criminal on any Zone. Leaving active warp inside of a container instead of cleaning it out...? Well, luckily for all of us, that cauldron is self-cleaning. Let's go."

Jake vanished, and no matter how carefully Joe scanned the area around him—with or without Essence Cycle active—he could not spot the Alchemist. Rubbing at his neck, Joe decided that he simply had to assume that the man had escaped, and that it was time to make a break for it himself. One of the benefits of owning the area, as well as the active ritual that was saving all of these people, was that he felt perfectly okay about skipping the line. He Omnivaulted right back over to it, diving through the distortion as a Lord Checkoff called out at him furiously for not properly waiting his turn.

With a burst of iridescent light, he was traveling over the ruined Elven capital city. As it burned or melted, Joe was struck by how tragic the view actually was. This city had clearly been built up as one cohesive whole. Anything that was not grown naturally into a building was supplemented by beautifully carved quartz or other translucent stones. Unlike the cities of the Dwarves, this was a winding forest with lazy switchbacks, and was intentionally designed for aesthetics far more than defense.

That made Joe pause in thought. "There is no way that this place *isn't* designed with security in mind. They've been at war for centuries. Most likely, the whole thing can attack autonomously. I bet they have all sorts of Druids, nature Mages, people that can pull elementals out of that stone, and so many natural defenses that I likely couldn't think of all of them on my own."

With that in mind, it was easy to shift his perspective of the city below as he passed over it. Those trees that were on fire were not moving around naturally; the wind was blowing opposite to the direction they were shifting. They were likely some kind of living tree, or inhabited by Dryads. The quartz no longer simply appeared to be a beautiful, if somewhat dazzling display—instead he searched deeper and found enchantments woven into it that would summon elementals, send out spikes of earth, or trap attackers within rapidly-filling pits. "Then again, that might just be my imagination going wild. At the speed I'm moving, and with how little I know of this… well, I can only assume."

He relaxed in his bubble as it approached the energy of the Bifrost. The way he had set up the end point, his bubble should pop just as it entered into the energy stream. Mentally prepared, he waited until his entire body was caught in the light, mentally slamming 'yes' as the notification appeared.

You have entered the Bifrost! Would you like to travel to the next destination: Jotunheim? Yes / No.

Joe felt his momentum shift from forward to *up*. In an instant, he was breaking through the atmosphere and rocketing into space, following the rainbow bridge to the next Zone. Confident that he was safe from harm for the next while, he settled into his thoughts and pondered what to do next.

"As soon as I land, I need to help in subjugating any Elves that got through." He ticked off the list on his fingers as he went. "From there, setting up rituals around the area that will attack anyone who is not a human or a Dwarf. That should give us some protection, however meager, from whatever the local wildlife looks like. Then I need to see what it is going to take to bring buildings across; maybe I should start by testing it with the guildhall? Yeah… let's do that."

His mind drifted away from the Dwarves, and onto the thing that was *truly* the most important to him. "I need to figure out how to rescue Jaxon. As soon as the Dwarves are safe, I'm getting right back on this Bifrost and figuring out where he's being held."

Then he got a *most* unwelcome notification.

You have contributed to the death of a Dwarf on Alfheim by holding them in place to be slain! For the purposes of removing your mandatory title, this counts as one half of a kill! Kills remaining until the title achieves the next stage: 9.5!

You have contributed to the death-

You have-

"No! It must have counted my ritual as 'trapping' them!" Twenty notifications appeared in the span of only a dozen or so seconds. With a sinking heart, Joe realized that the Elves must have launched a large-scale counterattack against the stream of bubbles. With how many Dwarves had been slain, he knew that the Elves must have been putting everything they had into stopping the escape. "I only wish I could have done more for them."

Title removed: Excommunicated!

Trait lost: Dwarven Superiority!

You may now apply to an Elven chapel or temple for re-education into Elven ways!

Even though the message was horrific, Joe's eyes glowed with passion as he realized that he had just been given a great boon. "Got rid of the title, didn't need to kill any Dwarves personally, and now when I go back for Jaxon... the red glow that marked me as a Dwarven sympathizer is gone. They'll never see me coming."

CHAPTER FORTY-FOUR

The starry expanse that surrounded the Bifrost soon gave way to the first glimpse Joe received of Jotunheim. Having been on two Zones so far, the second being a collision of Alfheim and Svartalfheim, he had certain expectations for what the area would look like as he approached it.

Every single one of them was blown away as the new Zone came into view. "Is that... a gas giant?" He wasn't flying toward a single flat zone like Midgard, nor toward two spinning discs as the previous Zone had been; instead, this one was formulated to resemble Jupiter in appearance.

Instead of reds, oranges, and yellows like the giant planet back in his universe, this one was awash in greens and blues. Soon the dense cloud layer was in front of him, and he shot through a massive storm that was sending everything from acid to diamonds sparkling through the air. "This planet is a treasure already... what is going *on*?"

After a solid handful of seconds—which was impressive at this speed—he finally passed through the clouds and sighted the ground far below. The planet was so large that he couldn't see the curvature of it even from this great height, but he knew that it was a sphere due to the path that the Bifrost had taken to deposit him on the planet's surface. "Maybe that's why this is known as the world of giants in mythology? Because it is simply so massive?"

He was slowing down, approaching the exit point, and started to discern Dwarves in front of and behind him. There were sure to be Elves waiting below for them, but the amount of time between the opening of the rainbow bridge and the Dwarves beginning to travel along it had been minuscule at best. Since there were tens of thousands of Dwarves that would be coming through, they had a good shot at holding this location.

Joe landed, the impact shattering the ground. Even so, none of the force was transferred to him, the energy of the Bifrost cocooning him until he had fully stopped. Without missing a beat, he activated ritual after ritual, hurling them into the distance like frisbees. The tiles were strong and would survive landing easily, and they would offer basic protection against anything that was coming for an easy meal or a quick kill. He continued on until he had created a huge radius of rituals, some of which activated immediately.

Quest update: Student Ritualist II. Creatures killed: 14/100.

There was no indication of what the spells were attacking, but they wouldn't be running unless a hostile monster or an Elf was present in the area. As the counter slowly continued to tick upward, Joe selected a more defensible location and searched for a group that he could work with. In the distance, he spotted Major Cleave commanding the last of the Legionnaires that had been able to make it through, which had been one of the first groups through the bubbles.

He considered moving to assist, but it appeared that they had everything under control and were patrolling with calm, practiced motions. Soon, the area was secure, and he hadn't done anything more than wasting a few rituals that were simple to replace. Thousands more Dwarves were arriving every few minutes, and the circumference that needed to be protected continued to rapidly expand.

Joe had planned to continue on with the fight, but Havoc unexpectedly appeared next to him between one moment and the next, gripping his shoulder and staring wildly into his eyes. "You *brought* the Alchemist with you? You were supposed to tell him that we were leaving, not invite him along!"

Completely dumbfounded by the abrupt start of this conversation, Joe could only push the Dwarf's hand off and throw his hands up. "It's whatever, Havoc! We are here, he is here, soon the building will be too. I just need to try out this new ritual-"

"Do. Not. *Practice.* On an Artifact-ranked building. Certainly not on one that is owned by... Jake." Havoc turned away and saw the swarm of people that was continuing to grow with every passing moment.

"I'm not gonna! I'll start with the guildhall, and make sure all the kinks are worked out before-"

"Stop. Why don't you round up as many people as you need and get the guildhall here immediately, instead of flapping your lips. It's going to be more important than practically any other building on this Zone. The sheer scale of this place means that transportation between any habitable location is going to absolutely require teleportation. Since most teleportation can be achieved through guildhalls or town halls, that is the number one priority."

Joe nodded along as another realization dawned on him. "It's also one of the buildings that is easiest to replace if it is destroyed, right? That's why I was *already* planning to grab it."

"Right you are." Havoc's focus snapped into the distance as a blood-curdling scream rang out, and his face turned grim. "Since the guildhall matters and *doesn't* matter at the same time, it's the perfect Canary Hog in a mine shaft."

"Guinea pig. Canary in a coal mine," Joe sputtered, trying unsuccessfully to untangle the metaphors that Havoc was using.

"Doesn't matter! Fine, I'll bring that one across soon—*ow*! Fine, right now!"

"Move fast. With the volume of people coming through currently, combined with Jotunheim-specific conditions, as soon as no one is actively using the Bifrost, it'll change locations and start depositing people on a different part of the planet. If we don't have a way to get them here, they'll be Elves before you know it."

With that cryptic and dire warning, Havoc vanished, leaving a trail of dust that followed him into the distance—directly towards where the scream had erupted from moments ago. Joe massaged his left shoulder, where Havoc-finger shaped bruises had formed, though they were already fading due to his perpetual healing effect. Gathering his nerves, he squinted up at the swirling clouds that seemed to cast this world in a perpetual twilight and shouted to everyone around him. "I need *volunteers*! As many people as I can get who are used to channeling large amounts of mana! On me, now!"

Perhaps it was the fact that his head was sparkling with shimmering, iridescent light and acting as a beacon, or maybe due to the reputation that he had created for himself, hundreds of people swarmed over to him almost immediately. "Stand back! I'm going to be dropping a chunk of metal."

The Ebonsteel metal block slammed onto the ground, sinking half an inch into the spongy surface of the planet. It was only then that Joe realized that the gravity of the world around him was easily triple or more of the previous Zone. Only the fact that he had boosted his stats to their current level, combined with Mind Over Matter, allowed him to function as easily as he was. A tap of his Essence Cycle orb revealed that the energy in the world around him was similarly as dense as it was on Alfheim... but he quickly realized that for it to be that dense over such a massive planet meant that this world was of *incredibly* higher quality.

As the ritual blazed to life, it shone with a much higher intensity of light than was otherwise present on the planet's surface, lighting up the surrounding area to early evening proportions instead of twilight. The effect didn't extend very far, but it allowed everyone to see what he was doing with perfect clarity. Joe stared down at the map, feeling a cold chill run down his spine as no options for bringing buildings across were visible. The only positive note was the fact that all of the land adjacent to his position was designated as 'unclaimed wilds'.

"There has to be an option for previously tied buildings to be pulled, otherwise what was the whole point of all of this?" As far as he could see, even as his searching became more frantic and intense, there was nothing. Then he touched the map and found that, similar to a tablet device back on Earth, he could move the map around. "Yes! If I can move it, that means I can zoom it out, right?"

A moment later, he was looking at Jotunheim from a satellite view, which allowed him to select the previous Zone to inspect. However, it didn't function as a map; it only showed him the various buildings that he had tagged with the child rituals. He tapped one of the small pink dots, and it expanded to show the guildhall and its specifications. Double-tapping it selected the building for relocation and returned him to his view of the current area.

A green holographic grid appeared above the ritual that he was using, turning red in the next instant. Joe wasn't exactly certain what to do, but it reminded him of his times playing strategy games. Mentally pushing the red outline of the building, it moved and came to rest on a location not too far from him, turning green, then alternately flashing back and forth with red. "Anyone under the light, get out of the way!"

Humans and Dwarves scattered, and the space became completely green with a ghostly silhouette of the guildhall hovering above the plot of land. "I think I've got it!"

He selected for the transfer to begin, and five Ritual Circles rippled out from the block of metal. Joe directed anyone who would listen to stand on the rings, arranging them in a pleasing prime-number array around the edges. "I have no idea what is about to happen, so hold on tight and *do not* get off of the circles!"

Accepting the transfer, Joe staggered as though he had been punched in the gut as mana was *ripped* out of him. Based on the wheezing that came from his surroundings, he was not the only one that had felt the intense yanking from within. A horrid buzzing filled the air, as though ten thousand wasps were closing in to sting someone right between their toes.

An instant after it started, yet another ritual circle left the metal block and raced into the air over the ghostly outline that was waiting for the transfer to begin. The circle shrank down to nothing more than a dot of light in the sky, then slowly began widening once more. As it began progressing downward, the tip of the roof of the guildhall appeared wherever it passed—hanging in the air with nothing below to support it.

The deluge of mana pouring out of the people supporting the ritual increased, and the circle continued to move downward, pulling the building across the massive space that separated the two Zones. On and on it went, until the entire structure had appeared and fully materialized on this plane.

Joe stared at the structure, waiting until the ritual was fully completed, then pumped his fist in the air and shouted, "*We did it!*"

A cacophony of cheering erupted in the area as the first building's arrival signaled the start of a new home, a new center of civilization for the Dwarven people. Joe got a message that he had been expecting, but even so, he was surprised at what he read.

You have built a guildhall on Jotunheim! Area upgraded from wildlands into: Tier 0 Camp! By placing a guildhall, you have declared ownership of the area. Area ownership will continue to extend unless it meets the ownership of another group. Continue to cultivate your location into higher town and city rankings to increase the land ownership faster! Current land claimed, due to no competition: 100 square miles.

Rituarchitect class experience gained: 1,000. (Bonus experience awarded for utilizing a new method of building creation for the first time!)

"That's... a lot more room to grow than I had been expecting us to get. I sure as the abyss didn't expect the system to consider this as a new building, either. Perhaps it's due to the teleportation paradox? Maybe, although this is the exact same building, it's *not* the building that was located on the last Zone?" Joe slowly nodded as he stroked his hairless chin. "Either way... I agree, even that much land isn't going to be enough for all of these people to thrive. I need to get the teleportation arrays in order, and then get my rear back to Alfheim. Can't let Jaxon think I abandoned him for one second longer than necessary."

"Major-General Joe! We captured an Elven-associated human." A Legionnaire ran up to Joe and gave him a crisp salute as he came to a halt. "While we would normally execute the captive immediately, Major Cleave has requested your input on this matter. Apparently you know this one?"

There were only a handful of people it could possibly be. Joe considered simply ordering the execution and not forcing himself to acknowledge the prisoner or hear them out, but although he hesitated for a moment, he eventually agreed to come to the interrogation.

CHAPTER FORTY-FIVE

It was Daniella. Of course it was her. As soon as he caught a glimpse of her face, Joe slowed down to a trudge as he contemplated how he would handle this interaction. She had betrayed him and his team, but as far as he could tell, she hadn't done it out of spite. There were sure to be a huge number of factors at play, and he had to wonder if—were he in the same sort of situation—he would have done the same. "No... I wouldn't, but how much would I have suffered because I didn't try to take care of myself? Is it fair to demand that she does?"

He kept his eyes on Major Cleave as he approached, even though his fellow human was working with increasing desperation to catch his attention. The Dwarf nodded at him, her axe practically vibrating at her side as she held herself back from slicing the captive in twain. "Found this one lurking around; looks like she was sent as one of the advance parties. Probably scouting out a location to drop a building."

"That is *not* why I'm here!" Daniella interjected, finally unable to contain herself while she was being spoken about as though she weren't present. "I disobeyed orders and jumped on the Bifrost, because I knew that this was the most likely place for me to find you again."

"You sure it had nothing to do with the super volcano erupting underneath the Capital city and sending a wave of lava at you?" Joe finally turned to look at her, feeling incredibly tired as he met her eyes. "That would seem more your style, avoiding either helping or needing help. You probably felt the first hint of an earthquake and beamed yourself up."

"*No.* I came here because I needed to make things right with you." Daniella sucked in a deep breath, clearly about to say something she felt was monumental, when one of the guards next to her clapped a hand over her mouth.

"Charisma-based skill activating," the guard informed them as he held Daniella's pie-hole shut. "From what I could tell, she's got some kind of persistent persuasion effect on her."

Mmph! Daniella shook her head as best as she could while she had a hand gripping her face like a steel vice.

"I say we break her legs and chuck her in a bush a good distance away from camp." The second guard—who was holding an axe to the back of her head—added his vote. "That way, the wildlife will take care of her, and she'll have a full-length respawn time. That should give us plenty of leeway before she is able to report any of this to her *actual* superiors."

Something about the interaction seemed… off. Joe felt that he would normally have agreed with the guard immediately, but in this moment, his methods seemed overly brutal and at least a *touch* unjustified. As he pondered what could have changed, he shook his head. "Let's make a decision on what to do with her first, then follow through, no matter what she has to say. That way, we'll know we're not being influenced by her words, and she gets to explain herself."

"In that case, she will be tied to a prisoner post and left there until her words prove true or she gets eaten by something local," Major Cleave announced. There was a unanimous consensus from the other Dwarves, so Joe could only sigh and agree with them.

Daniella's eyes widened as she realized that there was going to be no opportunity to change her situation. Joe motioned for the guard to remove his hand, and the Architect spat to get the taste of filthy hand off her tongue. "Seriously! It's a permanent effect; I *can't* toggle it off."

"At least I know why I had such issues with deciding whether to let you come with me or not." Joe tapped on the side of his bald skull. "Mental Manipulation Resistance. Clearly, it was too low of a level to warn me about what you were doing, but it was able to at least whisper that you were messing with my head. There you were, getting me all wound up and convincing me that you were going to make sure that the things I was doing had a conscience behind them. I guess I really *do* need to get better at listening. To *myself*."

"This was about *survival*," Daniella insisted to the people around her. "All I wanted was to have a nice, safe life, maybe a residence in a little upscale area where I could advance my class and skills without getting torn up by monsters and other people. I never had so much as a broken *toe* back on Earth! How am I supposed to get over being torn apart by monsters? *Eaten*? I was a *pacifist*. I don't know how you and the other combat classes do it-"

"I'm *not* a combat class." Joe shrugged carelessly as everyone around him turned doubtful stares on him. "Really. I'm a Crafter. In fact, I specialized as a Crafter three times in a row. Just because I can craft weapons out of thin air doesn't mean I am supposed to be a combat class. A weaponsmith can make swords; does that mean they are supposed to be on the front lines?"

There were a few non-committal noises that rose from the people around him, but Joe didn't feel any need to further justify himself. Yet, Daniella did make a good point. Joe at least had the benefit of his military experience, both the training and the end results of knowing how to handle pain and suffering. He'd been through all the highs and lows that combat could bring, and he had treated the fact that he could come back from any injury here as a way to mostly ignore the emotionally draining aspects of enduring battle. The fact that the system inherently helped to smooth over those experiences made it even easier for him.

"Then I'll get right to the point." Daniella stared directly into his eyes, not a hint of mirth to be found. "Capturing Jaxon was *never* part of the bargain. I had made sure that all of you were supposed to be free and clear, so long as you moved on to the next Zone as soon as it opened. That wasn't explicitly stated in the quest, only being a verbal agreement, so there is no way for me to enforce it. But I can, and *will*, do everything that I can to make it right. At least... *this* part of what I did."

"How are you going to do that?" Joe looked around theatrically, his arms extended. "I don't see my waylaid party member around here. I don't see Herr Trigger tied up in a corner with a smiling Chiropractor shifting his bones into the wrong position."

"Remember the whole 'I'm not a combat class' thing that I was just talking about?" Daniella shot back at him, obviously annoyed by his taunting. "I can't break him out myself, but I know where they're keeping him. There's a prisoner of war dungeon, and it's right next to the Capital to ensure access to the very best 're-educators' available to work on people."

"What... do they do to them there?" Joe slowly inquired, not sure if he wanted to know the answer.

"Their first thing that they do is to force any human affiliated with the Dwarves to kill off the Dwarven prisoners until they lose their trait." Daniela swallowed hard; but even so, her next admission came out raspy. "Then they keep them in small rooms and indoctrinate them until they gain the Elven Superiority trait. Because there is no way to lose that trait, since the Elves are now a Unified race, at that point they are subsequently set free. But... they are never going to be given access to the Bifrost, and they will never be allowed access to a class trainer or information on how to progress themselves. The idea is that by the time they finally are strong enough to fight back against the Elves and attempt to break into Jotunheim, they won't. They'll have settled into the Elven way of life and never have a way to escape it."

"Forced assimilation on a grand scale." Joe wasn't sure whether to be impressed by the fact that the Elves had such a practice in place already, or if he should be disgusted by that piece of information. "That's unfortunate... but the fact of the matter is, we can't trust you. All of this sounds accurate, and I'm sure it *is*, but you've betrayed us once before. Now you want me to willingly let you lead me to a forced assimilation re-education camp?"

"Actually, all she would be doing is giving you the location," Major Cleave interjected, startling Joe from his ranting. It had been quite a while since he had forgotten her presence when she was an active participant, but maybe it had something to do with the sheer amount of focus he was giving Daniella. Or... could that be a side effect of whatever power she was using all of the time? Perhaps it wasn't *his* fault that he'd accidentally snubbed his once-guardian, now-companion so many times?

He was going to roll with that and hope it was the truth. Joe turned to Daniella after acknowledging the Major's words with a nod. "Alright. Fine. Go ahead and tell me where to go, and how to find him. For your sake, I hope that I can rescue him and return before a local predator catches your scent. Something tells me that no one here is going to try too hard to fend it off."

That made the captive gulp, but even so, she remained steadfast and passed along the details that Joe needed. After double-checking the information, and a barrage of cross-examination questions from the other guards, they could find no holes in her story. Without thanking her, Joe and Major Cleave walked away, leaving the other guards to truss up the human and leave her exposed to the elements.

When they were a safe distance away, the two of them tried to decide how to handle what they had just heard. Joe locked eyes with his friend. "I'll be going after Jaxon. Even if this is a trap, I owe him that much."

"*Absolutely*, you do," Cleave agreed instantly, causing Joe to choke on his next argument. "Let's discuss what you are going to need in order to make it back in one piece. First off, if the rumors I have heard about this place are true, the Bifrost won't bring you back here after you leave."

"That's what Havoc was saying," Joe agreed, recalling his discussion with the grumpy Grandmaster. "We set up the guild-hall right away to circumvent that issue, but I-"

"Here's what you do." Cleave interrupted him by shoving him to the side, "You take one of the teleportation pads that was keyed to the guildhall—you had extras to give to the Grandmasters, right? Good. Figure out how to use that to either guide you back here, or bring you back directly. I'm not some kind of fancy enchanter, but that seems like something you can do."

"It…" Joe furrowed his brow as he processed what she was implying. "Yes… I suppose that even if it was inactive, the sympathetic link between the two could act as a kind of lode-stone to indicate the correct direction. A compass, if you will. The problem is going to be the sheer scale of this world. If we get dropped somewhere else, it could be months before we make it back, even if we sprint the entire time and run into no issues at all. That seems unlikely."

"Then figure out how to *open* the portal. It shouldn't be too hard, since they're already linked." She grunted and abruptly turned the conversation away from what she had been saying. "Like I said, magical crafting and the like is not my forte. I cut stuff up. So that is escape plan number one; what are you going to do to make it into the prison camp and get Jaxon out?"

"You know…" Joe looked at the sky, watching as the storms far above traveled along, and remembered how they had been throwing around everything from acid to diamonds. "I think I just had an inspiration for a ritual that can cause enough of a distraction for me."

CHAPTER FORTY-SIX

Joe passed thousands of Dwarves as he rode the Bifrost back toward the previous Zone—toward his friend. Since he and they were moving so fast, they were only tiny blips of light, resembling nothing more than passing energy. Even so, he knew what they were. For every one that he saw, the weight of responsibility that he felt pressing down on his shoulders lightened considerably.

He had spent a few hours working with Grandmaster Snow, but it was Havoc—a dedicated killer of Mages—who finally gave him the key component for his new ritual. It was... *dark* was a good way to put it. Despite that aspect, he wasn't going to hesitate to activate it in an attempt to free his friend and any other captives he could save at the same time. Locked away in his storage ring, he also carried a teleportation pad that should eject him into a nice open plain just to the left wall of the guild-hall when he came back.

His hope was that he would be coming back with lots of other prisoner-of-war Dwarves that he had been able to rescue. If not, it was still a good idea *not* to teleport into someone else. Havoc promised to keep that area clear, and Joe shivered as he tried not to think of what methods the possibly insane Dwarf might use to make that happen. With nothing else to do, and quite a long time left in the energy stream that was bringing him back to the Elf-dominated world, Joe decided it was a good time to look over his character sheet.

Before that, he decided that he needed to activate his Knowledge skill. He found that it was the first time that he would be able to upgrade two of his lore skills at the same time after they had reached the Student rank. Since it had been a while since the last boost to his Ritual Lore, he was looking forward to making that happen. Choosing that skill, as well as Calculus And Number Theory for his second option, he activated his skill.

Instantly he regretted it.

Mana tried to swarm in from the ambient area around him, but all of the free energy in the Bifrost stream was being used to propel him forward and continue his travel. The clashing influences resulted in the ambient mana being forcibly pulled to focus on his head, and his pace increased *drastically* without the protective resistance to temper his fall.

Caution! Speed safeguards deactivated!

"Well, that's certainly not a fun message to see," Joe grumbled as his Knowledge skill continued processing. In the next moment, he had received a message that Ritual Lore had reached Student three, and Calculus And Number Theory had reached Beginner six. He ignored those in favor of anxiously watching a slight bend in the upcoming Bifrost, wondering if he was about to be ejected into the chaotic space between worlds.

Previously, he had considered that area as empty space, but a simple glance with his Essence Cycle-bound Ritual Orb was enough to convince him that it was anything but empty. Most likely, that space had *things* in it, similar to the abyss where he had accidentally reverse-summoned himself. He could only hope that he was not about to be chucked out there, feeling both relief and concern as he was *almost* thrown into space, but was yanked back at the last second by the rainbow bridge.

Unfortunately, that only increased his speed further and made his travel more unpredictable. Soon, he was ping-ponging between the outer bounds of the energy stream, constantly moving faster. For the first time ever, he was getting motion sick, and he popped open his character sheet just to be able to focus on something that remained at a static distance from him. As soon as it appeared, he was able to relax into the knowledge that at least he would be able to respawn if he was blasted into the emptiness in the next short while. "Maybe I will somehow land on the moon?"

Name: Joe 'Chosen Legend of Occultatum' Class: Reductionist
Profession I: Arcanologist (Max)
Profession II: Ritualistic Alchemist (1/20)
Profession III: Grandmaster's Apprentice (14/25)
Profession IV: None.
Character Level: 23 Exp: 279,833 Exp to next level: 20,167
Rituarchitect Level: 10 Exp: 54,700 Exp to next level: 300
Reductionist Level: 4 Exp: 10, 986 Exp to next level: 4,014
Hit Points: 2,327/2,327
Mana: 3,957/8,160
Mana regen: 67.83/sec
Stamina: 1,837/1,837
Stamina regen: 6.64/sec

Characteristic: Raw score

Strength (bound): 176
Dexterity: 177
Constitution: 169
Intelligence (bound): 185
Wisdom: 168
Dark Charisma: 123
Perception: 173
Luck: 110
Karmic Luck: 14

It was interesting to see that because of his rapid recent growth, the only things that had changed were the experience values he had earned. His eyes definitely were caught on the Reductionist class experience, excited to see that he only needed three hundred more before reaching the next level. Seeing the details laid out confirmed that working on increasing his skill levels, especially to and through the Master ranks, was going to be the best—and possibly only—way to progress from now on.

The Zone came into view, and he rocketed toward the ground, leaving a trail of energy that resembled a bolt of lightning cascading down the Bifrost. When he hit the ground, he *hit* the ground. He could feel the energy of the rainbow bridge attempting to reduce his inertia to zero, but since he had damaged the speed regulations, it was only able to *partially* mitigate the damage to both his body and the impacted terrain around him.

A massive wave of cascading energy ballooned out from his impact point, creating a miniature mushroom cloud as it collapsed back inward. Dozens of Elves surrounding the entryway were turned into ash as the energy cloud enveloped them, but Joe didn't receive even a single point of experience. Most likely, their deaths were counted as terrain damage.

As for himself, between his Exquisite Shell and the bridge actively working to keep him safe—one of its only tasks—he survived the landing with only a token set of injuries. The fractures in his femur, left ankle, three ribs, two lower lumbar vertebrae, and a minor crack in his skull were a slight price to pay, especially when he was able to tap his orb of Lay on Hands and bring himself back to combat-ready vitality in the next instant. He couldn't help feeling grateful that his landing had resulted in opening his escape route for him.

Title gained: Superhero Landing! By surviving a cataclysmic fall and wiping out at least five opponents, you have proven you have what it takes to fall outrageously heavily without killing yourself! When you jump or fall from a high enough location, you are now able to expel half of the total terrain damage to the area around you instead of taking it yourself. Anything killed by this damage will not *count as your kill!*

"Well… it was useful once, so I'm sure it will be again in the future." Even though he tried to act nonchalant so that the system would not increase the associated detriment, all he could think about was how perfectly he could pair this new ability with his Omnivault. He also played it off as not the accidental result of breaking the Bifrost, but something that he should have naturally gained. In his mind, he knew that if he were to make a big deal about it in this moment, he would gain another curse that he would need to work off.

Turning his focus strictly to his mission, the Ritualist attempted to orient himself, but found it difficult due to the copious amount of smoke in the air, combined with the fact that the overall landscape of the Elven capital city had been shifted drastically, certainly for the worse. The secondary problem that he was encountering was the fact that he had been deposited in the center of the city, instead of riding in a bubble floating over it. There was a strong likelihood that simply getting out of the city would require careful maneuvering, dodging traps, and evading patrols on the lookout for any Dwarven-affiliated people trying to sneak through and access the Bifrost.

He started to walk and realized at that moment why—during his conversation with Daniella—he had disagreed with the punishment the Dwarves had been planning for her. "Celestials above, I totally forgot that I had already lost the Dwarven superiority trait. That'll certainly make it more difficult to interact with the Dwarves going forward, but… it might become a huge benefit in getting out of this place. So long as I don't go attacking any Elves, I shouldn't regain a red murderer's glow."

In an environment where the Elves were on high alert, especially after the grand entrance the Shoe had made into the city, anything that made him stand out would bring an immediate attack. Instead of trying to skulk around and act shady, Joe strolled down what remained of the main street that should eventually lead out of the city and take him where he needed to go. There were multiple instances when shining armor-clad Elves sprinted past him, not sparing him more than a glance. A single human wearing a shell-shocked expression and wandering down the road as though greatly confused about what was going on was no threat or concern to these paragons of the Elven forces.

At least, that's what he kept in his head as he strolled along. Vacant expression firmly in place, he was able to make it to the border of the city without any issue. Unfortunately, that was when things got... dicey. The gates were closed, and no one was being allowed in or out unless the guards had orders to do so. Joe peered at the top of the wall, trying to decide if he could jump over it, even though a forty-foot drop on the other side would be difficult to manage, even for him.

However, a telltale shimmer in the air revealed that there were more than simple physical protections in place. If he wanted to get over this wall, he would need to either exit through a gate... or make his own point of egress. Joe knew that what he was about to do was incredibly dangerous in a place filled with magically sensitive, highly educated Elves.

He also knew he was going to do it anyway.

The Ritualist followed the ring of buildings until he was a solid half mile or so away from the nearest gate, then pulled out an inscribing tool and set up a Ritual of Raze. It was complete in an instant, swiftly followed by a Ritual of Remote Activation. Targeting the wall itself—which most likely had all sorts of protections in place against this very thing—Joe hurried back to the gatehouse, then slipped into the shadow of an abandoned home to flick a mote of mana into the ritual.

Moments later, a klaxon call went up as the Ritual Circle was spotted in the distance. The entire section of wall lit up bright red as the protective enchantments attempted to neutralize the foreign magic, and troops began pouring out of the gatehouse and sprinting toward the distortion as the wall ever so slowly crumbled. "So long as they don't have anyone with them that can cancel that effect instantly, it will continue for at least a little while. Hopefully, they'll be so focused on that that they don't have the manpower they need in other areas. Places like…"

Joe walked casually up to the gatehouse, and though they had stopped him previously, now they only gave him an annoyed glance as he left. Clearly their focus was on whatever was attacking the wall, and the fact that he wanted to leave was fairly natural. Frankly, *they* probably wanted to leave as well and saw his escape as a frustrating reminder that they could not do so themselves. "Okay, got out, and I even remembered to remove all of my passive enchantments so I wouldn't appear suspicious by getting those ripped off of me."

He could only assume that the Elves had as good or better protections than the Dwarven cities did when it came to magical defenses. Now that he was outside, he searched around for the landmark that Daniella had told him to watch for. The 're-education camp' was off the beaten path so that normal Elven citizens wouldn't stumble upon it, and its entrance was protected from casual passersby. "Now, why would a government not want their citizens to see something? Nothing suspicious here, *totally* not doing anything against their own laws."

After finding the set of stones that looked like a pair of butcher knives—totally not ominous—he found a small trail that led into the woods. Following that path should bring him directly to the camp. Daniella had warned him not to leave the trail, as the protections surrounding the camp had been set up by Druids and similar classes, and were designed to capture looky-loos and escapees alike. So long as he stayed on the path, he shouldn't run into any issues or traps. He could only snort at that thought. "Only as long as this entire *thing* isn't a trap."

Regardless, he had started down this path, and for the sake of his friend, he would continue to walk it until the bitter end.

CHAPTER FORTY-SEVEN

Against all of his expectations, Joe didn't run into any enemies. Even though the cynical part of his brain was screaming that he was a fool, he truly hoped that Daniella hadn't lied to him or intended to put him in a bad position. Before long, he encountered a small fortification, which looked far more Dwarven in construction than anything else he had seen since entering this territory.

Everything surrounding the hasty construction was lush, verdant vegetation and seemingly natural rock formations, even though it was clearly designed with a specific purpose in mind. It appeared to Joe that this place had been built by whatever Dwarven captives had been rounded up, and there was a good chance that was exactly how it had been made. If this truly was a prisoner-of-war camp, it wasn't like the Elves were just going to let their captives sit around drinking tea and eating crumpets all day.

Ironically, the Dwarves would have hated that far more than working, he was almost sure of it.

An average wall was no real impediment to a Rituarchitect who had mastered Omnivaulting, especially since he could tell at a glance that no magical barriers had been placed over it. There certainly were some enchantments, but most of them were various alarms and such meant to alert the guards if there was an escape attempt. Repeating the diversion he had used in the city proper, Joe set up yet another Ritual of Raze, tied it to a remote activation, then Omnivaulted over the wall.

This was the most dangerous portion of his current plan. If he had read the enchantments correctly, someone going *into* the camp wouldn't set off any of the alerts. However, if he had guessed *incorrectly*... he was about to have a very bad day. The other concern was the fact that he was jumping over the wall blindly, bouncing off a tree and Omnivaulting over a twenty-five foot obstacle in his path. There was a better than zero chance that he was going to land directly in front of a guard, so he had his Ritual Orbs out and ready to attack as soon as he was able to peek over the well itself.

To his relief, as well as his growing concern, no one was near the wall at all. Most of the activity he could see was from further in, but the smell of blood hung thick in the air. "They must be forcing their captive humans to kill Dwarves... that's the only possible explanation for this."

Scanning the area, he didn't see any guards at all, but several elegantly ornate buildings stood at each corner of the camp proper. One appeared to be a guardhouse, another looked as though it were at least an Uncommon-ranked apartment building, a third was likely the actual education center, and fourth... as far as he could tell, it was another guardhouse. The interior courtyard of the camp was filled with cots. Humans and Dwarves alike—in various stages of health and well-being—were either sitting or lying on them, exposed to the sun and humidity.

"If there are no guards around, there must be another way that this area is being watched and protected. My bet is... Earth Elementals playing watchdog between the buildings." With that consideration in mind, Joe gazed around the area until he noticed something that he could use: a thick cloud of smoke was billowing from one of the buildings, and thanks to the light wind of the day, it was fairly close to the ground. Sprinting toward it, he Omnivaulted over the open area, then— employing his Master bonus—tried to push off of the smoke and into the center of the camp.

Unfortunately for him, smoke was not water. Until he achieved a higher Mastery, or perhaps an even higher Tier than that, he had only earned the ability to jump off *water* in any state, so the attempt resulted in him sailing directly through the column of burning gases. Joe barely managed to tuck and roll as he hit the ground, immediately jumping as soon as his feet were under him.

It was good that he did, because as he pushed off the ground, a pair of hands reached out of the cloud where he had landed and clapped together with enough force to shatter his legs if he had still been in reach. The resulting slamming and grinding of stone was more than enough of an alarm to rouse the lazy guards... at least enough to get them to peek their heads out of the windows. By that time, Joe had landed among the prisoners and was sitting dejectedly on one of the cots.

Either out of sheer disinterest, inability to think clearly, or excellent acting, the captives he had landed among weren't looking at him with any surprise or excitement. Moments later, the Elven face in the window made an expression of disgust and vanished. Joe took a few moments to let the adrenaline pass, and as he paused, the people around him began to shift and look around in confusion. Before his very eyes, their faces seemed less haggard, and their skin was filling out slightly.

"I'm... I'm not dying of thirst anymore?" one of the humans muttered out loud, and that by itself was enough to clue Joe in: his Neutrality Aura had a ton of beneficial secondary effects. Beyond healing the people around him of their terrible sunburn and removing whatever debuffs they had accrued during their incarceration, his Neutrality Aura also eliminated their need for water, directly hydrating them from the humidity in the air. There was certainly more than enough of *that* to go around.

Realizing that his presence alone was giving the prisoners the strength that they would need in order to escape, Joe slowly began circulating throughout the courtyard. He never called out or informed them that he was the reason they were getting better, and he quickly decided to throw his Robe of Liquid Darkness over his set of the Silkpants Mage gear. Although everyone else was wearing whatever clothes they had been captured in, only *his* were pristine and white. Of course, being within range of his aura made the prisoners clean again, but it wasn't something noticeable to a casual observer in the context of their general shabbiness.

To the affected people, who hadn't been able to get clean for days—or possibly weeks—no longer having swampy underwear was certainly a giant boon. The overall mood of the detainment camp was rapidly improving, and the people were becoming more energized, clean, and healthy. Unfortunately for Joe, his main goal of finding Jaxon was proving fruitless, even though he was moving along and searching every prisoner's face. He had no doubt that no matter how terrible his friend was feeling, he would be sitting upright with perfect posture. Since no one was sitting so precisely, Joe realized too late that he may have thrown himself into prison for no reason.

Eventually, Joe had to break his streak of non-interference with the people around him, kneeling beside a grizzled Legionnaire and asking him a quiet question. "Lieutenant. Have you seen a human that had a proper beard, wide smile, and a somewhat disturbing fascination with the skeletal structure of the people around him?"

"You're looking for Jaxon?" While Joe hadn't been expecting instant recognition, he didn't know why he *hadn't* been expecting it. The Chiropractor was anything but subtle. "They took him into the re-education building… no Dwarf comes out of there, and no human comes out without being changed.

From what little I was able to understand about his situation, they were going to be chucking him into solitary for a while."

The Dwarf had perked up significantly since Joe had come over to talk to him, a direct result of becoming well-hydrated and healing all of the various bumps and bruises that he'd accrued during his stay. Joe nodded his thanks and slunk away to get closer to the building the Lieutenant had indicated. He wanted to warn everyone that he'd be attacking soon, that they should be prepared to revolt and make a run for it... but he'd never do that. The sad truth was, there was always a chance that someone in the crowd was a plant, or that one of the humans wanted to get in good with their captors while they had the chance. Secrecy was safer, and he could allow everyone to make their own choices when the opportunity presented itself.

Pulling out a quill and sending his intent into it, produced a flash of light that resolved into a Novice Ritual Circle in the air in front of him. Joe activated it, and a moment later, the outer wall started to fall apart, chunks of stone lifting into the sky with almost no sound at all.

At first.

Then the alarm spells were either tripped or torn apart and forcibly activated. A cacophony of noise filled the air, and would have caused Joe to slam his hands over his ears were he not prepared for it. Elves sprinted out of the building in droves, far more than he felt should have been occupying each of them. That spoke to the buildings being a higher rank than he had initially gauged them as—ones with potential spatial expansions. While that was not a happy thought, it was within expectations.

Next came the fun part.

Joe pulled out one of the copies of the ritual that he and Havoc had designed together. Holding his breath in expectation of a calamitous ending, Joe targeted a point where a large number of Dwarves were congregating and activated the Journeyman-ranked ritual. The outpouring of mana didn't go unnoticed: dozens of Elven heads snapped to the side to stare in his direction. Unfortunately for them, it was too late to stop what was coming.

Five circles appeared in the air above his target point, shimmering and transforming into a mass of roiling black clouds. An instant later, the ritual judged the people underneath it as 'not human or Dwarf'. Then the tribulation began, near-silent lightning falling on them like raindrops, streaking dozens of bolts per second. The ritual didn't stop there. Instead, the storm clouds lowered until they shrouded the ground, coming up nearly to the chests of the average-height Elves among them. With no escape from the lightning, and no way to see where to go to avoid it, the captors helplessly trapped as the storm cloud began crawling along the ground.

"Ritual of the Crawling Storm." Joe felt a hint of disgust, which was quickly overwhelmed with pride in his creation as it functioned exactly as he had intended. He had infused it with a healthy dose of Scattering Special aspects, allowing it to be super-effective against magical protections. In this instance, as the storm dragged itself along the ground in a nearly sentient fashion, it ripped apart Arcane Shells, Divine Barriers, and even magical lightning resistance, as exhibited by the Earth Elementals.

Screams and shouting broke out among the guards, and the prisoners all perked up. Most of them were on their feet in short order, and soon a full-blown riot and escape attempt was in motion. Upon seeing Elemental after Elemental pulling themselves from the ground, Joe decided that it might be a good idea to bring his full arsenal to bear. His Ritual Orbs flew into the air, unspooling into metallic Ritual Circles as he activated Planar Shift, summoning his Pseudo-Lich to join combat for the first time.

Quest update: Student Ritualist II. Creatures killed: 23/100.

With the prisoners attempting escape, the guards and guardians otherwise occupied by being magically fried, and the confining walls literally being razed, Joe ran in a direction that none of the other people were attempting: the re-education center. He kept his Ritual Orbs in ready positions and reached the front door without issue. No one tried to stop him, and it appeared that this particular building wasn't overly well-defended compared to the others.

He paused, then reluctantly sent the summoned being up to a hidden vantage point of the building, hoping it could alert him if the enemy was closing in. If not, at least he would have a secret weapon if things started to go wrong. Trump cards laid out, Joe kicked the door open and ran into the re-education building.

Once more, he was struck by the lack of defenders. Most likely, that had something to do with the building's true purpose, and perhaps the threat of the Earth Elementals was usually enough to keep any of the prisoners from attempting to break in or escape... but it reeked of a trap. Joe scanned the building with his senses, frowning at what he found. This place wasn't what he had been expecting from the outside. Instead of a jail or containment cells, the interior of the building held a large arena that was sunken into the ground—more like a fighting pit than anything else. The door he had entered turned out to lead to a spectator ring, far above what went on below.

It was also the source of the scent of blood that had permeated the entire camp, the ground in the pit being more churned mud than anything else. The coloration allowed him to determine that it wasn't *water*, but lifeblood that had been spilled for a specific purpose. There were many offshoots from the entryway that he could choose to follow down, and he was *almost* positive that the lower areas would be populated with various cells, or perhaps larger rooms where teachers and high-ranking members of the Theocracy could come and attempt to convert the captive humans to achieving an Elven superiority trait.

He could see some activity below, and it was apparent that the Elves had been in the process of preparing a Dwarven sacrifice for whatever human was being forced to lose their Dwarven superiority trait. There was a very familiar voice echoing up from the lower levels, and even amidst all of the dire circumstances, Joe could not help but allow a grin to stretch across his face. "Classic Jaxon."

"No, no, *no!*" Jaxon was chiding whoever was with him. "You have this completely backward! As a Chiropractor, *my* hands go on *you*, *your* hands dangle to the side or are put in the position that I need. They don't hold my wrists, and certainly not my throat-*gak*!"

"If we don't get this one out of here in the next couple of days, I'm putting in for transfer," a resigned voice rang out, earning a few chuckles from melodious Elven throats.

Another voice piped up, "That's what you say every time we get an oddball in here. You know these humans are all off their rockers; they need this experience to show them the light. If what I heard is true, they don't even hear the words that we speak. They have no idea of the true *majesty* that they're missing out on."

That gave Joe pause, as he realized that he indeed wasn't hearing them with the odd Boston accent and strange caricature-like shouting about 'face' and positions in society. If this was what they normally *naturally* sounded, it was no wonder that they were exasperated by reacting to how Dwarven-affiliated people treated them. "Enough introspection. They still need to die."

He had been planning to rush around like a chicken with its head cut off and hope that he somehow magically ran into his friend, but he decided instead to simply wait as they dragged Jaxon out into the open pits and threw him into the mud. His arms were bound behind him, which *should* have made rising from the mostly-liquid ground very difficult, but Jaxon simply bent his spine backwards until his face was free, then began shifting his hips back and forth to slither through the mud like a black mamba.

"I might say that I'm requesting transfer a lot, but I think I really *mean* it when it comes to this guy." The first annoyed Elven voice sounded unsettled. "That's just unnatural… are we *sure* that we checked his magical signature? There's no way that he's something other than human?"

There were noises of confirmation, and one person even griped about it. "You made me do the test four different times, with three different instruments. He is human, guaranteed."

Joe could understand their concern, as well as their confusion. There were many times through his association with Jaxon that he had wondered the exact same thing. Now that Jake the Alchemist had been proven to be something... other... of course his doubts about Jaxon were cropping up once more as well.

Quest update: Student Ritualist II. Creatures killed: 41/100.

Holding off on his rescue attempt until all of the Dwarves had been added into the pit didn't mean he couldn't prepare for it. By the time the final Dwarf came sloshing into the floor pit, Joe had four rituals set up. Two of them were designed to attack anyone that came to stop him, one was a Ritual of Bubble Travel that he frankly thought was a slight wasted for the short distance that it would need to cross, and the final one was a barrier ritual that should protect all of the people *down* there until they were able to get *up* to him.

He activated them one after another, then shouted and drew far too much attention. "Jaxon! I'm here to rescue you! Head for the distortion in the center of the pit, and bring as many of the Dwarves as you can!"

"Joe! It's s~s~so good to hear your voice!" Jaxon was putting a little too much sibilant stress on his S's. "S~see you S~soon!"

The Ritualist shook his head as Elven guards started swarming out of wherever they had been resting, coming after both him and the prisoners. "Yeah, I need to get you out of here. You're *really* not suited to being stuck in solitary."

CHAPTER FORTY-EIGHT

Before Joe even saw a lock of golden hair, a pointed ear, or a signature expression of smug superiority, all of the captives were traveling up to him in bubbles. While all of the chaos was unfolding within the building, his Ritual of the Crawling Storm was going about its grisly business outside. There was a sudden spike in kills, racking up so fast that Joe knew something was up.

Quest update: Student Ritualist II. Creatures killed: 63/100.

Experience gained: 7,440.

"Abyss, if I am getting experience for the kills, it must be either Elementals or monsters spontaneously popping up in the area." Joe pulled his friend out of the bubble, quickly using his Ritual Orb of Intelligence to slice through the ropes binding his arms behind his back. As soon as the Chiropractor was free, his body shook all over and aligned itself into a better position. "Grab the Dwarves; we need to get out of here!"

As they worked to free the other captives of their bonds, both of the defensive rituals activated. Lightning bolts and acid shot out in equal measure, followed by screams and wails of pain from below in short order. Jaxon turned around to look at the result, but Joe pulled him back, and warned him with a shake of his head. "I figured out how to make it only prey on Elves... essentially. Don't look; all that'll do is give them a target to aim at."

As the others were rapidly healed by his aura—their thirst quenched, their stench removed—the pick-up party ran outside to join the rampaging escapees, hoping to make a clean getaway. They burst out the door, skidding to a stop as they gaped around in horror.

"*Guten* tag," a smug Herr Trigger called out to them cheerfully, enjoying their confusion at being surrounded by a full platoon of high-level Elven warriors. Joe tried to turn and run back into the building, but the ten 'Dwarves' that had been rescued from the arena had revealed themselves as armored Elves. In an instant, Joe and Jaxon were gripped by multiple sets of concerningly strong hands and had various blades pressed up against sensitive areas. "I see that you found our little camp. You know, there is nothing better than a *predictable* foe. My first prediction was that the people here would have a terribly difficult time convincing your slippery friend to remove his Dwarven superiority trait, and my second prediction was that you would be coming for him. I will say, you impressed me. A full-blown assault on the capital just so that you could create a distraction to make it happen? A *masterstroke!*"

"Please do not compliment the accused." One of the Elves spoke in a hollow tone, his helmet distorting his words slightly. "Their actions have earned them a place in the deepest pits of Tartarus. The Ascetic herself will be present to judge them."

"Well, yes. *Eventually.*" Herr Trigger was practically dancing in happiness at the thought of Joe being locked away forever. "I am so pleased to have completed my quest. You know, I thought I had done it *twice* already. I either needed to kill *you* a certain amount of times, or a Grandmaster once—still wondering how that didn't happen—or capture you before you attained your goal on this Zone. Truly, I thought I had failed. Thank you for so kindly delivering yourself to me once more."

"So this entire place was a trap? Were *any* of the Dwarves

even real, or were *all* of them Elves under an illusion spell?" Joe's teeth were grinding as he wracked his brain for a way to escape. Unfortunately, as he peered into the distance, he spotted another complement of Elves approaching at high speed. His Ritual of Crawling Lightning was still doing *work*, and every time one of the Mages tried to cast dispelling magics at it, the ritual would scatter the spell and chase after whoever had attacked it. That was unexpected, but it made sense with the knowledge that Havoc had a personal vendetta against casters and had helped design it. To be frank, it was quite pleasant to see them scream and run, only to still be caught in the end.

Quest update: Student Ritualist II. Creatures killed: 93/100.

There was another wild card that he had yet to play, in the form of his summoned Pseudo-Lich. He reminded himself to be careful not to lose the orb that it was floating around on, as that one was not yet bound to him. If he lost it, it was gone. To that end, he kept his mind trained on it as he gingerly lifted it off the building where he had placed it, electing to keep it floating nearby but out of sight.

"It is time to remove the equipment from the prisoners." The no-nonsense Elf that seemed to be in charge of the operation motioned someone forward, and Joe winced as he recognized the face. The last time he had seen this particular Elf, he had been lit on fire by pulling raw aspects out of Joe's storage, and the Ritualist had made a daring escape by swimming through lava and hoping his Exquisite Shell would be able to hold out.

He had no misconceptions that this would be a pleasant meet and greet. The Elf strolled ever so casually over to him, a wide smile on his face, then slapped Joe so hard that the human was knocked out of his guards' hands and onto the ground. "Ayy, good to *finally* see you again. I've been looking forward to meeting up. You always had the most interesting stuff laying around, didn't you?"

The Elf ignored the return slap that bounced off his passive shield. That was a significant difference from the last time they had met, and Joe saw his chances of getting the Elf to light himself up a second time become defenestrated. Acutely aware that the Thief-class Elf was going to start working on him immediately, Joe subtly shifted his hand wearing his spatial ring to within two inches of his codpiece. That was the maximum distance he could use to transfer between the two spatial storage devices. In an instant, he moved the most important things that he carried—namely the Grandmaster's book on Mana Manipulation and Coalescence—into the codpiece. Now, it was one more of the one hundred thousand objects within the same storage device; if he were counting each aspect individually.

A few other things were transferred, almost entirely books, as well as a pamphlet. The Elf noticed what he was doing with alarm and grabbed his arm. In a last-ditch effort, Joe managed to send his survey tool into the codpiece before his hand was wrenched away. "None-ah that now. You think you're some kind of smart guy, don't ya? Well, let's start *right* away."

Cores, Ritual Tiles, half-created Talismans, rocks, interesting bits of ore and various plants that Joe had planned to break down into aspects started flying from his hand. As the treasures and baubles pinged off the stone, Joe found himself somewhat surprised that no one was bothering to collect them. It wasn't until they ejected an object that Joe recognized, his eyes widening slightly in horror, that the Thief stopped and took a more careful look at what he had managed to grab.

"'Ello, *'ello*! What's *this* now?" The Thief held up a large, flat tile that had an array carved into it. It pulsed with magical light, and a Mage class Elf was called for. The Thief had let go of his hand for a moment, which gave Joe the moment he needed to transfer over the Keystone that he had been given by the Grandmaster. He was quaking internally; he had nearly completely forgotten its existence. If he lost that... he might have lost the chance of a lifetime.

After a moment, the Mage ran over, relief etched on his face. Apparently, he had nearly been the next one in line to try to dispel the Ritual of Crawling Lightning, which was still chasing an extremely nimble Elf around—nope, it caught him.

Quest complete: Student Ritualist II. Creatures killed: 100/100! Congratulations! You have slain 100 creatures with a ritual in an astoundingly short amount of time! You really are the teacher's pet, aren't you?

Reward: Journeyman Design Diagram for Ritual of Slaughter. Access to Student Ritualist III.

Quest gained: Student Ritualist III. You have obtained a War Ritual! Give it a... whirl! Hah! Okay, that'll make more sense when you use it. Only by really going for it and trying out everything can you determine the path that you want to pursue until Mastery! This will give you a good jump start in understanding what it is like to be a Ritualist during wartime! Slay 1,000 creatures with the Ritual of Slaughter! 0/1,000.

Joe didn't exactly have the luxury of time at present, otherwise he would have been reading through every detail of the ritual that had just appeared in his mind. Currently, his eyes were focused on the teleportation pad that the Thief Elf had just stolen out of his ring. That was his ticket back to Jotunheim, specifically to the place where the Dwarves had relocated. More specifically... to the place the Elves should never have been able to find. Finishing the Dwarves off should have been a locked door, forever closed to them.

Yet now they had the key in their hands.

With pure fury filling his thoughts, instead of careful and intelligent planning, Joe sent his Pseudo-Lich swooping down at the Thief. Morsum opened its mouth wide, slamming its jaws closed around the clavicle of its target.

The two-and-a-half-inch long fangs pierced through the Elf's barrier as though the protection wasn't even there, although the edges of the puncture marks blazed with crackling mana as it attempted to repair itself. The Elf screamed and tried to pry the head off, but blood, mana, and what had to be stamina were being sapped from him at an excessive rate. Before everyone's eyes, the Elf was drained to a withered husk, and only mere seconds had passed. He fell to the ground, and the Lich head hovered into the air once more.

Blam!

Only to be blasted into smithereens by Herr Trigger as if he were shooting skeet at a range. The initial blow was followed up by two spells and a lance through the eye, and the head was fully dispelled and unsummoned. Before it vanished, the Lich sent a feeling of intense *satisfaction* to Joe. The Ritualist ignored all of that, his entire attention focused on forcing the Ritual Orb into his bandolier as soon as the head was gone. The orb zipped over, settling into its pouch in an instant. Now that the Thief was dead, there was no way for him to lose his current gear to his captors. They were infuriated and seemed at a loss of what to do with him, but Joe wasn't worried.

It wasn't like they could punish him more than they already planned to do.

"Keep a close eye on that one. Even captured and bound, he's got *teeth*." Herr Trigger giggled at all of the annoyed glances sent his way, but the Elf inspecting the teleportation pad soon regained everyone's attention as he got back to work, flipping the magical item around a few times, then using a long index finger to poke himself in the center of his forehead.

With his eyes closed, he seemed to be following something away from the item, and soon he was staring into the sky with a peaceful, serene expression. An instant later, his lids opened in surprise, and he regarded his contemporaries with a wild smile on his face. "It's a teleportation array! It leads to Jotunheim… and the other end is active!"

Herr Trigger could only casually shrug as the others around him began to celebrate. "I knew Joe would mess up. He's a *killer*; not a person who can successfully save others."

With this discovery, the Elves felt that there was no time to lose. Joe and Jaxon were trussed up in ropes and chains, then hauled out of the camp at a sprint. Joe's head bowed in shame as he listened to the celebration of the Elves around him. If they were correct, the main Legions of Light were converging on the Capital city at that very moment. With the teleportation array in hand, they would be able to expand it to a massive degree… and march their armies through the portal directly to Jotunheim.

The Bounty Hunter had been correct. Joe had just bungled his way into offering their enemies the final hope of the Dwarven race on a silver platter.

CHAPTER FORTY-NINE

The entire time they were being manhandled back to the devastated capital city, Joe stared up into the sky, caught in the swirl of negative emotions that had come upon him. All he wanted to do at that moment was figure out a way to resummon Morsum and send it to sink its teeth into the gunslinger's neck.

Joe wasn't sure who would enjoy that more: the Pseudo-Lich, or himself.

Sadly, that wasn't a viable option anymore. He was out of tricks to use, and being bound in blessed mana-disrupting manacles was incredibly jarring for the man who had come to rely on magic in nearly every aspect of what he did. The only positive to the journey was that it was incredibly swift. The Elves weren't targeted by any of their own defenses, allowing them to beeline directly to the city, and soon Joe found himself being watched by hundreds of sets of furious eyes.

"Is *that* the one who set off the spell that damaged the wall?" One of the guards that Joe might have recognized—if every single Elf did not look exactly the same to him—slowly pulled out a razor-sharp knife. "Do you mind if I take a piece of him as a souvenir? It's going to take *weeks* to repair that section of the barriers. We had to get a High Cleric out here just to get rid of the spell, and they demanded a hefty tribute from our salaries over the next few months. Said that *we* should be able to take care of it ourselves... well, *I* want something to remember this one by."

"Remove yourself from our presence immediately," the officer in charge of their group demanded of the guard. "This one has already been judged and will soon face the wrath of the Ascetic, separated only by a *single* intermediary."

That didn't sound so bad to Joe, but by the gasps and rapidity of everyone else's departures, he didn't think that it was going to be a pleasant experience. Although, it appeared that he was going to be forced to wait for whatever the punishment was going to be.

Instead of being tossed in a cell or a dark hole and left alone until his bones turned to dust, he was instead surprisingly placed next to Jaxon in a strange, circular stone area between several buildings. The Bifrost wasn't far away at all, and Joe thought that if he had access to his mana, he would be able to reach it in five or fewer Omnivaults. But the fact of the matter was that he *didn't* have access to it. Unlike every time he'd been caught in a bad position before, Joe didn't see a way out of this one.

Moments after the final captor had stepped out of the stone area, the light reflecting off the quartz buildings around them intensified. The heat began to increase, and a cylindrical barrier of light sprang up around them.

"Oh, so *that's* how they're going to keep us in here!" Jaxon touched the barrier with one of his fingers, then pulled it back to inspect the damage. Turning to Joe, he offered his injured digit. "Look at that! Straight through the bone with the lightest of touches! Lightest... *hah*! See, it's kind of a pun? I'm *laser* focused? I'm on a roll!"

"It's really, um, something. Great jokes, Jaxon." That level of damage wasn't something that Joe had been expecting, not when they clearly wanted to keep their captives alive. That degree of security indicated that there was likely something else going on here that would cause them to respawn inside of this circle if they tried to shove their heads through the barrier of light. It was nothing he hadn't experienced before, but it was just as annoying as always. "What is this... the third time that I've been put in a prison? Fourth? No, third. The last time on Midgard wasn't a prison; I was there willingly."

"Maybe you should think about just *not* breaking the law?" Jaxon offered innocently, a suggestion that Joe had no intention of taking.

"If they keep making stupid laws, I'm going to keep breaking them," Joe snorted through his nose, deciding to sit down and relax for a while. He glanced over at Jaxon, noticing that the flesh of his finger was slowly repairing itself. That was when he realized that the passive spells that he had previously activated were still going. A quick look at his character sheet informed him that Exquisite Shell, Neutrality Aura, and Retaliation of Shadows were spinning along in full swing. That was excellent news for him, as it meant that the slow torture of increasing heat was going to be nearly ineffectual against the two of them.

Their thirst would be quenched, their burns would be healed, so all they needed to do was wait. Eventually, they would be brought somewhere else, if for no other reason than to get them out of the public eye. Or they would be rescued, the Elves would slip up, or some other opportunity would present itself for escape. "The plan is, we wait and we stay ready."

"For the death of the king?" Jaxon clapped his hands over his mouth while gasping in excitement.

"What? No. It's not like we were captured by *Mufasa*." Both of them got a chuckle at that. Sometimes it was nice to remember simpler times, and it didn't get simpler than children's movies from back on Earth. That was the last time they spoke, much less laughed, for the next several hours. As the day wore on, the light around them continued to become ever-more intense. Even so, as long as they didn't move around too much, it was completely bearable. They stayed clean, didn't get thirsty, and all of the micro-damage to their dermis was repaired as quickly as it occurred.

It wasn't until evening began to fall that one of the guards who had been watching them realized that something funky was going on. "Why are the prisoners lounging instead of bleeding and burning? This is a kennel given to the most rabid of dogs! By now, the gods should have started to display their displeasure!"

Joe decided that this was as good of a time as any other to taunt his captors. "I guess they just like me more than they like you! In fact, I'm pretty sure I heard one of them whispering to me that they were all excited about having some round-eared friends. I bet if you stuck your head in the light, you would be able to shape yours perfectly. Plus-ten divine favor, if you know what I mean."

"I am always... *always*..." The Elf locked eyes with Joe, a curling grin on his face making Joe think he was about to try stealing Christmas, "excited to add blasphemy to the charges of my captives."

"Oh no! I hope you don't throw me in a prison made out of light—*oh wait*." The human's sarcasm caused the smile to decrease slightly, but it took on a grim edge, and that did succeed in making Joe's heart sink a little in his chest.

"Let me explain to you how excited I truly am." The corners of the perfectly sculpted Elfish mouth kept twitching, as though he were barely holding himself back from laughing. "I traded shifts with someone so that I could make sure I was here when *this* started."

An instant after he finished speaking, and just before Joe became puzzled enough to risk asking, music started playing in the distance. Thousands of voices began echoing through the evening air, so loud and so harmonious that the lazily drifting smoke that was choking the air of the ruined city was blown away as though a storm was rolling in.

"We always knew Dwarves were non-essential, rude, and unspeakably

crude." As soon as Joe was able to decipher the lyrics, he rolled his eyes and shook his head at his personal guard.

"Really? You stole Havoc's thing?" When there was no reaction forthcoming from the guard, Joe tried again. "Let me guess, you guys heard about how cool the Dwarves sounded and made up your own wartime song? How cute. Nothing like a little cultural appropriation to make you feel good about yourselves, am I right?"

"Silence, prisoner." Clearly the Elf wanted to hear the next verse, because he was humming along before the next lines even reached their ears.

"A shining new order; is sprinting right toward her. Meticulous planning, millennia spanning, the Ascetic's blade and ambitions are bared! No Dwarf will. Be. Spa~ared!"

From there on, the song repeated itself with a few tiny variations. It always came back to the fact that the Elves were on a mission of extermination, and Joe could only shake his head in disappointment. Not at the Elves, but at himself. He was the reason that this massive army was marching toward the center of the city right now; *his* actions and thoughtlessness were responsible for a full army gaining the ability to march into a barely defended civilian encampment.

His eyes drifted over to Jaxon, and Joe could only crumple slightly in defeat. The fact of the matter was: he would have done it again. There was no way that he could leave behind someone that he trusted, that trusted him. He had lost companions before, but only because they had *chosen* that path. Jaxon had specifically wanted to come with him, to grow and progress, and to see how far they could push the bounds of humanity. "Only thing I would have changed? Probably should have hidden that teleportation array a *little* bit better."

"If it were me, I wouldn't have been caught," Jaxon told him soothingly, patting Joe on the back. "That's what *I* would have changed if I were you and only had one thing I could have changed. I would have changed it to a perfect escape, you know?"

Joe stared at his friend, trying to convince himself that he still would have come back to rescue the man, even knowing what he knew now. The distorted sympathy definitely was not helping his case. "As always, your logic is… impeccable."

At the speed that the Elven armies could move, there was only a short time between when they could first be heard, and when they were visible. Hundreds, then thousands, then tens of thousands. As far as Joe could tell, this was the core army of the entire Theocracy. This was the elites, those tasked with protecting their own lands against the Dwarven threat. Every single one of them was not only a veteran, but a powerhouse in their own right. As more of them marched closer, the very air became more densely packed with power and bloodlust. Soon, the psychological effects were making Joe want to throw himself into the light barrier, and that was with all of his characteristics, including his Mental Manipulation Resistance, working on his behalf.

The front ranks of the army came to a halt not fifty feet away from Joe, the lines standing ten abreast… and every single one of them was glaring at the human that had been instrumental in destroying the gem of the Elven Theocracy: the Capital city.

"Joe. *Joe!*" Jaxon whispered into his ear, loudly enough that he knew for certain that the highly sensitive Elven ears twitching in the distance could easily make out the conversation. "Do you think that they know you intentionally wrecked their city, and that you believe their entire society and way of life is based off of a lie?"

Watching the Elves tense up in the distance, their mouths drawing into firm lines, Joe could only nod slowly as he rubbed at his temples. "Yes, Jaxon. I *do* think they know that. Now."

"Well, *that's* not great for you."

CHAPTER FIFTY

"Brothers and sisters of the Army of *Light*!" a High Cleric screamed from his position, directly adjacent to Joe and Jaxon's prison. The humans, caught unaware, flinched and came within fractions of an inch of being swallowed by the deadly barrier around them. "Today is a glorious day, a wondrous day! Today you find yourselves equals, for you are all equally blessed. As soon as the last glimmer of light from the sun above is hidden behind the horizon, a new source of light will appear on Jotunheim!"

"*One people, one purpose!*" The shout rose with perfect synchronicity as every Elf in the army slammed their fists to their chests.

Spreading his arms and graciously bowing his head to accept the show of faith, the high Cleric paused dramatically before continuing on with his clearly prepared speech. "Even as we speak, the brightest sparks among our enchanters are working to open and stabilize a portal that will carry us directly to the Dwarven encampment! A city's worth of Dwarves awaits, ready and waiting to be converted to our cause!"

"*We will show them our peaceful ways by force!*" Joe was starting to think that the speech was even more prepared than he had expected, as the rank-and-file Elves evidently had their own responses written and ready.

"That we will, that we *wi~ill!*" the Cleric sang out. "Any loss is acceptable, except the loss of one of our brothers and sisters trapped in the substandard form known as 'Dwarf'! When the doorway opens, know that with every swing of your blade, every cast of your spell, we are not cutting down unarmed civilians... we are cutting our family out of the prisons of flesh they have been trapped within!"

"Never again led astray!"

"Correct! Every single one of you will be brought back, the price for your salvation paid immediately. If you must die to take only a single one of them with you, make that sacrifice *willingly!*" The Cleric didn't wait for a reply this time, instead turning his head slightly to look at the humans trapped within the barrier of light next to him. "Once we have every member of our estranged family returned to us, the decades of work and millions of resource units required to restore our city will seem a trifle. With the resources of two Zones in our hands, we will finally be able to advance past this warlike facade we wear and spread our light throughout Eternium!"

"Don't like *that*," Joe muttered as the Cleric came closer. "Throwing away the facade of warlike behavior, so that you can spread to every other Zone like a disease and take them over by converting them?"

"We will convert them through faith," the Elf informed him calmly, his palms pressed together as though he were about to begin praying. "If that fails, we will convert them into radioactive ash."

"Ye~eah, that's pretty much what I was expecting to hear." Joe grunted as the Elf touched the light barrier, which sent a beam of scintillating radiance into the base of his shoulder. His Exquisite Shell brightened to the point that it could compete with the sun, and shattered. His left arm fell off, the wounds completely cauterized behind it. The injury produced a surprisingly small amount of pain, likely due to all of the nerve endings being destroyed instantly. His right arm followed, and he was expecting his legs to be next. Instead, the same injuries were imparted to Jaxon, and the barrier around them fell.

A platoon of guards stepped forward, grasping them in multiple locations to ensure they couldn't attempt an escape. Thus secured, the manacles on their legs were removed, and the extremely damaged humans were marched over onto a platform that grew out of the ground as they came nearer. The Cleric didn't bother to address the humans; instead, all of his words were for the army as a whole. "When the door opens, we will march through as rapidly as possible! As we will not be crossing via the Bifrost, not only will the assault on the Dwarven refugees be a perfect surprise, but we will appear directly within their midst! Destroy anyone who does not have their ears pointed toward the celestials!"

"One people, one purpose!"

Joe inspected the area around him, watching as a ramp was created from stone to lead directly up onto the platform. He was one of the first people to the top before being pulled off to the side as his ankles were re-shackled so he would not be in the way. It was set at a perfect height and grade to launch the Elves that charged into it up and over whatever defenses might have been set up around the receiving end of the teleportation portal. He had to hand it to them, as much as he was irked by being defeated so easily; they had put quite a bit of thought into every aspect of this attack.

"One of the main contributors to the destruction of our home, this human, is here to see the error of his ways!" The Cleric gestured grandly to Joe as he made his pronouncement, and the question that tried to erupt from the human's confused face hole was muffled as a guard stuffed a rag in his mouth. "Without him, we would not have driven all of the Dwarves into a single location, away from all defenses and protections! We would not have a path that brings us directly to them! A handful of Grandmasters, a plentiful supply of Masters! Yes, his actions against us will need to be penalized—and greatly so—but someday, when his penance is complete, he will be lauded as a hero for what he has done!"

"Ewe sutck!" Joe's muffled shout could only be heard by the High Cleric, who had a grin playing across his face. For the first time, the Elf turned to speak directly to him.

"It wouldn't do to make you out as a monster forever." The High Cleric gestured into the distance at some building that likely had special significance to them, but meant nothing to Joe. "The Ascetic herself has declared that you will become a great asset for us. Something about your ability to do damage on such a grand scale being balanced with the wonders that you can create. Say nothing now, but recognize that this is an opportunity for you. Would you not rather be loved and cherished by the society that you are going to be a part of... forever?"

Joe wasn't sure what to say about that. The question practically *burned* inside of him. The fact of the matter was, if the Elves really did wipe out the Dwarves, especially the ones that he had been making all of his promises to... wouldn't it be a good idea to start working with the people that replaced them immediately? He didn't want to be thrown into a deep dark hole forever, and if that meant... no! He shook his head, throwing off the intrusive line of thinking that was worming its way into his brain.

Mental Manipulation Resistance has reached Apprentice II!

Just as he had thought, there was more to that offer than mere words. He glared at the powerful Cleric, who simply shook his head sadly at the anger in Joe's eyes. "Don't worry. Right now, this likely seems terrible to you, but we already have a plan. Would you like to hear it? Of course you would. Here is what is going to happen... you are going to watch with your own eyes as every Dwarf is annihilated. Then, over the coming weeks and months, as they are pulled from the Ledger of Souls and returned to our society, we are going to parade them in front of you."

The Elf leaned in, his eyes glowing with slowly releasing

power. "Think of that, Joe, Chosen Legend of Occultatum. Think of what it will be like when hundreds of *thousands* of families are reunited, all because you were able to assist us in bringing their lost ones home. Some of them have been lost to us for decades or centuries. Will you be able to resist all of the thanks? All of the *love*, the *gratitude?* The Ascetic has deemed that you are to be an asset, and that means you will be very well treated. Your class will advance, the resources you need to do so will be handed to you. All for the low price of simply... *watching*."

Joe's heart began to break as his mind was pulled in different directions. Chief among them was the people that he had already evacuated to Jotunheim, the people that he had done everything for to this point. All he had been trying to do was help them escape extermination in this world and give them a chance to prosper once more. Directly after that, aided no doubt by some kind of coercive skill the High Cleric was using against him, came the thought that all of the families were going to have their brothers, mothers, fathers, and daughters in their arms once more when this mission was completed.

For some reason, even though he knew that the punishment for death had been switching sides, he had never considered what that actually *meant* to these two warring civilizations. It had always seemed to focus around resources, technologies, and ideologies. Had he been missing the point all along? Was this war actually about bringing home their lost loved ones? If so... was he actually planning on denying the joyous reunion of familial love to a city's worth of people?

Seeing the pain and indecision in his eyes, the high Cleric nodded solemnly. "I am glad to see that you are taking this matter seriously. Once this night has ended, and the light has come once more, the Ascetic herself will guide you in learning how you may right the wrongs that you have inflicted upon the Theocracy."

Joe wasn't sure if his conflicting feelings were the result of a spell being used against him or the indecision in his own heart, but hearing that he had a chance at redemption, even with all of his failures... it sent his mind into a tailspin. Finally, he looked up at the Cleric and steeled himself.

"Whenever possible, I have always followed through on my promises." He strained against the Elves holding him in place, attempting to lunge at the Cleric and bash the perfectly sculpted nose in with his forehead. "I don't need your *forgiveness*. As long as I do the right thing as well as I can, I'll hold my head high. Take your empty promises, your easy-way-out platitudes, and *shove* them up your-"

"The portal is opening!" A magically enhanced voice shouted to the side of where this personal drama was unfolding, so loud that it caused Joe to stumble. "You are ordered to never retreat, for any reason! Kill all the Dwarves, every last one, before you rest!"

"*One people, one purpose!*"

"All units... *charge!*"

CHAPTER FIFTY-ONE

He had seen portals open before, but he had never seen the fabric of the world *shredded* in a manner quite like this. Joe flinched back as the portal from Alfheim to Jotunheim ripped open and stabilized. Everything about it felt wrong, like a violation of not only the natural order, but his personal space. Until he was looking through the severed air revealing the open plain where the Bifrost had dropped the Dwarves onto Jotunheim, the only way he could describe the feeling was as if an extremely large, four armed man was looming behind him, breathing heavily on his neck while sweating profusely and dripping onto him.

There was something else tickling the back of Joe's mind as he watched the Elves step through from one world to the next in an instant, but... he couldn't remember what it was.

In reality, there were only a few seconds where the portal was open and he could see through it. Since the portal opened facing away from the guildhall, all he could see was a distant line of Dwarves that were protecting the perimeter, having no idea that they also needed to watch their backs. Once the charging front line of Elves blasted through the opening, it seemed as though the ranks following behind them were upset that *they* hadn't had the opportunity to go first. They piled through, just under two hundred Elves per second, every last one of them sprinting by the time they stepped onto the new world.

Through the flashing bodies, Joe watched as the stream of people reached the back ranks of the Dwarves, slaughtering them almost in passing as they began to spread out and move down the lines. The Elves had been nearly completely silent until an alarm went up, their blades flashing up and down, only the sounds of meat being chopped and blood splattering across their faces echoing into the otherwise silent environment. It was only after the first of the surprised defenders began shouting that spells and other 'noisy' tactics were employed.

"Twenty thousand Elite Elven Warriors in just under one minute and forty seconds, and still the portal is holding strong." The High Cleric spoke in a reverent tone, lifting his hands to give thanks to his Pantheon. "Even the best estimates only gave us three minutes, and we had expected to need nearly that entire time in order to get the same amount of troops across. You helped motivate them so well!"

"Three... minutes?" Joe's words could not be made out, as his mouth was still stuffed with a rag, but something about the Cleric's remarks resonated with his earlier thoughts.

"Yes, plenty of time to accomplish what we need." The Cleric was making a *whole* lot of assumptions based on the context of what Joe was seeing, but the human noted a sheen of sweat on the Elven face in front of him, which belied the fact that the Elf was as calm as he appeared. "Once our army has secured a foothold in that world and captured the location, they will remain there until such a time as they have ensured that the Dwarven infestation has been stamped out. From there, each of them will complete the ritual of the blade and be reborn once more among their people on Alfheim."

"Stheppuku is'snotta ritual." Joe managed to gurgle out around the filthy rag that had been shoved in his mouth. Actually, his Neutrality Aura had converted it into a perfectly clean rag, but he still wasn't happy about having it there.

"Your Grandmasters, your plans, all of them are going to come to an end right now." The cleric began humming, only pausing every few seconds to chide Joe or attempt to 'guide' him. "Soon the Ascetic will be here, or at least her representative: the newly-appointed king. It was still a surprise to see such a low-ranking Cleric given such an important post, but it's *exciting* for the rest of us. Someday, the Ascetic has made it clear, any one of us could be raised from our lowly positions and given such glory to hear her words directly—*Pop.*—what was that?"

Pop.

The unexpected sound resonated through the opening between worlds clearly, visually accompanied a shower of multi-hued blood rising into the air. For a moment, Joe was under the impression that Havoc, or perhaps Grandmaster Snow, had joined the battle. But the murmurings of the High Cleric didn't seem to indicate that was the issue. "What is happening? What have you done? Did you lay a trap within this teleportation formation? No… you are not that smart. There's no way you could have snuck that past our enchanters as well as the-."

A bedraggled body, bound to a log, was bodily heaved through the portal. The person and log bounced once, twice, then came to a rest on the mostly-empty platform. A few of the guards knelt and began cutting the bindings holding Daniella in place. The High Cleric's eyes landed on her, and he loudly proclaimed, "Ah, yes! There *had* been a human component that got sucked along in the excursion to the next world during the initial attack. It is good to see that you made it back, as clearly you were not there by choice. That is good; we were planning to excommunicate you if you did not attempt contact soon."

Daniella rubbed at her wrist, and Joe winced when he saw how swollen and red her hands were. "Of *course* I wasn't there by choice! For that matter, do you always punish people who were captured? I see you managed to nab the person who caught me; excellent. If I had to guess, this portal is the product of what he brought back with him so that he could return to the Dwarves on Jotunheim? I expect a full reward for sending him back and convincing him to take the portal with him."

Joe glared daggers at the Architect, who kept her attention carefully focused on the High Cleric. The Elf closed his eyes and muttered a soft prayer for the human in front of him, his eyes turning hard as they opened once more. "You humans and your demand for ever greater rewards. Can you not simply be happy with the fact that you have enhanced our people, saved thousands of lives, and are safe at the end of the day? No? What a delightful race... no doubt you're not able to put the needs of the Theocracy first because you have needed to remain undercover for so long. Yes, you will have your rewards."

"Excellent." She turned and stared at the open portal, which looked like it was starting to break down. "Now... correct me if I am wrong, but it looks like you have a problem over there."

Pop.

Pop. Pop.

Pop. Pop. Pop.

Pop. Pop.

Pop.

"What... what is happening to them?" The Cleric ran closer to the portal, his hands unconsciously reaching up and pulling out fistfuls of golden hair as he stared in horror at what was happening to the Army of Light. "How is this possible? They are just... they are just *dying*! I see nothing that is hurting them, and the protections they are wearing should be enough to last against even the heretic Snow. *You*! What is this?"

He rounded on Joe, appearing in front of the human in a flash. His eyes blazed crimson as he tore the rag out of Joe's mouth and threw it to the side. Enraged, his hands clamped down over Joe's throat and he began to squeeze. "Answer me! What is this? How are you doing this!"

Grahghgh! Joe choked out as he was shaken, only for the

Cleric to realize what he was doing and released the human. The Ritualist rasped in a couple of deep breaths, slowly allowing a smile to crawl across his face as he sneered up at the Cleric defiantly. "You know, I had a real rough experience a couple weeks ago. I was trying to create a summoning spell and accidentally found myself pulled into the abyss because of spell backlash. Really, *thank* you. It's only because I was excommunicated that I know *exactly* what's happening right now."

"Explain yourself at once! Did you manage to infect the teleportation array with power from the *abyss*? You fool!" The High Cleric couldn't hold back, slapping Joe across the face so hard that he tumbled off of the raised stone platform. Even before his body hit the ground, he was caught by the Cleric once more and set on his feet. The guards, Jaxon, and Daniella were also pulled down. "What am I saying; of course you did. How do I *fix* it?"

"Can't help you." Joe's head lolled to the side as he was shaken like a rag doll. Only when it stopped did the human nod at the portal. "Take a look at your toy soldiers. Why don't you try to figure it out?"

The Cleric's eyes snapped to the open portal, though his hands stayed locked around Joe's shoulders. "All I see is hundreds, *thousands* of our soldiers being killed pointlessly! The Dwarves are fighting them fiercely, uselessly, but somehow they are still just... they are just dying!"

"Right... but *how*?" Joe's laughter at the situation earned him another brutal slap across the face, and blood trickled from his gums down to his chin. He didn't mind. His clothes and wounds were healed and cleaned in the next instant.

The earnestness in the human's question—as well as the laughter that accompanied it—served to infuriate the man in the position of power, but it also seemed to focus him. His eyes took in the continuous death of his soldiers, and he noticed a worrying trend. "I thought they were *exploding*, because of the blood... but they are not. They are being pulled to a single point inside of themselves, and the release of the pressure is causing the gory fountains."

"Yeah… and that's not even the worst that's going to come out of this." As Joe finished speaking, the unstable portal linking the two worlds collapsed. Only once the light had vanished did the storm clouds gathering in the sky far above become visible, their unnatural darkness highlighting them against the starry vastness. Joe knew that wasn't all that was up there. He'd only ever seen such a backlash a single time before, when a small town had made a promise it could not keep and the world had converted it into an instant dungeon. "Also, just so you know, to explode *inward* is called… Implode."

CHAPTER FIFTY-TWO

The air practically buzzed with anticipation and the ground rattled as though a second super volcano were about to erupt from beneath it. The High Cleric started screaming frantic questions in Joe's face, tossing him back and forth before finally throwing him bodily at the circular location that Joe knew would turn into a prison once he was inside of it.

One major issue was the fact that the light barrier was already active, which meant he would splatter against the energy as a bloody mist. With no arms and no access to mana, Joe was completely expecting to die in the next instant. Regardless, he threw everything he had into controlling his Ritual Orbs, and to his great shock... they responded.

The Ritual Orb of Strength lifted out of his bandolier, flipping around and allowing him to hook his right foot against the bar. While he couldn't use it to hover in place, he absolutely *could* use it to redirect his momentum, and he had never been more grateful for all his practice. Joe hit the ground and bounced twice, the edge of his robe fluttering into the light and burning away in an instant. He wiggled away, then stared down at the manacles around his ankles. They were the only thing preventing him from using his power, so without hesitation, he swung his legs into the barrier, holding them within the searing boundary until the mana-draining metal clattered to the ground.

Once again, the process was nearly painless, thanks to the extreme damage that was dealt in practically no time at all. Then Joe did something that the Elves *definitely* hadn't been expecting. He cast Mend on himself without using any somatic gestures, as well as focusing his will and casting Lay on Hands through his Ritual Orb at the same time. Brand new arms and legs shot out of his body like a fast-forwarded video of watching bamboo grow, and he leapt to his fresh feet. "How did I forget that I had been able to control my Ritual Orb even after they had put me in the mana-locking manacles?"

He was not sure if it was due to a different classification of skill, perhaps some form of psionic power, but in that moment, he only cared that it had worked. He faced the Elves, who were still holding Jaxon, and crouched into a ready position. Then he noticed that they weren't even looking at him, and he felt a little disgruntled that they hadn't seen his impressive regeneration. They were too busy gaping at the swirling 'clouds'. Though Joe wanted to attack immediately, even *his* attention was pulled upwards as the unnatural phenomena released a blood-curdling scream.

Zone alert! There has been an outbreak in the Elven capital city! An attempt was made to move a large number of Elves from one Zone to another in an unconventional—as well as rule-breaking—method! Anyone who went through the portal received a two-minute warning and chose to ignore it! Due to the sheer number of violations, as well as the blatant disregard for the rules, the punishment has been set at 5x the standard!

As soon as the two-minute timer ran out, the weight of moving through the barrier between worlds—which is only mitigated by riding on the Bifrost—crushed each violator. The standard punishment is a doubling of the time or resources required to resurrect them, as well as summoning a tiny demon to wreak havoc in the location they started, to dissuade future infractions.

"Those fools!" The High Cleric spat. "If they saw the warning, like this message states, they should have returned immediately! Twenty thousand troops went through... the cost to bring them back is going to be astronomical, and that means that cloud above us contains ten thousand tiny demons swirling downward to desecrate our lands!"

"Your grace, they were *ordered* not to retreat under any circumstances."

The Guard Captain that dared to speak out of turn received a blast of light from the Cleric and went flying through the air. "So this is *my* fault, then? Is *that* what you are saying?"

That left Jaxon with no one physically touching him, so Daniella seized the opportunity to grab him. Using her much-criticized and underutilized Judo skills, she hoisted the Chiropractor forward and threw him directly at Joe.

When his friend landed in his arms, Joe sent a questioning look at the Architect as he healed the man in the blink of an eye, then instantly Omnivaulted away. A guard shook Daniella, shouting, "By the Light, what were you *thinking*?"

"He was attacking the High Cleric! I needed to get him away while His Grace was otherwise occupied," Daniella protested, throwing off the hand that was clutching onto her. There was an instant of hesitation, as the Elves were unsure of the veracity of her words.

"My *hero*." Jaxon fluttered his lashes at Joe as they sailed away through the air.

"*After* them, fools!" A scream tore out of the High Cleric's throat, a spell building on his fingertips as he watched Joe activate Omnivault one more time, managing to redirect himself closer to the Bifrost.

From there, it was a race to the finish. Joe had a lead, and his Omnivault skill was incredibly impressive. Still, the Elves were built for speed and caught up quickly, since Joe was burdened by carrying his friend at the same time. They certainly would have managed to catch the humans, likely throwing them into a dark hole and forgetting them as they had once promised, but at that moment, the tiny demons arrived.

Like a cloud of bats, they swarmed across the ground, attacking anything that lived. Being of a dark alignment, they took more damage from light-based attacks as well as *hating* those that wielded such powers. The High Cleric, being the most potent source of Light Magic in the nearby vicinity, was targeted by a massive flight of the creatures.

Joe and Jaxon approached the Bifrost, and as they stepped into it, Joe glanced back and somehow managed to lock eyes with Daniella. Acting on a whim—*needing* to understand—he cast Message.

<*Why did you do that?*>

The return message was almost instant, the strange feedback of excommunication gone from the connection.

{*Please come back some day. Please save me.*}

That hadn't been the response that he'd been expecting, but before he could inquire further, he was shooting into the atmosphere. He watched the land recede below him: the swarm of tiny demons flooding the capital, the city ruined and smoldering, and... blinking in surprise, Joe saw a familiar, massive hand reach through the ground to grab The Shoe.

It was nothing more than a volcano that had been torn out of the world, and the hand was only a fraction of the size of the mountain, but it still managed to slowly pull the volcanic shell down into a deeper part of the world's core.

"No idea what *that's* about, but the first thing I'm doing when I get back is pulling the pyramid across. I hope it can survive mostly intact till then. What do you-" Joe turned to find that Jaxon was already asleep next to him, and could only chuckle. "Onward... to Jotunheim."

———

It was a rare thing for the intermediaries of the Ascetic to venture out personally. Still, the invasion was on such a scale that they felt their presence was justified. Each of the five members of the new Royal Family had a direct connection to *her* and were in constant communication as they slowly pushed back the tide of evil that flew through the skies.

Extermination was unnecessary; they could issue quests for that. No, their purpose was to examine where things had gone wrong. Where their mission, and prophecies, had failed them. It was bad enough that the homes and livelihoods of those that lived in the Capital were destroyed, but it was a true tragedy that the civilians would need to wait in the Ledger of Souls for an extended time as the Elite troops were resurrected before them. Still, they needed to move quickly before the Shadow of Doubt could form in the hearts of the masses.

For the truth was, the *Ascetic* had failed.

Now, she had not been wrong. She had simply trusted that the people she had assigned tasks to would follow through on them with all of their being, along with understanding all of the intent that she had poured into her words. That they hadn't? A slap across the face of the Theocracy as a whole.

Each of the five spoke in unison as they interpreted the words of the Ascetic. "The Chosen of Occultatum truly is a Legend, able to avert the eyes of the Divine and twist prophecy by his mere presence. His final act on this Zone was a success, despite the success of the one who had a quest to stop him? Herr Trigger has yet again succeeded, and failed."

Now they spoke one at a time, though all of them were so similar that it could easily have been any among them that voiced their interpretations.

"Hiding the city was never a concern, for it had always been hidden."

"Collecting Dwarven allies, while it would have slowed our plans, would never have stopped us."

"An enclave of Dwarven resistance on another world, while troubling, would never have been enough."

"Even the destruction of our fair city and its people were within acceptable losses."

Then the one among them that had the most seniority—the new King of the Theocracy—spoke, his voice aged and terribly sad. "If only we had managed to remove the key to the Completionist's success, our chances of winning the eternal war would have moved to better than half! If only…"

A tear tracked down his face as all five of them lifted their faces to the sky, the Bifrost barely visible behind the dense smoke of their childhood homes crumbling to ash. As one, they spoke once more, their words blending with the world and echoing unnaturally.

"If *only* we could have ensured that Jaxon wasn't able to leave Alfheim."

EPILOGUE

Joe and Jaxon landed on Jotunheim in a lush valley filled with the sound of insects, the fluttering of wings, the squeal of pigs. That was concerning in its own right, as any of the creatures that they actually spotted were approximately the size of a garbage truck, and that was only the smallest of the bugs.

"That's impossible!" Jaxon pointed directly at one of the invertebrates as though it had personally evolved to be such a size just to spite him. "You don't have any bones; you only have an exoskeleton! *Disgusting*! None of you should be allowed to live. At that size, if you don't have a skeletal structure, your internal organs should be turning into *jelly*! Rahh!"

"*Easy*, Jaxon." Joe was already hard at work, spinning up Ritual Circles and pulling out blueprints. Aspects flew out of his codpiece like a stream of water, and with a thought, he was holding a heavily depleted core in his hand. "We are only going to be here for a couple of minutes, but we need to move fast before we get swarmed. The two of us alone here? Death sentence, for sure. This is a world where we need a massive number of allies in order to live, let alone thrive."

"What if I want to live, laugh, and love?" Jaxon questioned

intently, moving to the spot Joe indicated without another word. He knew what he needed to do in order to make Joe's rituals successful, and usually the man didn't start one up without a good reason. "Question for you: what is this?"

"Well, this is my plan 'C'." Joe didn't make eye contact with his friend, because he did not want him to know that he had only thought this up because he'd had no other options. Cruel desperation truly was the mother of innovation. "Since we are nowhere near our people, I'm going to build a town hall—technically different than a guildhall, according to the blueprints—and we're going to use the attached teleportation array to get back to the Guildhall."

Jaxon could only stare at Joe, his mouth slightly agape as he thought through what they were actually doing. "Let me get this straight. You are going to build an entire massive building… as a single-use teleportation spell?"

"Right, so, *that* attitude is why none of us thought of doing this beforehand." Joe grumbled at the sheer wastefulness of the strategy. "Who would ever think of doing something like this? Unless there was no other option, obviously. I can't believe how incredibly poorly it went back there due to the fact that being a little frivolous with my resources never even crossed my mind."

"Wiping out of the capital, slaying a massive army, infesting the Zone with demons that'll make life harder for our enemies, or finding out that the Architect you can only think of in tandem with a fireplace and bearskin rug isn't as bad as you thought she was?" Jaxon quizzed the Rituarchitect with a grin on his face.

"Kinda… okay, the *end* result was good, but it was pretty sour there otherwise." Joe growled as deep in his chest as he could manage. After a moment of intense concentration, mana began to pour out of him, and a building was erected over the course of a few dozen minutes.

As soon as it was complete, he got another message informing him that he had claimed the surrounding one hundred miles for himself, but that this would count as a secondary town and would contend with a higher difficulty of monsters due to not yet having a higher-tier settlement in place. The Ritualist ignored all of that, as he never intended to return to the location, and they stepped into the building.

Almost immediately, a disturbing *crunch* came from the wall, and the building's durability took a large hit. "Time for us to go!"

He and Jaxon ran over to the teleportation area and stepped onto the magical array that was built into the great hall. There was only one option for teleportation, which got Joe wondering how they would ever be able to escape Jotunheim. The Bifrost moved fairly constantly unless it was already in use, and he couldn't use teleportation to move between Zones... it appeared the only option for escape was to defeat whatever tasks the Zone had for him.

Carrying that thought with them, they activated the teleportation array and stepped into the guildhall half a world away. Instantly, dozens of blades were at their throats, crackling spells were tickling the goosebumps on their arms, and everything seemed to go still for a moment. Then they were recognized, and a cheer went up. In moments, they were surrounded by jubilant Dwarves and drinking hot coffee as they told their tale of the destruction they left in the wake of their escape from Alfheim.

They were lauded as heroes, and Joe was completely okay with that. As the rapid-fire explanations wore on, someone finally asked the big question that everyone had been avoiding until that moment.

"What do we do next?"

Before Joe could answer, a notification appeared in front of him, and by the blinking expressions all around him, everyone had just gotten the same message.

Welcome to Jotunheim, the World of Giants! As you may have noticed, the odds of being able to reach the Bifrost in its current state are nearly zero. This world bears another name: Jotunheim, the Prison World. The monsters here grow in intelligence as well as size and are territorial to the extreme. So long as you never attempt to build a settlement past a Tier 1 Hamlet, you will only need to contend with whatever hostile monsters you encounter.

If, for some unknown reason, you wish to leave this world and either progress to higher realms or return to lower ones, you must create and maintain a Tier 5 settlement, a city, and clear the cloud layer above it in order to form a new stable connection to the Bifrost.

Be warned! As soon as you attempt to grow past a Tier 1 settlement, you will need to fend off monster waves of increasing intensity and numbers. Live well, and enjoy the bountiful resources and beautiful locations the World of Giants has to offer!

A sober mood filled the air, as the thousands of Dwarves that had crowded around Joe shared a long, hard look. One Dwarf, a smith that Joe recognized from his time working in the Forge, boldly stood up and clapped him on the shoulder. "Looks like we have our answer, Bros and Dudettes! There's plenty of work to be done!"

A riotous cheer went up in response, because what did any Dwarf love more than hard labor? The smith continued, excited to have the eyes of so many of his contemporaries upon him. "Best part is? We aren't going to have to worry about those Elves ever again! None of them managed to make a foothold here, and it's going to be-"

He quaffed the rest of his drink and swiped an arm across the foamy mustache that had been left behind, "a long time before they can, thanks to Joe getting in position over their cereal bowl and dropping that massive Imp load!"

ABOUT DAKOTA KROUT

Associated Press best-selling author, Dakota has been a top 5 bestseller on Amazon, a top 6 bestseller on Audible, and his first book, Dungeon Born, was chosen as one of Audible's top 5 fantasy picks in 2017.

He draws on his experience in the military to create vast terrains and intricate systems, and his history in programming and information technology helps him bring a logical aspect to both his writing and his company while giving him a unique perspective for future challenges.

"Publishing my stories has been an incredible blessing thus far, and I hope to keep you entertained for years to come!" -Dakota

Connect with Dakota:
MountaindalePress.com
Patreon.com/DakotaKrout
Facebook.com/DakotaKrout
Twitter.com/DakotaKrout
Discord.gg/mdp

ABOUT MOUNTAINDALE PRESS

Dakota and Danielle Krout, a husband and wife team, strive to create as well as publish excellent fantasy and science fiction novels. Self-publishing *The Divine Dungeon: Dungeon Born* in 2016 transformed their careers from Dakota's military and programming background and Danielle's Ph.D. in pharmacology to President and CEO, respectively, of a small press. Their goal is to share their success with other authors and provide captivating fiction to readers with the purpose of solidifying Mountaindale Press as the place 'Where Fantasy Transforms Reality.'

Connect with Mountaindale Press:
MountaindalePress.com
Facebook.com/MountaindalePress
Twitter.com/_Mountaindale
Instagram.com/MountaindalePress

MOUNTAINDALE PRESS TITLES

GameLit and LitRPG

The Completionist Chronicles,
The Divine Dungeon,
Full Murderhobo, and
Year of the Sword by Dakota Krout

Arcana Unlocked by Gregory Blackburn

A Touch of Power by Jay Boyce

Red Mage and
Farming Livia by Xander Boyce

Space Seasons by Dawn Chapman

Ether Collapse and
Ether Flows by Ryan DeBruyn

Dr. Druid by Maxwell Farmer

Bloodgames by Christian J. Gilliland

Unbound by Nicoli Gonnella

Threads of Fate by Michael Head

Lion's Lineage by Rohan Hublikar and Dakota Krout

Wolfman Warlock by James Hunter and Dakota Krout

Axe Druid,
Mephisto's Magic Online, and
High Table Hijinks by Christopher Johns

Skeleton in Space by Andries Louws

Dragon Core Chronicles by Lars Machmüller

Chronicles of Ethan by John L. Monk

Pixel Dust and
Necrotic Apocalypse by David Petrie

Viceroy's Pride by Cale Plamann

Henchman by Carl Stubblefield

Artorian's Archives by Dennis Vanderkerken and Dakota Krout

Vaudevillain by Alex Wolf

Made in United States
Troutdale, OR
04/19/2024

19304260R00224